FROM THE SILENCE OF THE SHADOWS

V.B. LACEY

FICTION & FATE PRESS

FROM THE SILENCE OF THE SHADOWS

Exclusive Digitally Signed Edition

V. B. LACEY

ISBN 979-8-9938088-0-2 (paperback); ISBN 979-8-9938088-1-9 (hardback)

Paperback & dust jacket designed by Fay Lane

Hardcover design by Charlie Arpie

Map illustration by Andrés Aguirre

Editing by Mountains Wanted Publishing

Interior artwork by Anamaria (Instagram: @gioviia) and @flavie5dub

Fiction & Fate Press LLC

www.vblaceybooks.com

AUTHOR'S NOTE

This book has scenes depicting violence, torture, on-page death, traumatic flashbacks, unwanted physical touch, dubious consent, self-inflicted pain, derealization, and child endangerment.

Please be mindful of these and other possible triggers.

———

To those who are walking through darkness,
may you find the fire that welcomes you home.

———

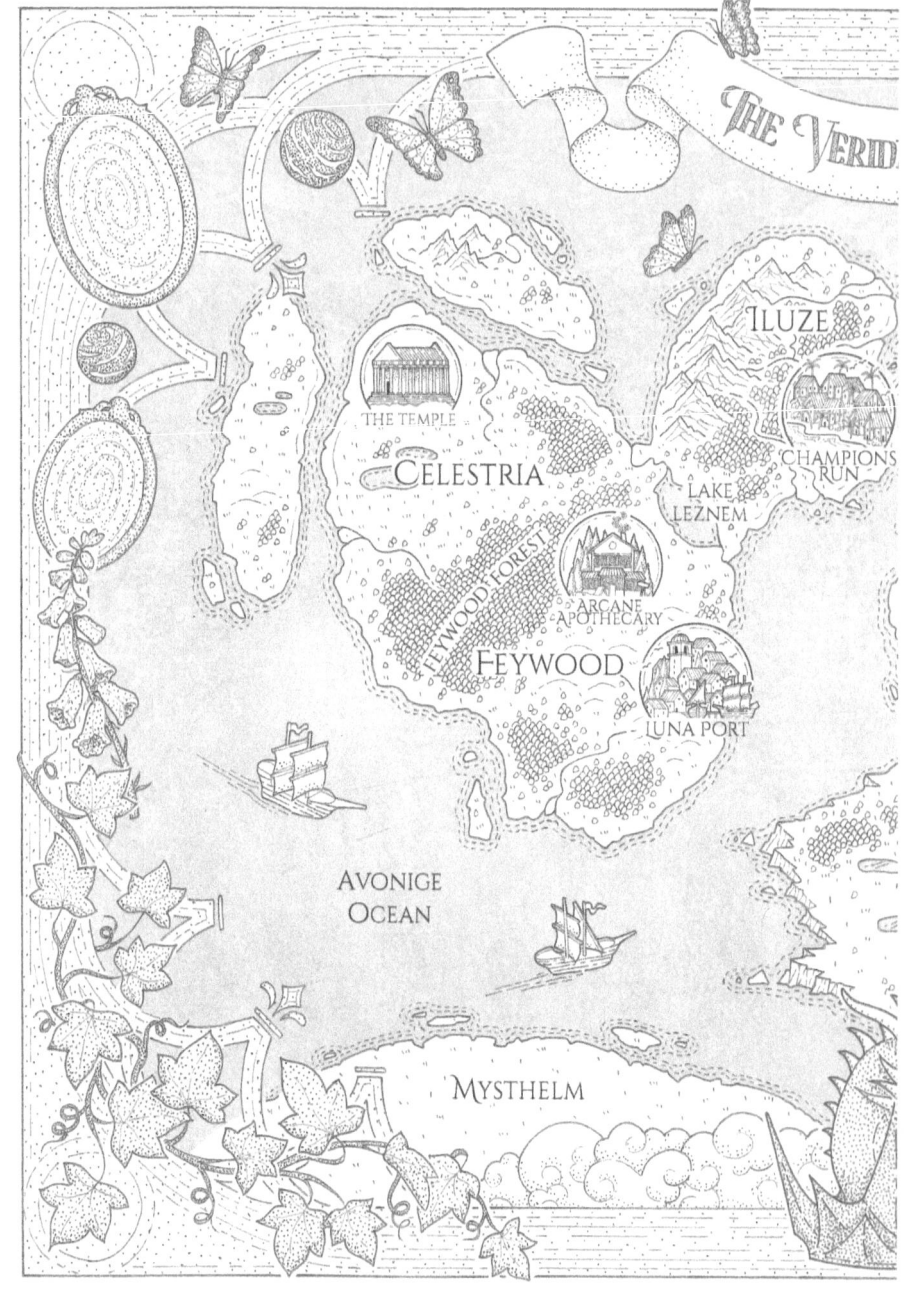

Even the darkest night will end and the sun will rise.
\- Victor Hugo

IN CASE YOU MISSED IT...

This is book three in the Veridian Empire series. While it *can* be read as a standalone, I highly recommend reading books one and two to fully capture the depth of this story and these characters. I'm including this recap in case you need a refresher of what happened in book one *(In the Wake of the Wicked)* and book two *(Of the Curse or the Crown)*. If you haven't read book one and/or two yet, you can either skip this section (spoilers!) or read at your own discretion.

In the Wake of the Wicked (1) follows Rose Wolff, a twenty-five-year-old Alchemist and outcast in her province of Feywood. Six provinces exist in the Veridian Empire, each with their own unique strand of magic:

Feywood: home to Alchemists, people with the power to cast spells and enchantments using the nature around them.

Celestria: home to Striders, who can transport themselves from one place to another in the blink of an eye.

Iluze: home to Illusionists, who can create illusions in the minds of others.

Emberfell: home to Lightbenders, people who create and bend light to their will.

Drakorum: home to Shifters, who can shift into a given animal form.

Tenebra: home to Shadow Wielders, those who manipulate shadows.

Veridians came to possess this magic three hundred years ago when the Fates, the deities of this world, issued a prophecy to both the Veridian Empire and the kingdom of Mysthelm. The prophecy stated that whoever could conquer the uninhabited island that held the magic of the Fates would be given their power.

The War of Beginnings ensued, and the Veridians won, causing a rift between them and Mysthelm (*remember this for book two*). Veridians were granted magic, but it came with a catch: over time, its power wanes.

Rose's story picks up three hundred years later, right before the start of the Decemvirate, a magical tournament held every ten years in order to replenish their fading magic. One challenger from each of the six provinces is chosen to compete in three dangerous trials. Rose ends up volunteering as the Alchemist challenger and gets close to a couple of other powerful competitors—Nox Duma and Arowyn Garrolas. (*Hmm...could these be important players in our new book?*)

While competing in these magical trials, Rose and Nox become involved with a secret rebellion called the Sentinels. The Sentinels are on a mission to bring down the corrupt Emperor Theodore Gayl, restore the empire to its former glory, and rid their land of a terrible sleeping curse. They use Rose as a spy to dig up information on the emperor, where she uncovers a life-changing secret from her past.

Rose grapples with many challenges thrown at her, all while growing closer to her new found family and finding love in a certain broody rebel named Leo. Everything culminates in the final trial of the Decemvirate, where Emperor Gayl and Rose stand off in an epic battle of wills and Alchemy. He confesses to being responsible for the sleeping curse. Every time someone fell to the curse, *he* absorbed their power, making him nearly impossible to defeat.

At the last second, Rose performs a charm that siphons the magic from him and funnels it into her, leaving him dead. In the aftermath, she discovers she now holds the power to wake those who were under the sleeping curse.

While she and Leo embark on an adventure to rouse the sleeping victims across the entire empire, Leo's sister and the rightful heir to the Veridian Empire takes center stage.

Of the Curse or the Crown (2) centers around Clarissa Aris: fox Shifter, former rebel leader, and Empress-Elect of the Veridian Empire. She faces relentless opposition from her council, assassination attempts from the Shifter governor of Drakorum *(might need to remember him...)*, and the monumental task of restoring peace to her broken land. Seeking stability, Clarissa turns to Veridia's southern enemy, Mysthelm, hoping for an alliance. But its mysterious king goes one step further.

He wants to marry her.

Temporarily leaving her empire behind, Clarissa sails to Mysthelm to consider King Galen Grimaldi's proposal. She tours the kingdom with him, his advisor and best friend Lord Thorne Reaux, her mother, and two maids, Devora and Katrine. But strange events keep happening. More assassination attempts, threatening messages, unnatural cave-ins, and a deadly blight challenge her at every turn. Cut off from her Shifter magic in this magic-less land, she's defenseless—until she uncovers the kingdom's darkest secret.

The Fates cursed the Grimaldi line two hundred years ago when their ancestor tried to barter for magic. Now every Grimaldi heir inherits a brand-new curse upon ascending the throne. What is Galen's curse, you may ask?

Everything he touches rots and dies. And it's beginning to spread, endangering not just those he touches, but his entire kingdom.

The only way to break it is to marry someone from Veridia. Clarissa understands his desperation and knows she must go through with it in order to save his kingdom. But her heart belongs to his best friend, Thorne, a widowed father torn between loyalty and forbidden love.

As Clarissa and Thorne try to avoid their growing feelings, more and more revelations are made known. Clarissa learns Veridians are immune to Galen's curse. She can touch him and can even absorb the curse's magic, temporarily restoring her powers and purging the kingdom's rot. Her magic earns her the title of savior, but it also makes her even more of a target to those who oppose her empire.

It all comes to a head when the curse unravels and overtakes the entire Island Territory of Mysthelm. Clarissa realizes the only way to end it is to marry Galen and break the curse as quickly as possible.

Their wedding day comes, and the Fates told the truth: their marriage *did* end the curse. But it also killed King Galen.

Now accused of both murder and treason, Clarissa is sentenced to death. She's able to evade her punishment when the Fates send her a single cursed flower with enough magic for her to absorb and shift into a fox to get away.

In the aftermath, they discover Thorne's mother was behind all of the attacks. She administered the help of several others along the way, including Clarissa's trusted maid Devora. (*Remember this for book three...*)

Still, the secrets keep coming.

For Devora isn't a simple human from Mysthelm, as she'd thought her entire life. She's an orphan from the Veridian Empire with the power of *shadow wielding*. Upon this discovery, Nox, one of Clarissa's companions and a dragon Shifter, offers to take her back to the empire to serve out her punishment for betraying the empress.

Clarissa, Thorne, and his daughter return to Veridia. While she is officially crowned Empress of the Veridian Empire and their little family lives out their happily-ever-after, a very different ending awaits Nox and Devora.

Or perhaps it's not an ending at all...

PROLOGUE
DEVORA

Six Weeks in the Future

The world tilted as I crashed to my knees.

He will heal. He will heal. He will heal.

The blade sank into his side. His lips parted in stunned silence, his eyes scrambling to find mine as two dark blooms soaked the front of his shirt.

His mouth formed a single word.

"Tomorrow."

Our forever will start tomorrow.

My stomach turned inside out, the air torn from my lungs like I'd been gutted. I forgot how to breathe. I forgot how to do anything except scream. The world dimmed around me, and I barely saw the cloaked figures emerge from the surrounding shadows and race forward.

My body wouldn't move, wouldn't run, wouldn't do anything but shriek uselessly at the sky. My magic, however...

Shadows flailed inside me, a tidal wave of despair unlike anything I'd ever felt. They swelled and collided against my ribs, and I no longer cared about holding them back.

Magic *exploded* from me in a blast of energy, so strong my hair whipped around my face, and my chest caved in from exertion. A ripple of shadows coursed over the ground. It trembled beneath the dark wave, kicking up dirt and sending weapons flying through the air.

But the power was short-lived.

Something cold and hard bolted around my wrist, and as quickly as it hurtled from me, my magic died. The shock of its loss sent me reeling backward into a cloaked figure.

My head snapped to the black cuffs on my arm.

Not again.

I can't lose him. I can't lose him. I can't—

My stifled magic made my chaotic, raging emotions claw up my throat, trying to get out. They were going to flood me. Drown me.

Blood glinting off the blade in his chest practically blinded me, making my vision go gray at the edges. I felt myself struggling against my restraints, but it was as if I was watching it from afar as a soundless scream escaped me.

The dagger moved to his throat, and I lunged forward with all my strength.

When my assailant grabbed my waist to yank me back, something in my pocket shifted. I blinked, thoughts racing as quickly as my pulse.

The fatesprig serum.

I dug in my pockets for the cool metal cylinder and hauled it out, needle tip glistening in the moonlight.

His gaze met mine as he stumbled to his knees. Even in his pain, even facing his own death, he didn't attack. He didn't defend himself.

He was protecting me, as he always did.

My fault.

His eyes widened. His lips curved around my name, a blood-stained hand reaching for me.

I didn't think. As I watched the blade point to his throat, I plunged the needle into my heart.

The last thing I heard was the deafening, soul-wrenching roar of a dragon.

I

NOX

I loved the color yellow. A golden yellow, like the kind that beamed over the Sea of Scarab in the sunrise, or freshly baked sourdough glistening on Mother's hearthstone.

My third-in-command of our secret rebellion, Tessa, once bought me a pair of golden leathers. She swore it would make my tan skin positively *glow*—her words, not mine.

But I could never wear yellow. It showed blood far too easily. That was why I always wore black.

I wiped the blade on the side of my pants, clearing the viscous red away until the tip was gleaming again. The heavy body fell at my feet. It sent up a plume of dust from the rocky cliffside, and several pebbles went flying down the steep drop-off in the Guardian Range. Despite the sun hanging high in the sky, the cold winter wind still chilled my skin.

The scent of fear, sour and pungent to my Shifter senses, wafted around me. "What do you want?" the man before me asked, his voice shaking as he held an arm out to block another man and woman behind him. They all wore the telltale light blue of Emberfell, but their clothes were dirty and torn, with rusty daggers strapped on by cracked sheaths. "Why are you doing this?"

I sighed. Why was I doing *any* of this?

9

The answer was always the same.

"You know why," I responded. I barely recognized my own voice. "You made him angry."

The man didn't even look surprised, only resigned. "So he sent you."

My jaw twitched. "I don't want to do this, but you brought this on yourselves. You openly planned a siege against him. You know that kind of attack can't go without consequences."

His eyes flitted to the dead body at my feet, then met my stare. Sparks of light shone around his pupils, a sign of his type of magic —a Lightbender. "Is—is there nothing else we can do?"

I gripped the handle of my blade tighter. This was always the hardest part, no matter how many times I did it.

"No. There's no other way."

———

"ALRIGHT, Kieran. If I die, I hope you know it's your fault."

"Duly noted. However, I think it's possible you're being a *bit* dramatic."

"We'll see who's dramatic when you're stuffing my dead body in the ground."

"I believe that would still be you, Tessa."

The sounds of my second and third-in-command bickering in the workshop tugged the edges of my tired lips upward.

"And why, do tell, are you dying today, Tessa?" I asked as I trudged into the dimly lit room. I unlatched my cloak and threw it across the back of a dark gray couch where Kieran, my second, sat with one leg propped on his knee.

"Because I agreed to take Kieran's morning patrol shift for the next week," my third said with a sigh. Tessa was perched on top of my desk to the right, twisting the end of one of her long black braids around a finger. "You know I'm more of a night person."

"Well, we all know Kieran's not an any-time-of-day person. You'll be doing everyone in the Keep a favor." I tapped her nose before nudging her off my desk. "Imagine how much more the refugees will appreciate waking up to your beautiful face."

She shoved my elbow. "Your flattery doesn't work on me, Noxy boy."

Kieran piped up behind me, his deep, measured voice always threaded with calm authority. "And I find myself offended by your insinuation."

I twisted to give my second a quick wink. "You have a beautiful face too, Kieran."

"Thank you." He rose from the couch and buttoned the middle button on his black suit jacket. The man was *always* in a suit. Even when it was just the three of us meeting in the private workshop of my seaside manor, the Keep.

But I couldn't blame him—if I looked that good in a suit, I'd never take it off either.

Everything about Kieran Blackwell was put-together, from his slick dark brown hair, to his chiseled, tan jaw, to the perfectly tailored suit and shined shoes. Even his Shifter form, a white stag, spoke of elegance. The complete opposite to my third-in-command, Tessa Briar. Her long black locks reached down her back, often fashioned in thin braids like how she wore it today. Silver bracelets adorned her arms up to her elbows. Her deep brown eyes were full of mischief and mayhem, along with the ferocity of her jaguar Shifter form.

She was nearly eleven years Kieran's junior. They were the most unlikely duo to ever grace the Keep, much less be my closest companions.

But I trusted them with my life. As Shifters, loyalty like theirs was *earned*. And once you had it, it would take the fires of hell itself to break it.

"Did you just get back?" Tessa asked, and I nodded. "How did this one go?" Her voice softened as she gave me a concerned look.

I scratched the back of my ear, trying to mask my emotions. "Same as usual."

"Do you want to talk about it?"

"There's nothing to talk about." I cleared my throat and pointed to Kieran. "Status report? I don't have much time. Scarven expects me at the Governor's House in a couple hours."

"We shall make it quick, then," Kieran said. I didn't miss the way his gaze locked onto Tessa's for a split second, a silent conversation taking place between the two. "While you were gone, we received intel for a night that Scarven and his guards would be at the eastern docks."

I leaned forward, my curiosity piqued. "Another cargo shipment?"

He nodded.

"And?" I urged. "Did you find out what he's been importing?"

"Not exactly." Kieran shifted on his feet. "I know you're eager to learn what these shipments entail, but Tessa and I decided to use Scarven's absence to make another raid."

He was right, I *was* eager to learn about Scarven's nighttime rendezvous. The governor of Drakorum had been orchestrating covert imports for a little over a year now, but we hadn't been able to get a lead on *what* those ships carried.

Knowing Scarven, it wasn't anything good.

Illegal weapons that could take out entire empires, hordes of dead bodies, poison, slaughtered animals for sacrifice...my imagination had come up with a plethora of vile things our *dear* governor would covet.

But much of our attention had been focused on using those nights where he was distracted as opportunities to break into his stronghold for these *raids* Kieran mentioned.

Raids, rescue missions—same thing. They had one purpose: get as many of Kane Scarven's prisoners out as possible.

"You made a good call," I said with a nod. "How many this time?"

"Nine," Tessa said, and I let out a low whistle. "Most of them under twenty, some a bit older. He's added an entirely new wing, and it's *full* of test subjects. We tried to get more out, but that

Alchemist of his is getting smarter with his wards. Even Arowyn couldn't get inside some of them."

"That's still good. At least you saved some. Any more than that would've drawn too much attention," I said.

Bile crept up my throat as I thought about what he was doing to those people. His *experiments*. People he was supposed to be leading and keeping safe. His underground wings held hundreds of cells bursting with innocents who were subject to his myriad of tests.

Kane Scarven had always had a fascination with Veridian magic—how it worked, what powered it, how it could be changed. He wanted to strip it to its bones. To mutate it, weaponize it, or maybe even erase it entirely.

And he had an entire province at his *disposal*.

He started small, taking only those nobody would notice had gone missing. Homeless, elderly, orphans—sporadically and with caution, so as not to raise alarm.

But then he grew bolder. Over the past five years, I'd seen more and more innocents ripped from their homes and sent to his laboratories. Families exiled when they tried to get their loved ones back. Bodies from failed tests piled higher than the tower of my Keep.

People were too scared to stand against him, knowing their loved ones could be next to go.

It had become my mission to fight for them. To save as many innocents from their fate as I could.

Because I'd once been one of them.

"How are the new refugees settling in?" I asked. Long ago, we'd turned the Keep into a safehouse for those we rescued to live and heal. I had built upon my seaside home until it was hardly recognizable—an enormous manor with enough wings to host dozens and dozens of refugees, kept safe from Scarven's prying eyes by protective enchantments.

We always debriefed in our "workshop," a large room on the first level made of black brick walls and wooden floors. It was a sanctuary and a war room all in one, with space crafted for each of us to feel at home in the unsteadiness of our line of work. The walls were lined with herbs and tinctures for Alchemy, books and maps, and weapons for target practice, all humming with magic.

It made the perfect headquarters for my little group, the Veridians dedicated to keeping this province safe from our governor. The Ashen Order. Each of us with blood on one hand and justice in the other, willing to risk our lives to undo the terror Kane Scarven had rained down on us in the last two decades.

Tessa exchanged an uneasy look with Kieran. "They'll be okay. It's only been a couple of days," she answered slowly. "We're running a little tight on space in the nursery and children's wing, but there's plenty of room in the upper towers. And I think a few will be ready for reintegration soon."

"Everett told me this most recent group is taking longer to adjust," Kieran cut in. "There seem to be more mental barriers for him to work through. The young ones in particular are easily distressed."

"Has anything happened?"

"There's one seven-year-old who Scarven manipulated to shift prematurely, and she breaks a couple of bones every time she does," Tessa said.

I closed my eyes and fought back a wave of rage, silver and molten. Shifters didn't naturally shift until early teenage years, as their bodies weren't equipped to handle it at such a young age.

"And a teenager he made into a Strider and Lightbender hybrid, who can't conjure light without burning himself," Tessa continued. "Silas is working on a remedy for that. A potion of some sort."

I should be used to reports like this by now. Fates, I saw things much worse during my time in those very labs. It still made me sick to think of them suffering, though. And it was even worse knowing I had to play my part. That I had to *answer* to him.

I may have been freed from his cells, but I was still his prisoner.

Scarven wouldn't simply let me, his precious *dragon Shifter,* off his leash for good.

As long as he had my sister under his control, I never would be.

"What about *her?*" I asked, quieter this time.

Tessa's throat bobbed. "Nothing. I'm sorry, Nox. We don't know where he's keeping her."

I nodded curtly and took a seat in the tall chair behind my desk. It was the same every time. No news. Scarven's word alone was the only proof that Vera still lived. That my sister, whom I hadn't seen in five years, was still breathing somewhere deep in his hold.

That was what kept me in line all this time.

I'd only ever tried to openly defy him once, and it ended with the woman I had loved dead at my feet. I learned my lesson quickly: do whatever he wanted without question.

Perhaps this refugee program I'd started five years ago was a subconscious way to appease the guilt I carried for being in his pocket. When he said "fetch," I ran. When he said "jump," I said, "how high." The things I'd done for him, the things I'd *seen*...maybe there was no number of good deeds in existence to counteract what I'd done in the name of protecting my sister. And now, in the name of keeping him from *ever* finding out about this operation.

I was toeing a dangerous line, keeping his loyalty while still lying to him with every breath. But I'd keep doing it until the day I died. It was worth it. These people were worth it.

"Thank you for the update." My eyes stayed trained on the piles of notes on my desk, refusing to meet Tessa and Kieran's stares. "I have to meet Scarven soon. I should be back late tonight."

Tessa put her palms on my desk, forcing me to look up at her. "Nox, what you're doing here is nothing short of miraculous. Do you know how many people we've rescued this year *alone?*"

"Fifty-two," I said instantly. *Not enough.*

"Fifty-two people who would still be stuck in those labs if it wasn't for you. Fifty-two people who'd be dead by now, for all we know. Fifty-two people who can rejoin their families." Tessa paused, letting her words sink in. "You've created this safehouse for them, and I know how much you sacrifice just to keep it hidden and give them the best chance for survival. None of us blame you for what you have to do. You're twice the man and leader I'd ever be."

"I don't know about that, Tessa. I think you'd knock any man flat on their back." I offered her a small smile.

"Obviously." She tossed her braids over her shoulder. "Fine, you're twice the man *Kieran* will ever be."

"Ah, yes. Always the brunt of your jokes," Kieran said with a heavy sigh. The coils in my chest slowly began to unwind as he joined Tessa at the front of my desk. "She is correct, however."

"Tattoo that on my forehead," Tessa interjected.

Kieran ignored her. "You are relentlessly in pursuit of atonement, Nox Duma, and yet fail to see that you have become that very salvation for so many. We follow you not because you are the infamous dragon Shifter of legend, but because you are *worthy* of it."

"Through flame and ash," Tessa said softly, repeating what had become the mantra of my Ashen Order.

I shifted the tip of my finger into one of my claws and gently ran it along the top of the desk, feeling grooves catch beneath my talon. These two knew me better than I knew myself. It was unnerving. And a bit annoying.

And exactly the kind of people I needed at my side.

"You're more than a couple of pretty faces. Don't let anyone tell you otherwise," I drawled. I swallowed hard and tipped my head at them. "Thank you," I added, my voice suddenly rough. "I wouldn't be here without either of you."

"Are we going to make the big, bad dragon cry?" Tessa crooned, backing away from the desk with a laugh.

I grabbed the bottle of wine still on my desk from our last meeting and threw it at her. She snatched it midair, quick as lightning, then tossed it at the back of Kieran's head. He gracefully reached behind to catch it around the neck, uncorking it with a single motion.

"Oh, Nox? There was one more thing we forgot to mention," Tessa said. The hesitancy in her voice made my gaze flick up with a raised eyebrow.

She shot a look at Kieran. "Kieran?"

"Don't look at me. I'm not the one who brought this up."

She scowled. "Okay, fine. Coward." With a sigh, she finally said, "The maids said *it* happened again. Last night. Almost tore the door down this time."

A quiet growl built in the back of my throat. *Not again.*

A vision of red hair and brilliant blue-green eyes passed through my mind, followed by a wave of distrust. This was *not* what I wanted to spend my evening doing before I had to meet Scarven.

The normally vacant tower of my Keep was now occupied by Devora, a spy and traitor to our empire. That girl had been a thorn in my side ever since she betrayed one of my best friends, the empress of the Veridian Empire, at the end of summer.

Empress Clarissa had far too much going on to deal with a prisoner, what with her coronation, wedding, and trying to patch together our broken empire on the heels of her deranged predecessor. So I, being the *good friend* I was, volunteered to keep Devora under my watch until Rissa decided what to do with her.

I was a glorified holding cell.

I sucked on my teeth as I stood, keeping my palms planted on the desk. "Wonderful. Guess I need to pay our guest a little *visit*."

Tessa raised an eyebrow. "How much longer do you plan to keep her here, anyway? It's been months."

"Maybe until Clarissa and I are sure she won't turn around and stab us in the back. *Again*."

"Play nice, Nox," Tessa warned.

I narrowed my eyes in a wicked grin. "I'm always nice, darling."

2

DEVORA

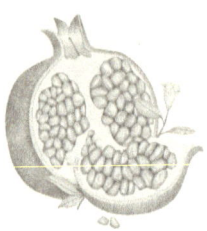

T hick tears fell from my cheeks and landed on the fur clutched in my grip. I pulled the dead creature tighter to me, burying my face in its red coat. Everything was stained with its blood. My hands, my clothes, the field beneath my feet.

"Get up, girl," a cold voice behind me said. "We don't have much time."

I could barely see through the tears, but I'd know that voice anywhere. I slowly turned to take in those stern features, the arched eyebrows, the brown-and-gray hair coiled into a tight bun.

Lady Reaux looked at me with disgust, sharp eyes full of dismissal. "Quit your crying. Don't forget, this was your idea, Devora. See it through, or we'll do things my way."

The dream shifted. I was standing before the skeleton of an enormous bonfire—easily three times my height. The fox dragged behind me, its weight making my muscles ache and my heart crack.

Every time was the same. I begged to skip this part of the dream, pleaded with my own mind to let me wake up.

It never worked.

I forced back choked cries as I hoisted the innocent animal onto a stake, its limp body giving way and falling back onto me. Once it finally stood tall, the fox stared down at me, golden eyes now lifeless and hollow. They swallowed me. Consumed me.

But the dream wavered once more. Blind panic crawled up my throat.

The image of the fox was replaced with dark onyx eyes. Long, wavy blonde hair cascaded over fair skin, with a crown of emeralds atop her head. The ends of her light hair were soaked in crimson. Blood seeped from her neck, turning her golden dress a fiery red.

Her dead eyes locked onto mine as a disembodied voice echoed around me. "How could you?" she cried, voice scratchy and rough to my ears. "You were supposed to be my friend. They're going to kill me because of you."

With a roar, flames burst from the firewood and leapt onto the stake.

"No!" I screamed, clawing at the wood. This wasn't what happened —she was supposed to live—

This is your fault.

You did this to her.

How could anyone forgive you?

There was a soft tap at the door.

My eyes snapped open, and the book I'd dropped on my chest fell to the floor with a thud. Out of the corner of my eye, I could've sworn I saw several wisps of shadows retreat back beneath my chair, but when I looked closer, they were gone.

I struggled to catch my breath as the door to my room cracked open. "Miss Devora?" The young maid peeked her head in. A brown curl came loose from her bun and framed her face. "I have your dinner ready."

"Come in," I said, voice cracking. I quickly cleared my throat. She opened the door just wide enough to slip inside, then hastily shut it.

I didn't know why she bothered. We both knew I couldn't get out, even if the door was wide open. My captor had made *sure* of that.

I threw the blanket over the cream bedsheets. The sight still made me snort. I never thought my prison would have *silk sheets*, but here we were.

A shiver raced down my spine as the memory of the dead fox resurfaced. If I was being honest, I never thought I'd be in a "prison" at all. After what I'd done, I thought my future lay in the gallows.

Instead, I was here. In a locked bedroom at the top of a tower in a cold, gray empire full of magical strangers.

Don't forget, you're now one of those magical strangers.

The maid set a tray of soup at the foot of my bed. "I'll just leave this here," she said in her bright voice.

"Thanks, Rebekah." I gave her a smile, which she returned with a slight curtsy.

We hadn't always been on good terms. No, back when I first got to the Veridian Empire, I was a menace. On my first day meeting her, I attacked her with little wooden shards I'd scratched off the bottom of my bedside table, then bolted for the open door.

I'd gotten about a foot before I slammed into some invisible barrier. It knocked me to my back and left me dazed for several minutes, long enough for Rebekah to retreat and call for the master of the house.

Nox Duma.

My would-be captor and, in a strange way, my savior. After all, it was thanks to him I wasn't left hanging at the gallows or rotting in the dungeons of Mysthelm after I betrayed his empress and almost got her killed. As a favor to the empress—and probably to get me out of the way—he'd offered to bring me back here to his province to serve out my "sentence." I didn't think he even knew *what* to do with me besides toss me in a room and hope I stayed quiet.

You deserve so much worse.

I silenced the voice with a wince and climbed onto the bed, leaning forward to see the murky brown soup on the tray.

"Bean soup again today?" I sniffed the air and grimaced. "Lovely."

"He heard how much you disliked it last week." Rebekah pinched her lips together. "He requested the kitchen make it as often as possible."

"Of course he did," I muttered. "Well, joke's on him. I *love* bean soup." I lifted the bowl, sucked in a greasy mouthful, and smacked my lips dramatically. "Mmm. Bean soup."

Rebekah shook her head with a smirk. "I'll be sure to pass along the message."

She took a few minutes to tidy up the room. I tried to tell her long ago that I could do that—I used to be a lady's maid in my kingdom of Mysthelm, after all. I liked having something to do with my hands. A goal, a task, a purpose. Sitting here in this tower, I had *no* purpose. No use beyond wallowing in my own guilt and imagining the life I was missing.

Perhaps that was the point of Nox's punishment.

I padded to the window at my right and gazed onto the choppy waters in the distance. The blue waves crashing against the rocky cliffside were darker in the fading sunlight. *Everything* in this province was darker. Colder. Lifeless.

With a shiver, I sat in the wooden chair next to it and pulled a quilt around me. I'd been in Drakorum, the mountainous province of the Veridian Empire, for three months now, and I'd barely seen the sun come out at all.

Every day was the same. Wake up, find a plain breakfast of oatmeal and pomegranates already sitting at the foot of my bed, pretend to sulk and refuse the meal, then give in because a girl needs to eat—and nobody was there to witness my silent temper tantrum, anyway. Then, I'd alternate between my many scintillating activities.

Pace the rug in front of the fireplace. Read one of the countless books on Veridian Empire history from the bookshelf. Take a bath. Pick at the bottom of my bedside table until I'd chipped off those little wooden darts that I could throw at the door. In Mysthelm, I'd gotten used to carrying a dagger at my thigh, just in case. I became somewhat proficient at throwing, having grown up as an orphan on those dark streets. But since the annoyingly arrogant dragon Shifter currently holding me hostage took my safety dagger, I didn't even have *that* to target practice with.

Sure, my prison was luxurious. Strangely so. But it was still a prison. Fancy sheets and golden bathtubs could only mask the truth for so long. When *you* were the one responsible for betraying the empress of this empire, someone you had the balls to call a *friend* even as you shoved the metaphorical knife in her back...you deserved worse.

I deserved worse.

Fates, that had practically become my battle cry at this point.

I still didn't understand why Nox kept me here. What was his endgame? To let me die alone up in this tower? Until he thought I'd *learned my lesson*? It seemed like all I did now was wait for the other shoe to fall.

I gnawed on my lower lip, which had grown chapped in the dryness of Drakorum. Even being stuck in this tower, I could feel it. The brittle air forcing its way through the cracks in the stone, sucking out the warmth and replacing it with a chill that settled into my bones with every breath.

Winter in the Veridian Empire was very different from back home in my kingdom, if I could even call it that anymore. I supposed the green, vibrant life of Mysthelm had never truly been my *home*.

A home was somewhere you could call your own. Somewhere that *felt* like yours. That welcomed you back again and again, no matter how long you were gone.

I had no home. Nothing to call my own. No friends, no family, no one to care.

That was all I had ever wanted.

Grabbing my glasses from my bedside table, I picked up the book that had toppled to the ground. I watched Rebekah over the top of the pages as she flitted around the room, tidying my dirty clothes, folding the blankets on the bed. When she stepped on her toes to dust the top of the armoire, I spotted a wrinkled piece of paper sticking out of her pocket.

With my glasses on, I could make out dark, messy script with the words "from your Milo" and a little heart next to it. *Hmm. A love interest?*

I wanted to ask her about this curious sweetheart of hers. It was the closest thing I had to entertainment in this dreadfully dull tower. But before I could, she gave me another curtsy and exited out the door, as quick and graceful as a bunny.

And *that* was the most exciting thing that would happen to me all night.

She was usually the only other person I saw, besides the strange horses and their riders barging onto the grounds beneath my tower at all hours of the night. Sometimes, when I was up late reading by the window, I'd hear hooves and look down to see newcomers dismounting, small figures making their way to the front of the mansion and out of sight.

I liked to pretend they were spies. Maybe assassins, sent by some far-off villain. Or workers from a brothel coming to pay Nox a visit in his mysterious lair. My imagination often ran away with me. That, paired with my annoying curiosity, used to get me in trouble at the orphanage.

I turned my attention back to the book in my lap. *From Peaks to Palaces: History of the Veridian Empire.* Real riveting stuff.

But it had helped me learn a lot about this mysterious land I was stuck in. *Drakorum.* One of the six provinces in the Veridian Empire, each home to a unique kind of magic I had yet to discover. Drakorum was where Nox and anyone with a Shifter bloodline originated from.

Shifters were evidently *massively* loyal creatures. It came from their innate wild nature, since they had the power to shift into whatever their animal form was. I'd only met a handful so far— Nox, of course, as well as Rebekah. And Clarissa, who was a fox Shifter.

Fox.

The image of those dead eyes, the bloodied fur, the limp body slammed back into me.

Your fault. Traitor.

I took a deep breath and squeezed my eyes shut to banish the feel of its fur beneath my fingers, then looked down at the book.

While Drakorum was where I currently resided, it wasn't the province that captured my curiosity. One word rang out in my mind.

Tenebra. The province just west of here, home to the Shadow Wielders. People who could turn darkness into weapons, who could control and conjure shadows from nothing.

My guilt morphed into something else. A deep, quiet, hesitant yearning. The only emotion that could distract from the shame, the only desire strong enough to outweigh my need for absolution.

Tenebra was the province that held the most intrigue for me because, as I'd only discovered three months ago, it was where I was born. It was where my real *family* came from.

And I knew absolutely *nothing* about it. Only that I'd been torn from whatever life I might have had and flung onto the shores of Mysthelm as a baby, with no recollection of my magic.

My magic. Against all odds, beyond my wildest dreams...I wasn't just an orphan from Mysthelm. I was a Shadow Wielder.

Knock.

The harsh rap on my door echoed for half a second before it slammed open.

3

DEVORA

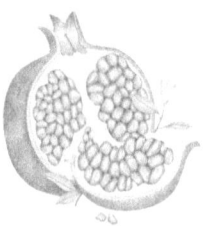

"Well, at least you bothered to knock this time," I said, barely glancing up at the tall frame in the doorway.

I felt those navy-blue eyes on me, saw those broad shoulders tightening as he bristled. Out of the corner of my eye, I watched him run a hand clad in glittering rings through his wavy, dirty-blond hair, then he crossed his arms over his chest to glare at me.

I thought it got on his nerves how little I seemed to acknowledge him, which was difficult, considering he took up *so much* space. I felt him in every inch of this tower; his presence was relentless, all-consuming, like a wave of heat beating at my skin.

But I ignored it.

Nox Duma was the kind of man used to commanding a room simply by entering it. He was all magnetic swagger and charm, with a hint of danger lying beneath the surface that intrigued you *just* enough to try and crack it.

I'd seen that side of him, once. Before he decided to hate me. Before he'd taken me to serve my punishment.

Before I'd ruined everything.

The first time I saw Nox was three months ago back in

25

Mysthelm, sitting next to Empress Clarissa at a campfire. The flames blazed in his dark eyes, accentuating that sinful smirk and catching the rings littering his fingers. He would toss a well-timed joke around the campfire when he knew the attention was on him. He had given his laughter so freely back then.

Suffice it to say, I didn't get that version of Nox. I didn't get the man who was all wit and charisma and handsome smirks.

I got the dragon with hatred in his eyes. The one whose claws itched to sink into me, whose teeth begged to draw blood.

I found my gaze straying to him, to the cloak draped across his shoulders, the tight pants tucked into sturdy black boots. I flicked my eyes back down to my book. "Going somewhere?"

He ignored my question. "It happened again."

I leaned back in the chair and propped my legs on the windowsill. "I hear it happens to a lot of men. It's nothing to be ashamed of."

A small growl rumbled from his chest, and I stifled a smirk. *Devora - 1, Dragon - 0.*

"Your shadows," he said, the words slow and deliberate. "The maids saw them again."

My grin slipped. I brought my legs back to the floor. "Again? I...I didn't feel anything."

"You were probably sleeping." He ran a finger along his bottom lip. "Magic can be triggered by strong emotions, like in dreams."

Or nightmares. I looked away from him and stared out the window, onto the rocky waves below. In the setting sun, the white foam could almost be mistaken for smoke. I saw it rising up a tall stake, eating away at flesh and fur—

"I'm not doing it on purpose," I said abruptly, shaking away the vision.

I knew what he suspected. That I was practicing my magic, preparing for some sort of escape or attack, maybe to finish the job I'd started with Empress Clarissa. About a month ago, the maids reported thick swells of shadows creeping beneath my door at night. Nox had instantly barged in to interrogate me, but it was useless. I couldn't control it.

My shadows hadn't shown themselves in months. Not consciously, anyway. I hadn't felt them since Nox and I crossed the border into the Veridian Empire. Magic didn't exist outside these borders, which was why I'd never known what I was while growing up in the powerless land of Mysthelm. I didn't find out until I was exposed to Veridian magic for the first time.

I had no *idea* how the shadows kept coming back. Sometimes, I would close my eyes and try to summon that same fleeting feeling, when the unfamiliar magic slammed into me and lit every inch of my body with this swell of intense energy. I remembered the shadows bursting from a hidden well in my chest, rolling down my legs in waves, and gathering in dark pools at my feet. I remembered how *right* it felt. Even while being so foreign, so terrifying, it still felt like *me*. A part of myself that had been unlocked after twenty-three years of dormancy.

It was one step closer to discovering who I was. Where I came from. What my family had been.

But just as quickly as it came, the sensation faded. And I had never been able to get it back, no matter how hard I concentrated.

In my sleep, however...my shadows reappeared. When the shame clawed its way to the surface, when the sorrow and bone-deep loneliness had nowhere to go, no snarky comeback to hide behind...that was when they showed themselves.

Little brats. Couldn't just come when called.

I cleared my throat. "Tell the maids I'm sorry if it scared them. I don't exactly know what I'm doing. If someone could *help* me—"

"We've had this conversation, Devora," he cut in.

"No, *you've* had this conversation. I don't get a say, remember? I get to stand here while you treat me like your prisoner."

He prowled closer, raising an eyebrow. "Devora, darling, if you think *this*"—he brandished an arm—"is a prison, then you really haven't got a clue." His tone was biting, the cutting edge of a sword balanced against my throat.

"Then what is it, hmm?" I stood and threw my hands in the air. "What *am* I?"

Who am I?

He held my gaze, eyes flashing dangerously. But he didn't respond.

My shoulders fell a fraction. "I just...I just want to learn about where I came from. You *promised* you'd help me find my family, Nox." His jaw clenched when I said his name. "I've stayed locked up in your pretty little tower for *months*. When will it be enough for you?"

"This isn't about *me*," he snapped. "This is about *you* and what you did to Clarissa. Actions like that have consequences. You're lucky we didn't leave you in Mysthelm to rot in those cells like your master."

"She is *not* my master," I said, voice rising. "I'm nothing like Lady Reaux. I did what I could to protect Clarissa from her. I tried to keep her *safe* when everyone else wanted her dead. She's my friend too, Nox, and—"

"Friend?" He scoffed. "You can't be serious. You lied to her. Made her trust you. Then you betrayed her, and burned the proof for the world to see. Do you think you can still call her your *friend*?"

That familiar wave of shame rose once more, coating my stomach and chest until nothing else could get through. He was right. I knew exactly what I'd done when I drove the stake through the fox's body.

"You don't understand." My voice cracked, but I held his gaze. "I didn't have a choice."

His navy eyes melted into the wrathful silver of his dragon. "I've heard that line too many times. It always comes from the guilty."

"Of *course* I feel guilty!" I snapped. "You think I wanted to spy on Clarissa? To get her accused of treason and almost *hanged*? Do you think I *wanted* to kill that fox? That was all Lady Reaux. *She* wanted your empress out of Mysthelm. She wanted to send a message. Lady Reaux dangled the only thing I ever wanted, and I was desperate enough to be her pawn. How can you possibly understand what that's like?"

His answering silence was louder than a shout. My chest heaved from my sudden outburst, and memories of the choices I made came flooding back.

When Clarissa came all the way to Mysthelm four months ago to marry the king in hopes of a peaceful alliance after centuries of animosity, she had *no idea* the adversaries that awaited her there. People of Mysthelm hated her kind—*Veridians*. Those with foreign, frightening magic.

My kind, too, I supposed.

The people didn't want her to be our queen. They didn't want to ally with the "enemy." That was where I came in.

I worked as a maid for Lady Reaux, the matriarch of one of the noble houses. I was the perfect, expendable pawn. The orphan with the shady past, the one who spent her formative years on the floors of taverns and in the streets of seedy towns. The nameless girl who would do *anything* to figure out where she came from. The moldable, impressionable, ambitious street rat.

Lady Reaux offered me what I wanted most in this world: answers. The truth about my past.

After I'd killed and staked that fox, the symbol for Clarissa's Shifter half, I hadn't been able to look at myself in the mirror for weeks. The guilt gnawed at me, eating me from the inside out. Clarissa thought I was her *friend*. And I wanted to be—just not as much as I wanted to find my family.

In the end, it didn't matter anyway. Nobody in Mysthelm had answers for me.

Now, only the man before me could help.

"I—I did horrible things," I said quietly, throat burning. "But I tried to protect her from what could've been so much worse. I never laid a hand on her."

"You're right." Nox's voice was slow, deliberate. "You just knew how to break her without touching her."

My eyes fluttered shut under the blow of his words. The worst part was, I couldn't even deny it.

"That's what I thought." He stalked closer when I stayed silent. "You think three months is hard? Up here in this *pretty little tower* with your warm bed"—he took another step—"and clean clothes" —his nostrils flared as his voice lowered into a growl—"and safety?"

He was close enough now that I could see the veins in his neck straining, could see the muscles in his jaw clench under pressure. "You know *nothing* about prisons, Devora."

I fought a shiver as I met his stare, refusing to back down. "I know they're not all made of stone."

The air crackled with anger and the scent of smoke from roaring flames, along with traces of something sweet and spicy. Like dying embers on a cold winter's night. Slowly, the silver in his eyes faded back into their normal dark blue, and the hint of fangs that had pressed into his bottom lip disappeared.

His lip twitched, and he sighed. "You're right about one thing. I made you a promise, and I intend to keep it. Trust *actually* means something to me." I flinched at the underhanded dig.

"I'll help you find your family," he continued, and my eyes widened. "But right now isn't a good time. Things in this province are...tumultuous." He rubbed a hand along the scruff at his chin. "I can't afford to have an outsider screwing things up. You may not understand right now, but you staying here is for the best."

His cloak swept across the floor as he moved to the door. I couldn't stop myself from following him, silently cursing myself for being so needy. So *curious*. I never could keep my mouth shut, especially when I sensed adventure.

And maybe, just maybe...there could be a way out of this. A way to get what I wanted.

"I'm not a child, you know," I said quickly. "I can handle whatever's happening out there. I see the horses coming after dark." I gestured out the window, where the edge of the estate was in view.

"I hear the whispers. New voices every few days, always at night. What's going on? What's so *dangerous*?"

He looked over his shoulder at me, his brow furrowing. "You can hear all of that?"

My lips parted, confused at *his* confusion. Why wouldn't I be able to hear them? They were incredibly obnoxious.

"Never mind," he said before I could respond. "It doesn't concern you. As much as you seem to hate this tower, it's one of the only things keeping you safe."

"Safe is boring."

"Spoken like a true child."

I rolled my eyes. "Don't give me that. You're barely ten years older than me."

He hummed. "Presumptuous."

"*Observant.*"

"Whatever you want to call it, you're still not leaving."

I let out a huff of frustration. "Just let me leave this Fates-forsaken *room*. I've been good. I haven't caused any trouble—*consciously*," I amended. "If you claim this isn't a prison, then let me see something besides these four walls. *Please.*"

He stared at me, one of his ringed fingers tapping against his thigh. I held my breath. I hated how dependent I was on this man. How my freedom lay in his claws.

I was so sick of others holding control over me. First Lady Reaux, now him.

"I'll have Milo loosen the wards," he finally said.

"You will?" My eyebrows rose in shock. I didn't think I'd heard him correctly. "Wait—who's Milo?" I blurted, suddenly remembering the name from Rebekah's love note.

"The Alchemist's apprentice. He can let the wards down enough for you to roam the manor. There will be rules," he added when a hopeful smile slipped onto my features. "You're only allowed in public spaces. And you still can't leave the property."

"For now."

An exhale that sounded like a low snarl left him. "I'm going to regret this, aren't I?"

I pasted on my most innocent smile. "I don't know what you're talking about. I'm perfectly well-behaved. Trust me."

Whatever antagonistic banter our hatred had morphed into disappeared at those words.

"After what you've done?" His features hardened once more, the brief warmth now sharp and icy against my skin. "I will *never* trust you, Shadow Wielder."

4

NOX

The evening winter air was biting beneath my wings, but I was used to the cold. Each gust of wind curled around me like an old friend. I soared above the darkening clouds, stretching my wings and savoring the release of tension. My irritation with Devora seeped away as I flew west, along with the sound of her sultry voice, the image of full lips curved on pale cheeks, of bright red waves spilling over a shoulder.

I didn't get to fly like this often. Scarven forced me to keep my dragon form a secret—unless it suited his needs, of course. He wanted me to stay covert. His Alchemist had charmed a ring that camouflaged my appearance when I shifted. It allowed me to blend into my surroundings, keeping me unseen as long as I was wearing it. I didn't like to use it unless I was meeting with Scarven or on one of his *missions*. I had a sneaking suspicion his Alchemist had infused some sort of tracker into the charm. The last thing I needed was him knowing my whereabouts at all times.

But, Fates, I missed flying.

It was the freest I ever felt. Out of reach from the rest of the world, with nothing but the night sky to watch over me. Up here, I could simply *breathe*. Unburdened. Weightless. Alive.

I remembered the first time I fully shifted. Young Shifters

showed small signs at first—perhaps a paw or an ear, fangs or wings, but often weren't able to control it.

I'd been trying to shift for hours outside our family's second home, a secluded little cottage by the sea. My father was the governor of Drakorum, and we often traveled to the shore when my parents wanted to get out of the public eye. On this particular day, I tripped and fell over a rocky edge of the cliff, but instead of plummeting to the shoreline below, I sprouted *wings*.

It was painful at first, the way this vicious creature broke free of my lanky body. Navy and silver scales exploded from my skin, talons cut through the beds of my nails, and my limbs stretched excruciatingly tight as my body elongated into something three—five—*ten* times my size.

But after the pain came euphoria. *Revelation.* For years, I'd had this other half inside, this invisible, gaping form that begged to be free...and I could *finally* see it. Could finally feel my magic unlocking.

But my parents...they didn't share my joy. They were *terrified*.

A dragon Shifter hadn't been born in two hundred and fifty years, not since a war almost broke out between the rest of the empire and the Shifters. They were wary of a dragon's immense power, fearing they would rise up to overthrow the other provinces. So a toxin to suppress a dragon's Shifter half was developed. It destroyed the gene entirely so it couldn't be passed on to their offspring.

Ever since that day, dragons no longer existed.

Until me.

I didn't fully understand the gravity of the situation as a child, but my parents did. I remembered the confusing guilt of watching their panic, knowing for *some reason*, it was my fault.

Someone claimed to see me in my dragon form, and rumors spread like wildfire. The people believed my parents had experimented on me. This led to more questions, more assumptions. Was Governor Caius Duma trying to build an army of dragon Shifters? Was I a danger to society?

When the voices escalated and began to turn the province against one another, someone else decided to take matters into his own hands.

Kane Scarven, only twenty-one at the time, challenged my father for his position. And when a Shifter was challenged, it was to the death.

I came out of my fog of memories and veered to the left to avoid a large storm cloud forming ahead, then began my descent into central Drakorum. Frost collected on my scales. I relished the cold and used it to clear the brutal images flashing through my mind. Claws slashing and pained roars and blood pouring from my father's—

A low growl rumbled in my chest. That was nineteen years ago, and I could still smell the sweat. Could still hear the cries of the crowd. Could still feel my mother's tears as she held my infant sister and me in her arms and watched my father die.

The only life I'd ever known ended that day. Scarven took us from our home and forced me into his gilded cage. The rest of the world slowly forgot about the Dumas, about the rumors of the mythical dragon. But as their lives continued on, I became his first prisoner. His first *experiment*.

He and his Alchemists did everything to me. They took my blood and tried to use it to make other dragon Shifters. They tore samples from my body—fangs, claws, scales. They forced poison after poison into me to figure out what made me *special*.

The worst part was that I couldn't do anything to fight back. Not when he had my mother and sister in the palm of his hand.

He gave up on using me as a test subject, deciding instead to make me his weapon. He spent over a decade curating this image of his fearful, mysterious guardian to keep those who would oppose him in line. Sending me off to deliver "messages"—ones that ended with blood on my hands.

Tessa and Kieran said they followed me because I was *worthy*. But my ledger was stained red. How could someone who had done the things I'd done ever be worthy?

With a powerful flap of my wings, I careened toward the wide stretch of land in front of the Governor's House. My feet landed on the cold, hard ground, claws digging into the earth. My limbs shortened, and the world became larger again as I shrank from my dragon form back to my human one. I quickly removed the ring from my finger, feeling the familiar tension snap around my chest that signaled the Alchemist's camouflage charm breaking.

The Governor's House loomed before me, a shadowed silhouette against an ever-darkening evening sky. Gray clouds swayed and swelled, the metallic scent of a storm flooding my nostrils with every inhale. I shrugged my thick cloak further over my shoulders and strode across the bridge leading to the entrance. A moment later, the clouds opened and rain pelted my skin.

Of course. I held in a sigh. Shifters did *not* like getting wet.

Up ahead, charcoal turrets clawed at the sky, shingles slick with water. Moss grew from the side of the mansion, and sharp, spired rooftops pierced the mist. The path to the front doors was littered with vines and fallen leaves—brown and brittle, as not much could survive the winters of Drakorum.

Water sloshed from my boots as I pounded up the steps. Two guards with metal lion's masks stood at attention at the door.

"He's waiting for you," one of them said. "In his antechamber."

Ignoring them, I threw open the iron double doors and strode through.

I was a fighter, but these hallways always brought out the flight in me. Memories of being dragged across the oak floors, watching my blood splatter against the walls, hearing steel from the guards' swords scraping the wood as they walked. The smell of those years spent in a cell came back to me every time I trudged these corridors. Sweat, piss, vomit, the bitter scent of herbs being ground to dust, the metallic tang of toxins in the needles before they pierced my skin.

And each time, I pictured my sister in my place. Vera was still down here, suffering in those cells. Somewhere we hadn't been able to find yet.

I forced all of it away.

I reached his personal wing. The stairs leveled off into a wide corridor with several rooms, and an enormous tapestry of a roaring lion hung along the center wall.

One of his mind games.

Like Scarven, my father had also been a lion Shifter. Every time I looked at it, I saw Scarven tearing Father's head from his body.

I approached the door to his chambers and steeled my nerves, slipping into the part I was forced to play: his willing and faithful servant, his sword and shield.

I opened the door.

Lounging in a burgundy wingback chair in front of the fireplace was a man dressed in black, swirling a glass of amber liquid in his hand. Firelight flickered off his sharp features, his high cheekbones and chiseled jaw. Those ice-cold black eyes lit with intrigue when he turned to stare at me. His lips twitched into a smirk above his trimmed, clean-cut facial hair.

"Hello, brother."

5

NOX

I gave him a stiff nod. "Scarven."

"You certainly took your time," he said, his full, rich voice rolling over me.

"I'm here, aren't I?" I drawled. "As you asked."

Being in his presence always made my stomach tense, my insides knotting with hatred. He looked more like our father every time I saw him. They had the same dark brown hair, the same gray streak on the right side, the same sharp chin and pointed nose.

Kane Scarven was the son of my father and an older woman Father had an affair with seven years before I was born. As Father was next in line for governor at the time, the Dumas—my grandparents—couldn't afford a blemish on his otherwise perfect slate. They paid the woman handsomely and let her keep the child, but refused any claim to young Kane. My father never saw him again. Caius Duma married a respectable woman who bore both myself and Vera. We were the only valid heirs to the province, or so they led everyone to believe.

Until Scarven turned twenty-one and decided *he* deserved to sit in his rightful seat as firstborn of Caius Duma.

I hadn't known of his existence until the challenging. After Father died, my mother told me the whole story of my bastard half-brother. The boy who came from nothing and took everything with one swipe of a paw.

I flicked water from the shoulder of my cloak, then rolled my head along my neck. About a foot away lay a black and silver rug leading to the fireplace, with large sconces on either side of it. A liquor cart stood next to his burgundy chair.

"Let's hear it, then." He brandished his glass toward me. "The Emberfell rebel leader?"

"It was quick," I said.

"Ah, your specialty."

"Well, I assume you don't just keep me around for my good looks."

He leaned back in his chair, propping one foot on top of his knee. I had to hide the way my features tightened at the motion—I knew how similar we looked. How similar our mannerisms were. And I *despised* it.

"It helps to make them suffer sometimes, brother," he said as casually as if we were talking about the weather. "Teaches them a lesson."

"I think seeing the dead body at their feet made the point quite clear." I kept my voice passive. This wasn't the first time we had a conversation like this. Whenever he sent me off to do his dirty work, to "send his messages," it was always the same.

This time, he had sent me to Emberfell, our neighboring province to the north where the Lightbenders lived—people who could create and manipulate light. Scarven had ordered some of his men to the border to act as guards, harassing those who tried to cross into our province. He was staunchly against free travel among the provinces, not wanting to "muddy the waters" between our people and theirs.

Emberfell, naturally, was pissed. Rumors of an uprising at the border had reached Scarven's ears. Their little group of rebels was planning a siege on Drakorum's patrol stations, and he wanted *me* to put an end to it.

Scarven nodded. "I don't need those Lightbenders thinking

they can strongarm me into anything. What did you do with the body?"

"Burned it." The words tasted like ash on my tongue.

"Good. They have a habit of raising their dead up like martyrs. It's better this way. Cut the rot before it spreads, you know."

I swallowed, forcing my features to remain neutral. He could never know the truth of what I did on these missions. "Do you need anything else?"

His lips tugged into a smirk. He lowered his leg and slowly stood to his full height, barely an inch shorter than me, although his frame was slightly larger. "Join me for a drink, brother. It gets rather lonely around here, you know."

Fates, I just wanted to get out of here. This place made my skin crawl.

I shrugged. "A quick one, perhaps."

He strode to his liquor cart and pulled the stopper on a bottle of clear liquid. Pouring a generous serving into a glass, he turned to me with a smile. A dangerous, feline glint shone in his dark eyes. "You've done well, Nox. Perhaps a visit with your sister is in order."

The words jolted through me, eliciting a sharp inhale as my spine straightened. Inwardly, I cursed myself for giving him any sort of reaction. It only fueled his control over me. But to see Vera again?

I hadn't laid eyes on her in five years. Not since my mother tried to break her out of Scarven's cells and was banished from the province. I hadn't seen my mother in that long either, but I knew where she was. I had Kieran hunt her down so Scarven wouldn't suspect anything. Mother was safely harbored in Tenebra, as close to our border as she could possibly get while still obeying Scarven's commands to stay out of Drakorum.

Scarven's men were watching her, though. Always watching. Always *right there* to suck any happiness from my life. So I still hadn't seen her, but at least I knew she was alright. Desperate, longing for her children, probably riddled with anxiety...but alive.

And I would bring her back home one day to reunite with Vera and me if it was the last thing I did.

Vera, however...I may have lived in this wretched mansion for many of my teenage years, but my sister had been *raised* here. Her first word was spoken in these halls. She took her first steps in her captor's manor. All because Scarven feared she would turn into something like *me*. A dragon. A rarity. A weapon.

He never imagined she would be so much more.

If Scarven had it his way, she would *never* see the light of day again.

"You'd like that, wouldn't you, Nox?" he drew out my name and handed me the glass. "To see her again. That can be arranged, of course."

I gripped the edges of the glass, reining in my emotions before my hand could shift into a claw. I merely dipped my head. "Thank you, Scarven."

His smirk slipped into a smile that didn't reach his eyes. Stretching out an arm, he touched his glass to mine, sending a sharp *clink* through the small room. "To loyalty, my brother."

I held his gaze. "To loyalty."

6

DEVORA

C rash.

        I shot up from my bed, mind foggy and heart pounding. I squinted in the dark for the sudden sound. Half of me hoped to see shadows curling around my body, finally showing themselves after months of silence.

No such luck. Just a bundle of twisted sheets, a frame knocked off the armoire, and an empty room.

But when my gaze slipped further down, a four-legged shadow stretched across the floor. It was unnaturally long in the moonlight. It crept forward inch by inch, its silhouette clawing toward me in silence.

I held my breath, pulse racing.

A small, tan and black-speckled head peeked its way around the corner of my bed.

"Holy Fa—how do you keep getting in here, girl?" I clutched my hand to my chest. The cat rubbed against the leg of the bed and flicked her tail in greeting.

She kept showing up, even when I knew the door was locked tight. Trust me. I'd tried it countless times, hoping to catch that pesky force field unaware.

"Did you come back to see me, little friend?" I cooed. I held out a hand, and she jumped onto the bed. Sliding her soft head under my fingers, she arched her back and purred louder. I chuckled as it vibrated up my arm. "My *only* friend, it seems."

Her first visit was a week after I'd arrived. Those glowing yellow eyes staring from the dark had nearly stopped my heart. Since then, she came and went, sometimes vanishing behind the tapestry by the bathing room. I'd examined the wall, but couldn't find anything out of the ordinary. It was simply a solid wall.

But I knew better than to trust anything in this magical empire. In Mysthelm, it might've been *just* a wall. Here...it was probably an invisible door that could only be revealed by the blood of a virgin on a full moon.

"You sure do like scaring me, Jaggy." I ran my hand through the silky fur of her neck. I called her that because she looked like a miniature jaguar I'd seen in picture books. I thought she approved. "You knocked over the—"

A click sounded from the door, stopping me mid-sentence.

I tossed the sheets aside and threw my legs over the bed, slowly padding across the floor. A small sliver of candlelight came from beneath the cracked door.

My eyes widened. I pulled on the handle and cautiously held out my palm to the empty space, waiting for the shock of magic to punch me back inside.

My arm fell straight through, and I stumbled into the hallway.

A laugh of surprise burst from my chest. He'd *actually* done it. Nox had gotten that Alchemist to lift the barrier.

"Jaggy, look—" I whirled back to my nighttime visitor, but she was gone.

I grabbed my glasses off the bedside table and barreled out the door, not even caring that I was still in my nightgown and slippers. The floorboards creaked beneath my feet as I ventured further, the single sconce on the wall casting shadows across the ground. A shiver of anticipation went through me.

At the end of the hall was a set of narrow stairs. They groaned as I hurried down them, spiraling for at least five floors before they finally leveled out onto solid ground.

Several silver chandeliers lit the space, much warmer and cheerier than my isolated floor. This must be where Nox allowed his *real* guests.

A long navy-and-green rug stretched across the polished floor. Decorating the walls were enormous mirrors and oil paintings of the sea and mountains. I took a few tentative steps forward, taking in the tall, arched doorways running down the length of the hall, and tugged on the handle of the nearest one. I was surprised to find it give way beneath my touch.

When it opened, my jaw dropped in delight.

It was a library. But not just any library. I worked for nobles of Mysthelm—I'd been in plenty of those *rich* people's libraries, with mountains of leather-bound books resting on gilded shelves, so delicate that if you so much as sneezed on them, you could be arrested.

This was not like that.

This library was well-loved, bursting with personality. Piles of books with broken spines were haphazardly stacked on shelves that reached to the ceiling. Potted plants that had grown unruly in their dwellings crept along the floor, with vines twining their way up the shelves. But what was most intriguing were the tables at the center of it all.

My brow furrowed at the pieces of paper strewn on top of one of them. Colorful paints swirled along the parchment, everything from small handprints to little flower doodles.

As I glanced around the room, I saw more and more signs that made me wonder where in the *world* I'd ended up.

The books here weren't the kind of history texts I'd been stuck with. Sure, there were plenty of those, but there was a whole wealth of other genres. Shelves full of adventure novels, children's books, guides on reading and arithmetic, coloring books, cookbooks, and even a small section of romance novels way up at the very top.

I climbed up a rolling ladder resting against the wall. Squinting, I read the spines and snagged one that looked interesting. The front featured a shirtless man with a short-cropped beard and abs that made my eyebrows hitch. I tucked it under my arm and carefully jumped off the ladder, continuing down the rows of books. My finger glided over creased spines and weathered covers.

I'd spent the last three months in the near silence of my room, but for some reason, I didn't mind the quiet as much out here. For the first time in as long as I could remember, I felt a small amount of comfort. I could pretend I was a normal girl in a normal house, perusing books I'd seen a million times in a home full of people that welcomed me with open arms.

I found a clock that showed it was ten minutes past eleven. With a sigh, I made my way back to the entrance and shut the door as quietly as I could, surprised I hadn't run into anybody yet.

I looked down the empty hallway and bit my lip. Well, if there wasn't anyone to stop me...

For the next half hour, I explored the lower floors. The one right beneath the library was some sort of guest wing. One of the doors was cracked, and when I peeked my head in, I saw a wall lined with bunk beds. Before I could investigate further, a female voice called out, "Get back to bed, Tilly!"

I yanked my head away and rushed back down the hall. Who in the Fates was Tilly?

The next set of stairs took me to the ground floor. These corridors were just as ornate, but mixed among the paintings and detailed moldings were strange drawings, leaves and sticks glued to paper, flowers made out of cloth, and a whole host of other... *unconventional* home decor.

What *was* this place?

I stumbled upon a narrow hallway in one of the back wings with a ceiling made entirely of glass. The scent of dirt and florals wrapped around me as I walked further down the path until it opened up into a beautiful greenhouse.

Rows and rows of pots filled with herbs and flowers lined the space, with vines crisscrossed at the ceiling and snaking down the walls. I remembered from books I read in my tower that Alchemists relied on the power of nature to source their spells and potions. Herbs, stones, plants, bones...anything derived from the world around them. I wondered if this was an Alchemist's greenhouse.

Nox had mentioned having an Alchemist *and* an apprentice. What kinds of people worked here? Why would Nox need an Alchemist?

Retracing my steps, I reentered the main floor of the mansion, wondering what other hidden treasures I could find. But as I neared the stairwell, voices caught my attention.

I scanned the hall but didn't see an open room, or even a door. Curiosity piqued, I followed the sound of voices, growing more and more intense by the second. Turning a corner, I saw a small iron door, so similar in color to the stone walls that I almost glanced right over it.

Hiding in plain sight.

I *definitely* shouldn't be here.

I turned the knob, waiting a moment to make sure nobody charged out to stab me, then pushed it open.

It was empty.

I opened it wider and took in the small room. It appeared to be a study, with a couple of desks and stacks of books toppling over the floor. Across from where I stood was a large tapestry and several maps of the empire hanging next to it.

I could hear the voices clearly now, as if we were in the same room. But where were they *coming* from? There wasn't anywhere else to go. No chambers, no doorways. No—

I raised an eyebrow at the floor-to-ceiling tapestry of a burning scroll with ashes swirling in the flames. Slowly, I reached out to move the fabric aside.

Behind the tapestry was a small hallway, barely large enough to walk through. I forced myself into the tight space and shimmied down until I came to the back of another tapestry, with shadows of moving figures on the other side.

"—that Emberfell will feel this loss. He was more than their leader; he was a *symbol*," a clipped, measured male voice was saying.

A female voice scoffed. "Yeah, well, everyone knows Scarven always gets what he wants, and he wanted their leader gone. Symbols don't last long against people like him."

"Evidently, that's the only thing I'm good for. Making people disappear." Nox's familiar drawl made me freeze. It was different than when he was with me—lighter and more sincere, void of the contempt I knew so well.

There was a pause, and then another male voice, this one quieter, said, "You did what you had to do, Nox. Scarven watches you too closely. You couldn't risk the truth getting out."

"Yes," the first voice said, his tone rich like honey. "He trusts you. That's what makes this work."

I tried to puzzle the small bits of conversation together. It sounded like they were saying someone important had died, and that Nox had something to do with it. I had no clue who this Scarven person was, but he and Nox must be working together.

The same female voice cut in again. "Anyway, we've got bigger issues than the Lightbenders. Mysthelm's next shipment has been confirmed—tomorrow night, east port."

Mysthelm. My heartbeat quickened at the name of my old kingdom.

"Same contact as last time?" Nox asked.

"No, someone new. Last guy apparently pissed off the wrong person and got his head detached from his body."

Nox hummed, the sound vibrating through the air. "That'll ruin your day."

"Tessa, did this informant have any more insight into what, exactly, this shipment contains?" the first man asked.

"Nope," Tessa said, popping the "p." "All I've got is a place and time. We'll be going in blind, *again*."

A new voice, a deep and husky male's, said, "At least we have an entire day to get ready this time. I swear to the Fates, Nox, if you try to barge up to the docks without a plan again, I'll—"

"Everett, you wound me," Nox said dramatically. "I always have a plan."

"You never have a plan," the first man countered. "*I* have the plans."

"Yes, and *that* is my plan. We all have our strengths, Kieran."

Tessa interjected, "All I know is, if Scarven wants it, we want it more. This might *finally* be our chance to beat him to the punch."

Okay, there was that Scarven name again. So they *weren't* working for him? I rubbed my temples, trying to keep up with the conversation. Maybe all of this had to do with the danger Nox wanted to keep me away from.

A familiar, broad-shouldered shadow suddenly appeared on the other side of the tapestry. I sucked in a breath, backing away as Nox said, "We'll meet back here in the morning to go over details. It's been a long day. You all should get some sleep."

"And what of *you*, Nox?" one of the men from before asked. "Will you be resting tonight?"

A pause. "Eventually. I'll be fine, Silas."

The group murmured their goodnights, and their footsteps faded as they left. I used the opportunity to sneak back the way I'd come before someone discovered me.

As I scurried down the short, narrow hall, fabric rustled against stone. I nearly screamed when a rough hand closed around my wrist.

"Leaving so soon, Shadow Wielder?"

7

NOX

I smelled her the second she stepped into the study. Those pomegranates she ate every morning clung to her fingertips, tart and sweet. It mixed with the scent of salt from a sea breeze, still embedded in her hair from her life on the beaches of Mysthelm.

Fear flashed in those bright blue-green eyes when I grabbed her arm. The smell of it was heightened with my Shifter instincts, bitter and sharp. I didn't think I'd ever seen her *afraid*. Angry and defiant, yes. Annoying and perceptive, constantly. But she was so quick to hide her fear. Behind those black-rimmed glasses of hers, her eyes were much more vulnerable, so easy to read.

I dug my fingers into her wrist. "Having fun playing the spy, I see," I growled. "I shouldn't be surprised. You've already proven how good you are at it."

Her fear swiftly turned to indignation. She yanked out of my hold, but the hallway was so tight, she didn't have anywhere to go. Her warm breath fell across my outstretched arm as she scoffed.

"You're such a hypocrite, you know that?" she seethed.

That caught me off guard. I raised an eyebrow, but she surged ahead before I could say anything. "You punish me for betraying Clarissa when I only did it to keep her alive, and yet you *brag* about what you did to that innocent man." She brandished an arm toward the workshop, her fingers so close, they brushed the side of my ribs. The contact sent a jolt through me.

"You don't know what you're talking about," I snarled.

"You act like you're better than me while spending your nights killing people for Scar—whatever his name is. The ends always justify the means with people like you. 'Doing what you have to do,'" she mimicked Silas's words from a moment ago. Her full chest heaved from her outburst, the space between her eyes creasing in mistrust. "What did that man even do to you? The Lightbender? Is that what you do while you keep me locked in that ridiculous—"

"If you would hold your tongue for five seconds, maybe you'd see you don't know everything," I growled, leaning toward her. She pressed back into the sidewall and glared up at me with contempt as I caged her in.

"I think I know enough," she spat.

"Do you, darling?" My eyes strayed to the pulse pounding erratically at the base of her neck, giving away her fright. I moved closer and relished the way her pupils dilated. *"Enlighten me."*

She swallowed, and I traced the path down the column of her throat. "I know you have some sort of secret operation going on. I know a lot more people live here than just you. Maybe even children. Are you hurting them too?"

Her words pierced my chest, sending enough shock through me that I took a step away from her to the side. That she could even *think* that—

Her eyes narrowed. She knew she'd hit a nerve. She straightened her shoulders, sending those long red waves tumbling down her chest and onto her nightgown.

Something hot and acidic flared inside me. I'd done what she asked. I'd given her free rein of my house, and here she was, sneaking around in the dead of night the first chance she got. *Spying* on my people. Accusing me of things she knew nothing about.

She was observant; that much was obvious. To be able to pick up on what little she heard so quickly was impressive. But she was brash. Presumptuous. *Mouthy.* With the wrong people, that could get her killed.

"You want the truth?" I snapped. "Fine. I'll show you the truth."

I closed my fingers around her wrist and hauled her out of the dark hallway into Tessa and Kieran's study. Devora tried to pull away, but I kept my tight grip on her as we exited onto the first floor.

"Where are you taking me?" she grumbled. I ignored her. We reached the entrance hall, where Everett had started hanging art projects of the refugees to brighten the corridors.

I dragged her to my side and pointed at a childlike drawing of a family—two parents and three children standing beneath a red sun. "This is Morpheus. He's a five-year-old boy who was taken from his parents by Scarven, the name you so callously threw out, and kept in a cell for six months. We still haven't found his family, but he's been living here ever since we rescued him."

Without giving her time to reply, I jerked her to another piece hanging on the wall. "This is a flower made by a fourteen-year-old named Juliette. She glued together pieces of her burnt clothing from when Scarven tortured her with fire. She's been here for two years."

I pivoted to the other side, pulling Devora with me. She stopped resisting, her lips parted and eyes wide. I motioned to three long chains made up of tiny pieces of paper twisted together. Each strand started at the ceiling and worked their way to the floor.

Devora reached out a hand to touch one of the strands. "These have names on them."

"One hundred eighty-two. One for every person we've rescued from Scarven in the last five years. Every person who found refuge in this place."

She looked over at me, her eyes softening for the first time since I met her.

That only made me angrier.

"*He* is the monster, Devora. Not me. No matter what you think you understand, I don't *hurt* these people," I said, my voice low as my nostrils flared. "I, unlike some, find ways to save those I care about. I do what I can to *protect* them. So the next time you want to accuse me of something, Shadow Wielder, I suggest you get your facts straight."

She crossed her arms over her chest, her features mingled with shame and a bit of defensiveness. "Maybe if someone had told me—"

"I don't owe you *anything*."

Her jaw shifted. "What if I wanted to help? In exchange for finding out about my past?"

I shook my head and chuckled darkly. "Of course, it's about what *you* need." That crease at her brow deepened, and I shrugged off the momentary guilt the look brought. "You've seen enough. We're going back to your room."

Her mouth fell open. "You're *unbelievable*."

I smirked. "You're not the first to say that, darling."

"You can't just order me back to my room like I'm some *child*. I've done nothing wrong. I have every right to—"

"Alright, we'll do this the hard way." I caught her around the waist, ignoring her thrashing fists, and hauled her over my shoulder before she could wriggle free.

She pounded her fists against my back, her voice sharp and furious. "Nox! What are you doing? Let me go!"

"So you can spy on me some more?" I started up the stairs, my grip tightening and molding to her curves. "Not a chance."

"You aren't seriously going to carry me up all those steps," she shot back.

"Watch me."

She struggled and kicked for another minute as I reached the next floor. I grasped the backs of her legs tighter, my fingers digging into her skin, and she inhaled sharply before letting out an annoyed huff.

She went silent until we were about halfway up to her tower, when she asked, "What was Scarven doing to them?" Her voice was small, timid. "To the children."

My shoulders tensed. "Whatever you're imagining...it's worse." Images of needles and blood, fire and darkness, chains and stone walls flashed through my mind.

When we reached her room, I flung open the door and dropped her onto her bed. The edge of her nightgown rode up her thighs, and I bit down on the inside of my cheek as I dragged my eyes up to meet her stare. Her cheeks were pink from all the blood rushing to her head, her hair wild and windswept around her shoulders.

She glared at me. "I still hate you, you know."

"Good." I strode back to the door, then turned to peer at her once more. "If I ever catch you spying on us again, I'll have the wards back up before you can say 'traitor.'"

She let out a heavy breath. "Fates, how many times do I have to apologize? Will you ever forgive me?"

My hand gripped the edge of the door. Instead of snapping back, I took a deep breath. "You betrayed my empress, Devora. My *friend*. Shifters aren't forgiving creatures. Especially when you hurt one of our own."

I faced her again. "I know nothing about you except that you're an orphan chasing answers. And I don't fault you for that. But you've proven you'll do anything to get what you want. You'll turn your back on anyone. Call it *protection*, call it the lesser evil, but betrayal is still betrayal."

She opened her mouth to reply, but I kept going. "You say you want to help, and I believe you. But I can't *trust* you. Not yet. I can't trust that you won't betray us if someone comes along to offer you a better deal. I can't trust that you'll make the decision to sacrifice your own desires for the greater good."

She looked down at those words, her hand curling into a ball at her side. I'd hit a mark, but it didn't feel as good as I thought it would.

I pointed down, seeing through floors and hallways to the

drawings that still hung in my mind. "My people risk everything to fight Scarven. To save the broken children you just saw. No matter how sorry you are, I won't gamble their lives on your loyalty."

My anger from earlier shifted into something less biting, but still deep. I didn't want to hate her. I didn't want to keep her locked up. But loyalty was the most important thing in what I did. The Ashen Order, the Keep, my family...they were the only things that mattered. And until someone *earned* that loyalty, they couldn't be my ally. They couldn't be my *anything*.

I supposed she'd been right all along. She *was* my prisoner. Because I would never give her the power to hurt what was mine.

"So hate me all you want, darling," I said, fingers digging into the doorframe. "It won't change a thing."

8

NOX

"Dance with me, Nox," Sage said, those dark eyes sparkling with mischief.

My lips curved into a smile. "With no music?"

"Music?" She chuckled. "We're rebels on the run. We don't get such luxuries." Her grin stretched across her face as she stood from our spot by the campfire and held out a hand. "Dance with me."

"As you wish." I pulled her into my arms. The wind whistled through the trees surrounding our tent, blowing her mass of black curls over her shoulder. Her sleeve had slipped down her arm, and I couldn't resist the urge to kiss her soft skin, my lips trailing up her shoulder and to the base of her neck.

Her head rested against my chest as we swayed to the sound of wind and leaves, buzzing insects and the distant river lapping at its banks. "Where are we going after this?" she asked softly.

I swallowed, thinking of Scarven's anger if he discovered what I'd done. The lengths he might go to in order to get me back.

"I don't know." I leaned away, cupping her face in my hands. "But I promise you, Sage, it will be a better life than the one we left behind."

She blinked once, long lashes brushing against dark cheeks. "I love you, Nox."

"I love you, darling."

I bent to kiss her. When my lips met hers, I tasted something salty. Metallic.

The vision wavered. Her skin went ashen, and crimson blood pooled at the corner of her mouth. She choked and inhaled sharply, eyes filling with dread. I let out a strangled yell at the blood coating my hands.

A slit appeared at her neck, long and gaping. She collapsed in my arms as we both fell to the ground.

"Sage! Sage—no—" I cried out, struggling to keep her in my grasp. Everything was covered in blood.

I scrambled back on my knees with shaking gasps and clutched my hair in my bloody hands. This wasn't real. This couldn't be happening. He couldn't have found us so quickly.

In the blink of an eye, the scene changed. Our moonlit campsite was replaced by sunny cliffs overlooking the Sea of Scarab. Ahead of me at the edge of the cliffs stood two figures I recognized in a heartbeat.

Mother twirled Vera in a circle, my sister's high-pitched giggles breaking the quiet air. They both shared the same blonde hair as me, but Vera's held a hint of rust.

"Noxy! Come play!" my little sister called, her voice rising above the waves crashing below.

My heart lurched in my chest. I stepped forward, reaching out to touch them. I hadn't seen them in five years. I was so close—

The cliffside began to shake. Rocks dislodged and crumbled into the sea below. With my next breath, my family disappeared.

I glanced around in a panic, then ran to the edge of the drop-off, my pulse pounding in my ears. When I blinked, I saw my father flying off the cliff.

I shouted for him, lunging forward as his body fell into thin air, his hand outstretched as if to grab mine. Before I could shift and catch him, the scene changed once more.

My body slammed into metal bars.

The sunlight vanished, and I was staring at familiar cold, dark walls, with the sound of water dripping from cracks in the ceiling. But this time, it wasn't me inside the cell.

I glanced up to find my sister—no longer the bright, giggling five-

year-old but a hardened teenager. She looked like she did the last time I saw her, when she was almost sixteen. Her cheeks were pale and gaunt, those golden eyes now lifeless and dull. Her dirty-blonde hair was tangled and matted, mixed with so much dirt and sweat that it appeared brown. My stomach hollowed when I saw how emaciated she was—her arms and legs were practically skeletons, the bones jutting out as if she hadn't eaten in weeks.

I reached through the cell bars to grab her hand when the shadow of a lion formed on the floor before me.

A dark chuckle echoed off the walls. "Hello, brother."

My eyes burst open with a gasp as I sat upright in bed, my fingers already shifted into talons. Moonlight from the window dripped off my claws, sharp as steel. Chest heaving, I took several deep breaths to calm my racing heart. I couldn't stop the tremor in my arms. The panic from seeing all of them was so *real* and visceral.

I hadn't dreamed of Sage in years. She had died a decade ago, after Scarven caught us trying to leave Drakorum. He'd given me a small taste of freedom, a blessed reprieve after nine years in his house, and I bolted the first chance I got.

It was all a test. He knew I'd run. And he made sure I paid for it.

Sage was a girl I'd met in captivity, an orphan they'd found on the streets of Drakorum and snatched up in one of their first batch of test subjects. She kept her radiance and light even when Scarven's men did everything in their power to dim her. My first love— my *only* love. The girl I'd given everything for.

He made me watch when he killed her.

"*The price,*" he said, "*for thinking you could be rid of me.*"

He slit her throat as she screamed my name. The first of many moments I would come to realize were my fault. If I had only done as he asked, if I hadn't let my pride make me think I could escape, if I'd just been *better.*

So I became better.

I learned how to deceive. How to hide my intentions with a silver tongue, how to get what I wanted without raising suspicion.

I became his subservient little lapdog while swiping his prisoners from beneath his nose. I played the part, did what he asked, and shed as little blood as possible while doing so. My loyalty gave me the freedom to move among the empire as I pleased, and eventually, I started the Ashen Order and led our group of rebels in rescuing more and more helpless people.

But that mistake had taught me well. Sage would still be alive if it wasn't for *me*. Anyone who meant that much to me, who got that close, who captured my heart the way she had...they were as good as dead. Scarven would make sure of it.

I would never let someone in so deeply again—not until Vera was safe and Scarven's head was hanging on my wall.

I scrubbed a hand down my face before remembering it had shifted into talons, and blood instantly welled to the surface of my nose and cheeks. I savored the sting, letting it bring me back to reality. Within seconds, the wounds had already clotted, courtesy of my quick Shifter healing. I forced my claws back into normal hands and threw the covers off my legs.

It was still dark out—half past three in the morning, according to the clock on my wall. I groaned. Tonight was the secret shipment from Mysthelm Tessa had found out about. It was going to be a long day, and I needed to be alert. But there was no chance of going back to sleep.

I padded to my closet and stared at the rows of shelves built into the back. They were full of hundreds of little wooden figurines in various stages of completion. Some fully rendered models of animals, ships, and people; many half-crafted designs still encased in wooden blocks that I'd given up on over the years; stashes of fresh planks of wood, blank canvases simply waiting for me to sink a blade into and carve something precious.

I grabbed one at random, a rich, hard chunk of maple wood, and swiped a carving knife from a chest on the shelves.

After making my way back to the window by my bed, I sat on the wide sill, turning the block of wood over in my hands. My fingers were already searching for the shape hidden inside. It was a habit I'd formed many years ago, when I desperately needed something to do with my hands and my mind. It was often the only thing that kept me from splintering.

With a quiet breath, I set the knife to the grain, letting muscle memory guide the first careful cuts. A curve here, a sweep of wings there. It took my mind off the memories that threatened to crush me, off the hopelessness that always reared back to life. All I had to do was keep my fingers moving, keep the image clear and ready in my head, and let the worries drain into curls of wood at my feet.

———

"You look like trash. You sure you're up for this, Noxy boy?" my third-in-command said by way of greeting as we made our way to the stables of the Keep. Everett and Kieran were already waiting for us with the horses.

I forced a smirk onto my tired features. "Trust me, Tessa, I have no problems keeping up. Tell me again what you found when you scoped out the port this morning?"

"The Mysthelm ship is scheduled to dock ten minutes after midnight," Tessa said. "The guards have a shift change right on the hour, and there's about a two-minute window of opportunity to sneak in and intercept the ship before Scarven's men get there. We'll have to be quick."

"Quick's my specialty," a new voice said as Arowyn popped into the empty space before me. Tessa jerked back with a cat-like hiss, still unaccustomed to the Strider being able to appear without any warning.

"Sorry, did I scare the kitty-cat?" Arowyn mocked.

I snorted. "One of these days, you're going to get a pair of claws to the face."

"Worth it."

When the others had settled, I went through their tasks. "Arowyn, you stay back with Kieran to keep our escape route cleared. We need you free to stride in and break us out if it comes to that. Tessa, you and Everett will come with me." I pointed to the two of them. "Everett will cast an illusion to keep us concealed while we take the south alleyway up to the port, and once we get close enough, Tessa will shift and slip onto the ship. We'll find out what they're carrying and destroy it."

Arowyn and Kieran went over the details of their escape plan while we all mounted our horses and took off north on the thirty-minute trek toward the port. The sun had set long ago, leaving us with the blustery, frigid night wind and the stars to guide our way to the water.

Silas, our head Alchemist and final member of the Ashen Order, had stayed back at the Keep with his apprentice, Milo, to reinforce the wards and protect the refugees. The Keep was made up of a wide variety of Veridians. The vast majority of them were Shifters, but Scarven didn't limit his experimentation to Drakorum citizens. Over the years, he'd captured many from all provinces, wanting a range of magic at his disposal to run trials on as he pleased.

One thing Scarven's victims had learned in their time under his hold was how to fight—for their lives, for their freedom, for those they cared about. And we taught them how to hone that survival instinct. We showed them they would never have to be weak or helpless again. If the Keep came under attack, they knew how to protect themselves.

We were all a bit uneasy about leaving them, but this mission was critical. We *had* to find out what Scarven kept importing from Mysthelm. If it was something he was this secretive about, it must be big. Deadly. Capable of putting even more destructive power into his hands.

We stuck to the cliffs that ran along the eastern shoreline. As we neared the small village off the port, the dark silhouette of a ship loomed in the distance.

A hint of worry flared to life in the back of my mind. Something was wrong. It was too close. It was half an hour to midnight—forty minutes early, if Tessa's scouting was correct. But this ship was already making port.

Tessa and I exchanged a glance before she, Everett, and I spurred our horses toward the village, cutting through the alley between two taverns that led straight to the cargo dock.

I looked to my left to see the hood of Everett's cloak fall to his shoulders, revealing short-cropped black hair and a hint of the numerous chains he wore around his neck. His dual-toned eyes, one dark green and one bright gray, found mine as he gave a sharp nod and said, "You're covered."

Having an Illusionist at our disposal certainly came in handy. He had the magical ability to cast illusions into the minds of others. To anyone looking, we would be nearly invisible—as if our bodies were blending into our surroundings. It was similar to what Scarven's ring did, but I was too suspicious of that *gift*. I didn't feel comfortable using his ring when we needed to be covert.

The three of us dismounted right as we reached the alleyway and tied our horses to a post. There was nothing in sight. The village was asleep, as expected. We made sure the horses were secure before we shot down the narrow street.

As we neared the entrance to the port, the hushed tones of dockworkers grew louder, the sound of feet pounding on wood and water splashing against the decks far too loud for this time of night. Warning bells rang in my head.

The alleyway opened into the wide port, exposing several levels of docks stacked on top of each other for both smaller and larger cargo ships. The mid-sized vessel I'd seen from a distance towered over the unloading dock, the crest of Mysthelm waving on their dark blue sail—a tree with four branches and a sword and sickle crossed at the trunk.

My hackles immediately rose. There were far too many workers. Firelight shone off several gleaming silver masks that some of the men wore, and I caught the familiar shape of a lion's face embedded in them.

Scarven's personal guard.

They weren't supposed to be here yet. We planned our intercept point perfectly—before the delivery was set and in between guard rotations. But here they were, littering the entire port.

"Tessa, we've been compromised. Fall back," I hissed to my third. "They can't know we're here."

"I got it, Boss," she cut in. "You stay. I'm not leaving until we find out what's on that ship."

I growled in response. "Tessa, I swear, if you—"

She gave me a quick wink before bursting into a sprint and shifting mid-air, her long, black locks disappearing into fur, her lithe legs shortening to paws. She landed on top of a low awning as a small cat, then rushed to the ground and took off toward the ship. Tessa had the unique ability to range the size of her Shifter form, from something as tiny as a housecat to a raging lion. It was particularly useful for getting into places she didn't belong.

I pulled my hood tighter over my face. "Remind me to have a little *chat* with her later."

Everett grunted. "Nox, you can't—"

I cut him off. "Is your illusion holding?"

There was a pause, and he sighed. "Yes."

"Good. Don't let it fall, or we die. No pressure." I tracked Tessa's shadow nearing the Mysthelm ship. "I'm going after her."

9
DEVORA

I nursed my wounded pride for the better part of the day, still reeling that Nox had the *nerve* to throw me over his shoulder the night before like I was nothing more than a sack of flour. Like I was his *property*.

The thought made my jaw clench as I traipsed back down the steps of my tower and to the library, the sun almost fully set behind the towering mountains in the west. After months of nothing but history books and almanacs, I was ready for a change of pace.

I ran into a few maids on my way to the third floor, but no other residents made an appearance. I spent a couple of hours browsing the books, reading the first chapters of some, then switching them out if I wasn't in the mood. I'd never had access to this many books before. Sure, the wealthy families I worked for had tons of them, but there was never much time for hobbies, and I wouldn't have been allowed to touch half of them anyway.

Before I landed my first big job with Lady Reaux's household, the only print I read was the Wanted posters hanging outside taverns.

The orphanage I was taken to after being found on Mysthelm's shores didn't hold the fondest of memories for me, but there was one nurse who took compassion on me: Miss Leigh. I was the most troublesome of the lot, always sneaking into the kitchen, drawing on kid's faces in the dark, getting my head stuck in the banister trying to spy on the adults. But Miss Leigh took me under her wing. She taught me to read and write, giving me direction for the stray thoughts running loose in my head instead of scolding me and sending me away without dinner.

Books were a solace now. A way to escape the truths of my life and dive into someone else's fantasies.

But as much as I tried to concentrate on the stories in front of me, a deep, sultry voice with a hint of a growl kept permeating my thoughts.

I'd been right—he *did* have a secret operation going on. And many more people lived here than I anticipated. I could hear them on the lower floors, the sounds of footsteps and slamming doors and clattering silverware from a nearby dining room. As the evening bled into night, the sounds dimmed, the occasional door creaking shut or whispered conversations from people outside the library being the only signs of life.

One hundred and eighty-two children rescued. That was what Nox said last night. He spoke of them as if he knew them—the ones with their art projects plastered to the walls, their families and lives and trauma reflecting in his eyes. It certainly wasn't what I had expected.

Then again, I barely knew him. Perhaps he was right, and I was too quick to assume I knew everything. But that didn't negate the other things I'd heard. How he'd hurt some innocent Lightbender on that *horrible* man's orders, and it didn't seem like it was the first time.

I prided myself on my observance, my ability to read between the lines and piece things together that others may not want me to see. It was a skill developed in childhood, bred by curiosity and loneliness and the need to understand when nothing in my life was understandable.

But even I found it difficult to reconcile all the sides of this dragon Shifter. His charm and charisma with those around him, his anger and disdain with me. The fact that his sole mission seemed to be rescuing others from such a horrid fate, and yet he was quick to draw a blade and snuff out someone's life.

I puzzled through the enigma that was Nox Duma while half of my attention was on the Alchemy book I'd chosen to keep me occupied, until my eyes strayed to the clock on the wall.

Half past ten.

I shut the book and put it back in its place, then crept to the only window in the vast room that overlooked the stables.

My real reason for coming here.

Sure enough, if I squinted through the darkness, I could see a group of hooded cloaks preparing their horses. Nox's tall, broad frame was unmistakable as he smoothly pulled a saddle over his steed's back and covered his own wavy hair with a hood.

The Mysthelm shipment. The one I'd caught them discussing last night.

Something was coming from my home kingdom. Something that this Scarven person they kept talking about wanted.

Call me curious. Call me *brash*, but I wanted to know too. If I could prove myself to be more than just a traitor in Nox's eyes, maybe he would finally work with me. Maybe he'd *finally* keep his promise and help me uncover the truths of my past.

There was only one problem: I couldn't leave the house.

But I had a plan.

I carefully snuck out of the library and down to the first floor, where I found the greenhouse the night before. I'd perused more books on Alchemy than I could count. I figured there had to be something in them about the type of ward Nox's Alchemist used to keep me locked inside.

I may not be an actual Alchemist (nor much of a Shadow Wielder, obviously), but I read how much of their power came from herbs or crystals themselves, paired with a recited spell. Maybe simply *ingesting* certain powerful herbs could dispel a charm, and I didn't have to actually cast a spell.

That was what I told myself, anyway. And I desperately wanted to find a way out of these walls.

The earthy scent of the greenhouse hit me as I hurried down the hallway leading to the glass chamber. What did that book say... something about dandelions being able to break curses? Wait, no. It was thistle.

I glanced around for the strange, jagged plant I'd seen in the book. Several of the sharper leaves with thorns pricked my finger as I—

"You're not supposed to be down here," a hesitant voice said behind me. "Does Nox know where you are?"

I whirled around to face a young man in tweed pants and suspenders over his white shirt. The fabric was smudged with dirt and bits of leaves. Keen, innocent eyes flitted from me to the entrance as he pushed his unruly blond curls from out of his eyes. He was a few years younger than me, maybe nineteen.

I instantly relaxed, sizing him up and seeing what angle to play. This kid didn't look like he would hurt a spider. And if the green marks on his fingers were any indication, he knew this greenhouse well. An Alchemist, perhaps?

An idea formed in my mind.

"Oh, I'm so sorry," I rushed out. "I figured if I wasn't allowed somewhere, the wards would stop me." I tilted my head to the side. "They must be broken or something."

His brow furrowed. "They're not broken."

I widened my eyes in mock innocence. "Well, it's best to be sure. You should bring it up with Nox. You don't want someone getting into—"

"I would know if they were broken," he cut in, chest inflating slightly. "*I'm* the one who set them."

"You don't say?" A grin unfurled on my features. "In that case, my name's Devora. It's *so* nice to meet you."

"We all know who you are," he said, eyeing me with distrust.

I stalked closer to him. "And *you're* Milo, right?"

He immediately stepped backward. "H—How did you know my name?"

"Rebekah, of course." I remembered the note I'd seen in her pocket the other day. *From your Milo*, with the hearts. The same name Nox used when saying he'd have the Alchemist loosen the wards. Put two and two together, and... "She talks so much about you, you know."

His lips parted. "She does?"

I nodded eagerly. "All the time. She wishes she didn't have to spend so much of her day up in that tower cleaning the room. She doesn't get much time for anything else." I took a shot with that last part, figuring if he'd resorted to writing her letters, he didn't get to see her often.

He swallowed. "They keep her so busy lately." His eyes moved toward the door again, then flitted back to me. "Wh—what else does she say?"

Fates, he was kind of adorable. I almost felt bad.

"That she misses you. But she's worried what they'll say if she tries to sneak off during work hours." I knew how big properties like this worked their schedules, more or less. The head housekeeper probably kept a close watch on her maids. Tight rotations, not much downtime in between shifts. Poor kid.

I slid closer to the row of flowers he stood by, absentmindedly fingering the leaves. "I could help cover for her so she can get away and see you." I looked up to see his eyes brighten. "If you wanted."

"You would do that?"

"Definitely. Now that I can leave the tower, I could distract the head housekeeper. Give you some privacy in my room while Rebekah's on her shift. I'd be happy to help you, Milo."

His lips twitched. "That would be—"

"If you do something to help me, of course."

His grin faded. He tugged on his earlobe, leaving faint traces of green behind. "You really shouldn't be here."

"Oh, come on." I propped my elbow on the nearest counter. "Don't you want to see Rebekah? I'm sure it's been a lonely few months. And if it works, maybe we can get a routine going. You'd never have to go this long without seeing her again."

He brushed back his tangle of curls. I could see every thought running through his mind, displayed to the world on his youthful, freckled features. I knew I'd gotten to him. He just had to take the bait.

His shoulders moved up and down as he let out an exhale. I watched him lick his lips, then swallow hard, eyes darting with his thoughts. I tapped my fingers at my side. *Come on, kid...*

And then—

"What do you want?"

There it is.

I smothered a smirk. "For you to drop the wards on the house."

He crossed his arms. "Absolutely not. Silas would kill me." The blood drained from his face. "*Nox* would kill me!"

Silas. One of the names Nox had said last night. I didn't know who the man was, but I filed it away for later. "Just for tonight, I promise. One single night for endless hours with Rebekah. That's more than a fair trade."

He shook his head defiantly. "They trust me. I can't let them down."

"Look, Milo..." I rested my hands on his shoulders to make him meet my gaze. I changed tactics, quickly thinking through my options. "You care about them, yes? Nox and the others? You must know where they are tonight." He blinked, then nodded. "So you know this shipment from Mysthelm could be dangerous."

His lips parted. "Wait, how do *you* know about that?"

"Because Nox told me." Okay, I'd crossed over into *blatant* lies, but I was in too deep to stop. "It's alright; I want to help them. I'm from Mysthelm, remember? Maybe there's something I could do if things go wrong. But I can't do it from here. Please, Milo. Drop the wards, just for a few hours, and I'll make sure they get back safely, *and* I'll help you see Rebekah again."

His light brown eyes, so sweet and naive, slowly took in my words. I saw the moment he made his decision.

"Just for a few hours?" he whispered.

I smiled. "I'll be back before you know it."

He let out a long, shaky breath. "Fine. But they *can't* find out." He reached for his pocket and pulled out a small burlap pouch, then shot me a warning look. "If they get mad at me, I'm telling them you tied me to a tree."

I let out a bark of laughter. "Deal. That was my next move, anyway." He jerked backward, and I laughed again. "Kidding, Milo. I knew you'd make the right decision."

He mumbled some choice phrases that had my eyebrows rising before he placed a few stems from his pouch onto his tongue. A string of unidentifiable words flew from him. There was a strange tightening sensation around my chest, almost like something was pressing on my lungs, and then it released.

He stared back at me grimly. "It's done. You're free to go."

A wicked smile curled on my lips. "Perfect."

IO

DEVORA

Fates, it was cold.

My (borrowed) horse flew through the night, following far enough behind Nox's pack that I could just barely see them cresting the small hills. I wished I'd grabbed a pair of gloves. My fingers were nearly frozen to the leather reins, and my entire body shook as the wind beat against me. Clenching my jaw to keep my teeth from chattering so hard, I raced north after the others.

I kept my distance when the five figures ahead of me came upon a small village and slowed. Three of them broke off and headed toward a town square. I recognized the back of the tallest, largest one to be Nox. Two smaller forms flanked him and silently made their way down the street and out of my line of sight.

I stopped my horse right on the outskirts of the square, dismounting and tying her reins to a tree. Her hooves would make too much noise, and even though Nox and his group were distracted, their Shifter hearing was strong. I didn't need them catching me just yet.

I wasn't even sure why I was doing this. Pride? Curiosity? The need to know everything? All were viable options. After being locked up for so long, the idea of an adventure was too good to pass up. And when I heard the name "Mysthelm" last night, my thoughts had spiraled.

What did my kingdom have to do with Drakorum? Mysthelm and Veridia *hated* each other. Our two lands had gone to war over three hundred years ago when the Fates, our mystical deities, promised the victor a wealth of magic never seen by humans before. The Veridians won, and Mysthelm was left powerless. They'd been holding a grudge ever since. There hadn't been any contact in centuries until the late King of Mysthelm reached out to broker a marriage of alliance with Empress Clarissa a few months ago.

Which was why I couldn't understand why Mysthelm would be sending cryptic shipments to one of the Veridian provinces.

A small part of me—okay, a pretty large part—entertained the idea of simply running away altogether. I had my freedom. I could get a headstart before Nox found out I left, and at that point, would he even bother tracking me down?

But I wasn't *that* reckless. A stranger who couldn't control her supposed "magical powers" on the run in a foreign empire wouldn't last long. I had nowhere to go. And as much as I hated to admit it, Nox and his group were the best chance I had of finding my family and learning my magic.

I just had to prove myself. Prove that I was more than a traitor, a backstabbing friend, and a liar. Prove that I was worth taking a chance on.

Prove it to him or myself, I wasn't sure.

I kept my sights trained on Nox and the two others as they slipped into a narrow alley. Following now would give me away—the path was too tight for them not to smell or hear me. Quickly scanning the streets, I saw a rickety ladder propped against a nearby building. I darted across and scrambled my way up onto the low rooftop. Keeping low, I tugged my scarf over my face and my hood over my bright hair. I'd foregone my glasses, afraid they would break or get in my way, but I could still see fairly well—I mostly used them for reading.

" —been compromised. Fall back," I heard Nox say from my viewpoint right above them. "They can't know we're here."

"I got it, Boss. You stay. I'm not leaving until we find out what's on that ship," a female voice I recognized from last night—Tessa, maybe—said. I risked a quick glance over the side of the rooftop and was so surprised, I nearly lost my balance.

I couldn't see them. Their voices filtered up to me, but nobody was there. I *knew* I'd seen them leave their horses and walk down this alleyway. And yet...it was completely empty.

A low growl echoed from somewhere on the deserted street. "Tessa, I swear, if you—"

Nox's voice cut off, and a moment later, the awning connected to the other end of the roof bowed beneath an invisible force. Almost as if something landed on it. I stumbled backward and held my breath, waiting for someone to catch me, but the weight disappeared from the fabric as suddenly as it appeared.

"Remind me to have a little *chat* with her later," Nox said, irritated.

A third male spoke, a husky voice I recognized from last night. "Nox, you can't—"

"Is your illusion holding?"

A pause. "Yes."

Illusion. That must be why I couldn't see them. I'd never witnessed that magic in action before.

"Good," Nox said, followed by the sound of heavy footsteps leading out of the alley. "Don't let it fall, or we die. No pressure. I'm going after her."

I peered over the rooftop toward the port beyond and saw a dozen workers moving about the various decks, with the daunting shadow of a ship spilling out onto the night. A sail with the familiar crest of Mysthelm billowed in the wind, and I involuntarily shivered.

The port was crawling with workers wearing eerie lion-shaped masks, concealing their true faces. It made my skin prickle. Rolling my shoulders, I cracked my neck from side to side and took a deep breath.

Life as a maid wasn't exactly conducive to late-night raids and climbing off rooftops, but before that, I'd done my fair share of sneaking around. When the orphanage kicked their inhabitants out at fifteen because there were too many mouths to feed, you were forced to roam the streets of Mysthelm. There were *plenty* of hours spent pillaging for spare coin or idiots with big pockets.

Never from quite so high, but still.

I lowered myself onto the awning, dangling my feet over the edge until they found purchase on the window lip. Grabbing on to the upper ledge, I shimmied down the wall, then braced myself and jumped. A brief pang jolted up my legs as I landed in a crouch.

The port was a wide, open space, with multiple docking stations leading out into the dark waters of the Sea of Scarab. The only ship in sight was the one from Mysthelm. Men moved to and from the gangplank, rolling large wooden barrels out from the cargo hold and into the backs of black carriages waiting in the center of the road.

Consider me intrigued.

I hugged the walls on the outskirts until I reached the railing overlooking the ocean. The gangplank to the ship was straight ahead. If I could just—

"You, there! Stop!"

The shout came from behind me, and I instantly tensed, my hands tightening on the railing.

But the shout wasn't for me. I peered over my shoulder to find three men swarming the alleyway I'd just abandoned. My eyes widened when they pulled out a cloaked figure with short black hair peeking out from beneath his hood. Was that the Illusionist? One of Nox's people?

Out of habit, I reached for my thigh, where I usually kept my trusted dagger—then remembered Nox had taken it. Glancing around, I spotted a splintered piece of wood lying on the ground. It was pointy, at least. It would have to do.

I tucked it under my cloak, but before I could make my way back to try and help the Illusionist, another shout rang out from closer to the Mysthelm ship. Sounds of a struggle echoed—fists on skin, creaking wood, cries of anger.

Nox and Tessa.

I stepped toward the sounds, about to break into a run when something else caught my eye.

The gangplank to the ship was empty. All the workers had converged on the disruption, leaving the entrance unattended.

Biting my lower lip, I flicked my gaze between the fights breaking out in the street and the clear pathway to this mysterious cargo Scarven wanted so badly.

My decision was made. Nox was a *dragon* Shifter, for Fates' sake. He could take care of himself.

With one last glance, I surged forward and onto the waiting ship.

II

DEVORA

T he quarterdeck was empty. The only sounds were the sail flapping against the mast above me and waves sloshing at the hull. Lanterns swayed in the corners, casting a golden glow over the weather-worn wooden planks. To my far right rested the ship's wheel, broad and rimmed in iron, with a compass and a spyglass hanging next to it. The scent of tar and brine hung in the air, thick with salt.

They'd cleared out most of the barrels already. A quick search revealed a couple of broken ones lodged near the stairs leading below deck. They were cracked down the center and turned on their sides, as if something had knocked them over in transit.

I took a step closer and squinted, unsure what I was seeing.

Spilling from the broken barrels were handfuls of...leaves. Or maybe flowers. An herb of some kind.

I knelt next to the barrel and stroked one of the brown stems. Four tiny, sharp green leaves branched from the center. Bringing it closer to my face, I noticed a faint red tint running through the veins, but other than that, it looked like a regular leaf.

That was...anticlimactic.

This couldn't possibly be what Mysthelm lugged all the way

across the sea. Why would Scarven be interested in a bunch of *plants*?

Without thinking, I grabbed several of them and stuffed them in my pocket. Nox wanted to know what the ship was carrying, and I found it. Whatever *it* was. Surely Milo and the other Alchemist would be able to figure it out. Not my job.

I hurried back to the gangplank and was about to descend onto solid ground when I spotted shadows walking toward the ship, their voices growing closer with every second.

Adrenaline raced through me as I stooped low to the ground and flattened my back against the inside of the ship, praying they hadn't seen me. Heavy boots thudded nearby, and a moment later, cloaks brushed against the floor, mere feet from where I hid.

"It's clear," the first man said, tapping the hilt of his dagger against a stack of empty crates. "You can tell Rolney it looks like the shipment made it intact this time."

"Thank the Fates. Last thing we need is another delay," the second one replied with a grunt. "Rebels slowed us down. Scarven wants this stock at the Hollow within the hour."

Scarven. So these were his men.

The first let out a low grumble. "Catch any of them?"

"No, they got away. He won't be happy."

Muscles I hadn't realized I'd been clenching slowly relaxed at the news. I wasn't sure when I started caring about the well-being of Nox, but I was glad they had made it out.

"What Scarven doesn't know won't hurt him." Their backs were to me, but I saw the first man kneel to pick up a stray leaf on the ground. "Think he'll notice if one of these goes missing?" he asked with a chuckle.

"I wouldn't put it past him," the second warned. "Stay away from that stuff, Brendyn. Fatesprig's nothing to scoff at."

Fatesprig. I looked down at the leaves in my hand.

"True, I saw what it did to that Duma freak," the first remarked.

My eyebrows shot into my head as I glanced back up. *Duma freak?* Were they talking about Nox?

Another thought occurred to me that made my stomach sink. If it *wasn't* Nox, who could they mean?

"Hey! What are you doing here?" The men whirled around to face me, the one with the knife lurching forward. The blade's edge gave a menacing flash. Cold scratched along my ribs as my lungs forgot how to breathe for a second.

Fates. Really wished I had my dagger right about now. Or magic. *Think fast, Devora.*

I reached out and pretended to feel along the floor, then shot up with a handful of leaves in my grip. I extended it to them, quickly sifting through the tidbits of information I'd overheard to see what I could use. "Umm...Rolney sent me. To get the last of the fatesprig."

The man holding the knife narrowed his eyes. "The boat's all clear. Why would Rolney send you?"

I shrugged. "There are still a couple of broken barrels over there." I nodded toward the other end of the quarterdeck. "Said Scarven would be pissed if a single leaf was missing."

"Go check," the first one, Brendyn, said to the second, jerking his head to where I pointed. His blade stayed trained on me. "Why don't I recognize you?"

I licked my lips. "I don't live here. I'm part of the Mysthelm crew. From the North Territory."

His eyes dragged along my body, interest sparking as if I were a toy suddenly dangled in front of him. "Mysthelm, you say? Maybe I should've stowed away on a ship with you months ago."

My lips curled up in disgust, but I schooled my features. "Look, my captain told me we're already late with the delivery, and he doesn't want to make Scarven mad. But if you're okay with that, then by all means, waste my time."

"She's right, Brendyn," the second one said as he made his way back. "Two broken barrels full of it."

Brendyn sighed, giving me one last look. "Fine. Get them out. I'll tell Rolney it's clear, then we can get going."

A weight lifted from my chest, and my shoulders sagged in relief. The two of them walked back down the gangplank and out of sight, the wooden deck creaking beneath their weight.

I slumped against the railing, pinching the stems in my pocket. *Fatesprig.*

A smile pulled at my lips. Perhaps this would be enough to prove myself after all.

12
NOX

T slammed my fists on my desk. "We were *this* close," I snarled. My fingers shifted into talons and scratched against the wood. "Why were they there so early?" I whirled around to face the others, then motioned to Tessa. "This new contact of yours must be a rat. Scarven knew someone was going to be there."

The four of them looked as dejected as I felt. We'd gotten away mostly unscathed. When Everett was cornered, his illusion over Tessa and me fell, and Scarven's men converged. Tessa and I took out a couple before she was able to shift into a smaller cat form and get away to help Everett, and Arowyn magicked herself to my side. Then we met Tessa, Kieran, and Everett in the village square.

Everett had a few scratches, and Tessa broke her wrist, but she'd healed by the time we met up. No lasting injuries. No identities compromised. Overall, it wasn't a loss.

But we still had no clue what Scarven wanted from that shipment.

My hands curled into balls at my sides. It was *infuriating*, not being able to use my power. Knowing he had managed to stifle the largest part of me and bend it to his will. If I gave away who I was among his men, he'd know I betrayed him. A dragon wouldn't exactly blend in. But *I* wasn't the one who would pay the price. The hold Scarven had over my sister's life threatened me every single day.

When I saw my people in need, I wanted to lash out. I wanted to do everything in my power to save them. Yet I was constantly reminded of what I had to lose, how I had to play it smart and protect the only advantage we had.

It felt like walking on eggshells, waiting for the moment when it all came crashing down.

Arowyn crossed her arms and cocked her head at me, her long, near-white hair piled at the top of her head in a bun. "I keep telling you to let me go at it alone. You're being an idiot."

Tessa snorted, and I shot her a look. "You're not wrong," she said to Arowyn. "But read the room."

Arowyn was completely unfazed. *Bored*, even, as she always looked. She simply shrugged. "Nothing to read. We failed, again, and Nox is pissed, again. I have a simple solution: let me go next time. I'll be in and out in under a minute. No need for all these illusions"—she waved a hand at Everett—"and testosterone." Her light blue eyes pierced mine.

My nose twitched as I held her stare. She was right. I *knew* she was right. But for all of my jokes and masks, my desire for control was immovable. If anyone was going to put their safety on the line, it would be me. Not the ones I cared about.

I sighed, struggling to release my frustration. "Arowyn, look—"

The door to the workshop burst open. A breathless Milo careened inside, nearly losing his balance as he cried, "I'm sorry, Nox! It's all my fault."

My second steadied him. Kieran's annoyingly perfect hair was intact as always, barely a hint of dirt on his cloak as he raised an eyebrow. "Calm down, Milo," he said in his smooth baritone. "Take a breath. What happened?"

Milo held a hand to his chest and inhaled, the color slowly returning to his cheeks. "I—I let her out."

A weight sank in my stomach. "Let *who* out, Milo?"

He licked his lips. "The Shadow Wielder. I dropped the wards. Just...just for a few hours."

In the corner of the workshop with his cabinets of herbs and potions, Silas the elderly Alchemist cursed. He swiftly crossed the room and grabbed Milo by the ear, yanking him forward. "I leave you alone for *ten* minutes..."

His words became muffled beneath Milo's whines. The two of them had a close, if not easily irritable relationship, and spent most of their time together. They'd even begun to dress similarly in the two years since the older Alchemist had taken Milo as his apprentice. Tweed pants, suspenders over a white button-down, the occasional vest or sweater. While Milo's messy blond curls constantly covered part of his eyes, Silas's brown hair was groomed close to his tawny scalp, gray creeping onto the sides.

He adjusted his glasses with one hand while keeping the other firmly on Milo's ear. "What did you do, boy?" Silas asked, his normally quiet, patient tone now heavy with disappointment.

Milo's brow furrowed. "Is—isn't that why the mission failed? Because she messed it up?" He glanced around the workshop. "Wait, where'd she go?"

My hackles rose, my spine straightening as I realized what he was saying. I took a step across the workshop to him, then another, my teeth grinding in an effort not to bite the boy's head off.

"You let her out of the Keep?" My voice was lethally quiet. If *she* was the one who got Everett caught—

"Down, boy," a voice said from the tapestry hanging on the wall. The scent of sunshine and pomegranates wafted toward me. My head snapped to face her, red hair tucked into the hood of a cloak, full lips tilted in a smirk. "He was just doing me a favor."

A growl rumbled up my throat as I stalked toward Devora. "Give me one good reason I shouldn't send you to the capital and let Clarissa lock you in a cell."

Her eyes sparked, and my blood heated. Instead of cowering,

she held out a hand, the tips of her fingers grazing my chest. Something green and leafy rested in the center of her palm.

She hummed as she stared me down. "I'm guessing you don't want this, then?"

13

NOX

I raised an eyebrow. "Did you...climb a tree?"

"If by 'tree' you mean 'big, scary Mysthelm ship,' then yes, I climbed a tree."

Murmurs broke out behind me as the other members of the Ashen Order took in her words. My eyes narrowed, gliding from her face to the leaf sitting in her hand.

"Start from the beginning," I ordered.

Victory shone on her features. She glanced around the workshop, those keen eyes not missing a beat. When her gaze reached Milo, she gave him a little wave, and he blanched.

"Listen, I heard you all talking last night about the Mysthelm shipment, and I got curious," she started. "I convinced Milo here to drop the wards on the—what did you call it? The Keep. But just for one night. I wanted to know what was going on." She looked back at me. "I wasn't lying when I told you I wanted to help, Nox."

My jaw twitched, but I said nothing. My Shifter hearing heightened the sounds of those behind me—Everett tapping his knuckles against my desk, the movement making his necklaces clink together; Tessa's little scoffs and sighs; the rustle of fabric as Silas took his glasses off and cleaned them on his shirt, something he often did in stressful situations. Milo's heart was beating like a hummingbird's wings. Kieran was silent, steadfast as usual.

Arowyn was the first to move. Her footsteps were heavy as she sauntered forward, curiosity lighting her normally uninterested features.

"So, this is her." Arowyn nodded at Devora. "The prisoner."

I rolled my eyes. There was that *word* again. "How did you find us?" I asked Devora.

"I watched you from the library, then borrowed one of the horses and followed you."

My features hardened. "Did *you* summon the men to attack Everett?"

Devora leveled me with a cold look and took a step closer. "What was that you said last night?" Her eyes flashed. "If you would hold your tongue for five seconds, maybe you'd see you don't know everything."

Kieran stiffened at my side, and Tessa's lithe shadow crept up beside me. Shifters knew their place in the pack. If someone disrespected their alpha, there were consequences. That was how our nature worked.

Heat unfurled like hot oil down my spine, but it wasn't mere anger. This Shadow Wielder liked a *challenge*. It sparked my blood, setting my chest on fire.

A menacing smile curled the edges of my lips. I towered over her, relishing the split hesitation that crossed her face, and slowly reached for her hand. My fingers shifted into claws as I scraped them down her arm, not breaking skin but enough to leave faint pink streaks.

Her breath caught. The scent of her fear mixed with something *else* wrapped around me as I forced her hand to open, and the feel of her skin against mine sent fire to my core. I grabbed the leaf's stem and dangled it in front of her eyes.

"Then tell me, Devora, darling," my voice was an icy whisper, "how this little plant is supposed to save you now."

The air around us snapped. She recoiled, slipping out from in front of me and clearing her throat. "That's what I was *trying* to do. Yes, I followed you to the port. But, no, I didn't summon anyone to attack Everett." Devora glanced around the room and stopped when her eyes landed on Everett. "You're him, right? The Illusionist?"

Everett nodded curtly, his shoulders shifting beneath his dirt-smudged tunic. Those dual-colored eyes narrowed on Devora, as if still trying to get a read on the Shadow Wielder.

He could get in line.

Devora bit down on her bottom lip, and she actually looked remorseful. "I was up on the rooftop next to you. I knew Nox and Tessa had left, so I followed. It wasn't until I was almost to the ship that I saw the men going after you. I—I had a choice to come help, but I decided to sneak onto the ship instead." Her throat moved as she swallowed. "I'm sorry. I should've gone back to help you."

Tension hung between the two of them. As much as I wanted to step in, this wasn't my apology to accept.

A muscle fluttered in Everett's cheek, but after a moment, his posture loosened. "We made it out. Just tell us you got something good."

Everett was almost as keen as I was about finding more information on Scarven's whereabouts. Besides myself, he was the only other member of the Order to have been one of Scarven's prisoners. He never spoke much of his time in the cells, but I had a feeling this was just as personal for the young Illusionist as it was for me.

"I did. At least, I *think* I did," Devora said. "I found some broken barrels carrying what Mysthelm is exporting. This stuff." She motioned to the leaf in my hand. "It's called fatesprig. I heard some of Scarven's men talking about it."

Tessa snorted. "Fates, you're good."

"Don't encourage her," I muttered.

Devora continued, "This is what he's been after. And it sounds dangerous. The men were afraid to handle it too closely. They didn't say what he's been using it for, only that..." She trailed off, pinching her lips with a strange look at me.

"What is it?" I barked.

"They said... They said, 'I saw what it did to that Duma freak.'"

It was like someone had dumped a bucket of ice water over me. The room went still, nobody daring to breathe.

I clenched my hand around the leaf. Whatever this was, Scarven was using it on my *sister*.

More experiments. More torture.

"Silas," I called, turning toward the Alchemist. "Can you figure out what this is?"

The older man extricated the plant from my grip. "Of course. I've never heard of it, so if they're importing it from Mysthelm, it's likely it only grows over there. I'll run some tests on it and see what I can find."

I nodded in thanks as Devora said, "Who were they talking about? The Duma—"

"Did anything else happen?" I curtly cut her off.

For once, she didn't press the issue. "They caught me before I could hear much more."

My eyes darted down her body, instantly checking for injuries. "And you simply walked away?"

"I told them I was from Mysthelm. They let me go when they thought I was part of the ship's crew."

Tessa chuckled. "Gotta admit, that's quick thinking."

Arowyn kicked off from the wall. "Great, so we know what Scarven's been buying, all because someone here finally had the nerve." She smirked at Devora. "I like this one."

"Why am I not surprised?" I rumbled.

"You should use her, Nox," Arowyn said. "She knows what she's doing. And once she gets a hold of her shadow magic, she could be exactly what we need."

"You don't have to talk as if I'm not right here," Devora said, quirking an eyebrow.

Two days ago, I would've shut Arowyn down and written off the entire exchange as ridiculous. I couldn't have someone on my team I didn't trust.

But tonight was our first breakthrough in months. A true step forward in figuring out how to beat Scarven at his own game.

Because of this Shadow Wielder.

An idea took shape in my mind. Slowly, carefully, the fringes of a new plan brushed against my doubts. A risky plan. A dangerous plan.

I didn't have to trust her. I didn't even have to *like* her. But I knew how desperate she was to prove herself, to discover more about her roots and her magic. It was what drove her to betray Clarissa in the first place.

I could use that desire.

The room seemed to hold its breath. "You want answers, Shadow Wielder?" I lowered my voice as my gaze raked up her form. "You'll have to earn them."

She squared her shoulders, rising up to her full height without breaking my stare. "On one condition," she said, and I cocked my head.

"I want my dagger back."

14

DEVORA

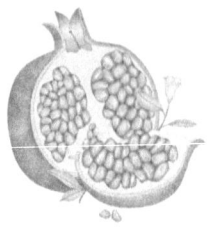

I didn't hear from Nox for two days.

I was restless. And irritated. It was beyond frustrating to be in the thick of the action, only to be shoved back in my tower without another word. What did Nox mean when he said I had to earn my answers? What was he planning?

I *wanted* to help. And it wasn't only because of what he could offer me. This entire operation, the mysterious fatesprig, this Scarven person, Nox's safehouse for his victims...I couldn't shake the feeling that there was something *more* here. Something important. Something Nox's people thought was worth fighting for.

I never had that before.

Thank the Fates for Arowyn, my new (figurative) best friend. If she hadn't vouched for me, he probably wouldn't have given me another thought.

The two days after the midnight mission were worse than all three months combined. I felt like I was going to crawl out of my skin with impatience. I was still allowed to leave my room, but every time I ventured down to their secret meeting space, someone was guarding it.

I kept my promise to Milo, at least. Poor kid looked like he was going to piss his pants when Nox found out he'd let me leave. I couldn't help but feel a little bad. I left him a note in the greenhouse the day after, telling him to meet Rebekah in my room that evening when she delivered my dinner.

The excitement on Rebekah's face when I told her he was going to come see her...I couldn't help but smile. They were so sweet. Aglow with that fresh young love that made butterflies erupt in your stomach and your cheeks hurt from grinning.

But it also pinched something inside of me. An old mark with so many scabs sewn across it that I thought nothing would ever get through.

I wasn't used to that kind of innocent affection. Where I came from, people were commodities to be *used*, not cherished. When I was starving or needed a roof over my head, I found the nearest bar with wealthy men seeking a distraction. For a little bit of attention, I could get a free meal or a warm bed. It was all about what you had to offer, how you could be useful to someone else.

That was how Lady Reaux had dragged me into her schemes. What I could do for her, and what she could do for me. It wasn't compassion. It wasn't anything akin to *love*. Miss Leigh from the orphanage was one of the only people to care about me simply because of who I was. An unconditional love not born out of necessity, but choice. Not survival, but sincerity.

The empress could've been that person for me. Clarissa was kind and genuine, with a loyalty that reminded me of Nox. I saw the way they both loved those around them, and I'd be lying if I said I didn't yearn for it.

But I'd ruined any chance for either of those relationships.

I shouldn't be surprised Nox wanted to use me for whatever the next mission against Scarven was. That was what I'd proven myself to be good at. A tool, a weapon. Something that was needed but not always wanted.

After two long days, there was a rap on my door before Nox abruptly entered the room.

I jumped and pulled the bedsheets up to my chest. "Most people wait to be let in, you know," I shot at him. "I could've been naked."

"As if you didn't spend an entire evening roaming my house in your lacy nightgown," he said without missing a beat, his eyes doing a quick scan of the room before settling on me. They flicked to the top of the sheet and back up to my face.

My cheeks heated against my will as I reached for my glasses on the nightstand. "Does the fact that you've *deigned* to come visit me mean I can finally know what you're up to?"

He let out a sigh that filled the air. "So dramatic. Come on."

"Come *where*?"

His large hand wrapped around the bedpost at my feet, dark rings glittering at me. "Are you always this obstinate?"

"More so, usually." I gave him a sweet smile.

"Fine. If you'd rather stay up here—"

"Fates, I thought you were supposed to be *charming*," I said with a disgruntled noise as I hastily threw off the covers. "I'm coming, I'm coming."

I followed him through the hall and down several flights of stairs until we made it to the bottom floor.

"So where are we going?" I prompted, tired of the heavy silence between us.

"Patience is a virtue," he drawled.

I rolled my eyes. "Yeah, well, so is not locking people up, but that's none of my business." When he glared at me, I held my hands up in innocence, then adjusted my glasses. "Is there a new mission?"

He hummed, and the sound dripped down my spine. "So eager to jump into danger?"

"I'm just as curious about what Scarven is using this fatesprig stuff for as you are."

His eyes examined me one more time before he spun and opened a door in the hallway. We were in the same large room as two nights ago, with dark brick walls and a wooden floor. Right by the door was a couch. Arowyn lounged on it with her feet resting on a small coffee table. Next to that was a whole wall of cabinets, where Silas and Milo had taken up residency. There were pouches overflowing with dried flowers and half-filled glass vials of liquid strewn across the cabinets. Their Alchemist den, I assumed.

My eyes kept roaming, taking in the space. To the right of Silas and Milo were a couple of bookshelves perched by the only window in the room. Along another stretch of wall was an area for target practice. Several circular targets were set up, with a cache of daggers, axes, bows and arrows, and little throwing stars inside a basket. Everett and a handsome man I hadn't met but who looked like he could kill me and bury my body without getting a drop of dirt on his impeccable suit sat at a table in the center of the room.

And finally, directly to my right, was a desk. Nox strode to it and leaned against the side.

An unexpected twinge went through me. I didn't know these people. This wasn't my home. This was my prison—it should feel cold. Unwelcoming. Hostile.

But it felt like *someone's* home. It was full of life and personality and mixed smells of herbs and steel, sweet alcohol and sweat. Watching these people so casual and unburdened, I could see this was a place where they let their guard down. Even Nox's shoulders relaxed as he swirled his glass in his hand.

Until their attention turned to me.

A combination of wary and curious eyes found mine. The outsider. The traitor. The broken Shadow Wielder. I could imagine their thoughts, and I didn't blame them.

I just had to prove them wrong.

"Official introductions might be unnecessary at this point, but this is Devora," Nox said. The way he said my name, the letters drawn out in that low, smoky voice, warmed the back of my neck.

"You already know who Arowyn is," he continued. I glanced at the couch where the woman sat. "She's a Strider. That means she can—"

"I know what it means," I cut in, then rolled my lips. "Sorry. Keep going."

"Silas and Milo are in the back," Nox said. The two Alchemists looked up at the sound of their names, and Milo's face immediately turned a bright pink. "And you know Everett, our Illusionist" —Everett stared at me from the table, something strange about his eyes that I couldn't quite place—"and Kieran, my second-in-command." He gestured to the last man sitting at the table with Everett. "He's also a Shifter. A stag."

Kieran's dark brown eyes pierced me, sizing me up as if he could see into my soul. It was unnerving having all of them focused on me. The insect under a magnifying glass.

To my surprise, something small and furry wound between my legs. I looked down with a gasp and then laughed.

"I was wondering where you'd been, Jaggy." I knelt to rub my fingers through her soft, speckled fur. She hadn't snuck into my room for several days now.

Nox chuckled. I looked over to see him giving me a curious look.

"What?" I stood back up with a furrowed brow.

Kieran, who had been stone-faced and quiet, put a hand over his mouth to cover a smirk.

I narrowed my eyes. "What is—" My question morphed into a strangled yelp. At my feet, Jaggy suddenly started to *change*.

Her fur sank into her skin as her four limbs elongated, her thin tail shrinking and vanishing before my eyes. Long, black locks grew from her head at an uncanny rate. Glowing eyes dimmed to dark brown until I was no longer staring into the face of Jaggy, but *Tessa*.

The Shifter stood a foot from me and wiggled her fingers, offering me a wink. She wore a sleek gray bodysuit and brown combat boots that managed to stay silent as she slunk over to the couch and sat next to a laughing Arowyn.

"It's been you this whole time?" I asked once I caught my breath. "*You* were the cat sneaking into my room?"

Tessa shrugged. "Noxy boy wanted someone to check up on you."

"Of course he did," I grumbled, shooting him a dirty look. He was still smiling. That might have been the first time I'd ever seen him truly *smile*. It made something clench in my stomach.

"Now that we're all here," Kieran started, rising from his seat and buttoning his suit jacket. "Might we know why you called us, Nox?"

"Always straight to the point," Tessa said with a dramatic sigh. "No time for pillow talk."

Everett snorted. "To be a fly on *that* wall."

Silas gave a loud *humph*. "We have children present," he scolded from his side of the room, wiping his green-stained hands on an apron.

Next to him, Milo rolled his eyes. "I'm nineteen, Silas."

"Exactly. A child."

The tension in the room drained little by little at their banter, until Nox spoke again. "I called you here because I wanted everyone to meet, since Devora will be joining us from here on out."

"*What?*" Kieran bit out. Next to him, Everett crossed his toned, dark forearms in front of a pair of chains hanging from his neck.

I didn't miss the pointed glance Tessa shot Kieran across the room, and neither did Nox. "What was that look for?" Nox snapped.

"What look?" Tessa asked innocently.

"You know what look."

Kieran responded this time, "It's just that we want to make sure you're positive this is a good idea."

"What Kieran means is, are you crazy?" Tessa added.

"They're just bitter." Arowyn flicked something off her shoulder. "The newbie got the fatesprig."

"We're not *bitter*, Arowyn; we're *logical*. Cautious," Kieran shot back.

"Logical would be saying 'oh, look, this person succeeded in something we've been trying to do for months. We should take advantage of her talents,'" Arowyn said in a mocking tone as she kicked her feet off the coffee table. "Illogical would be, 'oh, let's lock her back up and keep pretending we're making progress.'"

Tessa jerked her thumb at the Strider. "I mean, she's got a point."

"I know," Nox said. "Which is why Devora is here. I have a plan."

The authority in his voice made the whispers die down. I could tell Kieran and Everett weren't exactly in agreement, with the way their gazes kept shifting to me and narrowing slightly, but they were listening.

"We know what Scarven's been importing. And thanks to Silas, we're starting to get an idea of what this fatesprig does." Nox gestured to Silas.

Silas nodded. "It reacts strongly when exposed to Veridian blood. I've only tested it by dripping a couple drops of my own blood onto it. The veins in the leaves change color, indicating the composition of the plant physically *changes*. I can't test it further without risking someone's safety, but it stands to reason that the opposite would also occur: the fatesprig can change the physical composition of *our* blood. Our magic."

"So Scarven is using it for his experiments," Tessa said slowly. "To manipulate magic."

"That's what we think, yes," Nox said. "We just don't know exactly *how* it changes magic. Does it take it away? Mutate it? Make it stronger? Can it be applied to weapons or released at a widespread level? There are still many questions, the most important of which being how much he has and how we can destroy it before he does anything catastrophic."

"We can't break into his labs," Arowyn countered. "I haven't been able to get through those wards his Alchemist has up. If this stuff is so important to him, he's going to have it locked down even tighter."

Nox's next words made my stomach drop. "That's where Devora comes in."

"Me?" I asked, both eyebrows raised. "What do you expect me to do that all of you can't?"

Nox crossed his arms, wrapping his fingers around his biceps. "Get close to him. Make him lower his guard. Get him to *want* to show you his secrets."

I choked back a laugh, then sobered when I saw how serious he was. "That's the best you've got? You want me to what, *seduce* him? This murderous Shifter who experiments on people for pleasure?"

"Not *seduce*, just..." Nox trailed off, licking his lips.

"Make him want you as his next project?" Arowyn offered.

I huffed. "Yes, because that's *so* much better."

"You told us his men think you're from Mysthelm, yes?" Nox asked, and I nodded slowly. "If anyone were to recognize you, they would assume you're not Veridian. They would assume—"

"That she doesn't have magic," Everett finished, interest piquing in his features.

Nox nodded. "There's a contingency from Mysthelm coming soon to visit the provinces. Clarissa organized it as a peaceful way forward since she took the throne. They'll be in Drakorum in three weeks, and Scarven's planning a ball for them. He expects me at his side, but he would never expect *you*."

He took a step closer to me. "You can disguise yourself. We'll forge documents of passage to corroborate the claim. You'll pretend to be part of the group from Mysthelm—a normal, *magic-less* human. Get his attention and, trust me, he'll be interested."

It was suddenly too warm in the room. Heat crawled from my chest and up my neck at the look on his face. Did he really think I could do something like this?

"Scarven likes to collect things," he continued. "Especially rare things. *People*. Someone hard to come by, such as a human from Mysthelm. Defenseless and magic-less, completely at his mercy."

I licked my lips. "Only problem is that I *am* defenseless. I may as well not even have magic. I don't see how I could help."

"So we train you," Kieran said, moving to stand by Nox's side. "This might actually work, Nox. Shadows are one thing we have not yet attempted."

I shook my head and held my hands out, trying to wrap my mind around everything. "Wait. What's so special about shadows?"

"There are multiple sides to all our magic," Arowyn began, and I turned to the couch. "Everyone from each province has the same basic abilities. Here in Drakorum, they can shift, while those in Feywood practice Alchemy; those in Emberfell can create light, and so on. But sometimes, we develop..." She paused and twisted her lips. "Variations. Take me, for example. I'm a Strider, but I can also summon things." She held out her other hand, and I watched with parted lips as a faint shimmer appeared above her fingers, followed by a hairbrush popping into existence in her palm.

I let out a breath. "Did you just—"

"It's from my room upstairs," she said. "Not all Striders can do it, just like there are other variations among the provinces. Everett here is an Illusionist, but he can also dreamwalk," she added, nodding to Everett. "He's so good with the kids and their night-mares because he can literally enter their dreams to calm them down."

"Those two aren't the only ones with fancy tricks," Tessa said with a wink. "That's how I can shift into something as small as a cat or as big as a lion. It's pretty uncommon, but some other Shifters can do it too."

"We need to find out the extent of your powers," Everett jumped in. "I've read about shadow wielding variants before. Some people can do what's called shadow marking. There's also shadow melting and whispering, I think. Any of those would be helpful here. You could melt into the shadows to get into warded spaces, use them to eavesdrop on conversations, things like that."

"The perfect spy," Arowyn finished.

Everyone turned back to Nox, whose lips curved into a sinful, devious smirk. "The only trick is finding out what *you* can do."

I blinked, still reeling from all the information. "And how, exactly, do you propose we do that?"

"I know someone who can help." He looked around the room, those navy eyes dark and calculating. "Everett and Arowyn, pack your bags. You too, Shadow Wielder."

"Where are we going?" I asked, anticipation building inside me.

"You wanted to find out where you come from, yes?" He cocked his head. "Here's your chance. We're going to Tenebra."

PART ONE

THE

BAIT

15

DEVORA

Mountain after mountain passed by the carriage window, the same gray and dark brown landscape mixed with icy silver as far as the eye could see. White-capped peaks loomed in the distance on both sides. The solid doors did little to dispel the chill from the winds as we rode.

Everett, Arowyn, Nox, and I had left two days ago for Tenebra. It was all happening so quickly. I'd gone from months in a single room to days in a carriage, traversing miles and miles of foreign ground. We had less than three weeks until the ball in Scarven's mansion for the Mysthelm contingency. Less than three weeks for me to learn how to be a Shadow Wielder competent enough to spy on and infiltrate a sadistic Shifter's stronghold. Less than three weeks for me to find my family.

No pressure.

More than anything, I yearned to learn about where I came from and this magic that had been dormant inside me for over twenty years. But I was also curious about what Scarven had up his sleeve. If my magic could help, then I'd happily use it. I wanted to finally be seen as more than the mistakes of my past. I wanted *redemption.* A chance at a new life.

And I was terrified. Of the weight I now bore, the possibility of failure, the inevitability of disappointment.

My fingers ran along the handle of my dagger on the outside of my leggings. I was comforted by its weight back at my side while my mind ran through everything that had happened. I couldn't help but wonder what awaited me when we arrived in Tenebra in three days. The place I was born. The place my *family* may still be living.

What would they be like? What would they think of me? I often thought about *how* I would find them, but hadn't let myself think much on what I would do if I ever *did*.

I didn't imagine a particularly warm reunion with my family. I wanted *answers*. I wanted to know why they'd abandoned me in Mysthelm as an infant. Was it even their choice? Or was there something larger at play?

I leaned back in the carriage I shared with Everett and Arowyn, the latter of whom had dozed off next to me. Everett occupied the space across from us, his long legs stretched out as much as the cramped carriage would allow. Adjusting my glasses, I looked out the window to the west, where the orange sun began its descent beneath the mountain peaks.

The carriage slowly rolled to a stop, causing Arowyn to jerk awake. Nox tapped on the window before opening the door.

"We're at the Mistwood Mountains." He nodded toward the enormous mountain range separating Drakorum and Tenebra. He'd taken up the habit of going ahead of us each day to make sure the path was clear, then meeting back up with us at night.

"We'll stop to make camp in about an hour." His ear-length dark blond waves were tousled from the wind, making him look more roguish. His tan cheeks held a twinge of pink, and his eyes glowed from being outside. He didn't wait for a response before shutting the door, and a moment later, the driver started up again.

A strained silence spread over the carriage, so naturally, I decided to break it headfirst.

"So, how come you can't just whisk us to Tenebra with your

magic?" I asked Arowyn. We'd had a few exchanges over the past couple of days, and I'd grown more comfortable around her. She didn't seem as wary of me as the others did.

Everett glanced up as I spoke, then went back to his book. I didn't think he particularly wanted me here. He had mostly ignored me, splitting his time between staring out the window or thumbing through one of his books.

"Too much magic," Arowyn said with a shrug. "Striding four people over this great a distance wouldn't make any sense. It would take me weeks to recover."

"But you *could*, if you wanted to?" I pressed.

She gave me a smirk beneath hooded, pale blue eyes heavy with dark kohl. "Sure."

A woman of many words.

"You don't give yourself enough credit," Everett said in his husky voice without looking up from the pages. "I've seen you rescue half a dozen refugees in one go and walk away like it was nothing."

"Yeah, well, that was a much shorter distance."

Everett grunted, then gazed off into the sunset, running his thumb along his lip. Dark scruff had grown on his face in the days we'd been traveling. It made him look older than he was—his early twenties, if I had to guess. Probably around my age.

"Everett, how long have you been working with Nox?" I asked.

"About three years," he said gruffly.

"He was a rescue from one of their earlier missions. Before I got here," Arowyn added. When Everett shot her a stern look, she shrugged. "What? We're all working together. It's not like she can't know."

My eyes widened. "You were one of Scarven's prisoners?"

Everett adjusted in his seat and cleared his throat. "Yes. My parents died when I was a teenager. His men found me on the streets of Iluze and brought me back to his manor."

"I'm so sorry," I breathed out. "How long were you there?"

There was a beat, and his hands tightened around the book.

"Seven years, I think." He licked his lips, suddenly looking younger. Hesitant. As if those memories turned him into that fearful teenager again. "Time is...different there. I lost track of the years, until Nox pulled me out."

I knew better than to ask what kinds of torture he endured. That was none of my business. But the pain in his eyes told me enough. Something lurked behind the dual-toned green and gray, something that spoke of darkness.

The more I learned, the more people I met whom Scarven had hurt, the more I wanted to stop him. What people like Everett had gone through...it was becoming *real* to me. It made my stomach clench, an icy awareness tightening around my throat.

This was about so much more than just me finding my family.

Not wanting to dwell on Everett's discomfort for too long, I turned to Arowyn. "What about you? How did you meet Nox?"

"It was about a year ago. Both of us competed in the Decemvi-rate at the capital, and he and I became allies. Friends, I guess." She looked out the window at that last word, and something about her answer felt unfinished. Like there was more to the story.

"The Decemvirate? Isn't that a tournament your people have every year?" I remembered reading the word in one of the history books.

"Every ten years," she said. "But not anymore, if Empress Aris has anything to do with it." I squirmed at the mention of Clarissa. "When the Fates gave us our magic three-hundred-and-whatever years ago, there was a catch: it fades over time. There's this ritual the emperor can do to replenish it, and someone decided long ago to turn it into a competition." Arowyn rolled her eyes. "So, every ten years, each province had to submit their strongest challenger to compete in a bunch of trials. The winner's province received the most magic, all the way down to the person in last place, who barely got any. And then we did it all over ten years later."

I blinked. "That sounds..."

"Gratuitous," Everett offered.

Arowyn nodded. "It's ridiculous, I know. But that's how I met

Nox. He was Drakorum's challenger, and I was Celestria's. We were friends until..." She broke off and sighed, emotion flickering across her features. "Look, it was every person for themself. Those games aren't the kind you should make allies in. Not when there's only one winner. I cut ties before I did something I'd regret."

Perhaps Arowyn and I were more similar than I thought. "So how did you reconnect?"

"Nox came to see me in Celestria a few months after the tournament. Said he had a place for me, if I ever wanted to put some of my aggression to use." She snorted. "Told me about Scarven's operation and how he'd started a group of rebels set on rescuing as many people as they could, and eventually wipe Scarven out completely. They didn't have a Strider yet, and he thought I'd come in handy. Nox can be very convincing."

I shifted in my seat, remembering the carefree, charming yet commanding man I'd seen glimpses of in Mysthelm and with his Order. So very different from his wrath.

"I know what you did. To Clarissa," Arowyn suddenly said. There was no judgment in her voice, simply a statement of fact. "I probably would've done the same thing."

"I'm not sure that makes me feel any better."

She shrugged. "Wasn't supposed to. But I know why you did it. You were trying to make the most of a bad situation. I think everyone knows you did what you could to try and keep her alive, in your own way."

I let out a small scoff. "Then why does he still hate me?"

Arowyn gave me a curious look. "It's because you're like *us*. You're clever and resourceful and obviously not scared to get your hands dirty. You barely know anything about our cause, and you're already diving in headfirst. Sure, you're getting something out of it, but I have a feeling it's more than that." She crossed her arms over her full chest. "But you're unpredictable. I think he knows how great you could be, and the fact that he can't trust you scares him."

"Do you?" I tilted my head. "Trust me?"

"I don't really trust anyone," she said, a smirk in her eyes. "But I like you. So that's good enough for me."

My gaze trailed over to Everett. I knew he'd been listening, and my question wasn't only for her. If I was supposed to work with these people, I wanted to know where I stood. "And you, Everett?"

His eyes searched me, guarded and stoic, but with a hint of something more. Resolution, maybe. Determination.

"If you're our best hope for finding out how to take Scarven down, then I don't really have a choice but to trust you," he said slowly. "I made a promise to someone there. Someone I said I was coming back for. And I don't intend to break that promise."

A chill swept down my spine that had nothing to do with the cold air. The carriage came to a stop, and despite the heaviness in Everett's words, they lit a fire inside of me. For once, it felt like we were getting on the same page. Understanding each other. Learning to trust.

Perhaps I really could get everything I wanted. My answers *and* my redemption.

16

DEVORA

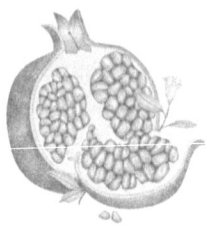

Every night on the road was the same. We'd stop in some secluded area, set up camp, eat a quick dinner of dried meat and fruit by a fire, then sleep until dawn and do it all over again.

Day three and part of day four were spent traversing the rocky mountain pass of the Mistwood Mountains. It was overgrown with twisted trees and wide bushes, with dangerous holes the carriage had to maneuver around. Strange howls and animals rustling through the leaves echoed outside my tent at night, making sleep impossible.

When we finally emerged on the other side into Tenebra, I didn't think life could possibly get any colder than Drakorum.

I was wrong.

"Holy F-Fates," I said, teeth chattering when we stopped to relieve ourselves and let the horses get some water. "Wh-why would anyone l-live here?"

I pulled my scarf up to cover my mouth and nose, tugging my cloak tighter around my shoulders. I should've brought five more of them. A thin layer of gray ice coated nearly every surface in sight, from the rocky ground to the treetops to the small hills in the distance. The dry, cold air sucked the breath out of me, making my lips crack and my hands throb.

"I suppose you can ask your family when you find them," a voice said from behind me. I whirled around, surprised to find Nox standing there. He'd been avoiding me since we left.

"Yeah, I'll p-put it at the t-top of my list," I replied.

His shoulders moved up and down as he let out a disgruntled sigh, then unclasped the cloak from his neck. All he was wearing underneath was a thin button-down shirt tucked into black pants. The muscles in his arms strained as he gripped the cloak in one hand.

"Here." He held it out to me.

I blinked. "Wh-what's this f-for?"

"It's called a cloak. You wear it."

When I continued to stare at him, his lips thinned into a straight line. With another sigh, he stepped closer to wrap the thick cloak around my shoulders. My breath hitched when he moved to secure the clasp at my neck. It always surprised me how *massive* he was. His frame towered over me, easily a foot taller, his broad shoulders blocking the view of the dreary landscape.

His warm fingers grazed my collarbone. "Your teeth are about to fall out of your head."

"W-would make it hard to talk. M-maybe then you'd like me better," I mumbled, the tremor in my limbs already beginning to settle with the weight of his cloak. That sweet and spicy scent, like amber and smoke, enveloped me when I took a breath.

The corner of his lip twitched, but he flattened his expression into a glower once more. "Are you ready for this?"

I raised an eyebrow. "To find my family, learn magic, or be your bait?"

"Take your pick."

"No," I said. "To all of the above. But I will be. I won't let you down, if that's what you're thinking." He hummed and turned to the side, crossing his arms over his chest. I reached out without thinking.

"Hey." I grabbed his forearm. He pulled away so quickly, it was as if I'd burned him. "I'm *not* going to betray you. That person you think I am..." I shook my head. "You don't know me."

His eyes landed where my hand had touched him, then back up to my face. I hastily pulled both my arms back inside the cloak.

"We'll see," was all he said. He looked like he was about to go back to his horse, when he pursed his lips and added, "You have eight days here. That's all I can give you. Eight days to train and hunt down whatever you can find about your past. Then we head back to Drakorum to get ready for the ball."

I nodded, then something occurred to me. "Does he know you're here? Scarven?"

He ran his tongue along his teeth, as if contemplating whether he would even bother answering me. I knew I was being nosy, but trust went both ways. Scarven had Nox *killing* people for him. I hadn't forgotten about that Lightbender rebel leader they spoke of. The others may stand by and blindly trust him, but I needed more than that. I needed to be able to ask questions and make judgments for myself.

"Yes," Nox finally said. "I made him think it was his idea to send me. There have been whispers coming from Tenebra of an embargo against Drakorum. They seem to be suspicious of what Scarven's been doing. He wants me to...take care of it."

I ground my teeth together in frustration. "So you're going to kill them. Like you did before."

He took a step toward me, and I could've sworn his dragon glared back at me from his navy-and-silver eyes. "Why are you so convinced you know what happened, Devora, darling?"

"I heard what you all said." My shoulders straightened. I refused to be intimidated, even if my heart was racing. "That Emberfell would feel this loss. That Scarven wanted him gone, and that you're good at making people disappear. What would *you* think if you'd heard that?"

"I would think," he said, his voice low, "that I was somewhere I shouldn't be. A habit you seem to have a difficult time breaking."

"It must not be too bad of a habit if you're so willing to give me to your sworn enemy on a silver platter," I shot back. "It's only inconvenient when it doesn't serve your needs, I guess. You can't have it both ways."

He clenched his jaw, then leaned away and ran his fingers through his wavy hair. "I didn't kill the Lightbender, Devora."

My brow furrowed. "I don't understand. I heard—"

"You *think* you heard," he snapped. "I removed him from his rebels, yes. I helped him and his family relocate to Feywood, far away from Scarven's suspicions. I killed one of *Scarven's* own guards in order to get them to safety. It was still a loss, in a way, since I took the Lightbender from his home and people. But he knew the alternative—that I *am* Scarven's blade, whether I want to be or not. I gave him a choice."

"Get out or be killed," I murmured, my lips parting as I took in his words.

"Scarven *must* believe I'm doing as he says. My actions—" Nox cut himself off, scratching the back of his neck. "I've been forced to hurt people. There were times I couldn't find a way out of it. But I've made every effort in the years since to give those Scarven targets a second chance at life."

I swallowed hard, shame snaking its way through my veins. Something else I'd misread. Something *else* I'd been wrong about. Why was I so eager to find the darkness in him?

Every piece I discovered seemed to lead me to the same conclusion: Nox Duma wasn't the man I once thought he was.

I saw what it did to that Duma freak. The memory from the ship washed over me, and I put the pieces together.

"Scarven has someone, doesn't he?" I asked softly, pulling his cloak tighter around me. "That's why you keep working for him. Why you can't leave him. He has someone you love."

Nox slowly ran a finger over his lips, and my eyes caught on his mouth before I jerked my gaze up.

To my surprise, he didn't look angry anymore. Merely... resigned.

"You know, that mind of yours is going to get you in trouble one of these days," he murmured.

I rolled my lips together. "Good trouble, or bad trouble?"

"I don't know yet." Those dark eyes held mine a heartbeat longer than normal before he looked away. "You're perceptive. That's what we need." He cleared his throat and took a deep breath. "Yes, he has someone. My sister."

My eyes widened. The pain in his voice hit me like a stack of bricks. I lifted a finger to push my glasses back up the bridge of my nose. "I—I'm so sorry, Nox."

He dipped his head curtly, and I tucked my hand into the crook of my neck. I was never sure how to handle these kinds of moments. *Especially* with someone like Nox. I had no idea where we stood—enemies? Captor and prisoner? Reluctant allies?

But no matter what we were to each other, nobody deserved to have somebody they cared about locked away.

"Is she—is she like you?" I asked. "A dragon?"

Nox stiffened, then shook his head. "No. She's not a dragon."

I waited for a moment, then realized he wasn't going to offer anything else. He was already beginning to retreat, the brief glimpse into the Nox that everyone else saw now covered once again by the armor he wore around me.

For the second time that day, I instinctively reached out a hand. I stopped it before I touched him. "Nox, I—I know this mission is important. For more than one reason. I'll do everything I can to help."

He gazed at me, his face unreadable. The air around us was charged even through the icy wind. When he didn't respond, I licked my lips and hastily unclasped his cloak. "Here. Thanks for letting me borrow it."

His brow furrowed slightly when he looked down at my outstretched arm. "Keep it. You need it more than I do."

Then he turned on his heel and strode back to his horse.

17

NOX

I pulled the reins to slow Tempest as I crested the final hill and the training grounds of Tenebra came into view. Five days later, and we'd made it.

The wheels of the carriage carrying Devora, Arowyn, and Everett weren't far behind me. My legs and back screamed at me for subjecting them to so many days on the back of a horse, but it was far better than being cramped in that carriage with them. *Her.*

My blood boiled every time I was near her, and five days together was far too much time to spend controlling the impulse to silence that smart mouth of hers before it got her into trouble.

Trouble. That was exactly what she was. But evidently, she was the brand of trouble I needed.

The brand of trouble *we* needed. Not me.

I shook my head of the thought as Tempest and I reached the outskirts of the infamous training grounds, where Veridians of all backgrounds and magic types had traveled over the decades to practice magic and hone their skills.

Some of the most powerful people to have ever lived once roamed these grounds. I could feel the magic vibrating through the earth, making my Shifter half lift its snout in curiosity.

It was an enormous rectangular base nestled right in the valley between two mountains. A stream ran from north to south, with small clusters of fir and evergreen trees dotting the landscape. The training grounds themselves were in the very center of the base, a wide, open-air expanse surrounded by dozens of connected buildings that served as living quarters, kitchens, and storage. The base was currently home to around fifty trainees and trainers.

And now, us. For eight days, at least.

Eight days. That was how long we had to train Devora into a Shadow Wielder worthy of meddling her way into Kane Scarven's highest security fortress.

This was never going to work.

I scrubbed a hand down my face, then guided Tempest to the nearest stables. Our carriage came to a stop behind me just as two strangers approached. The tallest, a tan female in deep red fighting leathers with three daggers strapped to her waist, stretched out a hand.

"Aurel," she said in a deep, resonant voice as she gripped my hand. "Aurel Vexley. And this is Elric." She jerked her head to the shorter, broad-shouldered man at her side.

"Nox Duma. Thank you for letting us stay here," I replied.

"We couldn't very well turn away a friend of Larken Everest," Elric said, wiping his forehead with a rag.

Larken Everest, a close friend of mine from my time in Veridia City last year during the Decemvirate tournament, was a powerful Shadow Wielder and now part of Clarissa's council. She was one of the first people I reached out to when I got back to the empire with a brand-new, inexperienced Shadow Wielder in my charge.

Everett, Devora, and Arowyn exited the carriage and stretched their legs. My eyes snagged on my cloak still around Devora's neck. I forced my gaze away and tried not to breathe in the scent of her skin, like pomegranates and sunshine, mixing with my own that still clung to the cloak. Something stirred in my chest, and I smothered it.

"We weren't sure what time you would arrive, so Thecae stepped out. He should be back shortly," Aurel was saying. "Our stable hand can help your driver if the rest of you want to grab your bags and follow me."

Our group followed the two of them down a path leading to the base, then through an archway and into a long corridor. The further we walked, the more rooms we saw branching off the main path—bunkers, dining rooms, kitchens, cupboards, armories. The vast space appeared mostly empty, but every now and then, a couple of people would walk by and nod politely.

When we made the first left turn, a tall man materialized in front of us, seeming to have emerged from the shadows themselves. Devora let out a surprised squeal and nearly stumbled. I reached out an arm to steady her, my hand grazing her skin as I backed away.

She met my gaze with wide eyes and pointed at the man, who was now retreating the way we came, his attention focused on the book in his hands. "Did he just—"

"It's called shadow melting," Aurel said without looking back at us. "Some of us can use shadows to travel between dark spaces."

I had to admit, that was incredible. "Can Thecae teach her how to do that?" I asked Aurel.

Aurel shrugged. "If she's strong enough."

Out of the corner of my eye, I saw Devora bristle. I hid a smirk. I had a feeling if there was one thing someone could say to ensure this woman would succeed, it was that.

Aurel and Elric stopped in front of an entrance to an armory full of fighting leathers and various weapons hanging on the walls. "Thecae will meet you here." Elric held an arm out.

The four of us stepped inside the gray stone room. Aurel and Elric dipped their heads before turning back down the hall.

"So, who is this Thecae person?" Devora asked as she took in the weapons.

"I've never met him, but he comes highly recommended by a friend. He's a trained warrior and Shadow Wielder who's helped others develop their powers," I answered.

"Was he the one behind the Southern Bridge Rebellion a couple decades ago?" Everett asked.

When I nodded, he let out a low, impressed whistle. "He's a legend. I grew up hearing stories about him. He once made a bridge of shadows over the Eldertide Ocean for his rebel group to cross from Tenebra to Veridia City."

"And it almost killed him," I added. "That much power can hurt even the strongest of us."

Devora looked down at her hands. "Well, let's hope he can work a miracle on me."

"That's entirely up to you, girl," a gruff voice said at my back. We all turned to find a tall, muscular man in his late forties walking through the door. His dark hair was shaved close to his scalp, with matching scruff that held hints of gray along his chin. Deep brown eyes took us in until they landed on Devora.

His lips parted, surprise lighting his features. "*Ceres,*" he said on an exhale.

Devora looked around in confusion. "Sorry, I—I'm Devora."

Thecae shook his head and blinked several times. "Of course. Apologies. You just...you like so much like her."

The blood drained from Devora's face. "Who?"

Thecae swallowed. "Your mother."

18

DEVORA

My chest caved in, all the air leaving my lungs. "You—you know my *mother*?"

The Shadow Wielder gazed at me as if he were seeing someone else. He had to be twenty years my senior, if not more. Probably around my parents' age. Was he friends with them? Could he take me to them? A tentative hope blossomed in my chest, unfurling at the edges like a blooming flower.

"I knew her, yes."

"Well, where is she?" I stepped forward in excitement.

He licked his lips, a deep crease appearing on his forehead. "I thought you knew."

My hands went clammy at my sides. "Knew what?"

"She...she died, girl." His throat moved as he swallowed. "Her and your father both. In a shipwreck a long time ago."

That flower of hope rotted and died in my stomach. My shoulders fell as I exhaled, the weight of *years* of longing now wrenched from my very bones with every breath. I rocked backward on my heels, reeling from his words.

They were gone.

I should've expected this. I should've put the pieces together. I was usually so good at that, at reading between the lines, taking information and twisting it till I got the truth. I was found on the shores of Mysthelm as a baby. If I was alone, what was the *only* reasonable explanation?

I was an idiot. A foolish girl holding on to the thread of a dream that I'd find my family one day. Not just that I'd get my answers, but that I'd find somewhere I *belonged*. I hadn't realized how much I wanted that until it was dangled in front of me, then ripped away.

Everyone in the room seemed to hold their breath. Even Nox's features had softened toward me, no longer full of the resentment I so often saw.

Pity was worse. I'd rather have anger.

"What happened?" I finally asked, barely holding my voice steady.

"Ceres and Malijah were part of a rebellion against the former emperor with me and some others over twenty years ago. Until she got pregnant," Thecae started.

Ceres and Malijah. My breath caught at the sound of their names.

"They didn't want to get involved in anything that could potentially endanger Ceres or the baby. We knew where things were heading in the empire, and they didn't want their child growing up in such a dark world." Thecae met my stare again. "So they and a couple other families set sail for Mysthelm shortly after you were born. The ship and its crew were supposed to return, but when weeks went by and we hadn't heard anything, we sent some scouts." He took a deep breath, his voice suddenly weary. "All they brought back was rubble from the wreckage. We thought everyone died."

I sat down on a large box against the wall, afraid my legs would give out if I didn't. "I was found inside a basket. There was a—a blue baby blanket with the name Devora S stitched onto it." My nose twitched with a sting, and I adjusted my glasses. "It was the only piece of my past I ever had."

"Sephorne," Thecae said, voice rough. "That's what the S stands for. Your last name."

Devora Sephorne.

I mouthed the words, letting them roll across my tongue. A shiver crept down my spine. I'd never had a last name. A jagged piece snapped into place, however small it may be.

"My mother stitched that blanket, you know." Thecae gave a soft smile that looked at odds against the hard planes of his face. "Our families were close. Do you still have it?"

I shook my head and glanced down at my feet. "I wasn't able to grab most of my things when I...when I left Mysthelm."

Movement to my left caused me to look up. Nox shifted, his brow furrowed as he stared at me. I quickly turned away.

"I'm guessing they were both Shadow Wielders?" I asked Thecae after a moment of silence.

He nodded. "Your mother was an exceptionally powerful one. Malijah was actually half Shadow Wielder, half Lightbender, although it's unlikely that both passed on to you. If anything, it would make you an even stronger Shadow Wielder. You've shown signs of the gift, I assume?"

I twisted my lips back and forth, slightly embarrassed. "Briefly, yes."

"My maids say she conjures them in her sleep on occasion," Nox offered. "They've seen shadows form beneath her door at night."

"But I—I can't make it happen again. I can't get them to come back," I admitted.

At that, Thecae grunted. "Of course not. Can you *make* your shadow do anything?" He pointed to the ground at our five elongated shadows, highlighted by the sun coming through a window in the far corner. "Can you make it disappear or reappear at will?"

"No, but...that's different," I said.

"Why?"

"Because," I squinted as I tried to form my thoughts, "because that's caused by the sun. It's not a force I can control."

"That's the second time you've talked about them like that. Why are you so interested in *controlling* the shadows, girl?"

I bit down on my bottom lip, torn between embarrassment and irritation. "I thought that was the whole point of this? So I could learn how to wield them?"

"That was your first mistake." He held out his arms, and I blinked several times as his real shadow, the one on the ground next to all of ours, wavered. It slowly furled in on itself and crept up his legs, then his torso, until it split and billowed out across his arms. The shadows twirled around his hands as if they were an extension of him.

"Until you learn that your shadows are *always* a part of you, not just something to summon and banish whenever you feel like it, you won't be able to access them. They won't answer you if you view them as nothing more than a weapon to wield."

"Okay." I scratched the back of my ear. I supposed that made sense. It explained why trying to force them never worked for me. "Well...can you help me?"

"For Ceres and Malijah's daughter?" His lips curved upward. "Anything."

19

DEVORA

I swatted at the gnat buzzing next to my ear, and a loud sigh across from me made me open my eyes.

"What, am I doing it wrong again?" I asked.

"The fact that you have to ask means yes, you're probably doing something wrong," Nox's voice came from behind me.

I craned my neck to shoot him a glare. "Why are you still here?"

He shrugged. "Curiosity."

Rolling my eyes, I faced Thecae again and squared my shoulders. He'd brought me to the far north edge of the training grounds and had me sit in a circle of dark, swirling shadows that he'd conjured, with the sun quickly setting to our right. Nox had followed us and took up a spot on a barrel right behind me. I could feel his annoying stare on my back the entire time.

For half an hour, Thecae and I just sat there with our eyes closed, breathing. I had no idea what this had to do with shadow wielding, but evidently, I was even doing *this* wrong, if Thecae's constant sighs were any indication.

"I thought I was supposed to be learning magic," I grumbled under my breath as I closed my eyes again.

Thecae grunted, a sound I knew almost as well as his sighs.

"Do you give a child a broadsword and say, 'Here, go fight your enemy'?"

"Why am I always the child in everyone's scenarios?"

This time, a rumble of laughter escaped him. "The answer is, of course you don't. You start small. Short wooden swords, then blunt ends, until one day, they're ready to handle something real. Something dangerous. Something that could hurt themselves and others. Your shadows are no different. If wielded correctly, they can be destructive weapons. You're nowhere *near* ready for that, girl."

I cracked an eye open. "Then how could I possibly learn any of this in eight days?"

"Don't worry about that yet. We're starting with the *mind*. You must quiet your mind so you can listen to the shadows. Feel them. Let them in and understand them before you *control* them, as you seem so intent on."

I scrunched my brow. "*Listen* to them?"

He nodded. "Close your eyes." I snapped them shut. "Take deep breaths. Empty your mind of everything else. Fear, rage, hope, doubt, yearning. Let it all slip away with each breath. Feel the weight spreading from your shoulders and into your chest, down to your hands, your legs, your feet. Once all the noise in your head is quiet, *listen*."

I did what he said. I shoved away my exasperation and tried to imagine all of my thoughts being siphoned out as I took several breaths.

At first, it felt pointless. Childish. Especially with Nox's weighted stare of expectation on me.

But I pushed that aside too. I let it go with my next exhale.

My shoulders fell. The clink of steel on steel and distant voices of the training grounds faded into silence.

And then...I heard it.

Soft murmurs, barely distinguishable at first. Like wind whistling through trees or fabric sliding over skin. The sound morphed into a deep, rough voice, one that almost sounded like

Thecae's. It wasn't words, more like...like whispers from the shadows in the circle around us, and when I concentrated harder, I could almost feel them. *Feel* their emotions. Fragments of memories, of desires and fears and pain weaving into a sound. A song my subconscious mind could understand, even though the rational part of my brain told me it wasn't possible.

I sucked in a breath. "I can feel you. Your shadows. Are you doing that?"

"They have a stronger presence because my magic is stronger. But it's a good sign that you can tell they're mine. Most can't decipher that on their first try." A hint of pride bloomed in me at Thecae's words. "Dig deeper. Try to put mine to the side and find your *own*. Our magic is tied to our emotions."

Well, that was a dangerous game. My emotions weren't something I particularly enjoyed sifting through. I liked to hide them with an ill-timed joke, perhaps a sarcastic comment.

I was afraid of what I'd find if I got too close.

But this wasn't just about *me* anymore. This was for all those innocent lives Scarven was ruining, all the people he'd hurt. People like Everett and Nox's sister.

I shifted in the circle and tried to shove the whispers of Thecae's shadows into a small corner of my mind. To pick out something different. Something *mine*.

There was nothing.

It was blank. I could still only feel him and his strange, foreign shadows curling at the edges. My hands were balled so tightly in my lap that my nails left crescent-shaped indentations in the skin.

"This isn't working," I mumbled.

"You're trying to force it."

I made an annoyed sound in the back of my throat. "You said to dig deeper. How else am I supposed to do that without forcing it?"

He let out a hum. "You're right. This approach won't work for you. You're too...aggressive."

Nox scoffed behind us. I ignored him.

"But until you can center yourself, your shadows won't

respond," Thecae continued. He turned to his right and nodded through one of the windows leading to the covered perimeter. A trainee rushed out with a long, shallow basin of water and set it in the middle of our shadow circle.

"Tell me what you see," Thecae instructed, motioning to the water.

I got up on my knees and peered into the basin. My own blue-green eyes stared back at me, framed in black-rimmed glasses. Thick red hair rested in a bun at the top of my head, with loose strands brushing my cheeks.

"I just see—"

I stopped myself. A shadow appeared at the very edge of the water. Deep gray mixed with black as it swirled, almost as if the ends of it were playing with the reflection of my hair.

"Are those your shadows again?" I asked Thecae.

"No." I didn't have to look up to hear the smile in his voice.

Mine, something whispered.

My shadows curled in on themselves, exploring the water. The ends of one tendril wiggled across like it was trying to leap out at me. But when I looked down at my body, there was nothing there.

"It's enchanted water," Thecae explained. "It shows your magic, even if it's not visible to the naked eye. Those are *yours*, Miss Sephorne." I jolted at the name. "If there was ever any doubt of the power you possess, let go of it. Your shadows are a part of you whether or not you can see them. They're simply waiting."

"For what?"

"For *you*."

He went quiet, letting me gaze at my shadows. A smile quirked one end of my mouth as I watched them. Small ribbons twisted together and floated beneath the reflection of my neck, while more billowed like clouds by my ears. I could almost feel them. Extensions of myself, in a way.

I reached out a finger to touch the surface of the water, and it rippled to the edge of the basin.

The shadows disappeared.

"It's alright, Miss Sephorne," Thecae said gently when I deflated and rocked back on my heels. "We have time."

No, we don't, I thought.

"I think that's enough for this evening," he continued. He rose to his feet and dusted his knees off, then held out a hand to me. "Would you like to come to the Noctus Vigil tonight?"

I took his hand and stood. "What's that?"

"A ritual we have every full moon to honor our dead. It's held in the nearest town, just outside the training grounds. All our trainers and trainees will be attending." He paused. "Many there knew your parents, Devora. I think they would like to get to know you."

The thought made my heart clench. I was desperate for any scrap of my past. Any scrap of my parents, of the life they lived—the life *I* could have lived, if they hadn't tried to escape.

Nox appeared at my side. Thecae shook his hand and said, "You're welcome to join us, of course."

"Thank you. We'll think about it," Nox said.

Thecae told us where to meet him and strode back toward the perimeter of the base.

I was about to follow him when Nox lowered his voice. "Are you sure going tonight is the best idea?"

I furrowed my brow. "Why wouldn't it be?"

"We don't know these people. It may not be wise to get too close to them."

I pursed my lips. This man just couldn't agree with me on anything. "Look, I'm doing what you want—I'm learning my magic so I can help you take down Scarven. *You're* the one who said I could find out about my family while we're here."

He rubbed his jaw. "We already know what happened to your family, Devora. What good will this do?"

My neck and cheeks heated. "I just found out they *died*, Nox. I want to know how they *lived*. I want to go where they went, talk to their friends, see the province I was born in. Why are you trying to take this away from me?"

"Always so defensive, darling," he said with a low growl that both warmed my chest and ignited my anger.

"It's hard not to be when I know how much you all dislike me."

He let out a breath and closed his eyes. "It's not that I want to take anything away from you," he said slowly. "But sometimes we're better off staying in the dark. Sometimes not knowing hurts less than the truth."

I examined him carefully. Beneath the standoffishness, he actually seemed...concerned. For *me*.

That was new.

"Maybe that's the difference between you and me," I said. "You have the luxury of choosing to be in the dark. I was *forced* there. I have to know, Nox. Even if the truth hurts."

"Fine," he said, lips thinning into a straight line. "Then I'm coming with you."

20

NOX

Our group ascended the small hill on the outskirts of the training grounds. With my Shifter eyesight, I spied cobblestone paths leading to a village, rocky paddocks with sheep, goats, and cattle, and right in the center lay a patchwork of bright, flickering bonfires. There were hundreds of people flocking to them, with all sorts of instruments blaring as the Noctus Vigil began.

Thecae and Devora led the way, while Everett and Arowyn stood at my side. Most of the other trainers and trainees had gone on ahead. The five of us quickly reached the top of the incline and made our way to the center of the town square.

Shadows from the nearby mountain ranges cloaked the town, but the full moon and lit torches carved a pale path through them. The stars twinkled above us without a single cloud to block the sky. The low hum of insects and night creatures, the rhythm of pounding drums, and the whispers of so many Shadow Wielders floated around me like music.

I couldn't help but glance at Devora. She'd taken her hair out of the bun, letting it flow in waves down her back. When she turned to look at us, her eyes sparkled beneath her glasses, her cheeks pink and lips parted in wonder.

My gaze was glued to her. I hadn't seen her like this before. She seemed...happy. Or at least, verging on something that could make her happy. Something like hope.

I hated the word she so often used. *Prisoner.* But the longer I saw her outside of the confines of that tower, the more I realized what I'd done to her. How I'd treated her.

She deserved it, a voice in the back of my mind kept saying. *Rissa is your friend, and she betrayed her. We've done much worse to traitors before.*

That reasoning was beginning to hold less and less power over me, now that I'd seen how willing Devora was to help us. That outrage, that grudge, that hatred of disloyalty...it was an innate part of my Shifter half. It was still there, churning and searching for an outlet. But it was slowly turning into something else.

Shame.

"It was the only piece of my past I ever had." The blanket Devora's parents had left for her, the single possession she had linking her to her family. It was funny how such a small item held such great significance. And I'd taken it from her. I hadn't even thought to let her gather her things when I swept her out of Mysthelm. I'd been so focused on what she'd done, so *angry* with her for hurting my friend.

I remembered when I'd been taken from my home. We were still mourning our father's death when Scarven's men burst into our seaside cottage and snatched my mother, sister, and me away.

Like Devora, I was taken with the clothes on my back and nothing more. No keepsake from my childhood, no favorite toy, nothing to remember my father by.

I scrubbed a hand down my face and finally ripped my eyes from Devora as we approached the rows of bonfires. I *refused* to be anything like Kane Scarven. Yet sometimes...sometimes I wondered if we had more in common than a shared father.

"The rituals are beginning," Thecae whispered, nodding toward the largest of the fires where a group had gathered. "They'll read the names of those who have died since the last full moon, and then families of the deceased will burn their tokens."

"And then what?" Devora whispered back.

Thecae flashed her a smirk. "And then we celebrate. These lives are not to be mourned. They're to be *remembered*."

Someone stood on a raised platform in front of the center fire with a scroll in his hands. A hush fell over the crowd. He cleared his throat, and the drumroll started again, quieter this time.

"Finnian Alabar." There was no introduction, merely names spoken in his reverent tone, with the rumble of drums as a backdrop. "Wynn Calestro. Loren Davros."

On and on the list went, and each time a new one was said, a cloud of shadows formed above the bonfire in the shape of their silhouette. The families of the deceased stepped forward, one by one, to burn their offerings in the flames. Some tokens were too small to see, while I could tell others were pieces of jewelry, letters, or books. The fire crackled louder with every item, emitting sparks and bursts of smoke.

When the list came to an end, the people all murmured as one, "You are not forgotten."

Hundreds of whispers washed over the space like rolling thunder. The drums fell silent. A long horn answered from somewhere behind us, and the crowd exhaled.

Silence.

And then—

The musicians started up in full swing. The Shadow Wielders around us burst into applause, separating into groups with hollers of excitement. Some called out names in greeting, while others broke out bottles of wine.

The atmosphere instantly shifted from melancholy reverence to raucous nightlife.

My lips curved into a grin. Now *that* was something I could get behind.

"Are you *smiling*?"

I jerked my head to the sound of Devora's voice and found her raising an eyebrow at me.

"Oh, Nox *loves* his parties," Arowyn drawled to my right.

Devora's eyebrows inched higher and higher up her forehead, as if she couldn't possibly believe *I* could have fun. I liked a little challenge, and this woman constantly asked for one.

"Arowyn, darling, remember the night last year at the capital when we snuck that bottle of Luxe?" I grinned at the Strider.

Arowyn snorted. "There are *young minds* present, Nox." She nodded toward Everett and Devora, who rolled her eyes.

My stare lingered on her. I sometimes forgot how young she was. Twenty-three—ten years younger than me. Only a couple of years older than my sister.

But there was nothing *sisterly* in the way I found my thoughts straying to that smart mouth of hers.

I quickly looked away. A passing Shadow Wielder held out a half-drunk bottle of something that smelled like raspberries, and I snatched it.

"Feel like sharing?" Everett's deep voice asked behind me.

I held the sweet drink out to him. "After you."

I hadn't spent much one-on-one time with the Illusionist since we rescued him from Scarven three years ago. He'd been a wonderful asset ever since then, especially with the children. His illusions and ability to dreamwalk soothed them.

Everett Swift wasn't a particularly outgoing fellow—mostly stoic and pensive, with occasional spouts of dry humor that had me laughing out loud. But he was compassionate, in his quiet way. When the children had nightmares, he always seemed to know. He was at their side in an instant, drawing on his illusions to craft visions of warmth and comfort in their little minds. He was a natural.

And fiercely determined. Something crouched behind those mismatched gray and green eyes, something desperate and long-ing. He was the only other one in our Order besides me who knew the pain, loneliness, and despair of those cells. After so many years as part of Scarven's experiments, he had a vendetta. A personal obligation I could see burning inside that closed-off exterior.

I could work with that.

We walked in silence to get away from the busiest area of the square. Arowyn and Devora had ventured to one of the bonfires still in my line of sight. I watched as Thecae introduced her to a couple of people, and she shook their hands with a smile.

People all around were dancing, cloaks and skirts swirling across the ground to so many different tunes that it made it difficult to concentrate. Shadows seeped from their feet and billowed up into the sky. To my left, one man grabbed a large stick and lit it in the nearest bonfire, then slowly lowered the flame down his throat to the cheers of many bystanders. He took a deep breath and let it out, and a cloud of shadows burst from his lips.

"You know," Everett said, "there was this girl I knew. Down in the cells." He paused, and I didn't risk looking at him and ruining this rare moment of openness. "I think she'd like this."

I hummed, absentmindedly watching as Devora twirled around a campfire. Her body moved like smoke, so natural and carefree. "Were you close?" I asked Everett, forcing my attention back to him.

"You know how it is." He cleared his throat and took another drink. The movement caused his tunic to shift, revealing the very tip of a black-inked design on his dark chest. "Nothing and nobody last long. We didn't even tell each other our names. It would've made the cells feel too...permanent." He paused, a far-off expression on his face. "But yeah. We were close. It was...it was real. As real as it could be."

I nodded in understanding. Down there, you had to keep things at arm's-length. It was the only way to protect your mind from giving in to the darkness completely.

"I had someone like that," I offered after a moment. "Her name was Sage. We planned to run off together, after everything."

"What happened?"

Grabbing the bottle from him, I took a long swig. "We did. Run away together, that is. But we were caught." I rolled my neck on my shoulders to look at the sky. "She didn't make it."

"I'm sorry, Nox."

A moment passed, then I asked, "What about your girl?"

At first, I didn't think he was going to respond. He crossed his arms over his chest, staring into the distant mountains. Finally, he said, "She's still down there."

My spine straightened. "What? Why haven't you said anything? We could try to get her out, Everett."

He shook his head. "I look for her. Every time we go back. But he must have moved her. I haven't been able to find her again." His voice trailed off as he took the bottle and drained it. "I promised her I'd come back for her. We were young, but...I promised."

We went silent after that. I was sure we were both thinking the same thing—if he hadn't been able to find her, she was probably gone.

But I knew better than anyone what that kind of hope felt like, and Fates help me if I was going to be the one to take it away from him.

I found Devora again. She threw her head back and laughed at something Arowyn said, then turned to lock eyes with me. Her smile fell, but it still lingered on the edges of her eyes, and she tipped her chin toward me.

"I'll help you keep that promise," I said to Everett, my gaze still on her. I blinked and shifted back to him, remembering my other motive for coming here. "But there's actually something else I wanted to talk to you about."

"Oh?"

"The real reason I asked you to come with us." I clapped him on the back when he raised an eyebrow. "I need a favor."

21

DEVORA

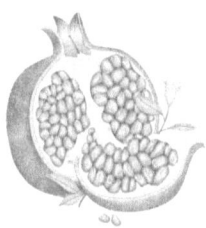

The buzz of power and excitement flooding the town was intoxicating. It took the edge off just enough for me to shake the nerves of being around all these strangers, to let my guard down and let loose, not worrying about magic or guilt or spying on a murderous Shifter.

Flames and shadows twisted together and rose into the sky. I couldn't tell what was magic and what was smoke from the fire. I reached out a hand, standing on my tiptoes to try and grasp a flickering tendril. It slipped through my fingers, but something inside me stretched. For a brief moment, a heartbeat, something *else* came to life.

"I have someone who'd like to meet you, Devora," Thecae said from my left.

I turned to see him standing next to an older woman with coarse gray hair curled around her head. Kind silver eyes stared back at me, with a smile deepening the many wrinkles along her face.

"I would know you anywhere," she said, her voice quiet but strong for her age. "Ceres's daughter. You were born with a head full of that fiery hair, you know."

A half smile formed on my lips. "You knew my mother too?"

"'Course. She was my most gifted scribe. Powerful as could be, with a mind to boot."

"I...I have so many questions," I said with a nervous chuckle, savoring every small tidbit of information.

Her grin widened, exposing a gap between her front teeth. "Come, girl. There's a log over here, and my old bones need to sit. Thecae?" she called, glancing behind her to the other Shadow Wielder. He approached and took her arm as the three of us walked to a nearby log.

"This is my mother, Calyra," Thecae said. Recognition dawned on me. She must be the woman who stitched the blanket I was found in.

"It's nice to meet you," I said.

"I always wondered if we'd ever see you again," she said softly. "I saw the rubble from the shipwreck, but I knew your parents. They would defy the Fates if it meant saving you, girl." Her wrinkled hand clasped mine as we sat. "The shadows have brought you back to us."

The sentiment made my heart lift. "You said my mother was a scribe? What does that mean?"

Calyra nodded. "A lifelong learner, that one. Shadow Wielders are big on tradition and history. Recording the lives of our ancestors, figuring out ways to keep their memories alive, that sort of thing. She loved uncovering new stories. Traveled all across the province, recording people's tales." Her smile faded as she gazed at me, then let go of my hand to cup my cheek.

"You have her eyes. Such bright eyes. And her hair too. You could see that girl coming from all the way across the valley. But your smile...that's all Malijah."

I swallowed. Her words clenched around me, pricking the backs of my eyes. "And what did he do?"

Thecae stepped in. "He was studying to become a shadow trainer, like me. At least, until we formed the rebellion. He was the only Shadow Wielder and Lightbender hybrid in the province. His magic was incredible to watch."

"And boy, did he know it," Calyra added with a chuckle. "Half the province was in love with him and the shows he'd put on for the ladies. Handsome and charming, always ready with a joke. But, oh, Ceres couldn't *stand* him."

I couldn't help but smile as I listened, watching their story unfold before me.

"Malijah only had eyes for her," Thecae said, a low laugh building as he shook his head. "He talked about her so much, I once knocked him off our bunk."

"You lived together?" I asked. "At the training grounds?"

"For a time, yes. We were in the same class."

"Ceres refused to give him the time of day, but I was always rooting for them," Calyra said, wagging her finger at me. "There are some people who are just meant to be."

Thecae grunted. "It wasn't until Malijah almost died that she finally realized her feelings for him."

My eyes widened. "Almost died?"

"A fight broke out one night on the border with Drakorum." Thecae motioned to the east where the Mistwood Mountains lay far in the distance. "An argument between the border guards, a group of Shifters, and some of our Shadow Wielders got heated. Several died. Malijah tried to step in and help his friends, and a Shifter clawed him across the stomach. Nearly killed him."

With a grave nod, Calyra cut in. "They had to hold his guts inside his body when they carried him back to the training grounds. He didn't wake up for four days. Ceres never left his side."

"They were married six months later," Thecae added.

Calyra's wrinkled hand found mine again, and she squeezed. "When you came along, everything changed for them. None of us blamed them when they needed to leave. This empire wasn't safe for a very, very long time. I just wish...I wish we could've known what would happen. We would have never let them get on that ship."

We sat in silence for a moment, them honoring their dead friends while I mourned a life I never knew.

Mourn was too strong of a word. I wasn't sorrowful, the way one might be when losing a loved one. Because I didn't technically have anything to *lose*. In reality...I had *found* them.

Piece by piece, I was gaining parts of the puzzle that were my past. Stories that rounded out my chipped edges, that gave me the feeling that somewhere, somehow...I *fit*. My mother's eyes and hair, her desire to seek out answers and observe the world around her. My father's smile and propensity for humor. Their passion and fire and nobility. I liked to think I had some of that too, when I wasn't swept up in my own selfishness.

In a strange way, the sounds of people laughing, feet pounding to the music, and drinks swishing against bottles was the perfect setting. Where the heady daze of the night made colors blend and shadows melt into your skin, where the world seemed less sharp. Less...cold. It was the way I wanted to remember these people I never knew. Thrumming with life, not hidden behind a veil.

After a moment, Thecae raised a hand into the air. Two strands of shadows shot from it, separating and forming into silhouettes of two people—one with short hair and broad shoulders, and one with a long braid down her back and a quill in her hand.

"To Malijah and Ceres Sephorne," he murmured. Calyra repeated his words, and the shadows slowly dissipated.

I stared at my hands, suddenly wishing, willing, *begging* for my shadows to emerge. To give me that one final piece, that one final proof that I'd finally found somewhere I was meant to be. I wanted *more* than just my mother's eyes and my father's wit. I wanted their magic. I wanted to know this part of them still lived in me.

As usual, nothing happened.

My throat burned from holding back desperation as I clenched my fingers into a fist.

Even my magic rejected me. Pushed me away. Wanted nothing to do with me.

I shoved my fingers through my hair, blinking rapidly to fight the dismay that swept through me.

To my surprise, Thecae crouched at my knees and yanked my

hands away in his callused palms. "Don't fight it, Devora," he urged. "This is what we talked about. You have to face whatever it is you're feeling. You can't keep trying to control them—your emotions *or* your shadows."

My hands shook as the first tear tracked down my cheek. I was so close. So close to shoving the sorrow away, taking several swigs of wine until it blurred completely, and tossing him a smile. Pretending like this never happened. Because it *hurt*. It hurt to face the truth.

Everything eventually rejected me. Used me, discarded me, or left me. Saw what I was good for, got their fill, and no longer needed me. Even though my family hadn't *chosen* to leave me behind, I was still alone.

Always alone.

These shadows didn't want me. And I didn't deserve them. That was what it all came back to, wasn't it? *I didn't deserve them.* Any of it. The things I'd done, the way I lived my life—I brought it on myself. Why would my shadows want someone like me?

Why would anyone?

A snarl broke through the sounds of revelry as a massive figure appeared on the ground before me. Thecae staggered to the side.

"What did you do to her?" Nox growled, taking Thecae's place at my knees. His eyes, more silver than navy, roved over my body.

"I'm not hurt," I said with a gasp. I hastily wiped the tears from my cheeks and turned away from him. "I'm fine."

Rough fingers came out to grasp my chin. Nox moved my head back to face him, his nose mere inches from mine, before his lips parted in surprise.

"Devora, your eyes," he said. "They're black."

Alarm blared inside of me, and I searched for Thecae, who'd been knocked to his side when Nox burst in.

"It's her shadows," he said, brushing dirt off his pants. "They're trying to get through. The emotions, the magic of the Vigil,"—Thecae motioned to the revelers around him—"it must have triggered something."

Their voices became muffled and distant as my heart pounded louder in my ears. Something pushed against my chest, desperate to get out.

I slammed my eyes shut, all my muscles clenching as if that could keep it inside. Could keep the pain from escaping. One of my hands shot to the log beneath me, and my fingers curled tight around the bark, nails digging into wood.

"But she's in pain," Nox said, voice surprisingly urgent.

"Magic is tied to emotions, boy," Calyra said. "Can you imagine going two decades without yours? She's *drowning* in them."

It didn't feel like I was drowning. It felt like I was *exploding*. Like a dam had crumbled as I choked back another sob. It was writhing inside me, all the self-loathing, the bitterness, the anger, the loneliness. The years I spent merely surviving, finding my purpose in the wrong people.

This is what you deserve.

Voices whispered in my mind, the same kind I heard in the shadow circle earlier with Thecae. They brushed against the raw wounds, making me double over as if I'd been struck.

Small tendrils latched on to those emotions and *tugged*. They ripped them into the open and twisted around them, growing, building, pushing—

I felt Nox move away from me, and without thinking, my arm lashed out and gripped his hand.

I glared at him. "Don't"—I huffed out a breath through gritted teeth—"leave me."

Don't leave me on these shores.

Don't leave me in this tower.

Don't leave me behind.

Don't leave me.

Don't—

His other hand clenched my arm. "I'm not going anywhere, Devora."

Something solid slammed into me. I let out a gasp as the gates opened and power flooded me.

Shadows tore out of our joined hands, rolling down my body and surging at my feet, sucking the world into its black tide. Nox was still on his knees in the dirt before me, but I could barely see the bottom half of our bodies through the darkness. Wind whipped at our hair and cloaks. Shadows pulsed in the air. They brushed against my skin while familiar voices drifted through my subconscious like music.

I stared at Nox, whose wide eyes matched my own, and for a moment, time stopped.

In my next breath, the shadows snapped back into my skin like someone had released a bowstring, and my muscles gave out. I slumped forward, falling from the log and into solid arms.

Everything went black.

22

DEVORA

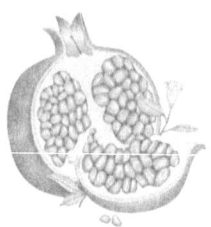

"You awake, honey?"

Wrinkled hands squeezed my arm, and my eyes fluttered open. I blinked against the bright sunlight coming in from the window, sluggishly lifting an arm to block my face. I was in a small bedroom with gray walls and a single window, with a closed door on the opposite side. The bed I lay in was just wide enough to fit me.

To my left sat Calyra, her silver eyes meeting mine with a smile. "That one knocked you right out. You've been asleep all night."

"What happened?" I asked, voice groggy. I tried to sort through my memories of the last few days. "Where am I?"

"The training grounds. Nox brought you back here after you passed out at the Noctus Vigil last night. Your shadows drained you, that's all. You went through a lot in a short period of time." She patted my arm. "You'll be fine, girl."

I furrowed my brow. "My shadows?" Had I truly conjured them? That was real?

She grinned. "Yes, honey. *Your* shadows. My son tells me they've been quite stubborn, but all they needed was a little push." Her eyes flicked to my hand, and I looked down.

Small wisps of smoke curled around my middle finger and

thumb, barely hovering over the skin. So soft I couldn't even feel them. When I sucked in a breath, they seemed to notice I was watching. The end of one of the tendrils perked into the air before the entire thing melted back into my skin.

"No—wait—" I reached out my hand as if I could chase them, but they were gone. I leaned further into my pillow with a sigh.

Calyra chuckled. "Stubborn and shy. An interesting combination. Reminds me of your parents."

"Are shadows always like this? So..." I searched for the word, still staring at my fingers. "Animated?"

The elderly woman shrugged. "They're a part of you. They have little personalities, as you'll quickly find out. You just have to get to know them. But now that you've found them, Devora," she leaned in and shook a finger at me, "they won't ever leave. They will *always* be with you. And that's a promise."

I nodded and swallowed, wondering if this woman could see to the core of my emotions better than even I could.

Don't leave me.

The last thing I'd said before my shadows finally broke free. As if they'd been waiting.

"Where is—" I bit my tongue before saying *Nox*, and instead switched to, "everyone else?"

"Waiting for you. But if you need the day to rest—"

I was already throwing the blanket off. "No more waiting." I swung my legs over the side of the bed and planted my feet on the floor. "I'm ready."

———

I WAS NOT READY.

These obstinate shadows made me want to jump off a cliff. I'd spent three hours staring at my hands so hard, I was going cross-eyed.

Thecae had me working on summoning. He made it seem so simple—as easy as breathing. His shadows came to him with barely a thought, wrapping around his arms and retreating at will.

We sat on the floor of the training grounds practicing my breathing. I worked on getting my mind to relax and opening myself up to what I'd let in the night before.

I had gotten to the point where I could get little wisps to come out and slide along my fingers, but any time I tried to conjure *more* or make them *do* something, it was like the little buggers freaked out and went into hiding.

"You have *got* to be kidding me," I said with a frustrated grunt. I'd finally managed to form a small ball of shadows in the palm of my hand, only for it to flatten back out and dissipate. "Is this what it's like to have children?"

Across the open space, Arowyn snorted. I shot her a bland look. She'd been sparring with other trainees all morning, both with physical weapons and with their magic. It was intriguing to watch. They would mold their shadows into weapons and shields, while she strode from one spot to another in the blink of an eye, getting in little swipes here and there with her blade. They were all so quick to react, their magic coming to them like second nature.

Other trainers filtered in around us from time to time, but we mostly had the grounds to ourselves. Calyra had made us all breakfast and now observed from a window overlooking us.

But Nox and Everett were nowhere to be found.

I pushed them out of my head and closed my eyes, shaking out the tension from my shoulders. I sent my mind back to the bonfire last night. To those feelings of hopelessness and rejection, the heartache of letting it all in after twenty-three years of repressing the worst of my inner fears.

The whispers started back up, like disembodied voices swimming to the surface of my subconscious. They hummed in my ear, and with it, I felt shadows licking at my hand.

I kept my eyes closed. They were too skittish. I couldn't let them think I was watching.

Something tickled the sensitive skin on the inside of my wrist. The corner of my lip twitched, but I didn't look.

Hello, there, I said softly in my mind. The voices hushed at the sound, and my shadows swelled, as if taking a breath.

I feel you, I thought, pushing my internal voice toward them. *You feel like a friend.*

Something warm wrapped around my wrist and slowly scooted up my arm. I smiled and tightened my shut eyes. Maybe they had the same fears and doubts I did. Maybe they, like me, needed a little push.

Thank you, I whispered to the thin threads. *For being with me last night. I don't know what it's like to have this magic, but Calyra says you'll always be there. That nothing can take you from me.*

The same feeling pulsed in my other hand, then twisted up to my elbow. *I'm sorry it took me so long to find you. But I won't let you go again, I promise.*

A warmth spread through my chest. I took another deep breath, and my shoulders sagged slightly. I wasn't used to acknowledging these emotions. It left me raw but filled at the same time.

"Open your eyes, Devora," Thecae murmured.

I opened them.

My shadows twined around both my arms up to my shoulders, thrumming to the beat of my heart. I grinned as they thickened with every passing breath, tiny wisps breaking off from the larger mass as if they were poking their heads out to wave at me.

I carefully stood and moved my arms, turning them and lifting them up and down. The shadows stayed. They tightened their grip on me, and when I nudged them with my mind, a small section extended to wind around my torso too.

When I flexed a hand, another piece floated off and formed a ball in my palm. It pulsed and writhed, but stayed in its compact shape, waiting for my command.

No, not *command*. Thecae was right. I kept thinking about them as something to control, when really, they were extensions of me.

It was like they knew what I wanted before I had to think it. They were *part of me.*

"I think the girl's starting to get it!" Calyra called from her position inside. I craned my neck to look at her.

Thecae, however, merely grunted. "We'll see."

As I turned back to him, a thin shard of shadow came flying at me.

"Hey!" I shouted, raising my hands to block my face. My shadows instantly disappeared. Thecae's shard shattered into fog against my bare skin. I could tell if he'd really wanted it to, it could have been sharp as steel.

"What was that for?" I snapped.

"Defense. Your shadows will be your best guard against an attack, if you can learn how to train them."

"You could've given me a warning," I mumbled, which earned me a soft chuckle. Straightening my shoulders, I held out a hand and called to my shadows again. To my surprise, they actually answered this time. Delicate and tentative at first, and then in a billowing mass like before, excitedly swirling around my body.

"Let's work together this time, alright, kids?" I muttered to them. A couple tendrils lashed out and swiped playfully at my neck in answer. I couldn't help but smile, until three huge balls of shadow came bursting from Thecae's hands.

I lifted my arms and imagined my shadows forming a wall in front of my face.

A second before his hit, mine faded into smoke.

"Seriously?" I shouted, right as his shadows slammed into me. I staggered backward with an exasperated sigh.

To my far right, Arowyn cackled. Narrowing my eyes, I shot her a crude gesture, and a sharp piece of shadow flew from my fingertip. It smacked Arowyn square in the forehead.

I raised my hands in mock innocence when she glared at me. "That was *not* me."

"Again," Thecae commanded. "Concentrate. Your shadows are

reacting because they sense your fear. Show them that you can stand *together*, and they have nothing to be afraid of."

"Great. Sounds easy. Are you going to tell them that weeks from now when they're facing an eight-foot-tall Shifter trying to eat me alive?" I grumbled.

Arowyn snorted. "Scarven's not eight feet tall."

"Well, I've never met the man," I said.

"He *would* eat you, though."

I scowled. "Not helping."

"Focus, Devora," Thecae said. "You can do this."

I nodded, and he struck.

23

NOX

Everett's illusion bent the sunlight around us as we moved through the narrow alleys of east Tenebra. The eyes of citizens strolling the cobbled streets slid right past us. I trusted Everett's magic, but my hand still hovered near the dagger sheathed at my waist the entire walk.

Every step closer to the cottage, the tighter my chest drew. I could face Scarven's guards without blinking, but this? This had me sweating through my clothes.

I glanced down at my hand, double-checking the instructions scribbled on parchment. Kieran had found her long ago, in case I ever needed to reach her. But it had always been too risky, what with Scarven's men keeping such close tabs.

Her home sat on the edge of the most eastern town, right up against the Mistwood Mountains. As bustling village life gave way to cold, rocky farmland, a distant cottage came into view.

"You ready for this?" Everett asked.

I swallowed, then gave a tight nod. "Just keep those illusions going. We can't let anyone know I'm here."

Whitewashed brick and a sagging roof greeted us. Scents of dried thyme and rosemary drifted on the icy air, their bundles hanging from the windowsill. The sight stirred something in my chest. She used to do that at our cottage, too. Echoes of a voice humming lullabies while herbs roasted on fresh meat flooded my senses.

I ventured closer, taking in the modest-sized home and small vegetable garden in a patch out front. Not much could grow in Tenebra's climate, but she'd always had a green thumb. I could see a fire crackling in the fireplace through the window, along with a single rickety chair at a wooden table.

I took a deep breath, then slowly released it as I mounted the step leading to the door. My knuckles hovered, shaking, before I finally knocked.

Silence permeated the air. Beside me, Everett twisted to look around the wide farmland, no doubt searching for signs of Scarven's men. If I listened close enough, my Shifter hearing could pick up on several heartbeats nearby—maybe a quarter mile from the property.

They were always watching. But Everett gave me a confident nod. His illusions would keep our interaction hidden, for now.

Quiet footsteps padded across the floor, and then the door creaked open. Just a crack, enough for a single navy eye to poke through.

That eye widened like it had seen a ghost. "Nox?"

The sound of her voice undid me. I dropped my head, trying to breathe through the wave of emotions, but it was useless. The dam broke.

"Hi, Mama," I rasped.

The door opened the rest of the way. Her arms closed around me, and I folded into them, sinking to my knees the way I had as a child, burying my face against her. She smelled of smoke and rosemary and baked bread.

Home.

"I thought—" Her voice cracked, words muffled against my hair. "I didn't think I'd ever see you again."

When I finally pulled back to gaze up at her, her hands cupped my face and traced the stubble of my jaw. "You grew a beard," she whispered, half laugh, half sob.

She stood there, five years older than my memories, but unmistakably her. Blonde hair streaked with gray, worn lines around her mouth, navy eyes that resembled my own.

"I'm sorry," I blurted. "I should've come sooner. I should've found a way—"

"Hush." She pressed a finger to my lips and shook her head. "You're here now. That's enough."

Everett lingered by the door, his head bowed to give us privacy. A surge of gratitude shot through me. We wouldn't be able to do this without him.

Mother's hand slipped down to grip mine, pulling me to my feet. "What of your sister?"

My chest squeezed. "Scarven still has her. I—I haven't seen her since that day."

The last time I saw either of them was the night Mother snapped and tried to break Vera out of her cells. My mother was a raven Shifter, a small, cunning little thing, and she devised a plan to sneak into Scarven's underground tunnel system and fly through the bars of my sister's cage. But she hadn't been prepared for the wards. They alerted Scarven of her presence, and he sent guards to capture her. They were able to subdue her, but not before she pecked out several of their eyes.

It had taken everything in my power to convince Scarven not to execute her on the spot. Instead, he banished her.

The light in my mother's eyes dimmed, but her grip on me tightened. "Not a minute goes by that I don't think of you two. Are you safe? Are you well?"

"I'm..." I didn't know how to answer that. Were any of us safe? Were any of us *well?*

"I'm fighting, Mama."

A sad smile nudged at her lips. "Of course you are, my son. I never doubted it for a second."

It was then that she seemed to notice Everett at the door. "This is Everett," I gestured to him, "an Illusionist and close friend. You can trust him. Everett, this is my mother, Freya Duma."

"It's nice to meet you, Everett." She gave him a warm smile and ushered him farther inside. "Come, come. Let me make some tea. I want to hear everything I've missed."

―――――

THE THREE OF us sat around my mother's cottage drinking peppermint tea, like something out of a storybook. It all felt so mundane. So casual. I missed this feeling, where I could finally breathe through the weights that crushed me and remember what it was like to be at peace.

If only for a moment.

I told her why we were here and about the Ashen Order, how I'd built upon our family's seaside cottage and turned it into the fortress it was today. Everett and I took turns recounting some of our rescue missions, the people we'd saved, the children who lived at the Keep. I tried to keep it on the lighter side. Focusing on the growth we'd had and lives we'd given back, instead of all the horrific things I'd seen from the victims coming out of those cells.

Mother told us what she'd been doing the last five years as well. She spent many of the initial months in the mountains, trying to find a way to break through the border, but Scarven's men were always there to stop her. Eventually, she settled into a new home, with one eye trained on Drakorum.

She had made friends, people she could trust and share her story with. She even had a booth at the village market selling recipes and spice mixtures—cooking had been a passion of hers for as long as I could remember.

But she was fighting too.

"There are a group of us here who have all had someone taken," she explained, sipping her tea. "Every once in a while, more people pop up missing. They suspect it's the Shifters. I've told them about Scarven's past, about what he might be doing to those people. Don't worry, I know I have eyes on me." She batted her hand in the air when I opened my mouth to warn her. "I know how to be *discreet*, son. But these people are angry. They want to do something about it."

I couldn't stop my smirk. "My mama and her little rebel group with their tea and biscuits."

She swatted my knee. "Everything can be solved with some tea and biscuits."

My smile faded. How I wished that were true.

Everett set his cup down on the coffee table, and his hand gripped the edge. I looked over to see his jaw clench, and something in the air wavered like the flames of a candle.

We'd been here too long. He was straining to hold on to the amount of magic it took to maintain such a strong illusion.

My mother hadn't missed it either. "You need to go, don't you?"

"It's fine," Everett said through gritted teeth.

"No, it's not. You need enough strength to get the two of you out of here without being seen." Her tone was final, but her forehead pinched in sadness.

I wanted to argue, to stay in this cottage with my mother and let the world fall apart outside. But Scarven's reach extended far, and I wouldn't risk her safety again.

She seemed to read the war in my eyes. She always had been able to pick up on my emotions so easily. Her palms framed my cheeks one last time, firm and steady. "Go, my son. Do what you must. I'll be here when you return."

I swallowed hard, then leaned forward to kiss her forehead. "We're going to bring you home, Mama. I won't fail you again."

"Oh, Nox." Tears swam in her navy gaze. "You have *never* failed me. It's your father and I who failed *you*. We should have done more to protect you all those years ago."

"It doesn't matter. I'm going to fix it." I pressed a kiss to her palm still clutching my face. "I'm going to get Vera back too, I promise."

Everett tugged at my arm. "It's slipping, Nox. I can't hold it for much longer."

Mother released me. Walking to her front door and down those steps felt like someone digging a hook into my heart and dragging me. She grabbed my hand one last time as we turned our backs on the cottage.

"I love you, son," she whispered.

"I love you, Mama." The backs of my eyes burned, a lump forming in my throat.

"I'm sorry," Everett said quietly as we slipped into the evening air. "I tried to keep it going as long as I could."

"You were amazing, Everett. This time...it was a gift." I cleared my throat. "I can never thank you enough. But I need to ask one more favor." He glanced at me warily. "Go back to the training grounds and don't tell anyone about this."

"And where are *you* going?"

I sighed, steeling myself for what was to come. "Scarven has a job for me to do while I'm here." I grabbed his forearm before turning away. "And...keep an eye on Devora. Make sure she's safe. I'll see you in a couple days."

24

DEVORA

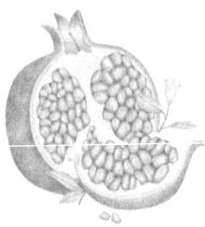

Four days had passed since the Noctus Vigil, and Nox was still nowhere to be found. Everett had reappeared, although he dodged any question I asked about their whereabouts.

I tried casually bringing it up with Arowyn at lunch one day, but all she did was shrug. They must be used to his sudden disappearances. But I thought he'd send word. Especially when he was putting so much hope in this plan.

Especially when he promised not to leave me.

One of my shadows that had taken to wrapping around the pinky of my right hand squeezed tight, and I flinched. "Just an *observation*," I grumbled under my breath. The dragon Shifter could do whatever he wanted. It didn't concern me.

"Who are you talking to?" Thecae asked as he planted his feet across from me.

"No one. Come on," I said, summoning shadows and lifting my hands in front of my face in a defensive posture.

He raised an eyebrow. "We've been going nonstop for almost four days, girl. I may be a harsh trainer, but even *I* say you need to rest."

"I don't have time to rest," I argued. We only had three days left

150

in Tenebra before we had to head back to Drakorum, and then it would be a whirlwind turnaround to the ball with Scarven and the Mysthelm contingency. I'd made progress ever since I learned how to connect with my shadows, but the most we'd done was defense and sparring. It would help me in a fight, yes, but spying? Not so much.

Thecae sighed. "You're more stubborn than your mother and father combined. Alright, fine."

His shadows moved before he did. I barely had time to breathe before they leaped, creating a sharp blade of darkness. My own shadows formed a wall without the slightest hesitation, seeming to know what I needed.

His false blade bounced off the barrier with a hiss, and the force vibrated through my ribs. Fates, he wasn't holding back this time.

Another lash came, this time from the opposite side—sleek shadows whispering through the air like a knife. I ducked and raised my barrier to soften the attack. Sweat broke out across my forehead as I concentrated. A cloud of shadows peeled away from me and reared up, striking Thecae's next attack mid-air. A thunderous sound rippled over us.

"Better," he said, impressed. "You're adapting."

I smiled and straightened, thinking we were done, when he melted.

Literally *melted*. Into a puddle of shadows.

"What the—"

He burst from the shadows at the edge of the training grounds to my left, balls of thick darkness blasting from his hands.

But I was ready.

My shadows caught them, two in each hand, and I faced them toward each other. The spheres slowly molded into one enormous circle, growing and crackling as I forced my own magic into it. Slamming my foot on the ground, I shoved the mass back at him.

He raised his own shadow shield with a lazy smile. I merely smirked back. I knew he'd expect a counterstrike. But after days of focusing, of diving into my bitter emotions and blending them with my shadows, I was getting better. *We* were getting better.

I twisted my finger in the air, and the ball of shadows flattened right as it met his shield, then forked into a hundred tiny branches up and over the barrier. They crawled along his arms and down his torso and legs, covering every inch of his body.

With a snap of my fingers, they froze, and him with it.

For a moment, there was silence.

And then a beam broke out across his face. He threw his head back and laughed, the sound rich and booming in the empty training grounds. The sun had set rapidly as we sparred, leaving only the torches scattered around the perimeter to light the way.

"Very good, Devora. We'll make a fighter of you yet," he said.

I let out a breath and dropped the shadows from his body, exhaustion seeping into my bones. I matched his grin. It was the first time I'd bested him.

"What was that thing you did? The shadow melting?" I motioned to the spot he'd reappeared from. "When do I get to learn *that*?"

He chuckled. "Do you think you're ready?"

I crossed my arms over my chest. "Wasn't it just yesterday you said I was one of your quickest trainees? I think I can handle it."

"Be careful, darling," a familiar drawl said behind me. "Don't let it go to your head."

I spun on my heels. Nox was leaning against an open archway, half in shadows, half in moonlight. His scruff was slightly thicker than usual, making him look rugged and tired. A black shirt clung to his broad shoulders and arms, those dark rings he always wore catching the light as he ran his thumb along his lower lip. I hated the way my breath hitched, the way relief made my stomach flip.

That relief quickly shifted to irritation. "Kind of you to join us," I said, tossing my sweat-slicked hair over my shoulder.

He pushed off the wall and prowled closer. "I see you've been practicing."

"What else did you expect?" I snapped.

Circling me, he eyed the dagger strapped to my thigh and the shadows swirling lazily at my feet. "You've gotten rather cocky."

I tilted my head. "I've gotten *better*."

"Shadows to shadows is one thing," he said with a shrug. "But what happens when someone hits you with their fist? Or a real blade? You can't absorb everything into your magic."

I slid my gaze to Thecae, then back to Nox. He had a point. Which I also hated. But—

"Square your feet," Nox instructed, rolling the sleeves of his shirt up his forearms.

I blinked.

When he lifted an eyebrow, I could've sworn a smirk flickered across his features. "Let's see how you do against something a bit more...*physical*."

That was the only warning I had. He struck faster than I thought possible, aiming for my hip. My shadows flared to my defense and slowed his fist enough for me to block him. His other hand swung at my neck, and I ducked. I pivoted on my heels to put some distance between us, panting from exertion.

"Where were you?" I seethed between breaths.

"Worried about me, darling?"

"Hopeful, actually." I sent several shadow shards at him, and he gracefully dodged each one. "Thought I might not be your *prisoner* anymore."

He darted close enough to grab my wrist. In a heartbeat, he spun me until my back was against his chest, my throat caught in the crook of his arm.

"You know how I feel about that word," he growled. "What are you going to do now, Devora? When your shadows can't help you?"

I struggled against his arms, but his hold was too tight. When I lifted a leg to kick him, he slid to the side, still keeping my upper half from moving. He applied more pressure to my neck. I didn't think he would really hurt me—it was more of a challenge. A way to see what I was made of.

He had some nerve, waltzing in here after disappearing for

days, not even bothering to say "hello" before criticizing my train-ing. Pressure built in my chest, my annoyance with him coming back tenfold.

I raised my leg and slammed it on top of his foot.

Only—it didn't hit his foot.

My body lurched toward the ground as half my leg melted into the shadows at our feet. The jarring movement made Nox release me, and I crashed to the ground.

He glanced down at me. "Not bad."

While he was distracted, I swiped my leg at his ankle, rein-forcing the blow with shadows strong enough to make his knees buckle. He lunged forward to try and pin me down, but I beat him to it. I used a rope of shadows to hold him to the ground as I strad-dled his waist.

"Don't underestimate me next time," I said, his face mere inches from mine.

Something silver flickered in his eyes. Just as I was about to get off him, he reached down between us, plucked the dagger from my thigh sheath, and held the blade to my neck.

I froze, my chest rising and falling with heavy pants. He was so close, I could see every tiny line of silver in his dark blue eyes, could feel his breath washing over my nose and cheeks. The tip of the blade dug into my sensitive skin.

"Is this the part where you fall in love with me?" I taunted.

"I don't fall in love, darling." His eyes slowly dragged to my lips, then back up again. "Not anymore."

I abruptly pulled myself off him, letting him get to his feet. My racing pulse still hadn't quieted. Without another glance at me, he backed away and nodded to Thecae.

"Good job. She's doing well."

"She's a natural," Thecae replied.

"Did you see that?" I asked Thecae, brushing dirt off my leathers. "Did I shadow melt?"

"More like shadow stumbled," Nox said, but it didn't hold as much of his usual bite. It was almost...teasing. When I shot him a bland look, his face was impassive.

Thecae chuckled. "Yes, I saw. I think you're ready to start working on some new techniques."

"Tonight?" I asked eagerly.

"No, not tonight. You need rest, girl."

"Maybe you two old men need rest," I mumbled, but the words turned into a yawn. I realized how exhausted I was, both physically and mentally. My shadows were fainter as they slunk back into my skin, settling heavily in my bones.

Thecae bade us goodnight, and I started to follow him into the base when a voice stopped me.

"I was handling something for Scarven," Nox said. "That's why I was gone."

I turned to face him. His shoulders were slumped, his features weary. That fire of his dragon had slipped away, leaving him raw. Open. Tired.

I nodded in understanding. He told me when we were traveling that Scarven had sent him to "take care of" a growing rebellion against Drakorum. But he'd also told me how he did everything in his power to help Scarven's targets. To give them a chance to get away and start a new life. If Scarven ever found out the truth, Nox *and* his sister could pay the price.

For the first time, it struck me how incredibly brave this infuriating man was. And he had trusted me with this knowledge, knowing I could ruin everything. That thought alone made my stomach flutter with unexpected emotion.

I licked my lips and swallowed. "But you're back now?"

He stepped forward and handed me my dagger. "I'm back."

His fingers brushed mine as he pulled away, then strode out of sight.

25

NOX

Fine. I was impressed. Devora was doing rather well with her shadows. I made a mental note to tell Kieran that perhaps *I* should keep making the plans going forward, considering this was my idea.

I watched hour after hour, day after day as Thecae trained Devora in her shadows. Arowyn and Everett occasionally jumped in with their striding or illusions to give her practice dealing with other kinds of magic. Even Calyra, Thecae's spritely mother, would commandeer Thecae's sessions to discuss some of the deeper elements of shadow wielding with Devora.

"You know, neither your mother *or* father could shadow melt," she said one evening, two nights before we needed to head back to Drakorum. She wagged her finger at Devora over a bowl of stew. "But Ceres was the best shadow marker I've ever met."

"Shadow marking? What's that?" Devora asked, adjusting her thick glasses on her nose. She didn't wear them when she trained. She said she was worried they'd get in her way. When she wore them, it made her look...softer, almost. Still fierce, but with this edge of vulnerability hidden behind the lenses. Either way, it was hard not to notice how beautiful she was. When—

I jerked my head to the side at the intrusive thought. Fates, what kind of a monster was I to have thoughts like that about the woman I'd kept captive in my own home? The woman I was training to send off to spy on my *brother*?

Something tightened in my stomach every time the impending ball came up. When I first devised the plan, I thought it would be easy to put her in certain danger. If she was willing, so was I. We had nothing to lose. She was a traitor to my empress, which effectively made her a traitor to my *people*. She meant nothing to me other than being part of the mission.

But now, it was almost as if I was *anxious* for her. I knew what Scarven was capable of, and the thought of her being in his clutches...

The lines were blurred. Things weren't as black and white with her as they were three and a half months ago.

"Shadow marking is where you leave a bit of your shadows behind," Calyra was saying. "Almost like an anchor to help you find your way back."

"Sounds kind of like my magic," Arowyn mused with a bite of stew in her mouth. "I can summon things to me if it has some of my essence connected to it."

Calyra nodded. "We may possess different magics, but it's all from the Fates, isn't it? Runs through each of our veins." She patted Devora's hand, who was gazing at her with quiet admiration.

"What else is there?" Devora asked.

"Well, there's shadow whispering," Calyra said. "Shadows carry sound, you know. If you're in a dark enough space, some can use them to tune into sounds from far distances."

"I think you've actually already done that, Devora," I said, and she looked over in surprise. "You told me once that you can hear whispers from my men all the way up in your tower. That's not something a normal Veridian can do."

"Impressive." Thecae nodded at her.

Devora moved a strand of hair behind her ear, her cheeks turning pink under the praise. "Okay, so, there are lots of different variants." She tapped her spoon against her bowl. "How could I use them against Scarven?"

We hadn't told Thecae and Calyra everything, just enough for them to get the gist of what we expected Devora to do: infiltrate the governor's mansion and learn his secrets. If my friend Lark trusted them, I figured it was safe. They certainly held no love for Scarven after the way he tried to control the borders between our provinces.

"You can't be too obvious with your magic," Everett pointed out across the table. "He's supposed to think you're from Mysthelm."

"Well, I'm *so* glad I learned all that shadow combat I can't even use," Devora said, cocking her head at Thecae with a sarcastic smile.

He tipped his cup at her. "You'll be thanking me when you find yourself at the sharp end of a blade."

"Nobody's going to be at the sharp end of anything," I cut in. "You'll get close to him and make him intrigued enough to want to show you more. Once you're past his main wards, it's just a matter of gathering intel. You're not trying to single-handedly bring his mansion down. We need to know where he's keeping his stash of fatesprig, what he's doing with it, and how we can get past the wards to destroy it." I ticked each item off on my fingers.

Devora turned to face me, locks of that red hair falling over one shoulder. "Why are you so confident he'd let me get close enough to find out any of this?"

"I told you, he likes to collect things. We only just allied with Mysthelm. It's been centuries since we've had magic-less people wandering our empire. He's going to covet someone like you. Someone he's never *had* before."

"So what, I smile and look pretty? How am I supposed to make sure I get his attention?"

"I don't think that'll be a problem," Arowyn said with a snort. Devora raised an eyebrow, and Arowyn shrugged. "You're hot, Devora. And young. And men are pigs."

Everett grunted. "Present company excluded, I hope."

"I said what I said."

"Look, Scarven is an intelligent man," I started. "But he's also incredibly arrogant. He rules this province with fear. And while that's satisfying to him, it's not enough. I think…" I trailed off, sorting through how to word this next part without giving away my proximity to him. Not many people knew of our relationship.

"I think in his quest for power, he's grown lonely. He wants someone to share it with. Someone who's *like* him. I've always wondered if these experiments are his way of trying to turn people into himself." I waved a hand in the air. "Most are either disgusted by him or are too scared to do anything other than blindly follow him. But very few are *interested*. I think if you were to show intrigue in his work, his desire for that connection would tempt him to share more than he's usually comfortable with. You just have to take advantage of that."

Devora stared at me, then blinked slowly. "How do you know so much about him, Nox?"

My jaw clenched, but I held her stare. She didn't know the truth. The fact that I shared blood with this vile man was something I hardly ever admitted.

"It's my job to know the enemy," was all I said.

For the rest of the evening, Calyra and Thecae talked through the intricacies of shadow melting, marking, and whispering. Calyra was particularly skilled at shadow whispering, and she had the rest of us move into the training grounds and speak near the shadows to see if Devora could train her own magic to carry the sound back to her. Arowyn told some rather questionable jokes, while Everett recited excerpts from his books on Veridian magic.

Devora couldn't hear a single one. But even I had to admit, the atmosphere was lighter than it had been since before Devora joined. In just a few short days, Arowyn and Everett had become as comfortable with her as they were with anyone in the Order. She fit in better than I could've imagined.

Part of me was relieved. As a leader, I wanted unity. Shifters were pack creatures, and the pack worked seamlessly when everyone was on the same page. But the other part of me still felt guilty. As if I was pardoning her betrayal, sweeping it under the rug like nothing had happened.

I didn't know how to *let go*.

But I was trying.

"Alright, last one. Nox, you're up!" Calyra shouted, her voice echoing to the far end of the training grounds where I stood.

With my Shifter senses, I could hear her saying to Devora, "Remember, all shadows are connected. They can speak to one another. Just imagine the shadows around *him* carrying the sound back to your own. Relax your mind—don't force it."

I heard Devora's soft inhale and exhale. A moment later, I leaned into the shadows in the corner.

"Look, Devora," I whispered, knowing she was far too tired for her magic to work. "The thing is, I *want* to trust you after everything you're doing to help my people." I scrubbed a hand down my face as I forced the words out. I was speaking more to myself than anyone else at this point. "But it's hard to give up that control for someone I barely know."

I took a deep breath and murmured, "I didn't think it was possible, but you're becoming one of us now. So...thank you. I know I haven't said it yet. Thank you for what you're doing. It—it means a lot."

As I headed back to the buildings to rest for the night, I thought I saw a tendril of darkness flick against my ankle as the whispered words "*You're welcome*" died on the wind.

26

DEVORA

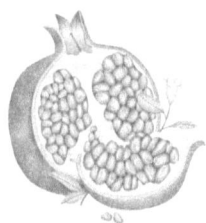

"Come here, honey," Calyra said, pulling me into a shockingly strong hug for someone of her stature. "We're sure going to miss you."

"I'll come visit, don't worry," I said. My heart constricted at the comfort of her hug. I didn't think I'd ever been hugged like this.

Like from a mother.

She pulled back and cupped my face in her hands, her silver eyes and thin lips lined with wrinkles. "You have Ceres and Malijah's spirit in you. It felt like we had them back for a few days." She patted my cheek. "They'd be proud of you, girl."

"You have to say that. It's the classic orphan pep talk."

"I don't *have* to say anything. It's the truth. Look at all you've done in *eight days*. You're quick as a whip, but your heart is what makes you a Sephorne." She lowered her voice. "I know you have your dark thoughts, girl. We all do. But shadows aren't just *darkness*. They aren't what's left when the light goes out. They're proof that light was there to begin with, and that it will come back again."

I blinked and cleared my throat, not used to this kind of emotion clogging my senses. "Thank you, Calyra," I whispered, pulling her into another hug. "For everything."

When she released me, I faced Thecae, who stood with his arms crossed over his large chest. He was an imposing sight, this shadow warrior, but when he smiled down at me, his features softened.

"You've done well," he said.

"All thanks to you."

He shook his head. "Trust me, I've trained plenty of Shadow Wielders who didn't amount to anything. It's not just about strength or magic. I think you could be powerful, sure, but there are others like you. The difference is that you're someone I'd want to stand beside."

I looked down at the ground, unable to meet his gaze. Nobody had ever said that about me. "You hardly know me, Thecae."

"You're a Shadow Wielder. You're Malijah and Ceres's daughter. Trust me, I know you." He tapped a knuckle under my chin to make me look up again. "Chin up, girl. Your father's watching. Make us proud."

My eight days were up. This morning, we were heading back to Drakorum. No one had thought I'd be a prodigy, but at least I knew what my shadows could do. I wasn't heading into the lion's den unarmed. I'd keep practicing, keep learning, keep getting comfortable with my shadows *and* my emotions.

But, Fates, I'd miss this place. I'd even gotten used to the cold. It wasn't so bad after a little while. These people filled it with a warmth I hadn't expected to feel in such a short amount of time. Compassion, cheer, friendliness. A sense of belonging. All things I hadn't had in...well, perhaps ever.

And a bit of the ice had thawed between me and the Ashen Order, too. Enough to make me think we could be allies after all.

We packed up our carriage and waved goodbye, heading into the rising sun.

———

WE WERE NEARING the last peak of the Mistwood Mountain range after almost three days of travel. Once we reached the base of the mountain, it would only take two more days to get back to the Keep, and then two more before the ball.

It was all happening so fast.

"You look nervous, oh great and mighty *Shadow Wielder*," Everett said with a faint smirk, glancing at me over the top of his book. The Illusionist had certainly loosened up between the last time we traveled and now. He was surprisingly funny. A dry, witty sense of humor beneath the stoic outer shell.

"I do *not*."

"He's right; you're paler than usual. And you keep biting your lip," Arowyn, who was next to me, pointed out.

I rolled my eyes. "You'd be nervous too, if you were about to have to cozy up with some evil maniac in his evil lair."

The two of them shared a look. "Are you *sure* you want to do this?" Arowyn asked.

"I'm fine; I'm just...dramatic." I waved away their concern. "How does Nox know so much about the way Scarven's mind works, anyway? He was incredibly specific."

Everett turned his eyes back to his book. "Trust me, if you had firsthand experience with what Scarven put us through, you'd see it too."

My elbow slipped, and I jolted forward. "Wait, did you say *us*?" I blinked back my shock. "Was Nox one of his *prisoners*?"

Everett glanced up in alarm. "You didn't know?"

"Smooth, Everett," Arowyn drawled.

My mouth fell open. "No, I didn't *know*. Nobody tells me anything."

My mind reeled. Both Nox *and* his sister were part of Scarven's experiments? No wonder he was so concerned about trust and protecting his people at all costs. The man had been *tortured*, for Fates' sake.

I let out a breath as guilt for all the horrible things I'd thought and said washed over me. "Everything makes sense now," I said. "He—"

The carriage suddenly lurched. We all instinctively braced a hand on the nearest wall, exchanging glances of confusion.

And then it slammed forward, throwing us all to the side.

There was a loud *crack* as Arowyn's head hit the far window. She dropped like a rock, crashing into the bench before I could break her fall.

"Arowyn!" I screamed. I put a finger to her pulse, relieved to find it still beating.

The carriage rocked again. I looked out the window to see us hurtling down the mountain at an alarming speed, narrowly avoiding the edge of the cliff as we swerved to the left.

"What's going on?" I shouted, struggling to regain my footing.

"It felt like a wheel came off," Everett said with a grunt.

I glanced out the window again, my heart thumping wildly. "We're going to go straight off the side if we don't slow down."

"We're going downhill," Everett pointed out, voice clipped. "There's no *slowing down*, Devora."

I squeezed my eyes shut. If Arowyn were conscious, she could easily stride us out of here. The carriage was moving far too quickly to jump out. What was the driver doing? Why hadn't he noticed?

"Grab my waist," I instructed Everett as I stepped over Arowyn and leaned into the door.

"Excuse me?"

"Just *do it*."

His hands came to my waist, planting me firmly in place. "Devora, what are you—"

I unlatched the door and let it swing open enough for me to stick my head out and get a better look.

Wind whipped my hair in a frenzy. The harness had come undone—the leather appeared faded and worn from overuse. The driver was frantically trying to gain control of the carriage, but with the horses detached, we were left at the mercy of the mountain.

Everett was right. We were going downhill, too fast to slow down.

I looked over and saw the front right wheel had broken. It was still partially affixed to the axle, but the top half was cracked and hanging by a few shards of wood.

Taking a deep breath to center myself, I summoned my shadows and sent them flying to the wheel. I concentrated on strengthening them, molding them to the cracks and pouring more power into them until they formed a semi-solid curve over the broken half. A small bead of sweat dripped from my forehead.

It worked. The carriage ceased its jarring motions. Letting out an exhale, my shoulders sagged in relief.

"Devora, watch out!" Everett cried, his hands tightening around my waist.

I looked past the wheel and nearly fell out of the carriage.

We were heading straight for the edge of a cliff.

I barely had enough time to throw out my arms before the front of the carriage careened over the side.

An enormous cloud of black shadows sprang from thin air. It supported the carriage as it dipped further downward, a split second from tumbling off completely.

My breaths came out in short gasps as I felt the carriage shift, but still, the shadows held. It was solid and smoky at the same time, with small wisps that broke off and stroked my arm. Energy poured out of me in droves, strengthening the wall as my heart hammered in my chest.

"Don't drop us," Everett whispered. His muscles strained from the effort it took to keep both of us from falling. One arm was wrapped around my waist, while his other clung to the inside of the carriage.

Slowly, painstakingly slowly, I urged the shadows to tilt us back on four wheels. Sweat slicked my clothes, and my arms strained from exertion, but I never loosened my hold. Inch by inch, the carriage righted itself.

With a motion that made my heart jump up my throat, we

were yanked backward and onto solid ground. A yelp left my lips before the carriage door was ripped off its hinges and rough hands encompassed my body.

All the fight left me when I saw Nox's face. Enormous navy wings loomed large behind him, blocking the sunlight while his arms dragged me from the broken carriage.

"Devora—"

"You didn't leave me," I mumbled, and my eyes fell shut as I collapsed in his hold.

27

NOX

I hadn't felt fear like that in years. One moment, I was riding ahead to clear space for the carriage, and the next, Devora's scream tore through the air.

I bolted back for them as quickly as I could, my wings already ripping free from my back. By the time I reached the cliff, the carriage was suspended on a cloud of shadows as if it weighed nothing. Relief hit so hard my knees nearly gave out.

Half-shifted, I wrenched the carriage to safety and tore the door off its hinges. Devora was barely conscious before she went limp in my arms again. Arowyn took a nasty bump to the head, and the driver had some bruises, but nobody was gravely injured. I sent the driver ahead to fetch help while we collected our supplies.

Arowyn took Devora's limp body as Everett and I loaded our bags onto the two remaining horses, but all my senses were tuned to the rhythm of Devora's breaths. I didn't know what exerting that much power in such a short amount of time would do to her, and until she woke up, I was on high alert, my nerves frayed and temper short.

Everett started to lift Devora onto the back of his horse with him, and I snarled, "*No.* Take Arowyn." I jerked my head to the Strider. "Devora's coming with me."

He raised an eyebrow, but I turned away before he could respond. I held Devora to my body with one arm as I mounted Tempest, leaning her against my chest and making sure she was fully in the saddle before grasping the reins in one hand. Her steady heartbeat and warm puffs of air on my arm eased my anxiety by a fraction, and the four of us set off down the last incline.

I didn't want to look too closely at the way my Shifter half purred in my chest when Devora stirred, her head nestling further into me. I was glad she was sleeping, even if it took being knocked unconscious to succumb. She'd been working too hard. Hardly letting herself rest while we were in Tenebra, and always ready for more training, no matter how big the circles under her eyes grew.

A stab of guilt pierced me. Again, that was probably my fault. I'd pushed her too far, put too much pressure on her role in this mission. Made her think success was the only path to her answers and her redemption. Assigned her worth to what she could do for *me*.

Wasn't that part of why I despised Scarven so much? Viewing my dragon as a weapon, ready to wield at any given turn. How was what I was doing any better than that?

Devora shifted in her sleep, and I tightened my hold. The end of her tunic rose when she curled her arms around my waist. My fingers accidentally pressed into bare skin, gliding above the waistband of her leggings.

She had complained about being cold this entire journey, but she felt like *fire*.

Heat spread up my arm, and when she let out a soft sigh, my dragon rumbled.

I had to hold on to her, or else she'd fall off. That was what the rational part of my brain said, anyway. I didn't *want* to be near her. I didn't *want* my skin to tingle everywhere her body touched mine.

The horse's trot pushed her deeper into the saddle, her side pressing and shifting against me with every motion. I tried to think of *anything* else. Anything other than her scent, or the way the top of her head brushed my neck, or how her fingers clenched my shirt in her sleep.

I didn't have to try for long. A moment later, she gave a shuddering gasp and jolted awake. I hastily loosened my hold. She jerked her arm away and looked up at me with confusion.

"Where—what happened?" she rasped, glancing around at the cluster of rocks and pine trees as we passed. The sun was beginning to set behind us. Its dark orange and golden rays cast the tips of the trees in shadows.

I cleared my throat. "Your carriage malfunctioned, and you nearly went off the side of a cliff, but your shadows stopped it. You passed out after using so much power."

"What about Arowyn? Is she alright?"

"She's fine. Everett is too. They're behind us on the other horse. We'll need to stop and make camp soon."

She blinked and looked down, seeming to just then realize we were sharing a horse. A hint of pink spread from her chest and up her neck. She tried to scramble away to put space between us, but my arm held her firmly in place. "Sorry, I—I didn't mean to sleep for so long—"

"You have nothing to apologize for," I said gruffly. "You saved them. You were—" I stopped myself and swallowed. "You deserved to rest."

"I didn't know what to do," she said, voice quiet. "I saw we were falling, and I just…reacted. I threw out my hands. It was like my shadows were trying to protect me."

I nodded. "Our magic knows what we need sometimes before we know ourselves. You're strong, Devora. Your magic is powerful."

She quirked an eyebrow. "Careful. That almost sounded like a compliment."

"Wouldn't dream of it, darling," I drawled.

Twisting at the waist, she grabbed the pommel and swung her leg around so she was no longer riding sidesaddle. The movement made her back press further into me, and I let out a grunt, instinctively tightening my grip on her waist.

She froze, back arched, hair spooling down one shoulder. My Shifter senses homed in on the sound of her heart picking up speed.

Something shifted between us, the air suddenly charged. My eyes fell shut for a moment as I strained to keep my hands away from her.

Fates, what was *wrong* with me? Not three weeks ago, I hated this woman. Now here I was, smelling her hair and anxiously awaiting the moment we could get off this horse so I could forget the way her skin felt against mine.

I let out a breath, forcing my muscles to relax. The strange tension snapped, and Devora scooted forward in the saddle.

"I'm just glad everyone's okay," she said breathlessly. "You know, we were talking about something before the accident." Her voice was hesitant, guarded. "Everett mentioned you were once one of Scarven's prisoners."

My spine straightened. "And?"

"And..." She cleared her throat nervously. "Well, I guess I wondered if it was true."

"Yes, it's true. It's not a secret, Devora—I'm not going to rip your head off for talking about it."

A small scoff left her. "You haven't exactly been forthcoming about your past."

I shrugged. "You never asked."

She twisted her neck. "Would you have told me anything if I did?"

"Probably not."

A smile stretched across the half of her face I could see before she turned to the front again. "Glad to see some things haven't changed. Well, maybe I've upgraded slightly. Now I'm a useful pawn."

My hands tightened around the reins, causing my arms to push her closer to me. "You're not a pawn, Devora."

"Then what am I?"

"You..." I trailed off, my jaw clenching as I sifted through the myriad of confusing thoughts rushing in my mind. "You're a Shadow Wielder," I finally said.

That seemed to be good enough for her. She let out a soft hum, and in that moment, I wished for nothing but to see her face. Was she happy? Did having an identity make her blue-green eyes soften, her lips curve, her shoulders relax?

"I'm sorry," she said after a moment. "About what you went through with Scarven. I can't even imagine."

We fell into silence again, but I could tell she wanted to ask more. Devora wasn't the kind to fall back when her curiosity took over. Her thighs clenched and unclenched around the saddle as her fingers played with the leather of the pommel.

She was always so quick to speak. Quick to try and make sense of the world around her. But now, she was quiet. A small part of me wondered if she was trying not to push too hard against the unspoken boundaries between us.

If she was trying, then I could too. Even if the thought of speaking about my past made my limbs lock.

"You can ask me, Devora," I murmured. "I won't bite."

I couldn't see it, but I could hear her swallow hard before she asked, "How did it happen? How were you...taken?"

A cold wind blew in, ruffling her hair against my neck. "I was fourteen. My father was the governor of Drakorum back then, but there was an uprising. People thought he and my mother had somehow illegally sired a dragon Shifter, which had been extinct up until I was born."

I paused, knowing her well enough at this point to expect fifty questions flying through her head.

"Wait—your father was the *governor*? And what do you mean, dragons were extinct? Aren't *you* a dragon?" She turned to face me in bewilderment.

"I'm the first dragon Shifter in two hundred and fifty years. The dragon line was eradicated after the emperor back then became afraid the Shifters would form an army and take over. Dragons were too powerful to let survive. Nobody knows how the gene got passed to me, but everyone suspected my parents had experimented on me." I grunted. "Kane Scarven challenged my father for his position and won. My father died, and my mother, sister, and I were taken prisoner."

"Fates, that's..." She let out a breath. "And you were only *fourteen?*"

"Many of his prisoners are far younger," I said, working to keep my voice even. "My sister was barely a year old."

"And he wanted you because you're the only one of your kind," she guessed. "You told me before that your sister isn't a dragon. But she must be powerful, if he's kept her locked up her whole life."

It wasn't a question, but I responded anyway. "She has all six."

"All six what?"

"Magics, Devora. My sister has all six magics of the Veridian Empire."

"*What?*" Devora nearly fell out of the saddle with how quickly she twisted to gaze up at me. "I haven't been here long, but I'm assuming that's not normal."

A snort escaped me. "No, that's not normal. Some Veridians have two types, and there have been maybe four recorded cases in history that had three. But nobody has ever dreamed of wielding all six."

I thought back to the first decade of Vera's life, where she, Mother, and I were still allowed to see one another in Scarven's manor. It was before her magic manifested, before Scarven knew what she possessed.

"When she was eleven, Vera showed signs of lightbending. We were all surprised, but it can happen—somewhere down the line, one of our ancestors could have been from Emberfell. But then she partially shifted. Scarven grew curious. Two years later, she created shadows." I paused when Devora's fingers started tapping anxiously against my thigh.

"When she was fifteen, she accidentally cast her first illusion on one of the guards. That was when Scarven took her away. For good. I haven't seen her since, and it's been five years. He would give me reports on her every once in a while, so that's how I found out she'd been able to cast spells *and* stride."

Devora's hand flattened out on my leg, and her thumb dug into my pants before she pulled it away. "I'm so sorry, Nox. Five years..." She shook her head. "I know I've said this before, but I need you to believe me. I'm going to do *everything* I can to help. And this isn't about what I can get out of it. I want to help you because...because it's the right thing. Because *nobody* should have to suffer like that. And if we don't help them, who will?"

I pressed my lips together, a lump forming in my throat. I wondered if she knew how many times I had the same exact thought.

I paused before quietly saying, "I believe you."

She turned so her profile faced me again, and a smirk climbed its way onto her face. "Look at us. Working together. Who would've thought?"

"I wouldn't go that far."

She rolled her eyes, then stretched out her back with a sigh. I inhaled as more of her body moved against me, tension building in my core.

"It's kind of nice, you know," she said, and I froze. "Not being your prisoner."

A snarl rumbled from my chest and up my throat. I slid my hand to her stomach and jerked her back so my lips grazed her ear.

"You know how much I *hate* that word." Her breath hitched when my fingers elongated into talons and gently brushed her side. "Call yourself that one more time, darling, and I'll show you what it means to be under a dragon's control."

When I released her, she lurched forward as if I'd burned her, the sound of her pulse pounding in my ears.

She was silent for the rest of the ride.

28

DEVORA

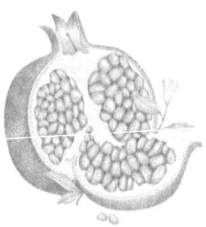

We stopped in a village at the base of the Mistwood Mountains to purchase two new horses for Arowyn and me for the rest of the trip.

Thank the Fates.

I could hardly sleep that night, what with the fear still pumping in my veins, the exhaustion of using all that power, the ghostly feel of claws scraping over my skin...

Things with Nox felt different. I couldn't tell if it was a *good* different. I still didn't think he trusted me, and I wasn't sure if I trusted him. There was all this lingering animosity mixed with something *new*, something heated and tense and raw, and I didn't know where it came from. Was it born of anger? Distrust? Curiosity? Desire?

We both wanted the same thing: to take down Scarven. But there was so much we still held against each other. I betrayed his best friend, and he kept me locked up for three months. How were we suddenly supposed to work together?

My body was confusing adrenaline with desire, that was all. My mind knew better. Nox Duma was a fuse waiting to be lit. All that restraint coiled beneath his charm, begging to be released.

I just needed to put distance between us.

I hung back with Arowyn the next day, our second-to-last full day of travel. Everett and Nox talked strategy up ahead. They would occasionally bring us into the conversation, which felt like an improvement from the cold shoulder I got on the way to Tenebra.

It was wild how much things had changed in two and a half weeks. I stared down at the reins, watching as my little shadows pulsed into view, wrapping around my fingers the way they liked to. It was as natural as breathing at this point. Thecae was right—they were part of me. Not something to control, but to complement. And after they saved us without a thought in the carriage accident, I trusted them implicitly.

My own shadows were probably the best friends I ever had. I couldn't decide if that was profound or tragic.

I knew they would help me with this mission. I hadn't been able to shadow melt ever since the sparring session with Nox, but I'd been practicing shadow whispering. I'd done it before—subconsciously back at the Keep, and then again in the training grounds before we left.

Nox's whispered confession still rolled through my mind. I knew he would never want me to admit I'd heard it.

"I didn't think it was possible, but you're becoming one of us now."

The words wrapped around me, warming the chill from the cold Drakorum air. I'd never been part of something like this. Something so important, so meaningful. I'd searched for this feeling in all the wrong places, hoping one day the answers to my past and my family would be that solace for me.

I was beginning to think that maybe there was more than one kind of family.

"What are you smiling at?" Arowyn asked as we trotted along.

"Nothing." I tucked my grin away. "So when are we stopping for the night?"

———

I DREAMED OF A ROCKING SHIP.

Waves rolling under a dark blue sky, stars reflecting off the crests like little diamonds. A blue blanket wrapped around a smiling baby. Shadows twirling and dancing between little fingers. It was one of those moments where I *knew* it was a dream, *knew* my body was lying in a tent in Drakorum, but I didn't want it to end.

Then whispers broke through the dream, carried on a dark cloud over the waters.

"No, please!"

"Not her. Take me—kill me—"

"Help me."

I thought it was part of the dream, until a familiar snarl burst from the shadows.

I jolted awake in my bedroll. Sweat dampened my brow, but the flap of my tent had come loose, letting in a chill.

"Help me."

That voice echoed again, along with a groan. My shadows circled my feet and twined up the blankets covering me. Something was wrong.

I hastily shoved off the blankets and grabbed the nearest cloak, throwing it over my shoulders as I crawled out of the tent. Tendrils of darkness unfurled toward the tent furthest from me, across the campfire that had long since dwindled.

Nox's tent.

The whispers grew louder as I approached. There was a silhouette of a candle still burning inside the tent, illuminating it with a golden glow. I hesitated, then reached out to undo the buttons of the opening.

When I poked my head inside, I sucked in a breath.

Nox lay in his bedroll, thrashing in his sleep. His pillow and blanket were shredded all around him. Silver talons extended from his fingers, scraps of fabric caught on their tips. Faint lines that looked like scars faded into his skin with every passing moment, as if he'd clawed himself in his sleep only to heal and do it all over again.

Without thinking, I rushed forward to kneel at his side and placed the back of my hand on his cheek. Fates, he was burning up.

I tried to keep my voice soothing. "Nox, if you can hear me, please—"

His eyes flared open, the silver slits of his dragon staring back at me.

In my next breath, he grabbed my waist and flipped me over so my back was on the ground and he was hunched over me.

He glared down, heaving breaths racking his chest. His ear-length hair hung wild and unruly past his forehead as he bared his fangs at me. Hints of fire and steel raged in his eyes. It was almost as if they were glowing, barely containing the power within.

Gone was the charming, silver-tongued man, and even the cold and angry captor.

This was the *dragon*.

I refused to be scared, not when I knew he was in pain. I lifted my chin and held his gaze. A devastating growl rumbled through the space between us, causing the hair on the back of my neck to stand on end.

"Nox, it's me. It's Devora. You were having a nightmare." When I spoke, he grabbed my wrists to keep me from moving, and I arched my back. "I—I promise, I'm not going to hurt you," I gasped.

He snarled again. His eyes flicked down to my neck, then to the cloak wrapped around my shoulders. His nostrils flared, but his breaths faltered.

To my surprise, he lowered his head to the fabric, breathing it in as his nose traveled down the length of it. The action was so predatory, so Shifter-like, that it made my muscles clench, nervous to flinch and risk his sudden movement.

"Devora?" he growled.

I slowly nodded. His breaths evened, but he didn't move, his nose still tracing a path where the cloak met my neck. Instead of fear, heat burned through my core. My eyes fluttered shut as I exhaled.

He was so close. So warm. The top of his head brushed my cheek, and the stubble at his chin was rough even through the cloak. I swallowed hard when he breathed in again.

The tension snapped.

Before I could blink, Nox threw himself off me with a grunt, almost bringing down the tent as he crashed into it.

"You shouldn't be wearing that," he said, voice so low and gravelly, I hardly recognized it.

I scrambled back and tried to catch my breath. "What are you—"

"My *cloak*. You can't wear that," he seethed.

My eyebrows flew up. "*You're* the one who gave it to me. What's wrong?"

"It smells like me," he forced out. "He—he can't know. Scarven. He'll smell it."

I got to my feet and moved closer. "It's okay, Scarven's not here. You had a nightmare. You need to calm—"

"*Don't!*" he roared, and I froze. "He's going to know. I was an idiot. You can't wear that anymore, Devora."

I shook my head. "I don't understand. How would he—"

Nox was before me in a flash, one hand wrapping loosely around my throat while the other tore the cloak from my shoulders. "You smell like *mine*, Devora. And he always wants what's mine."

I met his stare, startled by the fear in his eyes. Why was Nox so scared about this? With all the magic at our disposal, I was sure there was a way to mask my scent—a potion or spell, perhaps. No, something else was going on. Something deeper.

"Why does he care so much about you?" I whispered.

His lips lifted into a snarl. I didn't think he was going to answer me, but a moment later, he released me and backed away. Unspoken anguish lined his features.

"Because he's my brother."

Silence filled the tent. I blinked several times to wipe away my shock. "He's—he's *what*?"

How was that possible? How had I not known? What kind of person kidnaps and *tortures* his own brother?

"Half-brother," Nox amended, his voice returning to normal. He ran his fingers through his unkempt hair. "We share the same father. He's seven years older than me. We weren't raised together. I didn't even know who he was until he challenged our father for the governor's position."

"He killed his own father," I said under my breath. My shoulders deflated. The turmoil of Nox's past went deeper than I could've imagined.

I *finally* had all the missing pieces. I *finally* understood Nox's role, his unbreakable ties to this man who ruined his life. How Nox knew so much about Scarven and the way his mind worked. Why he'd dedicated his life to the Ashen Order and rescuing those who couldn't help themselves.

"Why didn't you tell me?" I asked softly.

"That my brother is a savage, ruthless murderer? Yes, I wonder why I failed to mention that part."

"That doesn't matter to me," I said. "You can't choose your family. None of that is your fault."

He said nothing, rubbing the back of his neck as he glanced toward the tent. The muscles in his shoulder flexed with the movement.

A strong gust of wind blew through the flap, and I shivered so hard, my teeth chattered. His gaze landed on the discarded cloak with a furrowed brow. He reached for it slowly, then crossed the space to wrap it around my shoulders.

I put a hand up. "Wait, I thought you said I couldn't wear it?"

He swallowed. "But you're cold."

My traitorous, ridiculous heart actually *stuttered*. "Nox, I—"

"I overreacted. One more time won't kill you. We'll figure out a way to hide it so he doesn't know." He clasped the cloak at my neck, then planted his hands on my shoulders. "He *can't* know, Devora. Do you understand? He *cannot* find out you're—" He paused and licked his lips, eyes scanning mine. "That we're

179

working together. He'll stop at nothing to hurt you if he even suspects you know me."

I nodded. There was something more there, something lingering in the back of his stare, but I didn't want to press. Not now.

"I understand," I murmured.

He backed away. "I'm sorry I scared you."

"I'm not scared."

His eyes flicked to my mouth, then up again. "You should be."

"Are *you*?" I breathed out.

He tilted his head, the fading firelight from the candle in the corner catching his eyes. "Devora, darling, I'm always scared."

A moment passed, the air so thick, it made it hard to breathe. I knew I should go back to my tent. But I was so desperate for *more*, to fill in the cracks of this man before me, to answer all the burning questions I had.

"Nox," I started, "what were you dream—"

"Good night," he said. Not angrily, not viciously. Simply resigned. His shoulders sagged, his features tired and haggard.

I nodded again, equally exhausted and exhilarated by what had just happened. I made my way to the tent opening and stepped into the frigid air. "Good night, Nox."

29

DEVORA

"Are you sure you're ready for this, Devora?" Tessa asked. Her legs were casually draped over the arm of a chair by my vanity, but there was a crease on her brow that gave away her concern.

"I wish everyone would stop asking me that," I said. I leaned closer to the mirror to swipe a line of kohl beneath my eyes.

Nox, Arowyn, Everett, and I had gotten back from Tenebra less than forty-eight hours ago. Since then, I'd been surrounded by members of the Ashen Order as they tried to talk me through the plan at the ball, how to hide my magic, and what to do if anyone became suspicious. They were all a bunch of mother hens.

Everyone except Nox, that was. I'd barely seen him since we arrived at the Keep and he stopped me from going up the stairs to my tower. Instead, he showed me to an empty room on the first floor. Evidently right down the hall from his, or so Tessa told me.

We'd been so busy, I didn't have much time to worry about where he'd run off to, or even to enjoy the new luxuries of this suite. The bed alone could fit four people, and the bathing chamber was *glorious*. The tub was practically a lake. If this was the room he gave me, I couldn't imagine what *his* chambers looked like.

Not that I thought about him. Or his bed. Or him *in* his bed.

"You okay?" Arowyn asked from my bed, where she lounged on her stomach. "Your neck's doing that thing again."

I looked down to see red splotches crawling up my neck from the top of my gown.

Tessa swirled a finger at me. "Is this one of your tells? Because we're going to have to do something about that with Scarven."

I swatted her hand away. "Trust me, I don't have any tells. I'll be fine." Lying was second nature at this point. Fantasizing about my ex-captor, however...

"Well, you look good, Dev," Tessa said, scanning my body as I stood. "Can I call you Dev?"

I raised an eyebrow. "I don't know, can I call you Jaggy?"

She threw her head back with a laugh, causing her dark braids to sway against the chair. "Fair enough. For what it's worth, I'd let you spy on me."

Arowyn snorted. "Yeah, especially when your breasts look like that."

I chuckled and turned to face the full-length mirror, taking in my reflection. She wasn't wrong—the girls certainly knew what they were doing when they picked out this gown.

It felt strange to refer to Arowyn and Tessa like that. *The girls.* As if we were some sort of close-knit unit who made a habit of doing each other's hair as we laughed and gossiped and ate chocolate. As if we were *friends.*

I wasn't sure what we were—what *any* of us were—but the way they barged in and made themselves at home in my new suite did something funny to my chest.

My hands slid over the deep red fabric of the gown. The sleeves fell off my shoulders, and the tight bodice crossed in an elegant twist between my breasts. It cinched at the waist and fit snugly down my legs until it hit my lower thighs, then cascaded into a floor-length skirt.

"I don't know how you expect me to move in this," I grumbled as I twisted to get a look at the back, where the smooth fabric strained over my backside.

"That's kind of the point. Also, you might want to get rid of that," Arowyn said, tilting her head to the slit on my right thigh where my dagger rested. "They won't let you take it into Scarven's manor."

I sighed. I figured as much. "Fine." I pulled the blade out and set it on the vanity next to my glasses.

Tessa stopped me before I unclasped the sheath. "Leave it. It adds intrigue."

Intrigue. The whole purpose of this evening. To catch Kane Scarven's attention and hold his interest enough to make him want to spill all his dirty secrets.

I still couldn't believe he was Nox's half-brother, *and* that he killed their father. That must mean Nox would have been in line for the governor's position. My mind had been barreling through all the factors and family dynamics at play since I'd discovered the truth three nights ago. How Scarven probably despised and envied Nox in equal measure, how he held his power over Nox using mind games, how his obsession with these experiments was driven by his hunger for *more*. How I needed to present myself as something *more* for him to want. To collect, as Nox had put it.

In a sense, this mission was perfect for me. A way to use the skills I'd learned when that was the only way to take care of myself growing up.

"You need to leave soon if you want to catch up with the Mysthelm contingency," Tessa said, glancing at the ornate clock on my wall. "You have to act like you came with them. Your story is that you're part of the ship's crew, and they let all of you have the night off to attend the ball. Have you picked a name?"

"How about Selena Nyte?" I offered as I pinned back one side of my hair.

"Oddly specific," Arowyn said.

"It's the name of one of the girls I used to work with. She was a bartender all the patrons fell in love with." I shrugged. "Felt fitting."

"I thought you were a lady's maid?" Tessa asked, cocking her head.

"I've been many things, Jaggy. Did what I had to do to put food in my stomach."

She unfolded herself from the chair and padded across the room to fix a few strands of my hair. "Well, *Selena Nyte*, stick with us, and we'll make sure you always have food in your belly and a roof over your head."

"Yeah," Arowyn called from the bed. "The only things you'll have to worry about are death by carriage and deranged Shifters who experiment on you in your sleep."

"Comforting," I said with a laugh.

But as strange as it seemed, the thought *was* rather comforting. *Stick with us.* After three weeks, I'd earned some semblance of trust from these people. We were all working toward the same goal, after all. And it felt...nice. Different.

"Nox will be at the ball, since Scarven always makes him stand at his side for things like this. Nox's letting Everett come as long as he disguises himself with an illusion. But the rest of us don't have access," Tessa continued. "Arowyn and I will be just on the perimeter of Scarven's manor, so I can hear if anything goes wrong, and Arowyn can stride in to get you. Remember," she gripped my shoulders so I couldn't look away, "don't do anything you're not comfortable with. If you need out, just say the word."

"Tessa, this entire thing is the furthest from comfortable any of us could be," I pointed out. "I have a mission. I'm not going to jump ship if things get hard."

"Devora—"

"What would *you* do, if you were in my position?" I pressed. "If you had the power to find out what Scarven's planning? If *you* could figure out a way to get all those prisoners free?"

She twisted her lips and sighed. "I'd do everything I could. Even if it got me killed."

I nodded tightly, and a nervous energy settled over the room.

Until Arowyn said, "Well, *I'd* cut his balls off."

I snorted while Tessa burst into laughter, her shoulders shaking as she grabbed my cloak from the bedpost.

"Come on, Miss Nyte," Tessa said with a chuckle. "Your carriage awaits."

———

I PEERED out the carriage window from around the corner of the Governor's House. The cloudless sky let the moon and stars cast enough light for me to watch the caravan of Mysthelm carriages pull up to the estate. I quickly signaled to my driver to follow, and we settled in place behind the others.

Everett sat across from me, his illusion making him appear a couple decades older and several inches shorter than his normal stature. Long, greasy black hair replaced his short-cropped cut. He had a hooked nose, sharp chin, and dark brown eyes instead of his ruggedly handsome, stoic features.

"That's still creepy," I said, pointing at him and his illusion.

He smirked. "But useful."

He had a point. I didn't want to admit it, but I felt far more at ease walking into this mess with someone I knew at my side.

The driver came around the side to open our door. The gray mansion we stood before was an imposing sight. Sharp stone turrets reached into the sky, nearly blending into the darkness. Moss overgrew along the walls, with gnarled vines snaking around columns all the way to the ground. A plethora of guards stood at the entrance. Drivers dismounted from their carriages and opened doors for the passengers, and Everett and I followed the wave of swishing cloaks and elegant ballgowns.

I saw the familiar faces of the regent families from Mysthelm— the lords and ladies who oversaw each of the four territories. A twinge of worry shot through me. I hadn't even thought about the possibility of any of them recognizing me. Although, if they did, that would only prove my standing as a citizen of Mysthelm.

We strode up the sleek steps to the manor, doing our best to blend in with the crowd. Nerves were beginning to churn in my gut and creep up my chest. Nox and his Order wanted me because of my magic, but also because they knew I had a *reputation* for playing the other side. For spying and remaining undetected. While this mission included those things, it also relied on the exact opposite: I was supposed to put myself out there. To be the bait on a line sinking into the depths of Scarven's madness.

What if I wasn't good enough? What if this failed before we even had the chance? Or worse—what if he discovered our plan, and someone got hurt?

What if *Nox* got hurt?

I swallowed hard, unsure when the thought of him being in pain made every fear inside me come alive. But as I walked across the shining oak floors, I thought about how he'd been held prisoner here. How he'd been ripped from his home and tortured. How Scarven made him come back as a glorified *lapdog*, reliving those moments again and again.

If Nox could withstand that for the sake of his sister and all the defenseless Veridians held captive here, then I could do this.

A wrinkled hand touched my elbow, and I glanced back at Everett, who gave me a quick nod of encouragement. I smiled and took a deep breath.

We were led to a grand staircase that descended into a two-story ballroom, where sounds of live musicians playing a hauntingly beautiful melody drifted up the steps. Light from a hundred candles flickered as I gripped the railing and forced my feet down the staircase to the mezzanine level.

Everett left my side with another quick touch to the arm. He was going to mingle and get the "lay of the land," as he put it. The magic-less humans continued down the steps on either side of me, where it leveled out onto the dark marble floor. A vaulted ceiling soared high over our heads, with arching beams and intricate bronze designs carved into the walls.

On the lower floor, four large lion statues rested in each corner of the enormous room. I watched from above as those from

Mysthelm and Veridia alike reached for glasses of sparkling wine. Chatter mixed with the stringed instruments playing on the far wall.

My eyes scanned the room from the balcony, instinctively searching for something. Some*one*.

At a tall table near the foot of the staircase stood three men. The first had his back to me and was deep in conversation with one of the lords from Mysthelm. And the second man...

Navy eyes flashed up to mine, and I could've sworn they narrowed into slits before widening again as his gaze raked over my form.

Fates, Nox looked good. *Too* good. He was in sleek black from head to toe, with a dinner jacket that hugged his muscular arms and a shirt with the top buttons undone. His gaze burned through me as he raised his glass and took a sip.

My breath caught as I remembered his body hovering above mine that night in the tent. Heat licked up my spine and bloomed to the place on my neck his scruff had grazed.

His eyes shifted to the man across from him. The stranger slowly turned his head up to the balcony, following where Nox had been looking.

Dark brown hair with a streak of gray, strong chin, sharp jaw, high cheekbones. A short, clean-cut beard that spoke of control and precision. Black eyes beneath a raised brow.

I instantly knew who this was.

Kane Scarven's gaze met mine, replacing the heat from Nox's stare with an iciness that chilled my blood.

I gave him a hint of a smirk before turning away.

Game on.

30
NOX

The *second* Scarven saw her, I knew this was a bad idea.

This was the plan. This was *my* plan. She had to get his attention. She had to intrigue him.

But when I saw her in that dress, all I wanted to do was grip her in my claws and fly us far away from this place. To shield her from the hungry, predatory gazes in this room. To rip out the eyes of every man who so much as *looked* at her.

Was it rational? Absolutely not. But the dragon stirring in my chest didn't care.

Scarven straightened when he saw what I'd been staring at. I knew it would work—anything I showed a modicum of interest in, he immediately homed in on. I wished I could say that had been my strategy, but truly, I wasn't able to look away from her.

I didn't know what this woman was doing to me, but I hated it.

Her hips swayed as she descended the steps to the lower level of the ballroom. That red dress hugged her curves, with thick hair pinned over one shoulder to expose the side of her neck. I hadn't been able to get her scent out of my head, the way it felt to run my nose along the curve where her neck met her shoulder, to feel her chest rise and fall beneath me.

My body remembered her even as I forced my mind to forget. It was intoxicating. It was *maddening*.

It was dangerous.

I took another sip of my drink, my fingers clenching around the thin glass.

"I've heard stories about your land and its Shifters, but I must say, no one said anything about the silk and chandeliers," Lord Silenus from Mysthelm was saying as he glanced over all the resplendent decorations. He seemed impressed, if not a little stiff.

Scarven hummed. His deep, rich voice filled the air as he asked, "And did you expect us to dine in caves, Your Grace?"

Silenus cleared his throat and dabbed a handkerchief over his balding head. "Of—of course not, Governor. There is so little we know, obviously. My eyes were opened to your kind when the lovely Empress Aris visited us this summer. Such a shame she couldn't meet us here."

Scarven's eyes narrowed at the mention of Rissa before he schooled his features. "Yes. A shame. I hope you enjoy your evening, Lord Silenus. If you'll excuse us," he said with a dip of his head. I nodded to the lord, then followed Scarven.

"Who was that woman?" he asked sharply.

My stomach tightened. "What woman?"

"Don't be coy. You couldn't take your eyes off her."

I shrugged and took another drink. "She was beautiful. Hard not to notice." I motioned toward the hordes of women in elegant ballgowns. "But there are plenty of beautiful women, if that's what you're after. Take your pick. I'm going to go *fraternize*." I gave him a lazy half-smile.

"Keep an ear out," he said. "We don't want these foreigners getting too comfortable."

I raised my glass to him, then sauntered off to chat with various members of Mysthelm nobility. I hardly heard a word anyone said to me. I simply smiled and nodded and exchanged pleasantries, keeping my focus on Scarven's movements. I was painfully aware of every step he took toward Devora, every table he made conversation at as he moved closer and closer to her.

We were as prepared as we could be. Silas had even cast a spell that covered any trace of mine or the others' scents, so Scarven would have no idea she'd spent time with Shifters. But there were still so many ways this could go wrong.

And so many people who would pay the price if it did.

"You look like you need something stronger than wine," an unfamiliar voice said. An elbow hit mine, and I looked over to see a man perhaps fifteen years older than me, with long black hair and a hooked nose.

I acknowledged him with a stiff nod, then moved to get around him.

"Nox, it's me," he mumbled under his breath. "Everett."

I quirked an eyebrow. "You've certainly looked better."

He raised his glass to his lips. "And you look like you're about to punch a wall."

"This place puts me on edge." My eyes roved over the crowd until I found Scarven's tall frame. He was right next to the table Devora lounged at.

"I know what you mean," Everett muttered darkly. "Knowing they're all down there somewhere while we're up here drinking and dancing..." He trailed off and downed his glass.

The prisoners. Somewhere on these grounds lurked more of Scarven's prisoners. I felt it too. The overwhelming guilt, the urge to act, the need for justice. It pounded in my head like a drum.

"We're coming back, Everett," I murmured into my drink. "This is only the beginning. We'll get them out."

It's what we kept promising ourselves when we were stuck in this in-between phase and couldn't risk taking action. I knew he'd told his girl he was coming back for her. I imagined it devoured him, the idea of being so close and yet so far away. It was probably why he'd requested to come tonight—to feel closer to her, even if there was nothing he could do.

"Showtime," he said softly, breaking me from my thoughts.

Scarven prowled to Devora, who was standing at a table by the grand staircase. His hand landed on her lower back as he leaned forward to whisper in her ear, and my vision tunneled.

"It's a rare pleasure to meet someone I haven't already grown bored of," he said to her, so low I had to strain to hear with my Shifter senses.

She turned, assessing him from his feet up. Her gaze flicked to his eyes, and she smiled a sharp, wicked grin that had me holding my breath.

"It sounds like you should keep better company, my lord," she said, spinning her empty glass between her fingers. "If you'll excuse me." She dipped her head, then twisted away from him and made her way to the nearest drink station, her hips swaying in a deliberate rhythm.

"Oh, she's good," Everett muttered.

She was. Just the right amounts of confidence, defiance, and reverence. In this moment, she held power over him. The difficult part would be keeping it.

Sure enough, a few moments later, he reappeared at her side. I turned my back so he wouldn't catch me watching, but my Shifter hearing was tuned in to their conversation.

"You're right," he said. "And I plan to rectify that immediately, Lady..." He trailed off.

Her low chuckle brushed against my ears. "Trust me, Lord Scarven, I'm no lady."

"Ah, but you're a challenge, aren't you?"

I heard his footsteps, then her heartbeat picked up speed. I squeezed my glass so tightly, it almost shattered in my grip. She was trying not to be frightened. I hated standing by while my people were put in uncomfortable positions.

"You seem to know who I am with merely one word, and yet, I'm still at a loss for your name, love," Scarven continued. "That's hardly playing fair."

"Of course I know who you are. This is your party, isn't it? Everyone here from Mysthelm has heard of the legendary Kane

Scarven." She sounded closer to him, and I resisted the impulse to turn around.

Everett was right, though. She was playing this perfectly.

Scarven hummed. "And what have you heard of me?"

"That you're powerful. A bit ruthless." There was a slow click of heels, and I imagined her circling him with that smirk of hers. "And you always get what you want."

"Not always, it seems," Scarven responded.

A pause. And then—"Selena Nyte, my lord."

"Ah, Miss Nyte," he said, the words practically a hiss. "Would you join me for a dance?"

I couldn't fight the urge to look away any longer. I turned, taking in the room in a wide arc, pretending to survey the guests when my gaze snagged on them. Scarven leaned forward to take the glass from her, then slid his hand around her hips.

My glass shattered.

I spun and gripped the edge of the table as those nearest me gasped.

"You alright?" Everett whispered.

I clenched my jaw. "Let's just get this night over with."

31

DEVORA

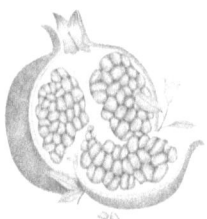

It was working. I'd gotten Scarven to notice me. Now...all I had to do was keep him intrigued. Show him I could be his next *project*.

I ignored the heads that swiveled in our direction as Scarven led me to the dance floor. It took all my energy just to keep my knees from giving out. I knew he'd be able to hear my racing heart, but I hoped it could be played off as innocent nerves. He probably liked that sort of thing—fear and admiration went hand in hand.

I swallowed and took a breath as he pulled me closer, one hand splayed possessively across my lower back. He smiled, a hint of his fangs digging into his lower lip, his black eyes glittering.

The motion reminded me so much of Nox, and yet...*not*. Nox was mostly playful. Charming with a hint of danger. No matter how fearsome his dragon form was, no matter how much we despised each other in the beginning, I never truly felt *unsafe* with him.

Kane Scarven may have had similar mannerisms—the smirk, the sharp teeth, the gleaming eyes. But there was no part of me that felt safe in his presence.

"So, Miss Nyte," he said as we moved across the dance floor to a slow melody. "Not a lady, as you've insisted. And yet you're traveling with Mysthelm's nobility?"

"I'm part of the ship's crew," I lied. "We're traveling with the regent families through the provinces."

"A crewmember," he said with a chuckle. "Not what I would have expected. And what is your role on the ship?"

"I'm one of the cooks."

"Ah, I see. Selena Nyte, mysterious cook of the galley. Is the rest of your crew here this evening?"

"Some of them," I said, my gaze roaming the crowd. "We were given the night off. Many chose the taverns or brothels in town."

"But not you," he murmured. "What brought you into my home?"

"Call it curiosity." I met his eyes. "Or perhaps I just like your food."

He hummed. "A lamb wandering straight into the lion's den."

I laughed softly. "I think you'll find I'm not a lady *or* a lamb, my lord."

His head cocked. Those eyes pierced straight through me, but I refused to squirm. "No, I suppose not," he said. He extended his arm, and I spun out in time to the music, then landed back in his arms. Both of his hands were on my waist now, and I forced myself to slide mine around his neck.

His voice was close to my ear. "You wear your beauty like an innocent mask, but I see something more. Something lurking beneath."

Fates, did he already suspect something? My pulse pounded, but I gave him a smirk. "You think I'm beautiful?"

"You *know* you are. But you also know how to play the game. You knew exactly how to get my attention." He lowered his head so his nose brushed the tip of my ear, sending an unwelcome shiver down my spine. "Tell me, Miss Nyte, now that you have it...what is it that you want?"

His voice hissed through me, sliding down my spine. I couldn't tell if he was suspicious, or if this was his way of "playing the game." Or both. I just had to play along.

"You're a powerful man, Lord Scarven." I squeezed his hand that rested on my waist. "Surely I'm not the first person who's been drawn to that power."

"So that's what this is for." He spun me again, and this time I landed with my back to his chest. "What my power can do for you."

I licked my lips. "No. What *we* can do for each other."

"Let me guess. You need something. Money, perhaps. Or protection. That's often why people come to me."

I raised an eyebrow, even though I knew he couldn't see my face. "Protection? You don't strike me as someone who's *safe*, my lord."

"So is that what you want?" he countered. "Safety?"

My brow furrowed slightly. I had never thought about it. I supposed my own safety hadn't always been at the top of my priority list. I was always focused on answers, on getting what I needed to survive.

"No," I said. "I...I want to *live*. And that doesn't always mean safety."

He twisted me in his grasp so I faced him once more. His answering smile was slow and full of dark promises. It felt like I had passed some sort of test.

"Then perhaps we *can* do something for each other." He leaned in closer, lips grazing my temple. I suppressed a shudder when he whispered, "I'm hosting another gathering tomorrow night. Something more...intimate."

The song ended, and he backed away, looking down at me with a gleam in his eyes. "You'll come, yes?"

I swallowed. "Is that an invitation or a request?"

He slowly reached for my hand. "I won't offer it a second time, Miss Nyte. You'll be there." He placed a kiss on my knuckles, his thumb rubbing across my skin before he released me. "Eleven o'clock. I'll tell the guards to expect you."

Triumph glowed in my chest, and I nodded as he melted into the crowd.

I wanted to sigh in relief, but I knew I was still being watched. Knew he'd be listening, waiting for anything he didn't like. I wouldn't even let myself find Nox among the guests, as much as I wanted to. *He* represented safety. A tether to my real reason for being here. An anchor to keep me from getting swept up in the heady lust of this music and wine.

I spent the next hour mingling with guests and dancing with strangers, being sure to catch Scarven's eye once as another man twirled me across the dance floor. It was all a game to him. The thrill of the chase, the power play, the back-and-forth.

This was just the beginning. A *successful* beginning. I was the bait, and he'd taken his first bite, exactly as we'd planned.

But it would take a lot more to reel him in completely. And while I knew what the end goal was, I also knew the inevitable would come.

Because the bait always bleeds first.

32

NOX

The nightmares came back that night.

This time, I was running through the forest with Sage the night we escaped. We were almost to the mountains separating Drakorum and Tenebra, where we could seek safety among the Shadow Wielders. But the moment we started up the mountain, Sage was killed.

The scene played on a loop in my dream—the same thing, every time. Except for the way she died. That was always different. In one dream, she was shot through the heart with an arrow. In another, a sword cut her head clean off. Still another, a pack of wild dogs ripped her limbs from her body.

In each of them, I was forced to watch. My muscles locked, unable to do anything as she was violently murdered for *my* indiscretion. I felt the searing pain as if it were my own. My throat was raw, my head pounding, my mind weak with anguish as I stood there. Over and over. Helpless.

A couple of times, I thought her dark hair blurred into bright red, but it was gone when I blinked.

The scene started up again. Sage and I sprinted over fallen tree limbs, freedom within sight as we approached the base of the mountain. She ran ahead of me, and I reached out an arm to stop her. A dagger whizzed past my hand and embedded itself in the back of her skull.

Tap. Tap. Tap.

"No!" I roared, my claws bursting from my skin.

Tap. Tap. Tap. "Nox," a voice whispered.

My breath faltered. "Sage?" I called out to her lifeless form, slumped on the ground with blood and bone sticking out from her wound. This...this hadn't happened before. She never *spoke* to me in this dream.

"Nox, please. It's Devora." The muffled voice cut through the nightmare like cold water.

My eyes snapped open.

I was in my bedroom at the Keep. The sheets were shredded beneath my claws, blood dripping from my quickly-healing wounds as I bolted upright in bed.

Heart racing, I took in gasping breaths to calm my senses.

"I can hear you, Nox. I want to help. Please," Devora said from the other side of my door. She sounded small and worried, so unlike the fierce woman I'd come to know.

But she *shouldn't* have been able to hear me. Long ago, I'd had Silas ward my private chambers so that no sound could escape. I said it was to protect against potential spies, but I always wondered if the wise Alchemist knew the truth.

I didn't want anyone to hear me scream when the nightmares came.

But *she* heard me. Her shadow whispering was getting stronger, if it was able to penetrate Silas's wards.

Tap. Tap. Tap.

I couldn't stop myself from throwing my legs over the side of the bed, then I slowly pulled myself up and staggered to the door. I propped my hand on the frame, my fingers gripping it hard enough to leave a dent in the wood.

"Nox?" she whispered again. So close, I could smell her just on the other side.

My forehead fell to the door as I squeezed my eyes shut. My

dragon half reached forward, clawing at my chest, aching to break through the wood.

It would be so easy to give in. To open this door and fall to my knees, to let her hands cradle my head and drive the nightmares away. That was what terrified me most—that this woman could give me comfort of any kind. Because the last person who had brought me peace...

She was front and center in my nightmares. She was *dead* because of me. And I'd rather let myself rot alone than bring Devora that same fate.

I turned and slumped to the ground, clutching my head in my hands until her footsteps retreated and the darkness crept in once more.

———

"Noxy, look what I did!"

I turned toward the sweet voice as a little body barreled into me. I caught her with a laugh and lifted her in the air, black braids swinging against my face.

"What'd you do, Zeph?" I asked the girl.

She beamed and wiggled in my grasp, then pointed a hand to her back. Small white wings with black feathers on the end protruded from slits in her shirt.

"And it didn't even hurt this time!" she exclaimed with her gap-toothed grin.

My heart clenched. "That's amazing, Zeph. It's only going to get easier, I promise." I set her down on the floor of the library with the other six, seven, and eight-year-olds.

Kieran had devised a system to divide the refugees into age groups for afternoon activities. It made it easier to keep an eye on all of them. Everett had even formed a sort of classroom schedule. As our numbers grew, so had the people willing to help get the refugees into a semi-normal routine. It aided their recovery to have something as mundane as schoolwork or training or playtime to latch on to.

I tried to visit with them as much as I could. It kept me focused on the ultimate goal. Watching the children make crafts or wrestle in the training grounds, learning to laugh again after all the joy had been sucked from them down in Scarven's dungeons...it filled me. Made it all seem worth it. All the heartache, the restless nights, the lost friends.

We were *building* something here. We were making a difference.

Zephrya nodded up at me and went back to her painting on the floor. She was one of our most recent rescues. Scarven had done something to her magic to make her shift prematurely—she was only seven. Usually, a Shifter's magic didn't emerge until much later. She'd been in incredible pain every time her emotions were heightened and she couldn't control the shift, sprouting her hawk's wings or talons and breaking several bones in the process.

She was one in *dozens* of stories. Innocent people whose bodies were violated and mutilated, their magic made to be a source of strife instead of the beautiful gift it was meant to be. I wanted to bring that beauty back. To make them feel at home in their own skin.

"Asher, how's your striding?" I called out to the nearby teenage boy who was overseeing a group of ten-year-olds.

He looked up, his mop of rust hair flopping over his face as he winked at me, then disappeared.

"You tell me, Boss," he said from right behind me.

I grinned and clapped him on the shoulder. "Looking good, kid. But I hear you've been causing some trouble in the girls' wing?" I raised an eyebrow.

Pink blossomed on his cheeks. He glanced over his shoulder at his friend across the room. "Seriously, Micah?" he yelled.

"Hey, don't blame him. Just remember the rules, yes?" I let go of his shoulder. "Keep the striding to public spaces. We don't want to make anyone uncomfortable."

He gave me a quick nod. "Yes, sir."

I took a moment to look around the large library, watching little hints of life twirl through the air. Beams of light and shadow twisted across the floor and up the walls. Giggles rang out from the younger groups. The scent of various herbs filtered in the space as Alchemists practiced their spells. Everywhere you looked were tufts of fur from Shifters still getting a handle on their magic, dried leaves from the greenhouse, broken pencils and small puddles of paint.

A sense of *home* swirled in my chest, pricking the backs of my eyes. It was rare that I felt moments like this, but sometimes... sometimes hope would leak through and cloud out the rest of the bad.

My gaze drifted over to the door, where Tessa leaned against the frame. She jerked her chin at me. "Time to go," she mouthed.

I nodded, then saw Devora move behind her. Her eyes roamed over the space, a look of wonder on her features. The corner of her mouth tilted up slightly as she watched Zephrya's group painting on the floor. I saw a flicker of that same emotion she had back at the Noctus Vigil.

I crossed to the two of them. "Ready?" I asked, and they both followed me out the door and down two floors until we reached the workshop.

The others were already there. Arowyn lounged on the couch next to the entrance, Everett and Kieran cleaned the weapons near the target practice area, and Silas and Milo were in the back with their Alchemist Grimoires perched on a work table.

"Well, I heard last night was a *raging* success," Arowyn said as Devora, Tessa, and I entered. "Someone very wise must've convinced you to let Devora help."

"I'll be sure to thank them when I see them, darling," I purred back to her.

"She was amazing," Everett admitted, returning several daggers to their cases.

Beside me, Devora blushed. "Tonight will be the true test, though."

"What is tonight?" Kieran asked.

Devora licked her lips. "Scarven invited me to a *gathering*. Something more intimate, he said. He requested I come."

Arowyn snorted, and I shot her a look. "What?" She shrugged. "We all know what that means. There's going to be a lot of food, a lot of women, and a lot of men whipping their—"

"*Children*, Arowyn," Silas chided, jerking his chin toward Milo.

"For Fates' sake," Milo muttered.

Arowyn smirked. "I was going to say 'dice.' You know. Gambling."

I curved my fingers around the edge of my desk, and the wood groaned beneath my hold. I knew what kind of party this was. What kind of *gatherings* Kane Scarven liked to host. And the idea of Devora being there, unprotected and vulnerable to Scarven's whims, made my dragon half rise to the surface. If he hurt her, if he tried *anything*—

I gritted my teeth. There was nothing I could do. That was the whole point.

Kieran raised an eyebrow at Devora. "I'm impressed. Perhaps this will not be a lost cause after all."

Devora chuckled. "Thanks, I think."

"Hey, coming from Kieran, that's about as high of a praise as you'll get," Tessa cut in.

"Alright, so what *is* the plan for this evening?" Kieran asked, rubbing his hands together.

I brandished an arm toward him, trying to act normal and not like a raging Shifter. "By all means. You're the man with the plans, Kieran."

My plan would be to lock Devora up in that tower where Scarven and his slimy paws could never reach her again. Or better yet, claw off every piece of his body that touched hers last night.

Which was why I left the planning to Kieran.

"We have to assume Scarven will have eyes on Devora at all times from now on," Kieran was saying. "He has proven that those he considers his possession must be treated as such."

Devora rolled her eyes at the word "possession," but nodded anyway. "Which is why Silas warded this place to be untraceable, right, Silas?" she asked the older Alchemist.

He shoved his glasses up his nose. "Yes. If Scarven did, in fact, have spies tailing you last night, my spell will make them believe they followed you back to the inn the Mysthelm contingency is staying at."

"So you need to leave from there tonight, Devora," I said. "Preferably in one of the carriages Mysthelm is using. Or in one that *looks* like theirs," I added, glancing at Everett.

He held his hands in the air. "I'm good, but I'm not *that* good. I can't hold an illusion like that from this distance. I'd have to be closer."

"That can be arranged," Kieran said smoothly. "It would be beneficial to have someone with her, after all."

"I can't walk in with her," Everett countered. "That would be too suspicious."

"No, but you could already *be* there," Tessa suddenly said, a wicked grin unfurling on her features. "At Scarven's manor."

Everett narrowed his eyes at her. "I really don't like that look."

"Oh, I *love* it," Arowyn said. "Means things are about to get interesting."

Tessa held a hand up to Everett. "Hear me out. Who would the guards let into this *intimate gathering* without batting an eye?"

"A woman," Arowyn said.

"An attractive, scantily-clad woman," Devora added.

"See where I'm going with this?" Tessa asked.

Everett's lips thinned. "I'm leaving."

"Oh, come on, Ev," Tessa cooed. "It's perfect. Just ride with Devora and illusion the carriage to look like Mysthelm's, then sneak in as one of Scarven's girls serving at the party."

"Why can't I just camouflage myself to blend into my surroundings?" he countered.

Tessa paused and twisted her lips. "Because this is more fun."

"*Because* I may need someone who can cause a distraction if I have to get away," Devora offered. "Nobody would suspect you."

Everett looked at me. "A little help here?"

"It would be nice to have someone else on the inside," I said with a shrug. "You're the best option for keeping her safe."

Arowyn stretched her legs on top of the table by the couch, crossing one ankle over the other. "Great. Operation Eve is a go."

"I hate all of you," Everett muttered.

"Is there a way for us to communicate with the rest of you while we're inside the manor?" Devora asked.

"Ah, yes, actually," Silas said as he dropped a stack of books on top of his work table. "There is. I can, uh—enchant this parchment —" He trailed off, patting his hand along his jacket as if searching for something. With a look of triumph, he pulled two pieces of paper from his inside pocket. "Yes. I can enchant these parchments to deliver messages between each other. Anything you put on one will appear on the other. Difficult to keep inconspicuous, I'm afraid, but if you get in a bind, it's the quickest way to let us know."

"This is great, Silas. Thank you," Devora said as she crossed the room to retrieve her piece of parchment. She folded it several times until it fit in the palm of her hand, then deftly slipped it inside her cleavage.

I followed on her heel and snatched up the other parchment. "Kieran, you and I will stay a few miles outside the perimeter, just in case," I said to my second. "Tessa, Arowyn, Silas—you're in charge of the Keep."

"We've got it, Nox," Tessa said with a firm nod.

They launched into details for the evening. We were well acquainted with sudden changes in plans, each of us able to adapt quickly and keep everyone safe. I trusted them without hesitation.

As I looked around the room, I realized that statement rang true with no condition. Before, it was "I trusted them, *except* for Devora."

Now, I thought I could trust her. Despite my pride telling me not to.

She had jumped into this assignment with no questions asked, even after getting the answers about her past she so desperately sought. She had saved my people in the blink of an eye. She had put her identity, her comfort, her *safety* on the line in order to get information the rest of us couldn't retrieve. She knew the worst was yet to come, and still, she hadn't complained. Not a single time.

I told myself it was only a sense of loyalty and protection that made my chest tighten when she stepped into danger. But *loyalty* didn't make my pulse quicken at her nearness. It didn't make me dream about her voice in the heart of my nightmares.

And loyalty hadn't saved Sage.

If Scarven laid a hand on Devora...my trust wouldn't matter at all.

33

DEVORA

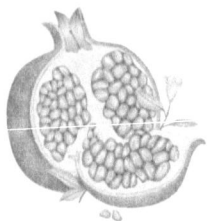

My heels clicked against stone as I walked up to the double doors of Scarven's manor. Everett had left once we exited the carriage, heading for the servants' entrance to create his illusion and get inside. Seeing the mansion again made nerves flutter in my stomach. Unease slid down my spine, pooling in my core.

Two guards with metal lion masks were stationed on either side of the entrance. They turned to face me when I approached.

I cleared my throat. "My name is Selena Nyte. Lord Scarven requested my presence."

Their heads tilted as those creepy masks moved up and down my body, assessing me. Tessa had put me in a black velvet dress that hung to my calves, with a small slit up the leg. The thin straps at my shoulders led to a ruched top that easily concealed the small, magical parchment Silas had given me. My cloak swung at my feet as the guards held the door open, and I strode inside.

Another guard was waiting for me. "Miss Nyte," he said, his voice muffled by the same lion mask as the others. "May I take your cloak?"

I shrugged it from my shoulders, and he took it, then led me down the vast corridor. We walked past the staircase to the same ballroom from the night before. I tried to keep track of all the turns we made, repeating them in my mind so I could jot them down on the paper the first chance I got. *Past the ballroom, left, right at the statue of the headless man, second right, left after the wooden door, straight under the arch, down the stairs.*

I heard the music before we reached the bottom step. It was different from the ball last night. This was slow and erotic, a rich, steady drumbeat that mimicked my pulse as a hallway came into view.

The long corridor was lit with torches and flanked by several stone archways leading to smaller rooms. Thick, sheer curtains draped over the arches separating the rooms, partially blocking whatever rested behind.

But as the guard led me down, I caught flashes of what was inside. Some rooms brimmed with partygoers gathered around tables, rattling dice and excited cheers ringing out. In others, silhouettes lounged on couches, whispered conversations tangling with a low drumroll. In still another, servants fed grapes to half-shifted animal forms. One servant raised a chalice to a half human, half tiger, and red liquid that looked disturbingly like blood dripped from the corners of their mouth.

So, it was *that* kind of party.

I had no idea what Scarven had planned for tonight. I didn't know what he would expect me to *do*. With the Order, I acted like it was simply another part of the mission, but the thought of being alone with him in any capacity made my skin crawl. I was playing a whole different kind of game here, where one false step would have me locked away for good.

Or worse.

Shadows flashed at my fingertips, responding to my heightened fear, and I took a deep breath to steady my pulse. I had to remind myself why I was here. What the end goal was. How many people we'd be saving. Slowly, my magic calmed, staying tucked beneath my skin but wrapping over my heart like a blanket.

I twisted a strand of hair around my finger as I entered the main gathering room. Couches were scattered throughout the space, with lacy fabrics tossed across them. On the back wall were tables sagging under the weight of an enormous feast. Roasted boars smothered in honey, mountains of fruits oozing their sugary syrup, wheels of cheeses, buttered breads, and tureens of candied nuts.

Every person in attendance wore masks bearing different animal faces. Everywhere I turned, I was met with tigers, snakes, wolves, and more dancing as they stuffed their faces with food. Other patrons watched from the couches. Some of the dancers had partially shifted, with tails that slunk along the ground, flicking back and forth.

The entire space overflowed with gluttony and indulgence, but instead of wanting to partake, it sent a shiver of discomfort down my spine.

My eyes snagged on a server in the far corner, next to a potted tree. Light pink fabric was draped over her large chest, crossing in the center and twisting down her body. She pulled off her mask to catch my attention, and mouthed "*It's me*," when my eyes met hers.

Everett.

I pinched my lips together to keep from laughing. Making sure nobody was watching, I mouthed back, "*Nice legs.*"

He scowled before replacing his mask. When I saw the animal he'd been given, I almost choked. Staring back at me was a goat, with little horns sticking out from his head and everything.

My hand twitched toward the magic parchment in my dress. My first instinct was to jot down a joke for Nox to commemorate this moment, but a voice at my back made me school my features.

"Miss Nyte," someone said, and I turned to find myself face-to-face with a fox mask. My heart picked up speed, my breath catching for a split second as I remembered Clarissa.

"For you," the servant said, holding out a black mask lined with silver.

I lifted the mask to get a better look in the torchlight. It was a panther. The material was lightweight and had a soft fabric on the underside. Delicate, feline ears rested on the top, leading down to the panther's nose. I carefully raised it to my face and tied it off at the back of my head. The small holes for my eyes severely limited my scope of sight, which I thought might be the point.

One of the dancers and a patron slid by me, heading toward the games and gambling room. I took a few steps backward to avoid them, and when I looked to the side, I saw a hallway obscured by more potted trees.

I glanced around the room. Scarven was still nowhere in sight. After wandering to the drinks, I grabbed one and took a sip, casually leaning against the wall until it was apparent nobody cared who or what I was doing.

Finally, a mission where my unhealthy desire to get into places I wasn't allowed *actually* paid off.

I slid down the unattended hallway. It was a relief to get away from the fog of perfume. That mixed with the constant music had made my head pound. I took a deep breath of clean air as my shoulders sagged.

I was in a narrow corridor, with several closed doors on each side of the hall. I looked over my shoulder, then reached for the handle on the nearest door. Unsurprisingly, it was locked.

Now was as good of an opportunity as ever to make note of my findings. I carefully pulled the enchanted parchment from my dress, along with a small piece of charcoal. Ensuring nobody was coming down the hall, I propped the parchment against the closest door and sketched a crude drawing of a map. I drew lines from the entrance to the mansion as best as I could to show the path leading down here. I wasn't sure if it would be important, but considering a private guard had escorted me, Scarven obviously didn't want this place open to the public.

When I finished, I waited several seconds for something to happen. Was I supposed to do something? Say a magic spell?

But a moment later, the drawing faded into the weathered

parchment. I blinked twice, once again in awe of these Alchemists and their powers.

I started to fold it back into its tiny square when something burned my hand. "Ouch," I muttered. The paper had a strange yellow glow. When I turned it over, four words stared back at me.

Quite the artist, darling.

That had definitely not been there before.

I grinned. I could practically hear Nox's insufferable yet charming drawl. I bit down on my bottom lip as I glanced toward the entrance of the hallway again, then wrote:

If only I could draw Everett in this outfit of his. There's not much left to the imagination.

I barely had time to look away before his response materialized.

Such a tease.

I smirked and put the charcoal back to the parchment.

Me, or him?

The words faded. I stared at the page for a moment longer than I should have, waiting for words that never came.

Embarrassment rose to the surface. What was I *doing*? Nox may be fun and quick-witted with his other friends, but we weren't like that. He was all business with me. Business mixed with a bit of trouble, something dark and sharp that kept drawing us together and pushing us away at the same time.

I knew he was still having nightmares. My shadows kept waking me from my sleep, summoning me to him with whispers of his cries. But he wouldn't answer the door. Not that I blamed him

—who was I to think I could barge in and solve his problems? Or that he would even *want* me to?

I wasn't sure why I cared, except the memory of him thrashing in his sleep that night in the tent played when I closed my eyes. He was a prisoner to whatever demons plagued his mind. I wanted to help him. But I knew when to take a hint, and he obviously didn't need me beyond the scope of my mission for the Order.

I shoved the parchment and charcoal back down the top of my dress, then spotted a series of portraits along the walls. Large oil paintings with ornate gold frames, each depicting scenes of battle. Human against human, animal against animal, humans against animal, all in various gruesome fights.

At the very end of the hall, however, were two matching portraits, the largest paintings of all. The one on the left showed two lions, one a vibrant golden color and the other a slightly darker, bronzed gold with a streak of white going down its side. Their throats were locked in each other's jaws while their paws wrapped over their shoulders, almost in a morbid embrace. And the portrait on the right—

The golden lion's head was clutched in the jaws of the darker one, ripped clean from its body.

The inscription at the bottom read *"The Challenging."*

I jolted back in horror. Was this Nox's father? Was this the day Scarven challenged him?

Disgust swirled in my stomach. The fact that he had these paintings done was *sickening*. I hoped Nox never had to see this memorial.

My fingers toyed with the edge of the frame, wishing I could tear it from the wall. Sorrow shot through me. Both for the boy Nox used to be, and the man he was now.

One of my shadows slipped from me and twisted around my extended finger. Before I willed it away, a faint whisper reached my ears. It wasn't a voice, but more like...a clanging sound.

Like chains.

A groan drifted to me in the shadows, but it wasn't coming

from the den behind me. It was distant and pained. Desperate. Longing.

I swallowed and let my shadows dig deeper. It was definitely coming from below. There was a grate in the wall to my left where my magic was picking up the sounds from. Someone was being held right beneath this wing of the mansion.

I closed my eyes, trying to push just a *little* further. My shadows tugged on that well of power deep in my chest. They urged me to follow. My body swayed forward in response when a hand clamped down on my shoulder.

"I was wondering where you were," Scarven's rich voice said at my back.

Releasing my hold on the shadows, I spun to face him with a pasted-on smile. "Up to no good, as usual."

He wore no mask, just a dark gray dinner jacket, matching pants, and a crisp button-down. I had to admit, Kane Scarven wasn't *un*attractive. He was classically handsome, even. He had strong, clean-cut features. Every hair was perfectly in place. His black eyes were like obsidian jewels, sharp and piercing.

But it was almost *too* perfect. *Too* put-together. I found myself imagining rough stubble on my skin, running my fingers through windswept hair, staring into a pair of navy-blue eyes that made fire lick up my spine.

I hurriedly blinked away the vision as Scarven said, "I'm glad you came."

"I didn't exactly have a choice, did I?"

He put a hand over his heart. "You wound me, Miss Nyte. Here I thought you simply enjoyed my company."

"I haven't seen enough to make a decision," I said with a shrug. "And please, call me Selena."

His eyes flashed. "Did my party run you off, Selena?"

I smiled sheepishly. "I'm sorry, I shouldn't have wandered. I got curious. Forgive me, my lord."

He assessed me for a moment, small wrinkles of scrutiny appearing around his eyes. I didn't think I would ever earn his trust, but if Nox was right, the man before me desired companionship—or at least, his twisted version of it. There was a degree to which he'd be willing to let me into his world, as long as it meant he could keep steady control over me. As long as there was something we could do for each other. *This* was part of his world that I could understand.

"Do you like it?" he asked, catching me off guard. I raised an eyebrow, and he motioned to the two portraits of the lions. "The paintings."

"They're certainly...intriguing."

He let out a low chuckle. "Some would call it distasteful, but I think it's part of nature. That's the way this world works. Survival of the fittest, after all. The strongest always come out on top."

I swallowed and nodded, unsure how to respond when all I wanted to do was scream.

"Come, Selena," he said, taking me by the arm. "Dark corridors are no place for a woman like you."

"Did you pick this out for me?" I fingered the edge of my mask as we walked back to the party.

"Ah, yes. The panther. A symbol of strength and mystery." He grabbed a flute of wine from the table as we passed. "What better mask for the beautiful Mysthelm cook with a taste for life?"

"You seem to think you have me all figured out, Lord Scarven."

He leaned in closer. "If I had you figured out, love, you wouldn't be here right now."

A chill swept through me. Goosebumps appeared on my forearm, and he smirked when he saw them. The power dynamic between us was shifting. He was beginning to take control, just the way he wanted.

I hated that I had to let him.

I lowered my gaze with a small smile, then turned to face the tables full of gleaming food, some of which now littered the floor. It smelled sweet, spicy, and rotten all at once.

Brandishing a hand to the room, I said, "Quite the party."

"What do you think?" he asked, tilting his head.

I licked my lips and thought about how I wanted to play this. He seemed to enjoy the "lamb in the lion's den" act. Innocent but interested. Like he wanted to push me to the edge and see what made me squirm.

I exhaled slowly, forcing my voice to sound breathless as I stared at the dancers. "I—I've never seen anything like it."

My eyes flicked over to the goat mask pouring water behind the table. Everett's eyes tracked me from a distance, easing my worries by a fraction.

With his hand still at my elbow, Scarven led me to the nearest couch. The heady scent of smoke and floral perfume struck me in the face as I sank into the soft cushions. Scarven's hand instantly splayed across the top of my knee. A heavy ring rested on his finger, and it dug into my dress. I resisted the urge to slap his hand away.

"I think you'll find this entire province to be unlike anything you've seen before, Selena." He summoned a servant in a serpent's mask carrying a tray of sugar-coated fruit.

"Shifters are complex creatures," Scarven continued. "Some believe we cannot control ourselves. That we're ruled by baser instincts and carnal desires. But, in truth, we have the most control of them all." He motioned for the serpent to come closer, and he took a vine of grapes. "You see, our instincts tell us to take what we want at whatever cost. Pleasure, violence, power." With each word, he plucked a grape off the vine.

"We must constantly fight against our very nature. We practice control in every facet of our lives. I wonder if you understand a bit of what that's like." Scarven shifted his hand to my chin, forcing me to face him. With his other hand, he pushed a grape to the edge of my lips, a silent command to open.

I obeyed. The grape glided into my mouth, and when I bit into it, its tart juice made my stomach coil. A mixture of fear, disgust, and temptation brewed at his words. I could see how his people got lost in these parties. It was easy to forget yourself, easy to let yourself sway to the music as food coursed through your system, easy to linger on masked faces instead of your own problems.

But your problems always came back to you. None of these desires could make things better. It was all a façade, a lie.

Scarven smirked. "I like to provide a safe haven, of sorts, for my people to let go. To give in to the passions that drive them, but that they must keep locked away from the rest of the world. To indulge." His finger traced my collarbone. "To feel." It trailed up my neck. "To *live*, as you said last night." His thumb came up to the other side, his hand wrapping loosely around my throat. "It can be difficult to get what we want. I'm merely making it easier."

"And what is it that *you* want, Lord Scarven?" I whispered, swallowing the grape as his grip tightened ever so slightly.

"What everyone wants," he said. "Power."

"You have *magic*. And you're the leader of an entire province. Don't you already have power?"

He removed his hand and waved at the serpent to back away. "There are different kinds of power. Some gained by fear, some by force. But what many don't understand is that the most absolute, undeniable power is gained by knowledge."

His words pricked the back of my mind. We were on the verge of something; I could feel it.

"Knowledge," I hummed. "Your books here must be very different from Mysthelm's, then."

He chuckled. "Ah, Selena. The kind of knowledge I desire cannot be found in *books*."

Oh, I bet it can't. I struggled to keep my breaths even, my face neutral. "Then where?"

He moved closer. "Do you really want to know?"

We were standing on a precipice. A door cracked open, beckoning me closer to the truth, but there was something in me that seized in fear.

"I don't know," I whispered. The words slipped from me before I could stop them.

Whatever hold I had over him broke like a spell, the tension dissipating as quickly as it came. He leaned back and propped one ankle on top of his knee. "Perhaps another time, then," he said, his eyes leaving mine to rove around the room.

"Lord Scarven?" A guard approached our couch, bending low to whisper in Scarven's ear. A pool of shadows on the couch shimmered and flicked toward me, bringing his quiet words to my ear.

"...latest caravan from the west has arrived. They're ready to be sorted in the Hollow," the guard said before straightening.

The Hollow. There was that word again. The same place the fatesprig had been taken that night I intercepted the shipment.

Caravan from the west. Could this be supplies? Weapons? More prisoners?

Scarven nodded curtly and got to his feet. "Escort Miss Nyte back to her carriage," he ordered the guard. He didn't so much as glance in my direction as he moved behind the couch.

My heart crashed to the floor. I'd ruined it. I'd shattered whatever bubble we'd been wrapped in and lost his attention. Was it something I'd said? Should I have been more forward? Less hesitant? More provocative?

Disappointment flooded me, and I imagined how I'd have to tell the others that I'd failed, how I'd have to tell *Nox*—

And then Scarven's voice appeared in my ear. "It's a pity you're leaving for Emberfell in three days, Selena."

I craned my neck up so I could look at him.

"There's an entire *world* I could have shown you," he said. "A world free of the innocence and naivety of your little kingdom."

I blinked. He thought I was going with the Mysthelm contingency on the rest of their tour. *That* was why he was creating distance.

Hope thrummed inside of me. Perhaps this wasn't over yet.

"Give me a reason, and I could be convinced to stay," I murmured.

"And what of your crew?"

"They don't need me until we set sail back for Mysthelm," I lied, holding his gaze. "Nobody would even notice I'm gone."

His hand fell to my chin, tilting my head back further. "Then it's their loss," he said. My chest clenched in unease as his fingers pressed deeper into my throat. "Stay. My men will come retrieve you in two nights, before your people leave. Be ready."

It wasn't a question. It was a command. An order I didn't think I was allowed to refuse.

"Yes," I breathed out. "I want to see your world."

He backed away, making me turn to watch him retreat. "Oh, little lamb," he hummed. "Be careful what you wish for."

My eyes followed him as he left for his mysterious meeting at the Hollow, and a plan formed in my mind. A reckless, stupid, dangerous plan that the others would surely yell at me for even trying.

I smirked. Perhaps Scarven was the one who should be careful.

217

34

DEVORA

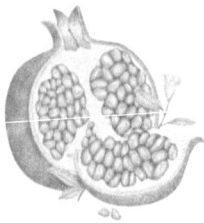

"**J**ust one more snack for the road," I said to the guard as he fit my cloak around my shoulders. I gave him my sweetest smile and held up a finger, then crossed to the table where Everett was cutting off slices of meat from the roasted boar.

"Get to the carriage," I muttered to Everett, popping a small chocolate pastry in my mouth.

His eyes furrowed in confusion beneath his goat mask. "What happened?"

"Go. *Now*. I'm being watched. I'll explain in the carriage."

He nodded and turned, disappearing down the servants' entrance. I shook out the nerves from my shoulders and strode back to the guard. We made our way through the twists and turns of the mansion and eventually arrived at the front. There was my carriage, bearing the (illusioned) flag of Mysthelm prominently on top. The guard bade me goodnight, and I had the carriage driver roll to a stop just outside the bridge leading to the manor.

Everett hauled himself into the carriage a few minutes later, his goat's mask and sheer fabric replaced by his normal pants and suspenders.

"Why so urgent?" he asked.

"I need you to illusion yourself to look like me and go back to the Mysthelm base," I said quickly.

"What? Why? Where will *you* be?"

"Following Scarven to the Hollow."

He snorted derisively. "Absolutely not."

I rolled my eyes. "Everett, come on. Scarven left because his men told him a caravan from the west is arriving at the Hollow. He's going there *right now*. What was the point of this whole thing if we don't use the information? If I can get my shadows to listen and find him, we'll know where the Hollow is. Don't you remember that's where he's keeping the fatesprig, and—"

"Okay, okay, slow down." Everett lifted his hands in the air. "If this is so important, then you should go back and *I'll* find him."

"Oh, sorry, I didn't realize you learned how to shadow whisper in the last two hours."

"Funny," he deadpanned. "Fine. We'll both go."

My jaw twitched as irritation built. He didn't get it. "You can't. Scarven expects me to go back to the Mysthelm base. If the carriage is being followed, *someone* has to pretend to be me and lead them away from here."

I moved to open the door when Everett caught my arm. "Devora, no. This isn't another one of your improvisations. If you're wrong, you'll get yourself killed."

"And if I'm right, we'll find the Hollow," I snapped, yanking free. "I need to act fast. We could lose the trail soon—it's been almost twenty minutes since Scarven left."

I could see the indecision warring in his gray and green eyes. What was best for the mission versus keeping me safe.

His chest swelled as he let out a sharp huff. "Write to Nox on your magical paper. He's only a couple miles away. Tell him and Kieran to come meet you."

I nodded. "I will, I promise."

"This is the worst idea ever."

I tapped my nose. "Or—hear me out—is it the best?"

"You've been around Tessa and Arowyn too long."

"That's neither here nor there. Are you in, or are you going to make us miss this once-in-a-thousand chance?"

He met my gaze. His eyes searched mine, hesitant and worried, and the column of his throat moved as he swallowed.

"Come on, Everett," I said softly, all humor and frustration forgotten. "Those could be new prisoners they're carrying. Don't you want to help them?"

He inhaled slowly, and on his exhale, he nodded. "Alright. Send the message to Nox, and I'll illusion you long enough for you to get into the forest. Wait for him and Kieran before you go running off."

"Yes, yes, I know." *Not a chance.* "We have to hurry. Is your illusion ready?"

He rolled his neck along his shoulders, causing his necklaces to rub together. "This is a bad idea. Alright, you're clear. Go."

I shot him a grin, threw open the carriage door, and jumped down. I made my way to the copse of trees bordering Scarven's property as the carriage rolled away.

I didn't lie to Everett—I planned on telling Nox and Kieran what I was doing. I just needed to wait until it was too late for them to make me turn back.

Staying within the shadows of the trees, I loosened my shoulders and took a few deep breaths. I'd never tried to shadow whisper over such a large area. I wasn't even sure where to focus my attention—for all I knew, the Hollow could be miles away. But I didn't think Scarven would leave in the middle of the night to go "sort through" this new arrival if it wasn't close by.

I pulled the hood of my cloak up to block the cold wind. The night was quiet, save for the sounds of insects coming to life in the trees and the breeze rustling through leaves. I closed my eyes and let my shadows come to life. They billowed across my skin, their form expanding and contracting with my breaths.

Find Scarven, I urged them. Just the sound of his name made them coil into a tighter ball. They seemed to share my aversion to the man. But, little by little, my shadows flitted away from me, curling across the dark grounds and searching out other shadows to latch on to.

It was hard to describe what this magic felt like. They were a part of me, even when they were detached like this. I could still *feel* them moving in my mind. Like something brushing or scratching against my thoughts. Soon, other sounds began to reach me.

Hooves stepping on straw. Hard bars of soap rubbing against a washboard. Metal creaking and footsteps pacing stone. Hints of the late-night servants and manor guards going about their jobs, all echoing back to me.

And in the distance was that sound again, the same one I'd heard in the hallway with the paintings—rattling chains, mixed with a mournful wail.

"Get them in here," a gruff voice said. So quiet, so far away, I thought I'd imagined it.

I sucked in a breath, willing my shadows to stay steady. I stretched my magic and felt them strain against my hold as if they were going to snap back into me like a bowstring.

The sound of hooves pawing the dirt was suddenly magnified. Several heavy feet plodding on straw, doors swinging on hinges, tails swishing, teeth munching on something.

Horses.

The stables. That was where I was hearing all this come from. The Hollow must be near the stables.

I hastily grabbed my parchment and charcoal from my dress and scribbled out a message.

Found the entrance to the Hollow. Meet me at the west stables on Scarven's property.

A reply burned in my hand almost instantly.

Whatever you're doing, stop. Kieran and I are coming.

I couldn't help but grin. So predictable, these Shifters. I jotted one last message before tucking it back in my dress, throwing off my heels, and sprinting through the night.

35

NOX

Too late.

I growled and crumpled the parchment in my grip. Squeezing Tempest with my knees, Kieran and I took off from the nearest village down to Scarven's property.

What did Devora mean, she'd found the Hollow? That hadn't even been a goal for tonight. She was still gaining Scarven's trust. There was no way he'd given her this information so freely.

Which meant she'd gone where she wasn't supposed to. Probably risked getting herself killed. And now she was heading there unprotected, like the stubborn woman she was.

"Unbelievable," I muttered under my breath as we raced closer to the mansion.

"You know what I find rather amusing about it all?" Kieran asked at my side, voice stilted from the horse's movement.

"What?" I snapped.

"That you would do the same thing in her position." A smirk appeared on his chiseled features.

I scowled and gripped the reins tighter as we sliced through the trees at the perimeter of Scarven's mansion. The stables were on the far west side, at the outskirt of the main property. They were massive, large enough to house not only Scarven's herd of horses but several of his carriages too. We didn't often venture that far in our raids. All the entrances to the underground cells we knew about were to the east and south of the mansion.

What if this was a whole new section of laboratories? Of dungeons and cells full of people who needed our help?

What if my *sister* was down there?

I urged Tempest faster until we reached the edge of the tree line, when I tugged on the reins to halt her. The enormous stables just beyond the forest were lit by moonlight and a couple of guards with torches standing outside them. Two carriages were stationed at the back in a line, waiting their turn to enter the stables. When I homed in on them, I heard dozens of hearts beating, but they were slow and sluggish, barely conscious. Accompanying them were the sounds of labored breaths and the scent of blood and sweat.

More prisoners.

I nudged Kieran's arm and pointed, then froze.

A flash of red hair peeked out from behind the last carriage.

"You have *got* to be kidding me," I grumbled. "Stay here, Kieran. I'll whistle if I need you."

Dismounting, I pulled Scarven's enchanted ring from my pocket. I didn't want to use it in case he could detect it, but without an Illusionist, I was running out of options. I slipped it over my finger and felt the pressure form on my chest as the spell snapped into place, and my body faded into my surroundings.

With as little noise as possible, I crept across the open grounds and to the stables, my vexation growing by the second. She was going to get herself killed. What was she *thinking*, coming out here on her own?

I approached her silently from the back, wrapping one hand around her mouth and pulling her into the shadows of the carriage. My hand muffled her gasp of surprise. She jerked against my hold, but I used my other hand to rip off my ring and reveal myself.

"Do you have a death wish, darling?" I hissed into her ear.

She shook her head free, and I lowered my hand. "I didn't want to lose their trail," she said.

"You could have waited for us."

She shrugged. "You took too long."

This woman. "What happened?"

"I was with Scarven, and one of his guards came to tell him he was needed at the Hollow. So Everett and I left the party. I used my shadows to find this place," she finished with a whisper, brandishing an arm toward the stables.

"And where is *dear* Everett?" I asked. I was going to kill him for letting her do this.

"He's pretending to be me." She twisted her head to look at me and raised an eyebrow. "You know Scarven is having me followed. We needed everything to appear normal. Don't give me that look."

"I'll give you whatever look I want when you go running off in the middle of the night to chase the most dangerous man in the empire," I growled.

"And here I thought that was you," she shot back.

My dragon thrummed with pride, begging to prove she was right. But as I was about to respond, the carriage we were hiding behind lurched forward.

"Oh, alright—this is happening now," Devora mumbled, nearly losing her balance as we stumbled to move along with the wheels.

"Maybe you should've thought about that earlier," I whispered.

"Let's save the bickering for when we're not hiding from a maniac, shall we?" she tossed over her shoulder, then jerked forward with a gasp when the carriage moved again. I instantly reached out and grabbed her waist. A ripping sound punctuated the air as her cloak, which had gotten stuck under the wheel, tore up to her sleeve. She spun on her heel to shrug it off before it took her with it.

I stopped in my tracks.

That *dress.*

It was black as midnight, a sharp contrast to her hair. It flowed down to her calves, and the material looked as soft and smooth as the skin of her thigh peeking out underneath. My hand flexed at my side with the effort it took not to wrap my fingers around her leg.

She smirked. "Not so mouthy now, I see."

"Just—go," I grunted. "Stick to the carriage."

"Hold on," she said, then tied the bottom of her dress into a knot. Together, we crouched low and followed the carriage, edging closer to the stables.

"What was your brilliant plan here, anyway?" I asked.

She flashed me a wry grin over her shoulder. "For you to come save me."

I shook my head but couldn't help the way my lips tugged upward. "For the record, that's a terrible plan."

"You came, didn't you?"

"I'll always come, Devora."

The carriage stopped, and so did we. She turned to face me, her eyes scanning mine. Her expression was guarded, hesitant, and a little something more that I couldn't quite place.

"Two more to go," a rough male voice said from up ahead inside the stables, making us both jump.

"Doesn't he know it's the middle of the night?" another grumbled. "Why does he have to inspect each by hand?"

"Wants to see how they'll respond to fatesprig. You're new here, but you'll learn how the boss is. Very particular about his subjects. Most end up going to the cells on the south side anyway. Only a few stay here at the Hollow."

Devora and I exchanged equal looks of revulsion. They spoke about these prisoners as if they were objects. Goods to be handled and stored instead of innocent people stolen from their homes.

But we'd learned something. Several somethings. This was, in fact, the entrance to the Hollow, and it was where Scarven kept his fatesprig and those he tested it on.

She found it.

The place we didn't even know we were looking for. This could change everything.

The carriage right in front of us rolled forward into the stables. I peered around the front, assessing the number of guards.

"Can you use your shadows to keep yourself hidden?" I murmured to Devora.

"I can try. Why, what are you doing?"

I took out my ring. "This will camouflage me. I'm going to sneak in and see what we're working with."

"I want to come," she said immediately.

I hummed. "It's good to want things, darling." Then I shoved the ring on my finger and disappeared.

I entered the wide stables. The opposite side contained a dozen stalls, all housing Scarven's horses, while the side closest to the entrance was completely empty. Except for—

A giant trap door, straight in the center of the floor.

It had two doors that opened upward. Large piles of hay and dirt rested on either side, as if they'd been moved to uncover the hidden passageway. A set of stairs led from the ground deeper under the earth. Echoes of movement, voices, and groans reached my ears from as far down as it went.

The Hollow. Hidden in plain sight.

The two guards we'd heard talking stood at the carriage ahead of Devora, and I quickly made sure she was still blocked from their view before turning back to them. Each had a sword strapped across his back and two daggers protruding from their waistbands. One of them put several herbs to his lips and whispered a spell over the opening in the ground. It was more than likely warded and needed a certain enchantment to get inside. I filed the spell away to tell Silas.

The other one yanked open the carriage door and dragged out half a dozen prisoners one by one, all bound together with black metal cuffs. The youngest one appeared to be around eight, while the oldest was in their twenties.

So young. All of them, so very young.

My hackles rose at the sight. Blood boiled beneath my skin, making my hands tremble and my nostrils flare. I wanted to rip off the guards' heads and whisk these innocent people back to their homes. I wanted to race down those steps, grab Scarven by the throat, and sink my teeth into him until his blood coated my hands.

I took a steadying breath and tried to calm my wrath. I had to play this smart, like Kieran would. Level-headed. I couldn't give myself or Devora away. We'd found the Hollow, so we could come back with better resources and make a coordinated strike. For now, my priority was these prisoners.

Walking back to Devora, I whispered, "Can you create a distraction?"

She jumped at the sound of my voice. "A distraction? I barely know what I'm doing with this magic."

"You can do it, Devora. We just need something that will draw the guards away from the carriages."

She nodded and bit down on her lip. "Right. I'll think of something. Then what?"

"I'm going to signal for Kieran. Get this back carriage full of prisoners"—I motioned to the one we knelt next to—"unhooked from the front one and attach it to Kieran in his stag form. He'll pull it out. I'll worry about the other carriage."

A swell of shadows formed at her feet as she nodded again. I raised both hands to my lips and blew through them, two sharp, quick breaths, creating an owl call to signal Kieran. Two calls meant to come in his Shifter form. I paused and strained for a moment to listen. Sure enough, the sound of four clopping hooves met my ears. A hint of white fur and gleaming, majestic antlers peeked out from the edge of the tree line.

"Now, Devora," I commanded.

Her brow furrowed as shadows seeped from her, gliding along the ground and toward the stalls at the far end. When she raised her arms, the stream of shadows broke off into a dozen trails, each leading toward the individual stalls. Small clouds of smoke billowed beneath the doors.

The horses went wild.

Hooves stomped as straw went flying. Panicked whinnies filled the air, and the animals banged against the stall doors in an attempt to escape.

The two guards spun around with bewildered expressions. One of them cursed. "What the—"

The doors on two of the stalls came crashing down, sending dust and hay flying. A couple of horses sprinted from their confines and out the other stable entrance. Several more doors creaked as hooves rammed into them.

"What are you looking at me for?" The first guard slapped the younger one on the back. "Go get them!"

He scrambled forward and grabbed a rope off the wall, then darted after the loose horses. Another one broke down its stall door and nearly trampled him. Shadows swirled in the empty stalls, licking at the walls.

I glanced behind me, relieved to find Devora hurriedly fastening a collar around Kieran's long white neck, then hooking the harness of the carriage to him.

When another pair of horses got loose, the remaining guard dropped the shackles connecting all the prisoners. "Stay put, or I'll cut your feet off before Scarven ever gets ahold of ya, got it?" he snapped at them, then turned on his heel to shout at the beasts.

I narrowed my eyes. I wouldn't mind killing *him*.

Still invisible, I rushed toward the group, knowing I had few precious seconds to make this work. "Don't be scared," I started, my voice making several of the children jump. "I'm here to help. Get back into the carriage as quickly as you can."

Some of them were more alert as they looked around for my disembodied voice, while others were still sluggish from whatever drugs had been pumped into their system. Their clothing was torn and dirt-smeared, many of them with wet streaks of blood and other body fluids. Half of them were shivering uncontrollably. Fates, how long had they been in these carriages?

I grabbed the oldest-looking one by the arm. His eyes flew to where my invisible hand touched him. "Get them into the carriage. We're going to get you all out of here. Do you understand?"

He nodded jerkily and beckoned the younger ones back toward the carriage, doing his best to keep them quiet as others finally started catching on. The pair of horses still harnessed to the carriage pawed anxiously at the ground, and I half expected them to dart off any moment. I just needed them to hold on a little longer...

I crept ahead to put myself between the carriage and the remaining guard as he slammed on the stall doors to try and quiet the horses. "Come on, come on," I muttered, looking back and forth between him and the prisoners.

They were moving too slowly. There were still two of them to go, but their motions were weak and stilted, their shackles dragging against the ground.

My heart hammered as I crouched on the balls of my feet, skin buzzing with anticipation. I barely allowed myself to breathe.

Just one more...

"What do you think you're doing?" the guard shouted, spinning to face the prisoners' carriage. He put his fingers to his lips and let out a shrill whistle.

Time to go.

Footsteps clanged up the stone steps, coming from deep within the underground tunnel. I seized a water trough that rested a few feet ahead of me, summoning my awaiting dragon as heat pulsed in my chest. With a snarl, I breathed a stream of my dragon fire directly onto the water.

An enormous cloud of scalding steam rose and blasted the trap door entrance right as four new guards strode into view. One of them fell to his knees, blisters erupting on his face. Two more staggered backward. The steam blocked their view for a few seconds as

I hoisted the last of the prisoners into the carriage, leaving only the older boy I'd put in charge.

Shifting my fingers into talons, I sliced through the cuffs on his wrists and tore them off. "Driver's box. Now. Get to the edge of the property and look for the other carriage with a big, white stag. He'll take you somewhere safe."

Still unable to see me with my camouflaging ring on, the young man nodded and darted to the box as I smacked one of the horse's backsides. The two of them rose onto their hind legs with a whinny and took off through the stables, zig-zagging between guards and bales of hay to the opposite end and out the wide entrance.

I looked back at where Devora and Kieran had been with their carriage to find them gone too. Relief soared through me. Nobody had been seen—there was no way to trace it back to us. It simply looked like an accident allowed the prisoners to free themselves. I just had to buy them enough time to get away without being followed.

"Why are you all just standing there?" the first guard snarled. "Track them down!"

Three of the guards raced for the remaining horses. Still invisible, I rushed ahead and threw open the doors of the nearest stalls, jumping out of the way as the animals surged forward. One of the guards with a torch approached the next set of stalls, and I let loose another blast of fire. The torch exploded into a blaze, making the man drop it with a shout. Fire spread to the straw on the ground. I swiftly unlatched the rest of the stalls to let the horses escape the growing inferno.

With a growl, the guard with burns on his face got to his feet and shifted into a hyena. He sprang over the fire and darted to the entrance where the carriage had disappeared.

My heart raced. If even *one* of the guards followed them to the Keep—

Out of nowhere, a whip of shadows descended upon his back. He howled and crumpled to the floor as thick tendrils of darkness wrapped around his throat and pulled like a leash.

I jerked my head behind me to find Devora standing before the trap door, arms outstretched and shadows dancing at her feet. The line of fire on the ground between us flickered, making her glow brighter in its orange and yellow haze.

"Where did she come from?" one of the guards shouted.

The man closest to me stopped in his tracks, peering at her in recognition. "Wait, isn't that—"

I reached out and snapped his neck.

He fell like a rock. The remaining four went on instant alert, grabbing their swords as they backed away from the spot where we stood.

I'd wanted to be discreet. Leaving a mass of bodies in our wake would raise too much suspicion. But now that they'd seen her, I couldn't let them go running back to Scarven and put her in danger.

They all had to die.

The realization of what I had to do settled over me. The bloodthirsty haze of my dragon half rose to the surface, gnashing his teeth.

I ripped the ring off my finger to reveal myself. Devora's eyes widened at the dead man at my feet.

"You shouldn't have come back," I said grimly.

Then I attacked.

Lunging, I grabbed the guard closest to the stalls and shifted my other hand into talons, slicing them down his chest until it was nothing more than mangled skin and sinew. I threw him to the side as another one pounced, his sword outstretched. This one must've been a Lightbender—lightning flashed around the blade, so hot I could feel it before it touched me.

He charged at me, and I caught the sword with my bare hand. With a menacing smile, I slowly pulled it from his grasp, the blade piercing deep into my skin. Blood trickled down my arm. The man's face was contorted in horror as I tugged the sword free, flipped it around, and plunged it into his gut. His own lightning crackled across his skin as his body went limp, then it fizzled out completely.

"Nox!" Devora called out.

I whirled to face her. She was all the way across the stables, with two guards advancing on her. A shield of shadows sprang up in front of her, but they were thin and weak. When she locked eyes with me, fear shone back.

My wings extended at my back with a stretch, their navy-blue and silver scales shimmering as they consumed the front half of the stables. I launched into the air with shifted talons and dove for Devora right as the two guards struck.

My claws pierced their backs, severing their spines.

They lifted a few feet until I shifted my claws back into hands, and they went crashing to the ground. I landed on the earth beside them in a crouch.

The night was quiet, save for the flames still blazing in the stables.

I turned to face Devora, my wings dragging along the ground. Hair hung in my eyes, and dried blood crusted my arms. I could taste the blood of the men I'd killed smeared across my face.

I looked like a beast. A wild, unhinged monster that Scarven so desperately wanted to create.

But it was for *her*. To keep her safe.

She stared at me, lips parted and chest heaving. Her shadows melted into her skin.

"Come on," I said gruffly. "We need to find Kieran."

Blinking twice, she gave a small nod. I turned to stalk into the surrounding forest when she gripped my elbow.

"Nox, wait..." She tugged at her bottom lip with her teeth, her eyes flitting between mine. The blue-green pools were just as bright, even in the dead of night. I swallowed as her fingers squeezed my arm before releasing me.

"Thank you," she whispered.

36

DEVORA

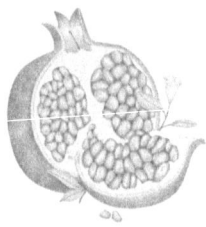

Our impromptu rescue mission at the stables was one of the most successful ones the Ashen Order had ever attempted, according to Tessa. Fourteen prisoners. All of them were Illusionists and Striders who had been captured by Scarven's men and carted across the empire for more of his experiments.

The Keep wasn't equipped to take on over a dozen more residents, but we made do. Makeshift beds were set up in the bunk rooms, and we moved some of the groups to the upper floors with the older ones and families. Tessa and Arowyn slept in my room for a couple of nights to free up their chambers. The newest additions to the Keep wouldn't be staying long, however; we were sending them back to their provinces once they recovered. It was a miracle none of them had any lasting effects—physically, at least. Dehydration and a few cuts and bruises were the worst of it, but I knew the mental and emotional toll from this trauma would remain long after the scars faded.

I was exhausted, but in a good way. Having so many mouths to feed and children to watch and people to care for helped keep my mind off what happened at the Hollow.

And the fact that tonight, I was going back.

"Miss Rora?" a sweet voice said behind me.

Turning from the basin I'd been washing dishes in, I found little Luna with her scraggly teddy bear in hand. I wiped my hands on a towel and smiled. "Isn't it your nap time, little girl?"

When I crouched, she ran forward to hug my knees. "Can't sleep. Phina keeps kicking me." She reached up to twirl a finger in my hair, then tried to pluck the glasses off my nose.

Luna and Seraphina were two young Strider sisters who had been in the carriage Kieran pulled all the way from the Hollow to here. They'd both latched on to me pretty quickly. Based on the tint of red in their hair, I wondered if their mother had hair like mine, and that was why they gravitated to me.

I scooped her up, and she rested her head on my shoulder. "Alright, you can come nap with me. Just this once, okay?" I tapped her on the nose.

We both knew I was a liar. I'd never been around kids much before to know if I liked them, but I was literally wrapped around this little girl's finger.

I carried her out of the kitchen and to my room. The little puffs of warm breath on my neck indicated she was already fast asleep. I shook my head with a smile as I reached for my door handle, then froze.

Nox leaned against the doorframe to his room down the hall, watching me with an intensity that burned through my skin. I hadn't seen him much in the last couple of days, what with our hectic schedules.

"Hello," I said. A small package with a letter was tucked in the crook of his elbow, and I nodded toward it. "What's that?"

He shifted on his feet. "Something from Clarissa."

At the sound of her name, I looked down and tightened my hold on Luna. I wondered if the empress still hated me. If she sent messages to him to keep up with my "imprisonment," or if she'd simply forgotten my existence—the lady's maid who stabbed her in the back, then moved on.

"She said she hopes you're doing well," Nox added, and my neck jerked up.

She hoped I was doing *well?* The last time I saw her, she practically spat in my face. My brows knitted together as disbelief swarmed me.

"She doesn't know the details, but I've told her things are getting better. That you've been a huge asset here." The side of his lip quirked into a small smile as he spoke. "Guess it's a good thing we didn't leave you in Mysthelm all those months ago."

"Yeah, why *didn't* you?" I blurted, keeping my voice low to not wake Luna. "Why didn't you just let them throw me in the dungeons?"

We'd never talked about this, not really. Everything was such a blur after they found out I'd been spying on Clarissa, when Nox volunteered to bring me back under his supervision. Now that he and I were on...*better* terms, there was no harm in asking.

"Because you're not from Mysthelm. You're *Veridian*. You were our responsibility."

"Ah." I wasn't sure why that made disappointment curdle in my stomach. "Just another part of the job, I guess."

He took a step forward. "And because I know Clarissa. As angry as she was, I could tell she didn't want to send you to the gallows. She cared about you, Devora. But she wasn't ready to deal with it, not after everything that had happened. I guess I wanted to...to give her time. I knew she'd want the chance to forgive you one day."

I hummed. "That day may not come for a while."

"Actually, it could be sooner than you think." He waved the letter at me. "She wants to extend an invitation to you."

That sent me reeling. "For what?"

"A royal wedding. She and Thorne have set a date, and they want us to come. *Both* of us."

I shook my head and let out a huff of surprised laughter. Her *wedding?* Was he serious? "Why would she want *me* there? Has she forgotten what I did to her?"

"You're not the sum of your past, Devora," he said quietly. "Forgiveness isn't about forgetting. It's about choosing to believe you're more than your mistakes."

A lump formed in my throat. That was a far cry from what he said to me weeks ago.

My nose twitched, and I quickly looked away. I wasn't sure what to make of Clarissa's olive branch. Part of me still felt I didn't deserve it, despite how much I was trying. I wanted to absolve myself of the terrible things I'd done, but now that I was doing it, it didn't seem real. The guilt that had weighed on me for so long wasn't easily moved.

I didn't know how to respond. Instead, I switched Luna to my other hip and asked, "When's the wedding?"

"A little less than two weeks, on the winter solstice."

"Oh." Anxiety trickled back in. "Well, it may not even matter. I might not be back from Scarven's by then."

His features darkened, but Luna let out a little snore before he could say anything. "I need to put her down for a nap," I whispered across the hall. "Will I—" I cleared my throat. "Will I see you tonight? Before I leave?"

He stiffened. Tonight was the night Scarven's men were supposed to pick me up from the Mysthelm base. Scarven believed I had nowhere else to go, so I had to stay with him to keep up a convincing cover. I had to admit that living at his mansion would make spying much more convenient, however anxious I was.

Nox looked like he wanted to say something else, but he merely pinched his lips in a grim line and nodded curtly. "I'll be there."

I slipped inside the room and gently laid Luna on my bed, tucking the covers around her small frame. The tension from the conversation with Nox hovered over me. Something was changing between us, but for the better or worse, I didn't know. He was hot one minute and cold the next. Fire racing along my pulse, then confusion leaving me hollow.

I had no clue how to feel. I once told him I hated him, and he said he'd never trust me. How did we get from that, to this?

Lingering stares, rough touches that lit my veins on fire, aching sadness for his past, longing for him to find happiness.

You didn't feel that for someone you hated. You didn't wake up in the middle of the night to the sound of their frightened cries, filled with nothing but the desire to take their pain away.

I glanced at my bag, packed and ready by the door, then flopped down on the bed next to Luna. My stomach churned at the idea of staying at Scarven's manor. I was scared of him; that was for sure. Scared of what he could do to me. Of what I might have to *let* him do to me for the sake of saving so many others. Scared of messing up and being a failure.

But the one fear that stuck out was that nobody would be here to listen when the nightmares came for Nox again.

———

THE EIGHT OF us were eating an early dinner in the drawing room— the first time we'd all been together since the rescue mission at the Hollow. The atmosphere lacked its usual unhinged camaraderie I'd grown to expect from this group.

Tessa and Kieran were hunched over blueprints of Scarven's manor they'd accumulated over the years, pausing occasionally to stuff bites of food in their mouths. Arowyn was flipping a dagger over and over in her hand while Silas jabbered to her and Milo about new tests he planned to try with the small amount of fatesprig he had left. Everett sat across from me, listening to the others while we ate.

And Nox was in a tall wingback chair in front of the fire, swirling a glass in his hand as he stared into the flames. He hadn't spoken the entire time.

Tessa folded up one of the maps. "The drawing you sent us the other day was helpful, Devora. We're connecting it with the network of tunnels we already knew existed, and seeing where it stands in relation to the new Hollow area."

I nodded. "I'll try to see if he'll take me to the Hollow itself.

That's the last big piece we need, right? If we can figure out how to get past his wards and where he's keeping his supply of fatesprig, we can destroy it and get the other prisoners out."

"Just be careful," Kieran said, and I raised an eyebrow in surprise. The stag Shifter had been the last one to warm up to me —although now that I'd gotten to know him, I wasn't sure if he was "warm" toward anyone. But the fact that he cared thawed something between us. "You still have your enchanted parchment from Silas, yes?"

I tapped the spot over my breast where it rested. "I'll check in every evening and send reports when I can."

"And what's the code word if you need me to get you out of there?" Arowyn cut in.

I rolled my eyes. "Arowyn, we don't need a code word. I'll just write, 'Help, I'm dying.'"

"Not funny." She pointed at me. "Code word?"

With a long sigh, I replied, "Sugar nuts."

She smiled. "Thank you."

"What did we ever do before you and your unbreakable codes, Arowyn?" Tessa asked with a snort.

"Two weeks," Kieran said, crossing his arms over his chest. He was always utterly unbothered by our ridiculous banter. "That's how long until the contingency sets sail for Mysthelm. You have two weeks to discover what you can so we can coordinate a final attack."

Tessa added, "And if we don't hear from you in any forty-eight-hour period, we're calling the whole thing off. Say the word, and we'll come in, through flame and ash."

"We've got your back, Dev." Arowyn tilted her head up in agreement with Tessa. "And your front."

A sudden warmth filled my chest as they all nodded. I pushed my glasses up the bridge of my nose, fighting off the sting in my eyes. "Well, let's hope it doesn't come to that."

"Be ready to leave in half an hour," Everett said, standing with his empty plate. He was escorting me to the Mysthelm base once again, where Scarven's men would pick me up.

The others followed his lead and cleared off the table, stopping to murmur their goodbyes and good lucks. Tessa pulled me into a tight hug, and Arowyn nudged my arm with a smile on the way out.

Only Nox and I were left.

I twisted my lips, listening to the crackle of flames and ice clinking against glass as he took a sip of his drink. Squaring my shoulders, I stood and made my way to the matching wingback chair next to him. "Mind if I sit?"

He glanced at me, then back to the fire, motioning to the chair with his glass.

"You've been particularly quiet," I finally said, unable to take the silence any longer.

"Haven't had anything particularly interesting to say."

"That hasn't stopped you before," I quipped, shooting him a half-hearted smirk. He didn't react. We went back to the tense silence, the ornate clock on the wall ticking faster and faster toward my impending departure.

I stared into the flames. My shadows came to the surface of my skin, twining around my finger as they liked to do. I flicked my hand and sent them toward the fire. I was entranced at the way the flames darted up the fireplace, the way my shadows moved around them like they were dancing.

"I wish you'd say something," I whispered after a minute.

Out of the corner of my eye, I saw his knuckles clench around his glass. He stood and paced to the edge of the fireplace, leaning against the mantel. "What do you want me to say, Devora?"

"I don't know. Something. Tell me a bad joke, or—or yell at me. Anything."

He raised an eyebrow. "You want me to yell at you?"

"No, I just..." I let out a breath and ran my fingers through my hair. "I just need a distraction."

His shoulders straightened. He put his glass on the mantel and took a step closer, eyeing me like a predator assessing its prey.

"A distraction?" he murmured. Another step.

My mouth went dry. I told myself to look away, but my eyes wouldn't obey. The fire was suddenly sweltering. My sweater clung to the edge of my shoulder, scratchy and hot and too tight under his stare.

He leaned forward, both hands resting on either arm of my chair, bracketing me in. "If I wanted to *distract* you, darling, I wouldn't waste my time yelling."

His voice scraped low, rough and dangerous. The air crackled between us. I could feel the warmth of his breath, the scent of spicy smoke clinging to his skin. My lips parted, but I couldn't breathe.

Fates, I didn't know why I had this reaction to him. How someone I'd once sworn to hate could make my heart stumble like this. There was always something waiting just beneath the surface, begging to be let out.

He lifted a hand and reached for something next to me. "Drink?"

And just like that, the tension snapped.

I blinked once. Twice. Then looked over to find a glass liquor cart next to my chair.

"Probably not a good idea." I shook my head and looked down at my hands, where my shadows twisted through my fingers. He released his hold on the chair and took a step back, as if he needed to clear his head too.

Now that I could think again, the daunting task ahead consumed me. "I don't know how you all do it," I said. "Risking your lives day after day, raid after raid. You act like it doesn't even faze you."

To my surprise, he scoffed. "Aren't you the woman who ran straight into Scarven's secret base with no weapon or back-up? You're fearless, Devora. You always have been."

"Then why am I so scared?" I whispered.

He stared at me for a moment, swallowed, then lowered

himself until his knees hit the floor at my feet. His hands rested on my wrists, my shadows hovering between us. "We're all scared. Every single time."

I rolled my lips together. "What if I mess this up? What if I do something wrong and—and he finds out? He could take it out on one of you, or his prisoners, or—" My voice caught, all my fears pouring from me in a tidal wave. Fears I'd pushed aside with false confidence and a brave face for the sake of the mission. "What if he tries to—if he experiments on me, or hurts me, and I—I can't stop him—"

Nox gripped the back of my neck, cutting me off as he pressed his forehead against mine. I gasped at the sudden contact. He hadn't been this close to me since the nightmare in his tent, and my pulse pounded at his nearness.

"I'm sorry," he rasped. "You don't have to do this. You're not a prisoner *or* a pawn. You're a *person*, and you have a choice. I'm sorry if I ever made you feel like you didn't."

I let out a shaky breath. "Part of me wants you to—to tell me to stay," I confessed, so quiet I barely heard it myself. "I'm selfish and scared, and I—"

He cut me off again with a growl. "You are *not* selfish. I was wrong about you, Devora. You've risked *everything* for people you don't even know, and I will never forgive myself for the way I treated you." He lifted his forehead and cupped my cheek, forcing me to look at him. A tenderness I'd never seen before shone back at me.

His thumb wiped a stray tear from the corner of my mouth. "Fates, I—I'm scared, too," he said. "I've been gone so much because I'm afraid if I look at you, I'll beg you not to go."

"Do it," I whispered. "Beg me, and maybe I'll listen."

His mouth curved into a sad smile. "We both know you've never listened to me, Devora, darling."

My tongue darted out to lick the corner of my lips, barely grazing his thumb. His arm went rigid, eyes locked on my mouth.

Fates, he was too close. Every breath tasted like him, like temptation and danger that I wasn't supposed to want. And still, I found myself leaning in, just enough to feel his warmth. His safety. To imagine what it would be like if I stopped fighting.

But that was the whole point of this. To *fight*.

"We both know I can't stay. Even if I want to." I paused on an exhale. "I can do this, Nox. I can help them all."

His fingers gently brushed my jaw. "I know you can. I trust you."

Those words poured through me, filling gaps I hadn't known existed. *I trust you.*

It was all I wanted to hear after everything that had happened between us.

My shoulders fell, and I gave him a tentative smile. "So, how about that drink?"

He rose from his knees, taking my hands and pulling me with him. Our time here was up.

"Come home, Devora," he said softly. "Then we'll have that drink."

PART TWO

THE

TRAP

37

DEVORA

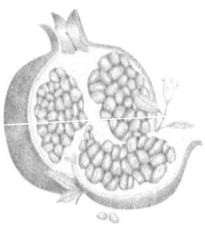

Scarven's mansion was even spookier the third time around. Shadows hung from the dark turrets, taking forms that looked like monsters hiding beneath their silhouettes.

Home, sweet home, I thought bitterly.

The guards who escorted me from the Mysthelm base dropped me off in a guest suite, promising that a servant would be by with dinner soon.

"Oh, is Lord—"

My question was cut off by the door shutting in my face.

"—Scarven here?" I finished, deflated. Guess that was my answer.

It seemed strange that Scarven would invite me here knowing I had no place else to go, have me hand-delivered to his home, then be absent. Unless something was wrong. Unless he was suspicious.

Anxiety spread from my throat to my core like sludge, dripping down my insides. Maybe he was angry about the rescue mission from a couple nights ago. Maybe he thought I had something to do with it. Had I been too obvious? Did he know I'd eavesdropped on his conversation?

I took a couple of deep breaths and tried to shake off the sensation of eyes watching me. If he thought I was behind it, he would've killed me, right? Not bring me into his sanctuary.

Unless he was toying with me.

I groaned and rubbed at my eyes with the heel of my hand. I was going to drive myself crazy if I didn't stop. I was here. I was *in.* The mission was working, and that was all that mattered.

Glancing around the room for the first time, I took in the four-poster bed with thick burgundy curtains hanging from the top, the nightstand trimmed in gold, the floor-length mirror next to a heavy armoire. The fireplace to my left was already crackling, and a chaise lounge in the same burgundy fabric as the bed loomed in front of the flames.

It dripped with opulence. The kind of lifestyle Scarven obviously lived, if his soliloquy about carnal desires from the night of his party was any indication.

There was a knock on the door, and I jumped, thinking for a split second it was him. But a servant girl poked her head in, carrying a tray with plates of food and a carafe of water.

"May I come in, miss?" she asked, her voice soft.

"Yes, please." I backed up so she could set the tray on the bench at the foot of the bed. "I actually had a question. Will Lord Scarven be—"

"The governor is busy. If that's all, miss, then I'll be back in the morning." She gave me a hurried curtsy before stepping out of the room.

I let out a deep sigh. Fates, these people were dodgy. That did nothing to ease my stress.

I devoured the roasted pork and steamed potatoes, washing it down with a glass of water. The clock on the wall read ten o'clock —it was safe to say Scarven wasn't coming tonight. I'd already checked in with Nox on the magical parchment when I got to the room. A quick "I'm here," followed by "Stay safe." Only two words, but after our goodbye at the Keep, they wormed their way through my chest and nestled among my shadows.

I dropped my bag on top of the bed and dug through its

contents, looking for a nightgown. Instead, my fingers brushed something soft and a little lumpy. Scratchy and fraying at the edges.

It was…oddly familiar.

I held my breath as I grabbed the fabric and pulled.

Out came a blue blanket.

It was thin and raggedy, with a touch of life left in it. The faded "Devora S" was stitched at the top right-hand corner.

I lifted it to my nose and breathed in the worn scent of salt and soap, of nights where sometimes all I had to my name were the clothes on my back and this blanket wrapped around my shoulders.

Tears stung the backs of my eyes. I sucked in a breath as I scrunched the blanket in my hands, a sense of serenity sweeping over me. It was just fabric. Tattered and barely large enough to cover my midsection. I didn't even remember receiving it, couldn't recall the hands that folded my body inside of it.

But it was the only reminder that those people existed. That once upon a time, someone loved me. Someone treasured me.

And someone had brought it back to me.

Words failed. There wasn't a doubt in my mind Nox had somehow secured this for me, and I didn't know how to tell him what that meant. How to tell him that it felt like my heart was about to crack open.

A few teardrops fell from my lashes and down my cheek as I grabbed my enchanted parchment and charcoal, my hands shaking as I wrote two simple words.

Thank you.

It wasn't until I'd gotten ready for bed and slipped under the covers, blue blanket clutched in my grip, that the paper heated with a response.

You're welcome, darling.

———

THREE DAYS. I'd been in Scarven's mansion for three days without a hint of the governor to be found. I was about to crawl out of my skin.

I convinced myself he somehow knew I'd been the one to help set his prisoners free and was now torturing me with some convoluted mind game. Seeing how long I'd last before I cracked under the pressure.

Every day, I worried he was gone because he'd found the Keep's hiding spot and had ransacked it. I thought Nox was getting tired of my constant checking in during the days, but it was the only way to ease my fears.

The servants and guards weren't treating me hostilely, at least. They weren't exactly friendly, but otherwise, I felt like a normal guest. The same servant brought me breakfast in the morning before drawing me a hot bath. I was allowed to roam the open, public spaces—the library, dining rooms, wine cellar, gardens.

Everywhere I went, guards were stationed up and down the halls, those lion masks they wore still eerily off-putting. If I tried to venture down an abandoned wing or darkened corner, they abruptly turned me away. When I followed the route we'd taken the night of his private party to get to the downstairs level, I was stopped. It was obvious Scarven had laid out certain rules. Even though he let me stay here, he didn't trust me. Or anyone, for that matter. I was scared to press my luck and raise any alarms by continuing to search where I was forbidden.

Personal growth, honestly.

But I could still practice my shadows. When nobody was around, I heard Thecae and Calyra's voices in my head, guiding me and my magic. I let it flow from me in the privacy of my room or the silence of an empty corridor. My shadows were as hungry for information as I was. They crept from my skin and along the cracks in the floor and doors, searching for sounds to bring back to me. For *something* I could pass along to the Order.

Truth be told, I was growing lonely. In a way, it reminded me of the months spent in Nox's tower, with only my festering thoughts to keep me company. At least I had my shadows now.

But when a knock sounded on my door on the fourth night, I found myself wishing for the silence.

"Selena," Scarven said when I opened the door, eyeing me like I was his next meal. "It's been far too long."

I shoved down the fear his presence always brought and slipped back into the mask of Miss Selena Nyte. Crossing my arms over my chest, I cocked my head. "I was beginning to think you'd forgotten about me."

"Never. Simply caught up with business. But no more of that— tonight, we're going out."

"Out? What should I wear?"

His gaze roved over me, lingering on my curves. He smirked. "Something you don't mind getting dirty."

38

DEVORA

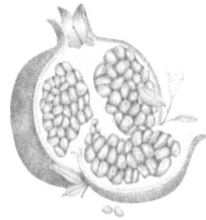

Apparently "out" meant a seedy tavern on the outskirts of the main village square, with cobwebs and some sort of dried bodily fluid I didn't care to question smeared on the outside of the cracked wooden door. When Scarven opened it, the scent of sweat and stale ale hit me in full force. I wrinkled my nose as I stepped over the leg of a man passed out in the entryway.

Gnats buzzed around my ear. I almost missed the small red coin Scarven passed to the bartender from the sleeve of his shirt. The bartender's eyes scanned the motley crew of patrons mulling around the tavern before he jerked his head, and without missing a beat, Scarven lifted a section of the bar top and held his hand out for me to pass through.

I swallowed my trepidation and stepped behind the bar, with him close on my heels. My shoes crunched over nut shells and broken glass as the bartender led us to a door in the back of the kitchen. I'd chosen a loose black tunic over leather pants tucked inside my calf-high combat boots. I had no idea what to expect of our little "outing," but I had a feeling my gowns wouldn't help me tonight.

The bartender inserted a key into the lock, then tugged it open to reveal a narrow tunnel curving to the right and out of sight.

I stopped at the threshold. There was *no way* I was going down there.

Was this it? Scarven's way of capturing me, lulling me into a sense of security before he struck and made me one of his experiments?

His hand slipped under my tunic to rest on the small of my back, against my bare skin. I tried not to flinch at the unexpected contact. "Don't be scared, Selena," he murmured in my ear. "I think you'll like this."

I think you're very wrong, I thought, but forced my feet to step into the tunnels. The path sloped down at an angle, leading us underground. Clammy sweat formed on my palms, even though the air dropped several degrees as we descended.

At first, it was mostly quiet. Water dripped to the stone floor, creatures scurried across dirt, and glass hitting tables echoed from the tavern we'd left behind.

Then...I heard it.

A low rumbling. Feet pounding. Voices shouting. Growing louder, like thunder rolling down my spine, the farther we walked through the tunnel, until suddenly, the path opened up into a large dome.

Hundreds of people were packed in the space. Bodies pressed in on each other, leering and screaming at something beyond my line of sight. I stood on my tiptoes to get a better look.

In the center of the raucous onlookers was a square stage raised on several platforms of wood. Two people stood on the stage. One male—shirtless, chest heaving, blood dripping from a gash in his cheek, and one female, her hands shifted into claws and teeth bared. Black hair was matted and clumped on one side of her head. The two circled each other in slow steps while the audience shouted, bags of money and betting slips raised above their heads.

It was a fighting ring.

I blinked against the onslaught of blood, alcohol, and adrenaline racing through the dome. Everything was so...harsh. It was palpable, tangible, grating against my skin.

"What do you think?" Scarven said in my ear.

Another test. *Everything* was a test. It was a good thing I was a great actor.

"It's...exhilarating." I let out a sharp exhale, keeping my eyes on the fighting ring. "A little frightening. What is it?"

"I told you I like to provide a means of escape for my people. There are many facets of indulgence. This is one of them." He tilted his chin toward the man and woman still circling each other. "For some, this is intoxicating. The rage, the suspense, the violence. The beautiful dance of two people locked in battle. Who will draw first blood? Who will be the victor?" A smile curled on his lips. "It's a game. One many of my people enjoy playing. I simply give them the ability to do so."

A cheer erupted from the crowd, jolting me back to the fight. The woman dodged something, but I couldn't see what the man had done. She let out a feral screech as she dove to the side.

The man just stood there watching her. That was when I realized he must be an Illusionist, casting an illusion only she could see.

She cowered on her side, and I sucked in a breath as he pulled a short dagger from his waistband. The noise from the crowd picked up. I could feel their anticipation, their thirst for blood, hammering in my ears.

The man lunged, but the girl was quick. A Shifter, if her claws were any indication. Her hand shot out to clutch his throat, and in one smooth movement, her other hand came up, claws ripping across his head.

He let out an anguished cry as blood poured from the center of his face. My hand flew to my lips. His eyes dangled from their sockets, the skin at his nose and cheeks flayed open.

"The trick to defeating an Illusionist," Scarven said at my side, "is to go for the eyes."

The crowd erupted. They stomped their feet, hands clapping as they screamed. The woman held her victim in her grip with flared nostrils. Before I could blink, she snapped his neck, and his body went crashing to the floor.

My heart pounded harder, mirroring the cheers from the spectators. I forced down my bile. I knew Scarven was watching for my reaction. I had to keep this pretense up—no matter how shaky my knees were, no matter how much I wanted to leave this Fatesforsaken province behind, I had to fake it.

I swallowed and faced Scarven, hoping the redness of my cheeks looked like frenzy and not my sudden nausea. "Are you in charge of all this?"

He waved a hand in the air. "My men organize it. Different times, different venues. We must keep things confidential. It's by invitation only, of course. But I provide the entertainment." He steepled his hands in front of his face, eyes locked on the stage in some sort of sick pride.

Another duo had just been brought out. Two males this time, one with long hair and a metal bracelet on one arm, and the other with a belt of broken weapons. They looked barely eighteen.

"Would you like to get a closer look?" Scarven asked. I gave a quick nod, barely feeling my neck move, and he pushed me through the crowd by my waist.

Bodies bumped against me, sweat rubbing my shoulders as we waded deeper. My feet slipped on something, and I clenched my teeth together when I looked down and saw splatters of blood across the floor.

Scarven stopped moving when we were right up against the stage, separated by several feet of wood and nothing else. Now that we were closer to the fighters, I could see their faces better.

They weren't angry. They weren't hungry for blood.

They were scared.

The long-haired one with the strange bracelet flicked his bloodshot eyes to the crowd, a deep furrow on his brow. The other had a twitch in his shoulder—it kept jerking, like an invisible string was pulling it up. He blinked rapidly as the announcer told them to get in position.

"They're all mine," Scarven said, watching the two men face each other. "Veridians from across the empire who have found their way into my fold. Their magic was weak, but I gave them strength."

He made it sound like these people had a *choice*. Like they came to him seeking help. Rage burned inside me, but I kept my features neutral.

"You see this one?" Scarven nodded to the long-haired boy on the left side of the fighting ring. He put his arms up as the second boy came running at him. "He was a child when I found him at the base of the Mistwood Mountains. A Shadow Wielder without a home." The second boy lunged, fist aiming for the long-haired boy's arm, connecting with the bracelet with a resounding *crunch*. "And I made him into something greater."

Light burst from the boy's bracelet, sending a shockwave through the crowd that temporarily blinded me. When the brightness dimmed enough for me to see the stage, my mouth fell open.

The long-haired boy had a whip of lightning in one hand and shadows in the other. Just when he slammed his lightning whip down, his opponent disappeared.

A Strider.

He rematerialized directly behind the first and jumped onto his back. They thrashed around the stage. The first one gripped the second boy's forearm and sent a beam of light into his skin. The Strider jumped down with a yelp, cradling his burned arm.

"What do you mean, you *made* him?" I asked Scarven slowly, my attention still on the fight.

"Magic is in the blood, Selena," he responded. "A mere tool at our disposal. If you can figure out how to bend it to your will, you can do anything. It's just like healing an illness. You take ingredients and mix them together to create medicine that heals the body. I combined this boy's magic with that of another, and made him into a Lightbender. One stronger than we could have anticipated."

At those words, the Shadow Wielder and Lightbender hybrid shot out both hands toward the other boy. Shadows and light collided in a brilliant beam of power, lighting the entire dome with enough force that I had to shield my eyes. The two coils twisted together in an arc, then dove straight for the second boy.

He opened his mouth in a scream, and they shot down his throat.

His arms flung out wide, his entire body shaking as a glow emitted from his pale, bruised skin. Then he went still, slumped to his knees, and landed face-first on the ground. The shadows and slivers of light snaked away from his body, back into the long-haired victor.

Cheers enveloped me from all sides. But the one left standing didn't appear *victorious*. He wasn't beating his chest in triumph. He slumped his shoulders, retreating back down the steps of the stage as workers came up to clear the dead body.

It was disgusting. It was heartbreaking. It was the worst thing I'd ever seen in my life. And I couldn't so much as show a *hint* of my true feelings.

"Ah," Scarven said, his features lifting. "My prized possession."

I tried to get a better view of the next fighter being brought to the stage. It was a girl—a woman, maybe a couple years younger than me, although with how pale and emaciated they all looked, it was hard to tell. Her hair was braided down one side, with streaks of dirt and red intertwined with the blonde strands. It highlighted her sharp cheekbones and even sharper jaw.

There was something familiar in the look on her face. The way she held her chin slightly raised despite the jeers from the crowd, the way her eyes glinted when they swiveled my way.

Dark gold, burning eyes.

But still, there was *something*...

The second fighter made his way onto the stage. He was *huge*. Easily three times her size, with his bare chest and arms shredded in muscles. A necklace of teeth hung from his neck. But the most terrifying part was his head—as he lumbered into the arena, it shifted from human to bear, his wide maw roaring and exposing sharp teeth.

"Is she supposed to fight *him*?" I asked in disbelief.

Scarven shot me a smirk. "Just wait, love."

The woman didn't even look scared. She didn't look much of anything. She stared at her opponent with a blank expression. He roared again—to the delight of the crowd—and cracked his knuckles, but she merely shifted on her feet.

When the announcer yelled for the fight to begin, I was actually *nervous*. I chewed on the edge of my fingernail, anxiety twisting in my gut for this woman I didn't even know.

The bear Shifter lunged, and I flinched.

But the woman evaporated into thin air. She must be a Strider.

Scarven glanced at me out of the corner of his eye, then tugged on my waist to reposition me in front of him. "Do you feel that?" he murmured in my ear. "The excitement, the anticipation, the hint of danger?"

I shivered against my will. I kept my attention focused on the fight, and not his hands hovering at my waist.

The woman was quicker than I gave her credit for. She moved out of reach of the Shifter's attacks with ease, and after the fourth time, the bear Shifter pounded on the floor with his fists. Spit flew from his mouth as he roared, but she looked as bored as ever.

He was getting smarter, though. Instead of hurling his entire body at her, he tried little jabs here and there, using both hands and feet to distract her. When he landed his first kick to her ribs, the crowd cheered. He aimed a punch to her other side when she turned, but right before he made contact, she sank into a cloud of shadows billowing at her feet.

My own shadows pulsed in my chest as my eyes widened. "Did she just—"

Darkness swirled at the base of the bear Shifter's shadow, and suddenly, a crack of lightning boomed in the air. From his shadow came a bright whip that snapped at his ankles. He whirled around with a yelp, and the woman emerged from the swath of shadows, holding a lightning whip.

I blinked. Was that possible? Could she be a Strider, Shadow Wielder, *and* Lightbender?

The Shifter grabbed the whip around his ankles, yanking it from her grip. Blood trickled from his hands where the light had cut his skin, but they healed within seconds. He staggered backward before finding his balance and squaring up to face her again.

I sucked in a breath as she darted forward, but...she didn't attack him. She leaned down and dipped her fingers into the trail of his blood.

She lifted his blood to her mouth. I couldn't hear her over the cacophony of the spectators, but her lips moved swiftly, words flying off her tongue. I'd only ever seen Alchemists do something like that.

Fire erupted at the bear Shifter's feet. Vines appeared from nowhere and spiraled around his limbs, making him unable to do anything but thrash around in the flames. He fell to his knees and tried to roll away, but the fire followed him.

Was she casting some sort of spell?

An icy numbness slipped from my spine all the way to my feet, coating my insides with horror.

Strider. Shadow Wielder. Lightbender. Alchemist. Four of the six magics.

A memory came back to me, Nox's voice echoing in my mind. *"She has all six. All six magics of the Veridian Empire."*

My breaths came faster as the flames consumed the Shifter, his wails mixing with the scent of charring flesh. It couldn't be. She couldn't possibly be—

The woman looked straight at me.

Or rather, above me. At Scarven's head mere inches behind mine. I glanced up and saw him give her a single nod.

She looked back to her victim and cocked her head. With one final word from her blood-streaked lips, there was a crack.

The Shifter's neck snapped to the side, and he went quiet. The crowd was wild, their cheers so loud they shook the ground.

"Isn't she beautiful?" Scarven asked, close enough that his

words reached me through the noise. "A stunning weapon. The only one of her kind."

I swallowed a heavy lump in my throat, trying to keep my voice steady. "It—it looks like she has many powers." I was hoping, praying, *pleading* it wasn't her. Anyone but her.

"You have no idea, love," he rumbled. "No one has ever possessed all the powers of our empire. She's our champion." The pride in his voice made me sick. "Defeats every challenger she has ever faced."

My heart dropped like a stone. It was *her*.

It was Nox's sister.

Everything around me felt too hot and close, pushing against me from all sides. I didn't know how I was going to tell Nox what I'd seen. That his sister was forced to fight in this revolting show-case, that she'd been turned into a weapon of destruction that murdered his other subjects for *sport*.

I closed my eyes. I had to remember where I was. Who I was supposed to be. I could spiral later—right now, I needed to be intrigued. Scarven's little lamb, thrown into the deep end and learning to swim. His new *project*.

The crowd was beginning to die down, shouts turning to animated conversations as they discussed the fights and exchanged money. That must've been the last fight of the night, for more bodies started working their way to the exits lining the dome. Scarven kept a hand planted on my back as he guided me to the tunnel we'd come from.

I licked my lips. "She was incredible. How did you make her like that?"

"This one was actually born that way, if you can believe it." We entered the dark tunnel, and the sounds of the fighting ring faded behind us. "She's been with me since birth. I've trained her to answer only to me." His features were smug, a dangerous gleam in his black eyes. There was this wild energy around him, as if the fighting matches had given him a high. "She's powerful. Her blood is the perfect test for our trials, since it allows my Alchemist to see the effects on each magic type all in one."

It took every ounce of control not to shudder at his words. *The perfect test.* How could I tell Nox? The torture she had to go through, the mind control he inflicted on her...it was too much.

But she's alive, a quiet voice in the back of my mind reminded me.

She was alive, and she was *here.* That was more information than the Ashen Order had before. Maybe I could use this.

I paused mid-step, making Scarven stop and raise an eyebrow. I opened my mouth as if I wanted to say something, then bit down on my bottom lip in fake hesitation.

"What is it, love?" he purred, taking a step closer. "Is this too much for you?"

"No, I just—" I let out a small laugh and leaned my back against the tunnel wall. "Have you ever tried these...*tests* on someone like...like me? Someone without magic?"

He blinked, then his lips curved into a dark smile. "Is someone a little curious?"

I flicked my tongue along my bottom lip, and his eyes tracked the motion. Lowering my voice, I said, "What if I was?"

He laughed, a low, thunderous rumble that sounded like a threat. My heart beat rapidly in my chest, sensing the danger in his proximity. But I held my ground. I was so close to something more. Something we could *use.*

"We haven't been able to test that theory before. There aren't many creatures without magic like you running around here." His thumb brushed my jaw, and I forced myself not to cringe. "But I have something new I've been working on."

"Can I see it?" I whispered.

He laughed again. "You really are a curious thing, aren't you? What was that you once told me?" His gaze pinned me to the wall. "I could be *convinced.*"

His breath smelled like rancid wine. The feel of him crowding around me on all sides made my hand ball into a fist so hard, my nails dug small crescent moons into my palm.

I knew what he meant. What a man like him *wanted*. And if I wanted to help all those innocent people, I didn't think I had a choice.

I steeled my spine and closed my eyes, tilting my head up to press my lips to his.

For someone who spoke of taking what they wanted, Scarven was surprisingly meticulous. He moved like he expected this—like he planned for it. One hand came to the back of my neck, angling my head up almost painfully far as he kissed me.

I fought the urge to recoil when his hand wrapped around my hair. I winced as he tugged harder, the force pushing my back further into the wall. Rough edges of rocks dug into my skin through my shirt. My palms lay flat against the stone, my nails grasping at it as if I could claw my way out.

Not for the first time, I realized how alone we were in this tunnel. How far we were from either exit.

My heart pounded faster in fear. I thought back to that night in Nox's tent, the way he'd lost control and pinned me to the floor. Even with the hint of a lethal dragon in his eyes as he'd caged me in, I'd felt no fear. I'd never been afraid of him. The most powerful creature in this empire, and I knew he wouldn't hurt me.

I wish he were here.

The thought of Nox made the pressure in my chest peak. Panic crawled up my throat as I struggled to get breath in my lungs. I couldn't do this. I couldn't—

I broke away, panting, using all my willpower to stop my body from shaking. I opened my mouth when Scarven's thumb came up to press into my bottom lip.

"As much as I want to continue this," he murmured, eyes hooded, "there are things I must see to after the fights." Straightening the collar of his shirt, he took a step away and cracked his neck, slipping back into his composed persona.

"My men will be waiting for you at the entrance of the tavern to take you back to the manor." He wrapped a hand around the side of my neck, pressing his thumb into the column of my throat. I held my breath, not daring to move.

"I'll see you tomorrow, Selena." He turned on his heel and strode back down the tunnel.

I waited until I could no longer hear his footsteps before I sank to the ground and buried my head in my hands.

39

D: *Just checking in. First full day in the books.*

N: *Anything new today?*

D: *No, I didn't even see him. I was too nervous to leave the room for long. Reminds me of another tower I was once kept in...*

N: *Hilarious.*

D: *Yours is prettier.*

N: *Don't forget bigger, darling.*

D: *Whatever you say.*

N: *Good night, Devora.*

———

D: *So, I was thinking...*

N: *This ought to be good.*

D: *What if S knows I was behind the rescue mission? What if he's biding his time, making me think I'm safe, but he's slowly poisoning me with tea and chocolate scones, and his maid is planning to drown me in my morning bath?*

N: *How many chocolate scones have you had this morning?*

D: *That's irrelevant.*

D: *Six. A girl's gotta eat.*

D: *Just make sure everyone there is safe. Please.*

N: *Of course, Devora. We're all fine. He can't find us.*

———

D: *Still nothing suspicious there?*

N: *It's been five hours.*

D: *Well, I'm bored. I tried getting into a couple of abandoned rooms, but his guards stopped me. I feel useless.*

N: *It's only your second day there. Have you seen S yet?*

D: *No. He still hasn't come. Neither my sneaking around skills NOR my immense powers of seduction have come in handy yet. Maybe I should seduce the guards...*

N: *Trust me, I've tried that before.*

D: *Are you sure it's not safe to use my shadows? I've been wanting to practice shadow melting.*

N: *Because that's exactly what we need—a novice Shadow Wielder accidentally melting into a room full of guards ready to kill you.*

D: *Aww, it almost sounds like you care.*

N: You made a promise. I haven't forgotten about that drink, darling.

N: Still alive?

D: Yes, sorry...I fell asleep early. You're up late.

N: Are you picturing me in bed?

D: Does that line actually work on anyone?

N: You'd be surprised.

N: Can't sleep, that's all.

D: Is it the nightmares?

N: They've been getting worse. It's just...everything going on. It feels like we're running out of time. Like we're on the verge of something big, but it keeps moving out of our grasp.

D: Have you ever talked to anyone about the dreams?

N: No. Not many know I have them.

D: Well...I do. So you might as well talk to me.

D: If you want.

D: You don't have to.

N: They're mostly visions of memories. I see things like my father's death, my sister and I when we were children, and the woman I once loved being killed. It's always the same, over and over.

D: I'm sorry, Nox.

D: What happened to her? The woman you loved?

N: It was a long time ago. We escaped S together, but he found us. Tracked us down and killed her so I'd go back with him.

D: Fates, Nox. I'm so sorry. He's a monster.

N: That's what he does. Takes those I care about and ruins them. It's why I can't let anyone get too close. Not since her.

D: I get it. But it doesn't mean it's always going to end that way. You deserve to be happy again.

N: Feeling sorry for your ruthless captor?

D: We both know that's never what you were, Nox.

D: Sleep well. I'll check in tomorrow.

———

D: That's it, if he doesn't show up today, I'm jumping out this window.

N: Good morning to you, too.

D: The suspense is driving me crazy. I need him to either kill me or give me something to do before I rot in here.

N: Not funny.

D: Sorry. I just don't do well with this. Feeling purposeless. Like I can't do anything to help. I know you're all waiting on me to find something.

N: I'd rather you be safe than efficient, Devora.

D: Distract me. What have you been working on?

N: Silas is down to his last bit of fatesprig. He's been trying to run magical tests without using it on anyone, since we don't know what effects it'll have, but it's not working. He's out of ideas. I'm thinking about letting him use it on me.

D: *That sounds like a terrible plan.*

N: *Never stopped me before, darling.*

D: *Such an inspiration to rebellious souls everywhere.*

———

D: *S just showed up. He's taking me somewhere tonight. Don't wait up for me; it might be late.*

N: *I'll be up. Stay safe.*

40
NOX

"Y ou're certain you want to try this tonight, Nox?" Silas asked as he pushed his glasses up the bridge of his nose.

"For the last time, *yes,*" I said. "You're running out of the fatesprig Devora brought, and we're getting nowhere. We need to try it on a human subject."

Next to Silas, Tessa crossed her arms, her black braids swishing against her wrists. "And you're sure this sudden demand to put your life on the line isn't because of something else? Something like, oh, I don't know—your inability to protect a certain redhead from danger and needing to grasp control in other areas of the mission?"

I blinked at her. Across the workshop, Arowyn snorted. "Stop being rational, Tessa. We don't do that here," the Strider said.

Kieran and Everett were on patrol duty and watching the children's wing, respectively. Tonight, it was just Tessa, Arowyn, Silas, and myself. Which may or may not have been why I decided to spring this on our Alchemist now, when the two most likely to convince me of my brashness were otherwise occupied.

It wasn't even "brash," honestly. This was practical. The next logical step in our testing. It had nothing to do with Devora.

I thought I felt the magical parchment burn in my pocket, and I reached for it so quickly, I cracked the arm of the chair.

False alarm. Nothing was there.

Tessa raised an eyebrow but kept her mouth shut.

Devora's last message said Scarven had finally come for her, after three full days and four nights of silence from him. She'd been so worried he'd discovered our hand in the rescue operation at the Hollow. I'd done everything I could to ease her fears, but truthfully, I was scared too. Scarven had a reason for everything he did. Every move he made. If he invited her to stay with him and then ignored her for half a week, that meant something.

My worst fears threatened to break the surface over the last couple of days. Fears that he had somehow traced Devora back to *me*. Sage's limp body appeared in my mind over and over again, every night when I slept.

But lately...Devora's had started to replace it.

She wasn't supposed to mean anything to me. She *couldn't* mean anything. Because those who did wound up dead.

I needed to keep my mind off it. So, human test subject it was. I just wasn't going to tell Tessa she was right.

"I trust you, Silas," I said, ignoring Tessa's glare. "We need to see what this stuff does. If we have a baseline, we can figure out how to counteract it." I settled back into the chair and nodded to the needle carved from bone that rested on Silas's work table. "Ready when you are."

"This is ground fatesprig soaked in a base liquid of spring water. I then boiled it to get rid of impurities and made it into this tincture." He waved the needle in the air. "Scarven's Alchemist could be adding all sorts of potions we aren't aware of, but this will give us its purest interaction. I have no idea what the reaction will be, Nox. I can't promise your safety."

Clearing his throat, he glanced at me again, waiting to see if I would object. When I stayed quiet, he came out from behind his work table. His protective leather gloves were smooth to the touch as he knelt to my side and turned my arm over. He pressed his thumb down hard over the crook of my elbow, then lowered the tip of the needle.

Before it broke the skin, he paused. "Nox, I—"

"Just do it," I said through gritted teeth.

He plunged the needle into my skin. I watched as the dark green liquid slowly pushed into my bloodstream.

Everyone held their breath. At first, I felt nothing. Barely even a pinch from the needle. And then—

Pain.

Blinding, ripping, piercing my body like a thousand knives embedded in my skin.

Fire.

Racing, burning, cleaving a path of molten lava through my veins.

It wasn't simple *heat.* It was as if every cell in my body was being scoured clean. Burned straight through until nothing was left.

My vision fractured from the pain, edges graying as I clenched my teeth together to avoid crying out. I doubled over and fell from the chair. My knees crashed into the ground, my fingers balling into fists, fighting off the current of fire flooding them. I inhaled sharply as I watched the veins in my forearm bulge. They quickly pulsed against my tan skin, a green so dark, it was like rot spreading.

My dragon recoiled in my chest.

Then it screamed.

I let out a roar, throwing my head back as my chest thrust forward.

My magic was trying to fight it. I could feel it twisting around the intruding force, a battle taking place in my blood. All I could think was pain. All I could see was red. It tore through me, shredding my magic, scraping every ounce of power from my body and leaving the edges raw.

I fell forward, barely holding myself up as I convulsed. Bile crept up my throat. I vomited, my stomach doing everything it could to expel the toxin, but it didn't matter.

Something inside me snapped.

I let out another scream through clenched teeth as I sank to the floor. After what felt like an eternity but could have only been seconds, the pain slowly morphed to something else.

Hollow. Numb. Like acid dripping into an empty shell where my magic, my *dragon*, once lived.

But it was gone.

41

NOX

I rolled onto my back and panted, staring up at the ceiling as my vision came back. The world was blurry and out of focus. Everything felt sore, every bone and muscle now brittle and tender. When the roaring of blood in my ears calmed, I could finally hear the voices.

"Nox, can you hear me?"

"Holy Fates. What just happened?"

"Here, drink this. Please, Nox." Silas held the back of my neck and pressed a vial to my lips, and I struggled to swallow the contents. Warm liquid rushed down my throat. "Carnation, flea-wort, and ginger—for pain relief and strengthening," he said in his panicked voice.

My head fell back on the ground with a thud. I groaned and blinked several times, trying to orient myself when all I felt was numb.

"It—it took away my magic," I finally rasped. My lips were dry, and my insides felt like they were about to break off.

And my dragon was *gone*.

I'd experienced magic suppression before. Magic only existed within the borders of the Veridian Empire, so once you left the boundaries, it disappeared. When I traveled to Mysthelm, it was as if someone had taken my magic and shoved it inside of a box, leaving a couple of holes to breathe so it didn't suffocate but was entirely inaccessible.

But this fatesprig...

This didn't just stuff my dragon half in a box. This *annihilated* it.

My breaths came out quick as I clutched my hair, panic overwhelming me.

What had I done?

It was *gone*, my magic was gone—I couldn't feel it, not a single spark.

This couldn't be happening. This couldn't be real. I didn't know how to live without my dragon half—the other part of me, my missing piece.

I staggered to my feet and shoved the chair out of my way, clawing at veins that had turned dark green. I crashed into the work table. I was blind, raging, unable to think straight as I lunged for any potion or herb Silas kept out.

"Nox, stop!" a distant voice said. Tessa, maybe. I didn't care.

Fingers trembling, I dropped the first potion bottle I could find. It crashed to the table and shattered into a hundred pieces. I gripped the edge of the wood to fight off another wave of nausea.

"Nox, please, sit down—I can find something to help, if you'll simply tell me what—" A hand landed on my arm as Silas spoke, and I wrenched myself free. The motion made me lose my balance. I fell to the floor and landed on my knees.

My shoulders sagged as my chest heaved. It was like I couldn't get enough air. Like I couldn't do anything to fill the void my magic had left.

It hurt. Everything hurt.

This was what Scarven had put countless innocent people through.

"Was that Nox I heard? What's—" A familiar voice stopped itself at the entrance, but I didn't bother to turn. Footsteps and voices drew nearer until Everett sank to the floor in front of me.

Those green and gray eyes stared back, dark forehead scrunched in concern.

"You idiot," he said quietly. "Did you take it? The fatesprig?"

I couldn't move. All I could do was blink slowly in response.

"Did it make your veins turn a different color?" he prompted.

I swallowed, nails scraping down my throat. "Yes," I croaked. "Green."

"Was it like it killed your magic?"

I nodded, unable to say the words.

To my surprise, he looked *relieved*. "It's not permanent," he said. "Are you listening, Nox? Your magic will come back. The fatesprig just needs to get out of your system."

It's not permanent.

Your magic will come back.

I blinked several times, his words sinking in breath by breath. "How do you know?"

"I've been talking to some of the kids, helping them work through what happened in Scarven's cells," Everett explained. "Several of them described an injection he gave them. It turned their veins green, and then it was the worst pain they've ever experienced. They said it completely took their magic away. But after a day or two, it came back."

Slowly, painstakingly slowly, the panic began to subside. It was just temporary. My dragon half wasn't gone forever. It would come back.

My heart returned to its normal speed, no longer threatening to jump out of my throat. Even the pain dulled to a mere whisper of the excruciating fire it was before.

My back sagged into the side of the chair I'd overturned. I leaned my head against it and closed my eyes. "Don't ever let me do that again," I mumbled.

The entire room let out a collective breath. "I didn't *let* you do it in the first place, you stubborn old man," Tessa said, but her voice was still filled with concern. She pressed a hand to my forehead. "You're burning up."

I ignored her, my mind now latching on to something else. "He did this to them. He's *still* doing it to whoever he has down there in his labs. To my sister. All of those people going through so much pain..." I shook my head. "We have to stop him."

"We will," Tessa said firmly. "But right now, you need to rest. It's almost midnight, Nox. And you look exhausted."

"No. Devora's still out there with him. I told her I'd stay up for her nightly check-in. I have to make sure she's safe."

"Give me the parchment. I'll monitor it, and I can come get you the second she sends something," Tessa offered, holding out her hand.

I instinctively reached for the familiar wrinkled edges in my pocket. "I won't be able to sleep. I can—" I cut myself off when my fingers met the paper.

It was hot.

I jerked my head down and snatched it from my pocket so fast, the room spun. She'd messaged me. I must not have felt it during the fatesprig episode. What if she needed me?

A breath left me when I saw what was on the paper.

There were no words. In fact, it was empty, save for two dark marks in the very center. They were small and slightly faded, nearly blending into the weathered parchment, but it had been enough to trigger the spell. And it definitely hadn't been there before.

"Silas," I held the paper out to him, "what is this? An ink blot?"

He adjusted his glasses and bent to take a closer look. "Any substance that touches the surface can be transmitted, not only ink or charcoal. Water, blood, sweat—"

"Tears," I finished. "What if she's been crying? Or bleeding?"

Blood roared in my ears, but for an entirely different reason than the fatesprig. Something was wrong.

I grabbed my piece of charcoal and hastily scribbled a message.

Are you alright?

I didn't think I breathed for the entire minute it took her to respond.

We need to talk.

That same panic trickled back into my gut, spreading through my numb muscles and coating them in another layer of dread. Visions ran across my mind, each one more horrible than the last.

What happened? Are you safe? Did he hurt you?

I would rip every limb from his body, with my magic or not, if he harmed her. This was my fault. I'd pushed her to do this. I'd made her feel inadequate, useless, banishing her to that tower until she resorted to *this* to earn our trust.

This incredible, brave, beautiful woman who was hollowed out by those who simply wanted to use her as a means to an end—and now *I* was one of those people, and I hated myself. I hated—

"Nox," Tessa said on a soft exhale, drawing my attention back to the parchment.

It's not me. It's your sister.

42

NOX

My fingers went numb, the charcoal slipping from my grip. *Vera.*

I got to my feet and righted the overturned chair, then sank into the cushion. In the blink of an eye, Arowyn appeared at my side with a glass of water.

"Thought you could use this," she said.

"Let's give him some space," Tessa added. "Let us know what you find out, Nox," she said as she, Arowyn, Everett, and Silas crossed to the exit, leaving me with several lingering, concerned stares.

I put the charcoal back to the parchment.

> *Tell me everything.*

I waited for her response with my head in my hands, occasionally sipping the cool water and letting it cut a path down the fire still in my veins. As her handwriting finally appeared, I downed the last of it in one gulp.

> *D: S is running an underground fighting ring. He took me there tonight.*

N: A fighting ring? We've never heard anything about that. Who does he have fighting?

D: The prisoners, Nox. He's using his prisoners.

My stomach soured, nausea swirling and crawling up my throat. Before I could respond, more messages came through, one after another as she told the whole story.

It was so awful. They were all so scared. I can't stop seeing them in my head. They don't want to be there, but he makes them. Everybody was cheering and betting on the winner as they killed each other, and I just had to stand there and watch. But then they brought out the final two fighters, and I realized who it was. It was HER. It was Vera. S said she was his prized possession because she has all six magic types, and I remembered you telling me about her, and...she looks like you. She's alive. He's changed her somehow, done something to control her, but she's still here.

I didn't respond. I was a mess of pain and frayed edges. I read her words over and over until they faded into the parchment.

My sister. She'd seen Vera.

My hand burned as another message came through, along with more tear marks.

I'm sorry this is how you have to find out. I didn't know how to tell you.

My sister was alive, and if she was in these underground rings, that meant she was strong enough to fight. That was more hope than I'd had in years. But Devora said Scarven was controlling her. Who knew what he'd done to brainwash her?

It made more bile creep up, the acid already on my tongue, but Devora's next message stopped me cold.

I think I've convinced him to take me to the Hollow. I can find out where he keeps her.

Her scrawl here was messy, uneven, as if her arm was shaking as she wrote. She was scared. And yet, she was doing this anyway. For me. An ache formed in my chest, different from the torment the fatesprig brought.

Devora, you don't have to do this. You've done more than enough. We'll find a way into these fighting rings and get him from there.

I waited, a plan already forming in my thoughts. This could be our way in. She didn't have to keep putting herself into danger.

D: He said they're never in the same place twice, and they change the date and time constantly. I don't know how to track it. You can't find out when the next one will be, not unless you're invited. There's no other way, Nox.

N: Whatever you promised him, whatever you did to convince him, we can stop this. You can come home.

I *needed* her to come home. I couldn't lose someone else.

Her next response took so long to come through, I was about to message her again. Until—

It's already done. Don't worry about me, I can take care of myself.

Anything else I sent, any quickly-scrawled, frantic message I wrote, she ignored. The woman was as stubborn as ever. I wanted to break out of these walls, fly to Scarven's mansion, and force her to listen to me.

But then I remembered—I had no magic. No way to protect her. No way to get her back.

All I could do was wait. Wait for the fatesprig to leave my system, wait for Devora to return, wait for my sister to be rescued.

And Fates, that made me a prisoner all over again.

43

DEVORA

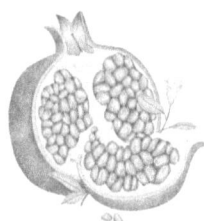

The knock at my door nearly made me jump out of my skin. Everything made me skittish lately. For good reason. I was living one hour to the next in this creepy mansion of doom, worried I was either going to be arrested one second or ambushed the next.

I could still see those young men and women fighting in that ring from last night, could still smell their blood and hear the roar of the crowd. I could still feel Scarven's hands winding their way up my back, his lips pressed to mine and his hot breath in my ear.

I wanted to burn the memories away. I wanted to wipe every touch from my skin.

"Ready, Selena?" Scarven's rich voice called out. In another life, it would've been the kind of voice I was drawn to. Deep, authoritarian, smooth like honey. But in *this* life, it made me shudder. It made me miss a different voice. One just as deep, but with an arrogant playfulness, a roughness around the edges I wanted to fall into.

"Coming." I hastily tucked the enchanted parchment under my pillow and laced up my boots. When I opened the door, I found Scarven waiting for me in black slacks and a crisp button-down shirt. His freshly trimmed beard was shaved close to his jawline, and those dark eyes sparkled back at me with a hint of desire and malice all in one.

"Are we going somewhere tonight?" I asked.

He raised an eyebrow. "I was under the impression you wanted to see more of my passion projects, as I call them."

That term made me sick. But I pasted on a smile and took his outstretched arm. "I didn't think it would be so soon."

"You gave me a very compelling reason not to wait." He covered my hand with his as we walked. It felt like a clamp. Something holding me down, something to claim me as *his*.

He guided me down the corridors of the guest wing, always staying half a step ahead, subtly pulling me along. We walked through the main entrance hall, down several more corridors, and up even more sets of stairs. Just when I was beginning to think he was taking me in circles, the stairs emptied onto a new landing.

We stood before a wide hallway, with a huge tapestry of a lion staring me straight in the face. By the look of the gold-plated doors and crown moldings, the lush rug running down the length of the corridor, and the two lion-masked guards at the top of the stairs, I would bet anything this was Scarven's personal wing.

My stomach immediately clenched. Why was he bringing me to his bedchambers? This couldn't possibly be where he kept his "tests." I tried to stop my heart from hammering in my chest, even though I knew he could hear it from a mile away.

"Relax, love," he said. "I want to show you something."

He strode straight to the tapestry of the lion at the end of the hall. I followed hesitantly, my trepidation growing with every step.

He stood, staring at the image with his head cocked in a feline way. Then he took a small blade from his pocket, swiped it along his palm, and pressed his bloody hand to the lion's maw.

I blinked. What just happened?

Before I could ask, the lion's mouth started to grow.

Shaking my head, I rubbed my eyes to clear away the vision. But when I looked again, its mouth had only gotten wider. It stretched and elongated, and I felt my face contort with both disgust and intrigue at the disfigured lion. Within seconds, the opening was wide enough to fit a person.

Scarven held out an arm. "After you. Be careful—the first time traveling by portal is quite a shock."

"A what?" I looked at him, then back at the lion's mouth. "I'm supposed to walk through that?"

He chuckled. "It won't hurt you. It's a magical entrance to my underground labs and office. Can't have just anyone waltzing in, now can I?"

I furrowed my brow and looked at the cut on his hand, which was already fading to a faint pink mark. His blood must be what opened this "portal." Why else would he have to cut himself?

That certainly complicated things for coming back. I doubted Scarven went around giving others his blood for fun.

He was waiting for me to enter, so I straightened my shoulders and stepped into the darkness of the lion's mouth.

It was like walking under a waterfall of ice. My breath caught in my throat, my skin so cold, I could barely move. I gasped at the sensation as the portal swallowed me whole, then spat me out onto a rough stone surface. Scarven gracefully appeared at my side, completely unfazed.

"Welcome to the Hollow," he said.

I swallowed hard, trying to hide my shock. *The Hollow*. Not only was there an entrance at the stables, but inside the mansion too—through his private quarters.

We were in some sort of lab. Gray-and-cream marbled stone surrounded us on all sides, with bookshelves and cabinets along every inch of wall space, save for two doors. A large table sat in the center of the room, where a man in a white coat hunched over a notebook and three thin glass vials.

The man straightened at our arrival, and a shiver went down my spine when his eyes met mine. From this distance, they looked pure white, with a small black pupil in the middle. The area around them was rimmed in smudged kohl, making the rest of his fair skin look even more pallid. A mane of black hair billowed around his face and past his chin. He appeared to be in his forties.

"Lord Scarven," he said, his voice quiet and measured. "I see you've brought a guest." His stare never left mine, his features blank as he tilted his head and peered at me. I quickly looked away.

"Malek, this is Miss Selena Nyte, a member of the Mysthelm contingency. Selena, meet Malek Mortep, my lead Alchemist and trusted advisor." Scarven nodded to the Alchemist.

Sure, because why wouldn't the creepy mansion of doom also have a creepy mad Alchemist?

"It's nice to meet you." I inclined my head to Malek.

He simply hummed. "I'm sure we'll be seeing more of each other, Miss Nyte."

Over my dead body.

On second thought, that probably wasn't too far from the realm of possibility.

"Let's leave Malek to his work," Scarven said, taking my arm. "He's developing a special serum for me now. But that's not what I wanted to show you." He turned us to the door on our left, fished a key out of his pocket, and inserted it into the padlock.

Behind the door was another large room, more of an office than a lab. A pine desk was situated against the back wall, with a leather wingback chair pushed into it. Other than that, a bookshelf, and a locked cabinet, the only items in the room were what hung from the walls.

I had to blink to take it all in, tamping down a look of horror.

There were drawings. Dozens and dozens of drawings, diagrams, and charts. Some mere sketches—dark, jagged lines of charcoal—and some were in full color, bright and glaring.

All were of his *experiments.*

A man with his chest cut open and a glowing green heart suspended in the middle.

Flayed skin with runes drawn on the surface.

A diagram of a body strapped to a table with what looked suspiciously like shadows being ripped from the skin by hooks.

A floating head with the eyes sewn shut.

Men, women, and children with burn marks and lacerations spread across their bodies.

Drawing after drawing after drawing, all depicting his *prisoners*. I wanted to vomit. But I could feel him gazing at me, studying me like one of his test subjects. Weighing the results. If I gave *any* undesirable response, my chance to find out more would be gone.

"You've been busy, my lord," I said, refusing to meet his eyes.

"Power takes knowledge, and knowledge takes time. I've always been interested in how our bodies and magic work." He brandished an arm toward the diagrams and charts with pride. "For the past three centuries since the Fates gave us our power, we've been limited, confined to the magic of our respective provinces. Nobody has ever bothered to seek beyond these boundaries. But *who* decides what power we possess? The Fates? Our own blood?" He laughed. "Nobody tells me what magic I can and cannot wield. Not anymore."

I raised an eyebrow at him. "One might think you consider yourself a Fate."

"Not a Fate. Simply a man who knows how to get what he wants."

I took a step closer to the nearest wall. "I never even knew something like this was possible." I forced awe into my tone. "You and your Alchemist can do all of this?"

He nodded. "I'm not too proud to admit that Alchemy may be the most powerful of all. But it's also the most underused. They use their abilities to what, make *tea*? Light fires? Mix their little potions? They have no idea." He shook his head. "We have created entirely new powers with Alchemy. Gone to the edge of mankind and back again, reshaping what it means to be a Veridian. If you can find *just* the right combination, pair it with *just* the right spell, be willing to go *just* a little further than magic permits, then you can do whatever you want. *Be* whoever you want."

A chill swept down my spine as I took in his words, then squinted to read the inscriptions below some of the images.

A teenage boy with symbols carved into each of his limbs—fire, water, a mountain, and wings. The expression on his face was frozen in agony. Beneath it read:

Ten drops of Alchemist blood mixed with fatesprig, dandelion, bay leaf, and blue vervain, injected into a Strider subject. Results of elemental magic test: chaotic, unstable.

There was another, a girl no older than ten, with red veins and pale skin that glowed like the sun was bursting inside of her. The note read:

Ten drops of Lightbender blood infused with vireroot, injected into the bone. Results of latent light magic test: bones now fragile and emitting internal Lightbender magic. Active.

Then one with three subjects, two male and one female, standing hand to hand. The note beneath said:

Linked using bonding spell and injected with three vials of Alchemist blood and crushed ashgrave. Results of coupling test: magical signatures have been forcibly paired. Physical symptoms are duplicated across all test subjects.

On and on it went. Dozens of tests, if not hundreds, all on display like some sort of morbid art gallery.

It was sick. Twisted. The results of a corrupt, cruel mind that would stop at nothing to gain power. To gain *control*. That was what this was—Scarven wanted to control this magic, to be a deity among men. And he took *joy* in it. He reveled in the pain of these people, torturing them and then watching them either die in his lab or in his fighting ring like animals.

I imagined Nox and Everett as one of the images on these walls, and I had to clench my hands at my sides. *They* had been through this. They had worn these chains and suffered in these cells.

I struggled to clear my mind and focus on what I could take away from this to help. There was one piece of long parchment on the wall that caught my eye, with rows and rows of drawings of various herbs. Some I'd heard of, like amaranth and thistle. At the bottom was fatesprig—I recognized the four green leaves with their sharp tips. There were a couple of others next to it that I'd never seen before.

"I don't know some of these names," I said, running a finger along the word "fatesprig" on one of the drawings, then "ash-grave" on the one next to it. "Are they flowers or something?"

"Or something," Scarven said. He came up next to me, his chest brushing my side. He fingered the edge of the fatesprig sketch. "I'm surprised you don't recognize this one."

My heart beat a little faster, paranoia seeping through me. "Why should I?"

"Because it's found in your kingdom."

I blinked. *Right.* "I've hardly left the North Territory of Mysthelm, to be honest. Where does it grow?"

"The island. We learned of its existence only a handful of years ago. It reacts with Veridian blood in a way no other element has before. Just as these do," he added, pointing to the two herbs next to the fatesprig. One was marked ashgrave, and one said vireroot.

"Are these from Mysthelm too?" I asked.

There was that chuckle again. It sounded more and more condescending every time. "Did you think the Veridian Empire and Mysthelm were the only two lands out there for us to draw inspiration from?"

I whirled to face him. I didn't even have to act surprised this time. "I—I don't know. I've heard people allude to there being *more* out there, but not many have explored the rest of the world."

There were whispers of places beyond ours. Uninhabited islands, continents ruled by less sophisticated groups, lost kingdoms outside our realm. But there had hardly been any proof. No records, no communication. For as long as our history could remember, the focus had been on the Veridian Empire and Mysthelm.

Was he saying he'd *been* to these places? That some of his herbs came from there?

His fingers slid from the drawing to my hand. "I didn't think you came here for a geography lesson, Miss Nyte," he murmured, leaning closer.

I closed my eyes and swallowed the lump in my throat. His lips moved down my neck, and I clenched my hand in a fist so tight, I thought I drew blood.

Blood.

An idea hit me. A stupid, reckless idea.

My specialty.

"Can't blame a girl for trying," I said as I wound my arms around his neck and pulled his lips to mine.

When his hands fell to my waist, I slid my tongue along his lips and nipped the bottom one—quick and light, just testing the waters. He responded by seizing the back of my neck, threading his fingers through my hair. I balled my fist in the top of his shirt right as I bit down on his lip again.

Hard.

A copper tang met my tongue.

I gasped and pulled away, wiping my lips with the back of my hand. "I'm so sorry, my lord," I said, feigning embarrassment.

"No need to apologize," he said, already leaning in again. "It's just a little blood."

As his lips met mine once more, a scream rang through the hall, coming from the other side of the door.

"What was that?" I asked sharply.

He glanced at the door with a scowl. "Nothing Malek and I can't deal with." Straightening his shirt, he let out a sigh. "Come, I suppose we better get you back to the main house."

He swiftly led me back into the portal to his private quarters.

He instructed one of his guards to see me to my room, but before he left, he yanked me closer.

His lips found my ear as he said, his voice low and heavy, "This isn't finished, Selena."

A promise. A warning.

It didn't matter. I got what I needed.

When he vanished back to the Hollow, I looked down at the small streak of red on the back of my hand and smiled.

44

DEVORA

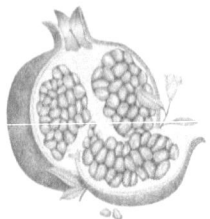

I ran straight for the bathing chambers in my room and carefully wiped the dried blood from my hand with a handkerchief. I had no idea if this would be enough to get someone back through the portal, but it was worth a shot. Then I got out the enchanted parchment to update Nox, describing where the portal to the Hollow was located and how he used his blood to open it.

N: *Convenient, considering Shifters rarely bleed.*

D: *Then it's a good thing you have someone as resourceful as me on the inside.*

N: *What did you do?*

D: *Got some of his blood.*

N: *WHAT?*

D: *Doesn't matter. The point is, I might be able to get through the portal now.*

N: *Devora, you are NOT going back there. And how the Fates did you get his blood? Did you stab him?*

D: Not exactly. I bit his lip.

It took several minutes for a response to come through after that. I toyed with the edge of the handkerchief with Scarven's blood, suddenly nervous about what Nox would think. The idea of kissing Scarven—of kissing *anyone*—and having to tell Nox about it made me feel sick.

When the paper heated, I scrambled to grab it from the bed.

What did you find in the Hollow?

I chewed on my bottom lip. I didn't want to describe everything to him or make him relive what he'd been through all those years ago. I would just give him an overview.

D: I only saw two rooms. The first one was a lab of some sort, with an Alchemist named Malek Mortep. S called him his lead Alchemist. Then he took me to a connected office with records of past experiments. Dosages, ingredients, results, things like that. Fatesprig isn't the only outsourced herb he uses. There are two others called ashgrave and vireroot.

N: I've never heard of them. I asked Silas, and he hasn't either.

D: That's because they're not found here or in Mysthelm. They get them from somewhere else. He didn't say where.

N: Wonderful, more for us to destroy.

D: N

Heavy footsteps in the hallway made me pause mid-word. I stuffed the cloth in my pocket and shoved the parchment and charcoal under my pillow right as the door swung open.

"Selena." Scarven smirked as he shut the door with his heel. The soft, deliberate click felt like a key locking. "You're still awake."

That same scent of rancid wine floated around me. I swung my legs off the bed, trying to calm my racing pulse. I felt the paper heat with a message beneath the pillow, but I didn't dare react. "I didn't expect to see you again tonight, my lord."

He stalked toward me with a hungry gleam in his eyes. "We have unfinished business." He stood between my legs, his large frame towering over me, so tall I had to crane my neck to meet his gaze.

Something felt different this time. Darker. His eyes were a wild frenzy of lust, control, and anger all in one. A terrified weight sank in my stomach when his hand came out to clutch the back of my neck.

"Has anyone ever told you how beautiful your hair is, Selena?" he whispered, my false name coming out as a hiss. He yanked my head back even further. "Like the blood of a fresh kill."

He captured my mouth, barely giving me time to breathe. His lips were rougher than usual. Demanding. Threatening. I gasped for breath, my fingers grappling on the sheets, struggling to keep up with him.

When he shoved my back down onto the bed, my blood froze.

He unbuttoned the sleeves of his shirt and rolled them up to his elbow. "You look good on your back, Miss Nyte," he said with a chuckle. "Almost as good as you'd look on your knees."

I slowed my breaths, matching them to the rhythm of my heart as I kept my gaze on the ceiling just beyond his head. I could feel my shadows writhing beneath my skin. Every instinct told me to use them. To fight back. To run.

But I would be endangering so many more people if I blew this cover. I couldn't let him find the Keep. I couldn't let him get to Nox.

His hands went to his waist and pulled at the belt buckle. He whipped it off in one smooth motion, then leaned back down to wrap it around my wrists. I sucked in a breath when he yanked them tight above my head.

Something hot flared next to my thigh.

Scarven's brow furrowed. He looked at the pillow, and my stomach dropped.

The parchment.

I couldn't breathe.

He lifted the pillow, his eyes locking onto the paper with what I knew would be another message from Nox.

"Well, well, well," he murmured, his voice icy. "It seems the lamb might not be so innocent after all." He flashed the parchment at me.

Devora, if you don't respond in five minutes, I'm coming to get you.

Crumpling it, he tossed it off the bed and gripped my throat in his large hand. "And who is this knight in shining armor, *Devora?*" he asked, drawing out my real name. He studied me coldly as he cocked his head. "Might it be my dear younger brother?"

"My lord, I—" My words ended in a choke as he tightened his hold.

"Let's see what else you've been lying about, shall we?"

Before I knew what he was doing, I felt a sharp prick on my arm.

I let out a yell as my magic instantly reacted. It thrashed and beat against every cell of my body until it burst from my skin in a billowing cloud of shadows, twisting around both of us.

He snarled, "*Shadow Wielder.*"

He pressed me deeper into the bed by my throat, cutting off my circulation. I tried to kick, but the full weight of his bottom half was on top of me. With his other hand, he reached into his pocket and pulled out something small and sharp.

Another needle.

"Did you think you could trick me, love?" he hissed. "Play me for a fool?" He rested the tip of the second needle against my neck. "I've known what you were up to since you left your cloak at my stables, reeking of dragon filth."

I jerked my head. I willed my shadows to curl at my fingers, shoving against his hold, but he was stronger.

With a growl, he said, "Now we'll see how my brother's play-thing looks strung up on my wall and screaming my name."

He plunged the needle into my neck, and the world went black.

45

NOX

"She still hasn't responded."

"She probably just fell asleep, Nox. It's late," Tessa assured me.

"But we were in the middle of a conversation."

"Then *perhaps* she doesn't hang off every word you say. You're not as riveting as you think you are."

I glared at my third. I knew Tessa was trying to ease my anxiety about Devora's sudden silence, but it wasn't working.

Plus, I didn't know what she was talking about. I was incredibly riveting.

"Believe it or not, I tend to agree with Tessa on this," Kieran said from the couch in the workshop.

Tessa raised an eyebrow. "Well, would you look at that."

"You cannot simply go bursting into Scarven's manor on a whim," Kieran continued, propping an ankle on top of his other knee.

"Especially since your magic hasn't come back," Tessa added.

"You've both made your point, thank you," I muttered. I ran my fingers through my hair, my eyes drifting down to the parchment every few seconds. Waiting. Pleading. Hoping for a response.

N

That was the last thing she sent. Then, nothing.

Tessa was right. And it *had* taken me a while to respond right before this. She could've just gotten tired of waiting and fallen asleep. It was late, and she'd had a long few days.

Kieran stood and walked to my desk, resting his hands on top of it before gently saying, "She is *not* Sage. She's going to be fine."

I let out a breath. She may not be Sage, but Scarven was still Scarven.

"Let's just wait until tomorrow, okay?" Tessa said. "That was the plan. She checks in every evening, and she already checked in tonight. We don't need to sound the alarms yet. Once we do, there's no going back."

"I know this is difficult," Kieran said when I anxiously twisted the ring on my little finger. "You bear the weight of so much, Nox. You feel that every decision is on your shoulders, and yours alone. If you decided to rain fire down on Scarven's mansion this very night, I would go with you to the end. But you must realize the precarious nature of this mission. If we react rashly, we could tip it over the edge."

I met his gaze, my talon-less finger tapping against my desk. He was right. He was one of the only ones who could force rational words through my chaotic mind. I gave a quick nod, and both his and Tessa's shoulders relaxed.

But as they turned to leave, I said, "There's only so much more waiting I can do. On any of it." I slowly got to my feet, fists resting on top of the desk. "A storm is coming, and we have to be ready to face it."

Tessa's lips thinned into a resolute line. "We will be, Nox. We will be."

––––––

I TOSSED and turned in my bed, fighting sleep and the nightmares that awaited me. I eventually gave up and, like most nights, sought solace in my blocks of wood. But my fingers were clumsy. I nicked my skin countless times, watching the blood bead and drop to the floor as my slow magic started to come back.

It had been over twenty-four hours since Devora's last message. The fatesprig was starting to wear off, and my powers trickled in little by little. Like hot oil dripping through my veins, filling the cracks its absence had left.

And it was impatient. Restless. Waiting.

My dragon half yawned somewhere deep within me, slowly rising from the dead. The ghost of talons scraped against my mind, its maw opening as a fire burned low in my gut.

It craved retribution. It craved bloodshed. And it craved *her*.

Here in these dark, quiet hours, I could let that part of myself admit my own desires. Admit that she was no longer just another member of the Order. Admit that she had come to mean something more to me.

And she was in trouble. I could feel it.

Tossing the half-formed figurine of a pomegranate to the side, I tugged a shirt over my head and left for the workshop. It was a little after midnight, and I knew Silas often worked late. He claimed his Alchemist magic was strongest under the moon.

Sure enough, when I strode into the room, I saw his brown-and-gray hair bent low over his table, those familiar glasses perched on the tip of his nose.

He looked up with a raised eyebrow. "Need another sleeping draught, Nox?"

I shook my head. "I'm not sleeping tonight."

His features turned grim. "You're going after her."

There was no use lying. "I need something to make my magic stronger. Do you have a potion? Some sort of spell?"

My question seemed to catch him off guard. His wise eyes grew larger behind his glasses. "Nox, that is a dangerous request."

I realized what it sounded like I was asking for. *Who* I sounded like. "No, no, not like *him*. Just...something to make my magic come back quicker. It's there; I can feel it, but it's not at full strength yet."

"And that's why you shouldn't take this on by yourself. Let's make a plan, get a team together," Silas urged. "Busting down doors and blowing up buildings isn't always the route to go."

"I'm not risking any of you getting hurt." I crossed the room to the target practice area where we kept extra weapons and examined a pair of knives before shoving them back in their sheaths. "This is my doing. My responsibility."

"You Shifters and your hot heads," he said with a sigh. "You don't even know where she *is*. She could be—" He cut himself off, and I turned to see what the pause was for.

"Silas, what is it?" I moved closer to him. His eyes darted across his stash of herbs, blinking rapidly as he rubbed his fingers against his apron.

His gaze finally fell to me. "I think I can find her."

"How?" I demanded.

"Can you get me something of hers? A strand of hair, or—or something she wore. Something that would have her signature."

I didn't bother responding. I stormed out of the workshop and headed straight for her chambers, already tuned into her scent. Wrenching the drawers of her dresser open, I was flooded with the smell of pomegranates and salt and sunshine. It opened up an ache in my chest, a yearning that threatened to break me.

I grabbed the first thing my hand touched—a gray sweater, the one she often wore when I visited her in the tower.

"Will this work?" I asked as I burst back into the workshop.

Silas took the sweater with one hand, his other busy grinding several herbs with a pestle. He laid it on the table, took the mortar, and sprinkled the crushed leaves onto the top of the sweater. An earthy, musty scent mixed with something spicy hit my senses.

Silas reached into the pockets of his apron and pulled out a piece of flint, then struck the side of a steel blade against it until it sparked. The small fire caught onto the bed of leaves, licking and spreading along the fabric of her wool sweater.

"*Vidia,*" he said under his breath.

I surged forward. "What are you—"

Silas held up a hand. "Wait."

I gritted my teeth and balled my fists at my sides. Flames danced in the air, consuming the herbs and sweater. The wool ignited slower than the leaves, the edges of it curling up and blackening under the orange haze. It left behind a dark, brittle ash that scattered as Silas leaned down, gazing in fierce concentration at the smoke.

He inhaled sharply, and I blinked. Where the flickering fire turned into smoke, an image appeared.

All the breath left my lungs.

"Oh, Devora..." Silas's quiet sigh of distress made the vision waver.

There was a flash of red hair, black cuffs on pale skin, steel chains nailed to a cracked stone wall. I gripped the edge of the table and got as close as I could, taking in every detail with sharp focus.

Devora's hands were held above her head by chains staked into the wall. Her arms strained as her body hung limp and her chin rolled along her chest, that fiery hair sagging down one side. Her shoulders were pulled so tight, I thought they were going to pop out of place. A small spot on the exposed side of her neck caught my attention—a red pinprick with dark lines branching from it.

The bastard *injected* her with something.

My dragon fully awoke inside of me, clawing its way to the surface. Talons erupted from my hands and shredded the tabletop. Chunks of wood broke off and fell to the ground, and it took every ounce of control I'd learned in my thirty-three years to force my magic to calm.

The vision showed her sucking in a breath, her neck jolting up when she woke. Dirt and smudged kohl lined her pale face. Her bloodshot eyes were wild as she jerked against her restraints, knees dragging the ground until she found her footing.

"Look who's finally awake," Scarven's muffled voice said.

A shadow appeared in the corner, and Devora's eyes narrowed in on her assailant as her jaw clenched. A spark of pride bloomed in my chest at the savage look on her face.

"Look who's finally figured it out," she snapped back.

There she is.

The shadow stalked forward until the back of Scarven's head came into view. A snarl of rage ripped from my throat.

"Ah, the little lamb has sharp teeth," he said. "That was what I liked most about Miss Nyte. Although, I suppose it's Devora now, isn't it?"

In a flash, he stood before her, clutching her throat in his hand. The workshop was filled with the sound of her scream. My stomach twisted, and it felt like my chest was caving in as red wrath clouded my vision.

But then something else snagged my attention.

On the wall next to her left arm were rows and rows of small scratches etched into the stone. Jagged lines, one after another after another, all down the side of the cell wall.

I knew those lines.

A memory reared to the forefront of my mind.

I was sixteen again, my back against the stone, sweat plastering my shirt to my body. My arm shook as I raised it, shifted the tip of my finger into a talon, and sank it into the wall, breaths laboring with the energy it took just to scratch the small line.

Footsteps pounded outside the cell door, and a second later, it swung open to reveal two lion-masked guards with rope and a needle. They took one look at my half-shifted hand and launched forward, one of them holding my arms back while the other plunged the needle into my leg.

That image vanished as the one of Devora wavered. The flames coming from the herbs began to dissipate.

"It won't last much longer," Silas warned.

"I know where she is," I said, my voice barely more than a growl. "He's holding her in the south tunnels beneath the servants' quarters."

"How do you know?"

I straightened my spine, my eyes never leaving Devora's face. "It's the same place I was kept."

He *knew*. Scarven knew she was working with me. He was sending me a message, keeping her in the same cell I spent years of my life in.

And he knew I would come for her.

It was an obvious trap—another one of Scarven's mind games, him laying the chessboard and letting me take my turn right into his hand.

"He's baiting you, Nox," Silas warned. "Are you sure you want to do this?"

I didn't care. There was nothing in this world that would stop me.

"Wake the others," I said, already charging out of the workshop. "We leave in half an hour."

I'm coming, darling.

46

DEVORA

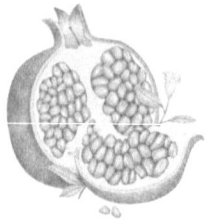

I woke with a gasp.

My eyes fluttered open, pain pounding through my head, my shoulders, my chest. I thrashed my torso back and forth, then sucked in a breath as spasms tore through me.

My arms had been wretched backward and strung up by a pair of cuffs, my entire body now hanging limp from the chains. But that discomfort was secondary to whatever Scarven had injected me with. It was like someone had shoved a dagger into the side of my neck. The spot radiated heat, pulsing down into my chest like a white-hot brand.

Dragging my legs along the ground, I tried to get to my feet and take some of the strain off my shoulders. I could barely support myself. My muscles felt as if they'd been beaten to a pulp and left as noodles.

It was safe to say the mission was compromised.

Terror gripped me, sluggish at first as my mind tried to catch up with what had happened. Scarven knew I was spying on him, *and* that I was working with Nox. Did he know about the Keep?

I let out a ragged sob as visions of what he might do to all of them raced across my mind.

It's my fault. It's my fault. It's my fault.

My chance to do something good, to prove myself, and I'd messed everything up.

I took in my surroundings. I was in a stone cell with iron bars allowing me a view of the dark hallway outside. If I listened closely, I could hear echoes of groans and footsteps from further down.

A shadow appeared outside the iron bars, one I'd begun to recognize easily.

"Look who's finally awake." Scarven's voice slithered over me as he turned a key in the padlock and slipped inside the cell. One of his masked lackeys followed close on his heels.

I steeled my nerves and stood straighter, shoving away the fear. He *wanted* me to be scared. He wanted to break me down piece by piece until I was trembling at his feet, like every other person he forced beneath him.

Well, I wasn't like every other person. And I'd *die* before I kneeled for this man.

"Look who's finally figured it out," I said between grunts as I struggled against the chains.

Scarven drew nearer with a chuckle. "Ah, the little lamb has sharp teeth. That was what I liked most about Miss Nyte. Although, I suppose it's Devora now, isn't it?"

I swallowed but stayed silent, holding his gaze.

He narrowed his eyes and lashed out a hand. His fingers wrapped around my throat, his thumb digging into the injection site wound. Before I could control it, a scream slipped from my lips.

"You thought you were so clever," he whispered, hot breath filling my ear. "You and Nox both. Sneaking around my house like a rat, thinking I wouldn't smell your deception. But you made a mistake, didn't you, love?" He ran his nose along my chin until he reached the other side of my face. "That night at my stables when you left your cloak. The destruction had my brother written all over it. He never could control that temper of his."

He had known all this time. It had just been another game to him. Showing me Vera while *knowing* I was working with Nox, letting me see what he was doing to all those innocent people, flaunting his torture in my face.

I let out a whimper when he pressed into the sore spot on my neck again. "He will soon learn that he cannot take what is *mine*."

"I was *never* yours," I croaked out between ragged breaths.

He hummed, then raised two fingers in the air and summoned the silent guard into the room. "Still snapping, even in chains. I wonder how long that spirit of yours will last after I'm through with you." Releasing his grip on my throat, he raised an eyebrow. "Or perhaps you could simply tell me what my brother is up to. You don't need to suffer. Not if you give me what I want."

I took in lungfuls of air, struggling to stay upright as I rasped, "What makes you think I would give you anything?"

Scarven shared a look with the masked guard, and before I could blink, the guard slapped me so hard across the cheek that my head banged into the wall behind me. A ringing formed low in my ears, my cheek pounding as blood filled my mouth.

"Don't make this harder than it has to be, Shadow Wielder," Scarven said.

I spat blood at his feet.

He sighed. "The hard way, then." He motioned to the guard again, who quickly left the cell.

My heart raced. I could only guess what was coming. "Why didn't you just kill me?" I asked. "If you knew I was lying, why let me keep going? Why let me stay in your home?"

"Keep your enemies close, they say," he mused. "And why should I deny myself the pleasures of your company, Devora?" He stepped closer and ran a hand along my neck, leisurely stroking down my chest and hips until he grabbed my backside. When he yanked me against him, I cried out as the chains bit into my arms.

"You may not be a threat, but you're still rather extraordinary," he murmured. "I can see why that brother of mine is so drawn to you."

"That's what this is about, isn't it?" I asked. "Why do you hate him so much?"

"Because he had *everything*," he said with a growl, that carefully curated voice of control beginning to slip.

"He had the life that should have been mine. *I* was Caius Duma's firstborn, yet my mother and I were thrown out with the trash. Do you know what it's like to be shunned by your entire society, simply for what you were born into? To watch your own mother suffer the consequences of her and my father's actions by herself, while he faced no scrutiny, no ire?" He cocked his head as if he were inspecting me.

Then his lips curved into a smirk. "No, you wouldn't, would you? Because your mother died before you could wipe your own spit from your chin."

My chest caved in, the backs of my eyes burning with the effort to hold back a sob.

"I did my research. Born to Malijah and Ceres Sephorne, a pair of gifted but ultimately unremarkable Shadow Wielders. It's a pity, isn't it?" He ran his hand up the bare skin of my back. "Growing up without an identity. Without a past or a purpose."

His guard entered just then, and Scarven finally released me. He looked over at the shiny, sharp objects on the tray in the guard's hand. There were several syringes full of multi-colored serums—black, red, clear, green. Their needles shone in the candlelight, primed and ready to break into my flesh.

"I had *nothing*, Devora. But look at me now." Scarven picked up a blade coated in an oily dark green substance. "I rose from the silence of the shadows to take my rightful place in this empire. I have full control over the *entirety* of Veridian magic."

He brought the blade to my ribs and pressed the tip into my skin, slowly dragging it down. That entire side of my body was lit on fire. I screamed in agony as my shadows themselves were split in two, writhing and shrieking inside my mind.

And then...they went silent. Dead. Gone.

My heart stopped in its tracks. Hopelessness and panic collided in my chest, mixing with the excruciating pain. Was it gone? Had he taken my shadows away? I only just found them, but the thought of losing them forever gutted me completely.

"Do you hear that, Devora?" Scarven asked softly, his voice carrying over the sound of my screams. "Your magic is mine. *You* are mine. I am *inevitable.*"

He removed the dagger from my side, leaving my shirt in tatters. When the pain passed enough for me to think straight, I rolled my neck on my shoulders to meet his gaze.

"You—are—a coward," I said on a gasping breath.

He drove the blade into my thigh.

I let out another guttural shriek. The pain reverberated in my very core, ripping and shredding through more than just skin and muscle.

A small part of me thought that perhaps I deserved this. *This* was the kind of punishment traitors endured. Nox's gilded tower was a mercy.

Nox.

I closed my eyes and tried to picture him. I could almost imagine him kneeling before me in front of the fireplace. His warm hands cupping my cheek, so gentle despite the strength of the dragon living inside him.

I never told him how brave he was. How much I admired him for everything he was doing for his people, how I'd been so wrong about him in the beginning. How he was the kind of man I was proud to stand beside.

I should have told him. Maybe then this wouldn't hurt so much.

As if Scarven knew who I was thinking about, he pulled the dagger from my thigh and leaned in closer. "Do you think your precious Nox is going to come save you now, love?"

I hope he doesn't, I thought to myself. Keeping the rest of them safe was more important than me.

I must have said it out loud, for Scarven smirked at me. "Well, *I* hope he does." He put the dagger back on the tray and grabbed a syringe with red liquid inside, then placed the tip to the same wound on my neck. I gasped as he drove the needle in.

"Because I have a surprise for him."

47

NOX

We moved through the night like wraiths. Tessa in her sleek black and tan jaguar form, Kieran in his brilliant white stag, and me. The dragon.

No longer hidden, but rising like a beacon in the midnight sky. A warning. A promise.

I'm coming for you.

There was no point in deception or concealment anymore. Not when Scarven knew I wasn't his submissive little lapdog. I wanted him to see me coming. I wanted him to *fear*.

My navy wings spread out at my side as I glanced down to find Tessa and Kieran still sprinting along the forest floor beneath me, pushing the limits of their Shifter speed. I'd expected them to tell me I was crazy, to try and convince me to play this smart or simply leave Devora behind for the greater good of the entire Keep.

But to my surprise, my second and third geared up without a single complaint, refusing to let anyone volunteer in their stead.

"Our place is beside you," Kieran had said to me.

"Through flame and ash," Tessa agreed.

A rumble shook the sky, right down to my very bones. I smelled a storm on the horizon—the clouds were laced with a sweet, metallic scent, and a spark of lightning struck to my far left. Within moments, the forest below me expanded into the outskirts of Scarven's manor.

We gave the property a wide berth and circled around to the south side, where the servants' quarters were. This was a fairly regular raid we'd made over the years. The tunnel system on this side of the land held his most commonly used cells. Usually, we broke in undetected, relying on stealth.

Not tonight.

I tucked my wings and dove, extending them at the last second as I breached the tops of the trees and landed with a resounding crash on the open grounds. The earth trembled beneath my feet, tree branches and limbs blowing backward from the force.

Tessa and Kieran bounded from the forest to stand at my side. A dozen guards came rushing out of the manor, some shifting into their animal forms while others wielded weapons of steel, shadow, and light. My rage and power twisted together in my core, rising through my chest.

When the guards charged, I opened my mouth and released my magic.

Dragon fire funneled up my throat and burst from me in a stream of white-hot flames, torching everything in my path. The blaze consumed the guards within a heartbeat. Their ashes scattered in the wind, still echoing with their final cries.

Kieran raced to the servants' quarters and shifted into his human form. Within minutes, the servants who had been inside fled the quarters, only stopping to take in the sight of me before Tessa snapped her teeth in warning. When Kieran came back out, he shot me the "all clear" signal, then darted out of the way.

With a growl, I covered the ground in a single step, my foot landing with another *boom*. I stretched out a wing and swiped it through the servants' quarters, bringing the entire building crumbling to the ground. Broken wood and stone scattered across the clearing, debris thick in the air.

Beneath the rubble rested a wooden door in the center of the ground. I elongated my sharp talons and shredded it from its hinges, exposing a set of stairs leading to the cells below.

A horde of arrows dipped in a green sludge shot from the underground opening. I batted them away with my wing before they could reach Tessa or Kieran, but one of the tips caught the very edge of my wing's underside. I let out a snarl as the dark green substance burned momentarily. *Fatesprig*.

It hadn't been enough to do damage, and my Shifter healing kicked in to banish it. But the distraction allowed other guards to emerge. They shot more of their weapons at me, which merely bounced off my scales. With another roar, I summoned my dragon fire and aimed it at them, smoke rising from my nostrils with each heavy breath.

Their weapons clattered to the ground as their bodies burned to ash.

I turned my snout to Kieran and Tessa, then motioned to the tunnel entrance. Tessa shifted to her human form as the two of them disappeared underground. I took one last look at the mansion and pushed off from the ground with a powerful flap of my wings.

I dove straight for the opening, shifting midair and sliding through the trap door.

A myriad of bodies already littered the bottom of the rickety staircase, courtesy of Kieran and Tessa. I quickly adjusted to the darkness of the tunnel and saw the two of them at the end of the path.

I caught up to them and took the lead. We moved as one, years of conducting raids together allowing us to instinctively know one another's patterns and habits. I stayed on the alert as we stalked forward, my claws half-formed and gleaming, waiting for a sudden attack. But we were met with only silence. No guards, no lion-masked lackeys, no traps.

It was too quiet.

Before long, we reached the start of the cells. The over-whelming scent of piss, sweat, and too many herbs to identify slammed into me, making me grit my teeth against the wave of memories.

I caught Tessa's eye and lifted two fingers, pointing them straight down the hall. She nodded and immediately shifted into her smallest cat form, her lithe figure able to slip between cell bars with ease. While she worked on releasing Scarven's captives, Kieran and I set off searching for Devora.

The halls were quiet, save for the occasional groan or screech of metal coming from behind us, indicating Tessa opening yet another cell.

My eyes slid over to Kieran, who was already looking at me with his lips set in a grim line. "This is far too easy," he hissed.

The hair on the back of my neck rose, suspense snaking through me. If this was a trap, where was the catch?

We stuck close to the stone walls, listening for anything out of the ordinary. As we drew nearer to the hallway with the row of cells I'd once been kept in, my muscles tensed. Even after more than a decade, it was as if my body was preparing for the torment that once awaited me. My Shifter healing made the scars vanish, but I'd never forget each dagger against my skin, each needle driven into my veins, each blow dealt to my flesh.

And now *she* had to endure it too. My Devora.

"Wait." I threw an arm out to stop Kieran. "Do you smell that?"

His nostrils flared, surely smelling the same thing I did. Something...decaying. Riddled with sickly sweet herbs. But it didn't smell *human*...

A scuttling came from further down the tunnel. Distant and quiet at first, and then louder, like several limbs skittering on a hard surface.

Red eyes appeared from the darkness. Tiny, beady little eyes, growing larger and larger by the second. The legs came next, followed by pincers, and—

Kieran cursed right as the first wave of spiders lunged at us.

They were twenty times faster, stronger, and *larger* than any spider I'd ever seen. One of them latched onto my neck. Before its enormous pincer could pierce my skin, I shifted my hand to a claw and shredded through it with a single swipe. Black blood and organs dripped from my talons. More crawled toward my legs, and I kicked them with enough force to send them flying down the hall.

One grabbed on to Kieran's back while another landed at his forearm. As I clawed through the one on his arm, something dark and furry came flying at us from behind. I nearly spun to knock it to the side when I realized it was Tessa. Her teeth sank into the spider at Kieran's back. It immediately let go, its legs flailing as she flung it into the sidewall.

She shifted and gagged, spitting out a thick, black liquid. "That's disgusting," she said with a grimace.

"Well, I don't think you're supposed to eat them," I drawled as I whipped a dagger from my belt and plunged it into another oncoming creature. "Did you get the prisoners out?"

"There weren't many, but I did what I could," Tessa said. I tossed her my dagger, and she sliced through two others before throwing it back to me. "Told them to get aboveground and to the village."

A dozen more spiders came scurrying from the end of the hall, some of them even larger than the last. Behind us, Kieran let out a hurried, "Move!" followed by the sound of pounding hooves.

I flattened my back against the wall right as he charged forward in his white stag form, his long, thick antlers pointing straight ahead. He shook his head back and forth, impaling at least seven of the spiders at the ends of them.

"You know what they say about big antlers," Tessa grunted as she speared one with her smallsword.

"That he's overcompensating for something?" I offered.

Tessa flashed me a feline grin. Faster than I could blink, her arm shot out and grabbed a spider midair as it flew straight toward my chest.

I winked before glancing at Kieran down the hall, where the remaining two were crawling up his hindquarters. My smile faded as one reared its head back, pincers aimed at his flank.

"No!" I shouted. I didn't think. I grabbed my dagger from its sheath and launched it.

It spun through the air, silver gleaming as it found its mark in the spider's head. The creature fell from Kieran's back with a crash.

"Nice throw, brother," a voice called out. The hair on the back of my neck rose.

It wasn't Kieran.

Chains rattled along stone, echoing around me as a torch ignited down the hall. A silhouette came into view. As Scarven stepped out of the shadows, he carried another with him.

"Devora," I choked out, staggering forward. She was on her knees with black cuffs binding her wrists and one around her neck. The skin on her throat and hands was raw. One side of her shirt was shredded, with a thin line of blood trickling from an open wound.

Scarven jerked the chain in his hand, and her body lurched forward. "Looking for this?" he purred.

He was dragging her along on a *leash.*

My control snapped. Blood boiling, my dragon fire rumbled through my chest with blinding rage. But when Devora's eyes caught mine, she frantically shook her head.

Scarven *tsk*ed. "Temper, Nox," he chided. "It must run in the family."

He stared straight behind me, a wicked smile curving on his features.

My stomach dropped as a scent wafted toward me. One I hadn't smelled in *years.* Smoky amber and rose, so achingly familiar, it nearly stopped my heart. But there was something else woven into it now. Something rotten. Poisoned.

I slowly turned. A figure emerged from the shadows at the end of the hall. For a moment, I was a teenage boy again, listening to the sweet laughter of a baby girl as she smiled up at me.

Scarven's voice rang out, "I told you it was time I arranged a visit. Say hello to your sister."

48

NOX

I barely recognized her.

It had only been five years, but gone was my near-sixteen-year-old little sister. In her place was a woman hardened by pain, by time, by whatever horrid things they had done to her.

Her legs were longer, but her frame was thin—too thin, the angles at her cheekbones too sharp and gaunt. Dirty-blonde hair was pulled back with a strap of leather, intertwined with red streaks of dye I'd never seen before. Her once golden eyes, bright and glowing from the power held within her small stature, were dark amber. Cold. Calculated.

But still, they had that defiant spark I'd always known. The one she had when hiding from Scarven's guards at six years old. The one she had when she burned one of my claws off with a beam of light at twelve. The one she had when she was fifteen, and they said we were no longer allowed to see one another.

"Vera," I said on an exhale, stumbling to her. I closed the space between us and took in her bony elbows, the worn, cracked leather of her bodysuit, the black veins at her neck.

I whirled to face Scarven, my snarl echoing down the hall. "What have you done to—"

A strong hand clutched my neck, cutting off my air and turning my words into a choke. Slowly, Vera twisted me to face her once more, nails digging into my skin as she lifted me inch by inch.

"Vera—" I gasped. "It—it's me—"

She simply cocked her head and stared at me.

"It's—Nox," I said, words garbled. "Your—brother."

Something red glinted in her dark gold eyes. "I have no family."

She thrust her elbow back and threw me forward. I soared past Kieran and Tessa and into the sidewall of the tunnel, my head bashing into the stone. Rocks crumbled around me as dust filled the air. A spike of pain shot down my spine, but I gritted my teeth and forced myself out of the rubble.

The air around her shimmered as she vanished from down the hall and reappeared before me in the blink of an eye.

"*I'm* your family, Vera," I said, forehead pinched as I took a step toward her. She didn't move. Didn't speak. Didn't seem to *breathe*. Simply held my stare with that empty look on her face. When I got close enough, I reached forward, slowly, slowly, to cup my hand around her sallow cheek.

There was a blur of shadow, and her fingers clasped mine, glowing bright yellow as she forced her light magic into my skin. The smell of burning flesh made my stomach clench, pain searing through me when I tried to jerk my arm away.

"Vera, let *go*," I said through my teeth. "You don't want to hurt me."

"She doesn't recognize you," Scarven called out. "Beautiful, isn't she? My masterpiece."

I twisted my arm, but she was too strong. I could feel my Shifter healing kicking in, trying to fight against the slow burn of my skin.

"I'm your brother, Vera," I tried again, voice labored. "It's me. It's Nox. Please, you have to let go."

I didn't want to hurt her. I *couldn't* hurt her. This wasn't the real Vera—she wasn't in her right mind. But the smoke coming from my arm told me she wasn't going to stop until she burned my hand straight off.

With a growl, I gripped her forearm with my other hand and carefully shifted my fingers into claws. They sank into her skin enough to make her loosen her hold. I quickly pulled away, my arm shaking as the fiery imprint of her hand branded itself deep into my flesh. Muscle and tissue peeked out from the charred skin. Within moments, it began to heal enough for me to flex my hand.

Vera narrowed her eyes and lunged at me, shadows at the ready. She swiped at my head while blades of shadow struck my torso, barely giving me time to dodge. I blocked her, but she shot another beam of light at my neck. It sliced the top of my collarbone like lightning.

When she moved to attack again, a large white animal burst from the side and knocked her to the ground.

"Kieran, don't!" I cried out. "She doesn't know what she's doing."

Kieran pinned Vera, his large stag form easily three times my sister's weight. Vera struggled against him for a moment before baring her teeth. In an instant, she vanished.

Kieran shifted back into his human form right as Vera reappeared behind him, grabbed the dagger from his sheath, and plunged it into his stomach.

A roar tore from me, so violent, it shook the ground. I launched myself at my sister and heaved her away from my second, whipping around just in time to grab Kieran as he sank to his knees. His hands were wrapped around the handle of the dagger, his face pale and eyes wide.

This wasn't happening. I couldn't lose one of them. Dread rushed over me, sweeping down my spine and curling in my gut.

"We have to get him out of here," Tessa said as she bolted to our side.

"Take—the sword out," Kieran said with a gasp. "I'll—heal."

"Not if it's too deep, Kieran. You're not immortal," Tessa argued.

Kieran ground his teeth together as he slowly pulled on the handle, his grunt muffled and nostrils flared wide. It came out of his stomach with a sickening squelch, and blood poured from the open wound.

"*Nox!*"

I whirled around to see Devora's terrified face, right as Vera surged toward me again. A spear made from lightning crackled in her grip. She drove it at my chest, but with a growl, I wrapped both hands around the end before it broke my skin. The light magic jolted through me with fervid force, sizzling over my flesh.

"I don't want to hurt you, Vera," I grunted out. "You've got to *fight it*. You're stronger than this!"

The golden light reflected off her eyes, hard and merciless. Whoever this was...it wasn't my sister.

"She's not yours anymore," Scarven said, his voice rich with satisfaction. "Her magic belongs to me." I caught his eye over Vera's shoulder, and he smirked back at me. "As does my new *pet*."

He rattled the chain tied around Devora's neck. She flinched, but her eyes held mine, those bright blue-green orbs shining with determination even in her suffering.

He could never beat the fight out of her. My fearless, obstinate, darling Devora.

I'm coming for you.

Resolve and rage flitted across my skin like sparks, making my vision go red. With a burst of Shifter strength, I gripped the lightning sword tighter and shoved it back at Vera. She lost her balance and stumbled as the sword disappeared.

"I'm sorry, Vera," I said, then summoned my dragon fire and shot a steady stream of it at her feet. She jumped to get away and slammed into the sidewall, where I caged her in with a circle of fire.

It wouldn't hold her off for long, but it was good enough. I broke into a sprint down the tunnel, aiming for Scarven and Devora.

"Behind you!" Kieran's weakened voice sounded. A split second later, his dagger ripped through the air beside my head, still coated in his blood. I reached out mid-stride to snatch it.

Scarven grinned as I drew nearer, but right as I launched the blade at his chest, he took a step backward.

"Till we meet again, brother," he said smoothly. "Unless your sister finishes the job."

The air around him shimmered, and he vanished into a portal. I watched as the dagger clattered to the ground in the empty space where he'd been.

"Nox," Devora breathed out, rising shakily to her feet.

I ran to her and crushed her to my chest. Her fingers clenched my back, tremors racking through her.

"I'm here," I whispered into her hair. "You're safe, darling."

"I knew you'd come," she murmured. The world around us faded as she looked up at me, those big eyes swallowing me whole.

I cupped her cheek, gently running my thumb over the tracks of her tears. "I told you once, I will *always* come for you."

Something thrummed in my chest at her nearness, at *finally* having her back in my arms. I didn't understand what she'd become to me until the thought of losing her made it feel like I couldn't breathe.

It was dangerous. It went against everything I'd sworn to myself. Her ties to me had already gotten her almost killed.

But in that moment, I didn't care. All that mattered was that she was *safe*.

Devora went rigid, and my heart dropped to my feet. I twisted her behind me to shield her as my sister stalked toward us like a beast released from her cage. A sword of lightning was gripped in her hand and one of shadows in the other. Both dragged the ground as she bared her teeth. Fire licked up her arms and legs, encasing her in an otherworldly glow.

But I knew that wasn't my dragon fire.

It was *hers*.

Phoenix fire.

She let out a shriek that turned into a birdsong—high, resonant, and laced with magic. It cracked the stone walls, sending shards raining down.

I glanced at Tessa and Kieran behind her, who had risen to his feet, leaning heavily on Tessa for support. It would take longer for a wound like his to heal, even with his Shifter healing.

"You two, get out!" I shouted.

Tessa's brow furrowed. "We're not going without you!"

"We'll be fine, just *go!*" I bellowed.

She glared at me, and I thought she was going to argue before she finally said, "You are *not* allowed to die on us, do you understand?"

I gave her a tight nod, watching as the two of them turned and limped their way as fast as they could back down the tunnel.

I faced my sister and took in her blazing tempest. I spent *years* dreaming of rescuing her. I couldn't leave her down here now. Not again.

"Vera, please," I begged, stepping toward her. "I came for *you*, too. Let me help you." When I reached for her, she held her lightning sword up in warning, and the walls gave a shudder.

"I love you," I said. "We can fight this together. I promise, I won't let him win this time. Just come with me."

She held my gaze, blonde hair whipping around her in the frenzy of her firestorm. Her lips parted, and with a voice that sounded more like the sister I knew and not this creature of Scarven's machinations, she whispered, "I can never leave. *This* is who I am."

Flames and rubble surrounded us, the tunnels shaking with the force of her power.

We were out of time.

But for a heartbeat, a single breath, Vera's eyes flickered. Recognition, sorrow, and deep, endless pain.

And then she lashed out, lightning and shadows blurring the air.

I unleashed my dragon with a roar. Magic exploded from me as my wings ripped from my back, every limb elongating and thickening with muscle and scales. My horns gouged the stone above us, sending more rock crumbling to the ground. I grabbed Devora with my talons, snapped the chains at her wrists, and tucked her into my massive side.

With a single lunge, I burst through the ceiling in a flood of gravel and stone.

The night air greeted me like a cool kiss across my scales. The ground cracked and ruptured as I spread my wings and hovered above the tunnel, Devora gripped in my claws.

I spared one last look at the rubble. With a heavy weight sinking in my chest, I watched my sister disappear in a flash of phoenix fire.

49

DEVORA

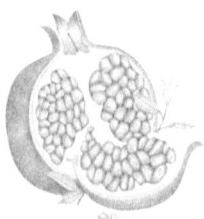

We soared above the clouds, the tips of forests and villages barely visible in the gaps. Nox's scales were like armor beneath my fingertips. Cool to the touch and hard as steel, deadly in their own right. Every inch of his dragon form radiated strength and power. It hummed through my veins with each flap of his wing, each dip of his massive neck.

It took all my focus to not fall off his back as the four of us raced back to the Keep. The adrenaline from the fight and seeing him again was wearing off, replaced with constant, bone-deep pain.

Every time I swallowed, I could feel the collar Scarven had put around my neck. It had some sort of spell on it that snuffed out my shadow magic, leaving me hollow. And the serum he'd forced into my system was still surging through me. Every breath hurt, every movement ached, and every beat of my heart made my vision blur at the edges.

I couldn't believe they came for me. They should've stayed back. It was such an obvious trap—they had to have known that. And if any of them had died because of me...

I couldn't handle any more guilt.

I pushed the thought away, forcing my muscles to grip Nox as tightly as my weakened form could. I thought he was growling when a rumble vibrated down his massive body, but then I saw lightning streak through the clouds beside us. More thunder sounded. It was so close, I could feel it in my teeth.

The tower of the Keep finally came into view. Exhaustion swept over me until a sharp pain erupted from the wound in my neck. I cried out as my vision wavered and a voice echoed inside my mind.

"I wonder how long that spirit of yours will last after I'm through with you."

Phantom spasms burst around my wrists and neck. I could smell the strong scent of wine that always lingered on Scarven's breath when he kissed me. I squeezed my eyes shut, my muscles too tired but crying at the same time.

I was weightless and floating, one foot in my memories and one in the uneasy darkness.

And then I was freefalling.

A bellowing roar broke through the fog right as a hand yanked my arm.

I sucked in a breath and nearly screamed. I was suspended in midair, with nothing but Tessa's tight grip keeping me from falling to my death. She slowly pulled me onto Nox's back.

"You alright?" she called out above the wind.

I nodded and clung to Nox's scales, panting from exertion. A dampness filled the air, heavy and suffocating despite the cold winter night, and then the skies opened to release a deluge of rain. It pelted us like daggers, instantly drenching our clothes.

Nox nose-dived for the perimeter of the mansion, landing more gracefully than I thought possible of his enormous body. I slid (very ungracefully) from his back. My knees buckled as a shock of pain radiated from my poisoned knife wounds.

The instant Tessa and Kieran were on solid ground, Nox shifted. He fell to the mud and cupped the back of my neck. My head pounded and my teeth chattered, which was strange, considering the wound felt like a hot brand coursing up my ribs. Nox's face wavered before me as my eyelids fluttered shut, but I forced myself to focus.

I licked my lips and swallowed. "Get them...off," I croaked. I clawed weakly at the collar around my neck.

His nostrils flared. In the blink of an eye, he shifted his hand to talons and sliced through the black metal at my throat and hands, then tossed them to the side.

The instant they were gone, the nausea began to subside. My body slackened in his hold. The pain was still there, but without the cuffs, it was like I could breathe again.

Nox pushed back the rain-slicked hair from my face. Without realizing what I was doing, I nestled my cheek against his hand. Fates, I had missed him. The frenzy in my chest settled when he was around.

"We need to get both of them to Silas," Tessa called through the rain. She supported Kieran with an arm around his waist, his hand still clutched over the wound in his abdomen.

I shook my head, and the movement sent a dull throb across my temple. "Just sleep. I just need to...to sleep. Please, Nox," I whimpered.

He nodded and gathered me in his arms. "Sleep, darling. I've got you."

———

FAINT NOISES FILTERED IN. Shuffling feet, whispered voices, something hard clattering against a wooden surface.

It sounded like chains rattling on stone.

"Now we'll see how my brother's plaything looks strung up on my wall and screaming my name."

My shadows flickered at the edges of my mind, but a cold wave pushed them away. Scarven was everywhere—his fingers digging into my back, his needles scraping my skin. My panic rose, but the heavy blackness kept me tied down, like weights dragging me under.

A different voice broke through the fog. "Her heartbeat is steadier, Nox. Her body is fighting the infection. She's strong, this one."

And then I heard *him*.

"You have no idea how strong."

Warmth brushed my hand. My muscles relaxed, and I faded once more.

———

THE BACKS of my eyelids glowed red, as if sunlight were shining down on them. Something soft rested on my legs. I moved my fingers, expecting them to be frozen in that liminal space, but to my surprise, smooth sheets shifted beneath my touch.

I slowly pried my eyes open. Golden rays of a sunset crossed over the blanket covering my legs. I no longer smelled the sour wine on Scarven's lips, but a different sweet, smoky scent that calmed my senses. I turned to bury my cheek deeper into the pillow, breathing it in, and a small whimper escaped me.

There was movement on the other side of the bed. I snapped my head to the sound, wincing at the sharp motion.

"It's okay; it's just me," Nox said, voice soft. He moved his chair as close to me as he could. His hand twitched toward mine, but he kept it on the edge of the bed.

"Where am I?" I croaked.

"My chambers. I wanted to be here when you woke up."

Tenderness bloomed in my chest. I took in the bedside table next to him, with a glass of water and several wooden figurines shaped like animals. When I squinted, I saw the outline of my glasses. He seemed to read my thoughts, swiftly reaching over and handing them to me.

I pushed them up the bridge of my nose. "How long was I out?"

"Almost a day. How do you feel?"

"Like I'm sick of constantly being the one to pass out." I

groaned when I took a deep breath and felt a pinch in my side. Looking under the blanket, I saw a bandage going from the side of my breast to my hip. Further down, my thigh was encased in thick gauze.

"You were exhausted, Devora. You needed to rest."

I sighed and reached up to scratch the injection site on my neck. When I lifted my hand, shadows twirled around my finger. I smiled faintly.

Hello there, I whispered to them. They grew with each breath, curling over my hand. *You're safe now. I won't let anything hurt us again, I promise.*

They squeezed my fingers in a soft embrace. I smiled wider and shut my eyes, the overwhelming relief at having my magic back making a tear track down one cheek. Something that, a month and a half ago, I didn't even know how to control. Something I didn't even *care* about, and now couldn't imagine being without.

"What's wrong?" Nox asked urgently. "Why are you crying?"

Another tear slipped out. "My magic's back. I thought after what he did, and that collar—I thought it was gone for good."

Nox flexed his hand a few inches from mine on the edge of the bed. He kept his distance, not letting our fingers touch. "What happened to you, Devora?" he finally asked. "One moment you were writing about how he took you to the Hollow, and the next..."

"He showed up in my room." I paused as the memory of Scarven taking off his belt and pinning me to the bed flashed before my eyes. "I hid the parchment under my pillow, but he was...he was on the bed when you sent your last message. He felt it burn and got suspicious."

Nox went lethally still. His other hand gripped the armrest of the chair, and something splintered. The end of it cracked off and fell to the floor as a hint of his silver claws glinted.

Growling, he asked, "Devora, did he—"

"No, no, he—he tried, but your message—it stopped him." I looked down into my lap and took a breath. My pulse raced with residual fear. "He knew I was working with you. He said they found my cloak that night at the stables. He'd just been toying with us the whole time. He pricked me with something that made my shadows go crazy. It proved I was lying, and that's when he took me to the cells." I glanced back at Nox. "How did you know where to find me, anyway?"

"Silas took something of yours—your sweater—and cast a spell that let us see a vision of you. I saw—" He cut himself off, his nostrils flaring. "I saw you hanging from chains. I saw *this*." Moving forward, he raised a finger to the puncture wound on my neck, but like before, he didn't touch me. I could feel the heat coming from every inch of his skin, those navy eyes alight with fire.

"I saw you wake up when he got there. I saw him grab you." Nox's eyes traced a path over my throat, the top of my collarbone, and to the other side of my neck where Scarven had gripped me. His gaze was as searing as any touch, and when he pulled away to sit back in the chair, he left a chill hovering over me.

"He kept you in the same cell I was in," he said. My mouth fell open. "There were marks carved into the stone on the wall beside you. Marks I left there over a decade ago."

It felt like someone had punched me. "Nox, I—"

"He was using you to send me a message. He hurt you because of *me*." He swiped a hand down the scruff at his chin. For the first time, I registered how tired he was. Purple circles gathered beneath his weary eyes. His tan skin was duller than usual, and his lips curved down at the edges.

I furrowed my brow. "If you knew it was a trap, why did you come?"

His eyes found mine again. Those broad shoulders shifted as he slowly leaned forward.

My heart pounded the closer he got. But not from *fear*. The man before me, this *dragon*, dripped power and strength. He could level an entire village with a single breath. He was a force of nature, a predator, a danger.

But with him, I felt safer than I ever had.

"Why did I come?" he repeated with a murmur. "For the last ten days, I've been unable to sleep. I can't get you out of my head, Devora. I know what that man does to the people in his possession, and the thought of him hurting you, of him—" He stopped, his jaw clenching as he exhaled sharply.

His eyes locked onto the bruise on my cheek, and his gaze darkened. "I will tear him apart for what he did to you," he said, voice deathly quiet.

He lifted his thumb and hovered above the mark. His entire arm shook with barely controlled rage. He'd been careful not to touch me this whole time, almost as if he was afraid of what would happen if he did. That I would crack down the middle like his armrest.

Maybe I would.

I reached for his outstretched wrist, needing something to ground me, right as he moved back to his seat.

A rock sank in my chest. I looked away before he saw the rejection on my face. He said he couldn't get me out of his head, and yet he kept his distance when he finally had me back.

He thought I was breakable. Damaged. And he was right.

"Do you know what *I* did these last ten days?" I whispered, gingerly touching the bandage at my neck so I didn't have to look at him. "I—I thought about *you*. I thought about the Order and what this all means to me. I thought about getting through this mission so I could come home. Every time I was scared, I remembered the other people he'd hurt. Every time he touched me, I—I wished—" My heart beat in my ears as the feel of Scarven's body on top of mine came back to the forefront. Pressure built in the backs of my eyes.

"But now I just want it all to go away. I want someone to take it away."

I turned my neck so my hair covered part of my face, shielding me from him. I wasn't used to this—to having someone watch when I fell apart. Unexpected emotion clogged my throat as a single tear trailed down my cheek.

"Devora," Nox whispered slowly. Before I knew what was happening, the bed dipped. His large body settled in next to me, and he carefully laid my head on his chest. I flinched for a split second before realizing where I was, and then wrapped my arms around his midsection.

"Is this alright?" He hesitated with his hand across my lower back.

I nodded and buried my head in his chest. When he pressed his lips to the top of my head, I couldn't stop the tears from coming. I let them flow out of me, all my fear, my helplessness, my distress. My anger and determination. My pain and silence.

He held me through it all, pulling me even further into his arms like he wanted to mold my body to his. "I'm so sorry, my darling," he kept murmuring, brushing soft kisses along my temple. "I'm so sorry."

Only when my head pounded and my eyes swelled did the tears subside, leaving me with shaky breaths as I clung to him. My muscles relaxed, releasing tension for the first time in weeks. The safety and warmth of being tucked into his side made the darkness weighing on my mind a little lighter, and as his fingers ran down the length of my spine, I closed my eyes and fell asleep again.

50

NOX

Faint voices from outside my door roused me from sleep.

"Is he *still* sleeping?" Kieran whispered.

"Hush, they both need it," Tessa shot back.

"Well, he won't be too pleased if he misses the empress's wedding. They need to leave in the morning."

Arowyn's muffled voice cut in. "Feel free to poke the sleeping dragon, Kieran. But I like my eyebrows the way they are."

Something warm stirred at my chest. Devora's body pressed against mine, her hair strewn across my arm. When she stretched, my other arm fell to her hip. Her soft curves melted into my grip. Her eyes were closed, still partially asleep, but her breath hitched slightly at the end of a sigh, and the sound made heat pool down my spine.

My fingers slid up her side and hit the rough edge of a bandage, and everything slammed back into me.

I recoiled, remembering how she'd gotten these wounds. *Who* had given them to her. And how that same man was the last one to force himself into her bed, to touch her so callously. How could I be so careless when *I* was the reason she'd been hurt in the first place?

My feelings for her were no longer something I could deny. I had wanted her from the moment I saw her, despite telling myself

I should have nothing to do with her. I *craved* her. In a way that had already been proven would ruin us both.

She was never my enemy. She was my *downfall*.

But I wouldn't let myself become hers.

Scarven took everything from me simply because I treasured it, and he knew how much she meant to me. Any second I spent falling for her, any proof I gave him that she was my weakness would only hurt her more.

I refused to be the reason she shed any more blood, even if it felt like tearing out my own heart.

I extricated my arm from beneath her and felt her stir.

"Nox?" Devora whispered, voice groggy as she turned and pried her eyes open. "What time is it?"

"We slept all night and morning. I just heard Kieran whispering about us needing to leave for the wedding soon." I tried to keep my voice level as I quickly left her side. I hadn't slept this much in...Fates, I didn't even know how long.

Devora went quiet, and I glanced back to see her watching me, a hint of sadness in her eyes. She schooled her features and asked, "What wedding?"

"Clarissa and Thorne's. It's in three days, on the winter solstice."

She blinked a couple of times, then rubbed her eyes. "Right. The wedding."

I sat back in the chair next to her. "You don't have to go if you're not feeling up to it. Nobody would blame you, after what you've been through."

And I didn't know how much longer I'd be able to hold on to my control if I was alone with her.

"No, I—I want to go. I mean, I know things will be weird between Clarissa and me, but..." She shook her head. "I think I need to get away for a little while. Not be so close to—to him, you know?" Her fingers played with the fringes of the bedsheet, and her shadows danced up and down her hands. They seemed to respond easily to her emotions. "Not that I don't love the Keep and everyone here. I do, and I'm so happy to be back. But it—"

"You don't have to explain yourself, Devora. I get it. If you want to get away, we'll go."

The words were out of my mouth before I could stop them. Fates, I was already wrapped around her finger.

"I'm a little surprised *you* still want to go. I figured you'd be planning an attack on the Hollow by now," she said, peering at me.

I'd thought about it. In the hours after we got back from the rescue mission and Devora lay passed out in my bed, the others had to talk me down from my spiral. How was I supposed to focus on anything when my sister was brainwashed? Vera Duma, phoenix Shifter and *truly* the most powerful magic-wielder in the history of the Veridian Empire, reduced to a puppet at the end of his strings.

Every time I closed my eyes, I saw her gaze void of recognition, and it hollowed me.

She probably wasn't the only one. He could be creating an entire *army*. That, combined with the destructive effects of fate-sprig we'd discovered, could make him unstoppable. A force that could both suppress magic and bend it to his will.

I soon realized any attack I made would have the same result until I learned how to counteract the magic-sucking fatesprig *and* how to break his compulsion over others. I would get nowhere with brute force. All these midnight raids and missions were point-less if he had some sort of enchantment over them—we could set him back, but not stop him altogether.

I had to think like him. Figure out what magic he was using, and reverse it. There was one thing we hadn't tried yet.

"Trust me, if I thought making a move on Scarven *tonight* would work, I'd be halfway to his manor right now. But it won't. He expects a counterstrike. He expects me to come in with every weapon in my arsenal, led only by my anger." I leaned forward to rest my elbows on my knees. "I can't fight Vera, and I won't lead anyone down there to our graves."

Devora's brow furrowed. "Then...I don't understand. We just do nothing?"

I shook my head slowly. "We have to break whatever magical hold Scarven has on her. We need *Alchemy*. Silas is wonderful, and he's done so much to help us and the refugees. But I've always known he would never truly be willing to do what it takes to get on the same level as Scarven."

"What are you talking about?"

"I need to talk to someone who's not afraid to get their hands a little dirty," I said. "We both know Scarven and his Alchemist don't have a clean bone in their body, and this might be the only way to figure out how they have such strong control over Vera." A strand of red hair fell onto Devora's cheek, and I had to fight the urge to move it behind her ear. "There are other kinds of magic, Devora. Darker magic that most Alchemists like Silas refuse to touch. But I know just who to talk to."

Her eyes darted between mine. "What does that have to do with Clarissa and Thorne's wedding?"

"Because this person will be there." I gave her a grim smile. "Have you ever heard of blood magic?"

51

DEVORA

ere we were in Veridia City, capital of the Veridian Empire and home to a conglomeration of people with all six magic types, the palace itself...and the empress I stabbed in the back four months ago.

The sun had been set for a couple of hours now, but the port was still brightly lit with torches along every path. From the bow of the ship, I could see colorful buildings dotting the skyline, like a rainbow of brick and stucco. Way less dreary than the shades of gray and brown in Drakorum. But the cheery sight did nothing for the nerves curdling in my gut.

Nox said Clarissa *specifically* invited me, but all I could think about was the betrayal in her eyes the last time I saw her. My shadows sensed my distress and rose to the surface, twisting along my fingers as I picked at my nails. They felt urgent. Restless. More aggressive than usual, which made sense, given my constant wariness.

We left early this morning by carriage from the Keep to the west shores of Drakorum, and then traveled a few hours by boat to arrive on the banks of the capital. I was thankful we chose to make the journey like *normal* people to keep a low profile. Riding bareback on a dragon for hours wasn't exactly my preferred method of travel.

Even if it was Nox's bare back.

My neck heated, and I turned away before he saw me staring. That was the last thing I needed to be thinking about right now.

When I left for Scarven's manor ten days ago, Nox said he trusted me, which meant more than any heartfelt declaration or words of passion. He wanted me to come home to him. He brought back my baby blanket, for Fates' sake. Waking up in his arms yesterday was the first time I felt safe in longer than I could remember.

But things were...complicated. He had more important problems to deal with, what with seeing his sister again. I couldn't imagine how he must've felt when she tried to kill him. To know his mortal enemy had turned her brain to mush and sired her to his every beck and call. To know he was *so* close, yet forced to let her slip through his fingers.

And me...

My shadows crept from my hands and wound along the railing of the quarterdeck. Last night, I woke up from a nightmare and found them hovering across my chest, like they were trying to protect me in my sleep. I saw Scarven every time I closed my eyes. Whenever a hand reached out to touch me, I thought it was him. The muscles in my arms were still sore from being bent back and strung up on a wall, a constant reminder of where I'd been mere days ago.

I didn't know if I could trust my own emotions or instincts. But if there was one thing I was certain of, if there was *one* thing keeping me from falling down that dark pit of fear, it was that I could trust *him*.

"Ready, Devora?" Nox asked, waiting several feet away with our bags in his grip.

"As I'll ever be."

I followed him down the gangway and to a carriage just beyond the docks. I was used to the fur cloaks, thick sweaters, and occasional training leathers of Tenebra and Drakorum. But the capital city was far less icy, even in the heart of winter. As we rolled through small villages to get to the palace, I saw citizens dressed in loose linen pants and long-sleeved blouses, barely a cloak in sight. My own heavy sweater was starting to make me sweat. There was a pleasant chill in the air, the kind that turned your nose and cheeks pink without freezing you.

"Tonight's a smaller gathering, just friends and family before they start greeting guests," Nox said across from me in the carriage. I kept my elbow propped up on the window as I listened, watching the tall, broad-leaved trees and shrubbery pass by. "Tomorrow night is the welcome feast, and the day after is the wedding. I'm hoping we can catch Rose tonight to talk before she gets too busy."

I squirmed in my seat, and my foot tapped against the carriage floor. *Rose Wolff.* The Alchemist who had experience with this blood magic Nox wanted to try. And, incidentally, one of Clarissa's closest friends.

I met Rose when their group of Veridians was in Mysthelm. Very briefly, but still. I liked the sharp-tongued Alchemist. She and Leo, her partner and Clarissa's twin brother, all had history with Nox as well.

Yet *another* reason I was nervous about this visit. Another person whose trust I'd lost.

"Devora." Nox put his hand on the edge of my knee to stop it from tapping.

My eyes flashed up to his. He'd been so careful not to touch me, besides holding me through my mental breakdown and subsequent sobbing.

"It'll be fine," he said. "They're good people. They know everyone makes mistakes, and they'll be able to see past that."

I tried to smile, but it probably looked more like a wince. "I know. I'm fine."

He snorted. "I thought you were supposed to be a good liar. Do we need one of Arowyn's ridiculous code words?"

I raised an eyebrow. "For what?"

"For if it gets too overwhelming, and you want to be alone."

My tight muscles loosened slightly. "What did you have in mind?"

His eyes flitted to my lips before meeting my gaze again. "Pomegranates."

A chuckle slipped free. "Pomegranates? That's the best you can do? Arowyn would be disappointed."

He shrugged. "What can I say? I've grown fond of them."

"Okay," I said, still smiling. "So if I say 'pomegranates,' you'll... what, shift and fly me out of there? Bust down the doors of the palace?"

His grin faded as his thumb rubbed circles into the side of my knee. "I'll do whatever you want, Devora, darling."

The heat of his fingers on my leggings suddenly felt searing. I held his gaze, the air shifting around us like a storm. My lips parted when I took a breath, and his eyes drifted down to them again. His thumb slid higher when the carriage jostled, his fingers digging into the space above my knee.

My heart was a drum inside my chest. The desire to be near him was always right there, like lightning in my veins, uncontrollable and dangerous.

The idea of anyone having power over me ever again was dangerous, and this man...he could ruin me.

The frightening part was that I would let him.

The carriage came to an abrupt halt, breaking the spell between us. I blinked and pulled away as the driver opened the door. Before us stood the palace, with rows of gilded spires stretching into the sky and a beautiful garden surrounding the entrance. Two guards in silver uniforms were stationed beside wide double doors at the top of a staircase, but before they could open them, two figures came bursting out.

Blonde waves fluttered around a freckled, heart-shaped face. Her loose pants billowed behind her as she skipped down the steps, with a blue sweater that hung off one shoulder and a dazzling diamond ring on her left hand. Close on the woman's heels was a huge brown dog with a lolling tongue and the sweetest eyes I'd ever seen. Mia, Clarissa's shepherding dog, had gotten close to me when I was her lady's maid in Mysthelm. The last time I'd seen the pup, she could still fit in my lap. Not so much anymore.

Mia instantly bounded over to me, wagging her large tail fast enough to leave a bruise. I laughed and scratched the back of her ears as she assaulted me with kisses.

"Hi there, sweet girl," I cooed. "I missed you too."

I could feel Clarissa's pointed stare on me the entire time. But when I risked a glance up, she had thrown her arms around Nox with a wide smile.

"You sure like to be fashionably late, don't you?" Clarissa asked.

He laughed. "You know I'm only here for the food." She released him, and he looked up at the palace entrance. "Long time, no see, lover boy," he boomed.

A new face was coming down the steps with a brown-haired little girl perched atop his shoulders—Clarissa's fiancé, Lord Thorne Reaux, and his daughter. I knew Thorne from my time working for his mother in Mysthelm. Lady Reaux was a piece of work, but her son had always been kind.

He and Clarissa were a good pairing. Both grounded and fair, neither of them with that air of formality or condescension I saw from so many wealthy nobles. I was happy for them, no matter how strained things were between us.

Thorne grinned and shook his head, his long, dark brown hair brushing past his shoulders. "It's only been a few weeks."

The statement caught me off guard, but Nox didn't see my questioning gaze. He beamed at the little girl on top of Thorne's shoulders.

"Yes, and look how much you've grown since then. You're practically a lady!" he exclaimed.

"I hope you're talking to Marigold," Thorne said.

His daughter giggled and patted her dad's head. "*You're* not a lady, Daddy. *I'm* a lady."

Thorne swung her off his shoulders, tickling her sides as she squealed with laughter. Mia's tail thumped against the ground at the excitement.

Nox took Marigold, and she squeezed his neck tight. "Daddy and Rissa let me stay up so I could say hi!"

"I'm so glad they did, darling." Nox ruffled her hair with one hand, and I cursed my stomach for bursting into butterflies. It was such a cliché, watching a rugged, handsome man turn into a puddle for a sweet child.

But, Fates, I fell for it.

"Nox is right. It's bedtime for you. We've got a busy day tomorrow," Thorne said, taking Marigold's hand. As she said her goodbyes and he led her back inside, I figured it was as good of a time as any to face the music.

I stepped forward until I was at Nox's side, stomach churning and shadows twisting anxiously between my fingers. His hand came out and brushed briefly against my elbow, enough to anchor me.

I gave Clarissa a small curtsy. "Hello, Your Majesty. It—it's good to see you."

Clarissa instantly sombered, the smile she'd had for Nox now guarded and hesitant. Those onyx eyes assessed me in that cunning fox-like way of hers, the one that said she was reading me like a book. I remembered the wrath they held just a few short months ago. The hurt. The instant distrust.

She finally raised an eyebrow and hummed. "Welcome to Veridia City, Devora."

52

DEVORA

Nox grabbed our bags, and we made our way up the entrance steps. I caught a glimpse of rich mahogany floors, dark green rugs, and dozens of sparkling chandeliers peeking out from the open doors. Clarissa was ahead of us, speaking with the guards, so I took a second to turn to Nox.

"What did Thorne mean when he said you saw them a few weeks ago?"

"Remember when I left Tenebra for a short while to take care of something for Scarven?" Nox started, and I nodded. "I brought the rebels he wanted me to get rid of here, to work for Rissa."

"Oh," I blinked back my surprise, "that was...that was good of you."

He winked at me before we walked through the open door. "Besides, how else did you think I got your blanket back?"

"Wait, Nox," I hissed after him. "Are you saying—"

"That he almost plowed down my palace to get me to send an emergency message in our next correspondence with Mysthelm? Yes, yes he did," Clarissa called. She waited for us just inside the doors. "I told him it better be important."

Nox, eyes still trained on me, said, "It was."

A blush crept up my neck and to my cheeks. The thought of

him roping in *Clarissa* just to get my childhood keepsake back hadn't even crossed my mind. And he did this when we were in Drakorum? That was so long ago—before he and I had any semblance of trust, any camaraderie or care for each other beyond the mission.

That somehow made the gesture more meaningful.

Clarissa cleared her throat. I jumped and tore my gaze away from Nox. "Sawyer here will take your bags to your rooms." She nodded to a guard who approached from the side. "Come on. The others are waiting."

———

"THERE HE IS!" a familiar female voice rang out from the drawing room.

"I was wondering when he was going to show up."

A booming chuckle followed. "The famous *dragon Shifter*. Now the real party can start."

"Quiet, Chaz. Nobody else knows he's a dragon."

I didn't recognize the owners of the second voices, but the first two, Rose and Leo, stood to greet Nox as he followed Clarissa into the room. I stood back with Mia still sitting at my feet, watching while Nox hugged his friends. A faint smile spread across my lips at seeing him in his element. I knew he and Rose were close—the beautiful green-eyed, dark-haired Alchemist and her partner had spent a lot of time with him when we were all in Mysthelm. I only hoped she'd be able to help us with Scarven's mysterious Alchemy.

Rose caught my eye as she stepped back from Nox. Her grin faltered slightly, but she nodded at me. "Devora. We weren't sure if you'd come."

At her words, six pairs of eyes turned on me.

This wasn't awkward at all.

A brown-skinned woman I'd never met before wheeled herself toward me in a large wheelchair. Black locks fell down one side of her full chest, and a blanket rested in her lap.

She stared at me with a curious look. "Is this her?" She spared one glance at Nox. "The infamous Shadow Wielder?"

Nox flashed her a smirk. "That's her."

The woman appraised me with sharp, discerning eyes. "Thecae was *quite* impressed with you. And it takes a lot to impress that man."

My eyes widened at the mention of the Shadow Wielder trainer. "You know Thecae?"

"Who do you think told Nox to take you there?"

"Devora," Nox said, holding an arm out to the woman. "Meet Lark Everest."

I remembered how Nox said a friend recommended Thecae teach me how to figure out my shadows. I shook her hand. "It's so nice to meet you," I said. "I guess I should be thanking you. Without Thecae, I would've never learned about my magic or where I came from. He's incredible, truly."

"He is. And he's often a good judge of character." She still eyed me with that guarded look, sizing me up. "I hope you've been using the shadows well."

I could tell these people were fiercely loyal and protective of Clarissa. I didn't blame them for being so wary. But they hadn't kicked me out yet, so that was a good sign.

A very large, muscular man with a trimmed black beard and three daggers attached to his belt stepped forward, feet thundering and dark eyes piercing. His imposing form towered over me, arms crossed over his chest as he stopped barely a foot in front of me. I held his stare and lifted my chin, despite my shadows trying to dart out from my fingertips.

"So you're the one who crossed my empress?" he asked, his voice deep and gruff. Out of the corner of my eye, I saw Nox straighten and step toward me, but I held out a hand to stop him.

"Yes," I said simply.

"You put that fox in the fire? You ratted her out and almost got her hanged?"

I bit down on the inside of my cheek before responding, "Yes."

He paused. "Do you regret it?"

That one didn't take any thought. "Every second of every day."

He hitched his thumb toward Nox. "And now pretty dragon boy over here has you working against Scarven?"

"That's right."

To my surprise, his scowl shifted into a bright smile. It transformed his entire face, taking him from burly, aggressive guard to friendly and playful in the blink of an eye. "Great. I hate that guy." He stuck out his hand, and I blinked twice before realizing I was supposed to shake it.

"This is Chaz," Lark said. "Tact isn't his strong suit."

"Sorry for being the only one with the balls to address the elephant in the room," he said, shrugging. "The way I figure, she was put in a tough position by someone abusing their power over her. Come on, we've all been there. Do I *like* what she did? No. Do I think it's possible to work with her because we're all on the same side now? Sure."

He glanced back at me. "And I think you know if you try anything like that again, Nox over here will be the least of your problems. Don't you, gorgeous?" He winked at me with that same grin still on his face.

"I would *never*. I—" I tore my gaze from Chaz and found Clarissa, who was still by the door with her arms crossed. "I promise, Your Majesty. I don't expect you to forgive me. I know I can't undo the wrong I've done, but I *can* choose what I do next. That's what these last five weeks have been about. Building trust and... and learning what I want to fight for." The words came to me without thinking, ones I'd wanted to say to her since I found out what Scarven was doing to his people.

"*This* is it. I want to fight for Veridians. I want to fight for the ones who have only known fear. I want to fight so people like me aren't taken advantage of again." I glanced at Nox at that part, then back to Clarissa. "You all may not believe me, but that's the truth. And I'm so sorry, Clarissa."

The entire room held its breath. I knew this moment would

come, the awkward apologies, the testing, the laying it all on the line. If they wanted me gone, it was better to do it before the celebrations began. I just needed them to *know*.

Clarissa's stare weighed on me, a flicker of uncertainty in those dark eyes. Each passing second caused a string around my heart to tighten further. She quickly glanced over at Nox, and the corner of her eyes narrowed by a fraction. Observing. Sifting. Calculating.

And then the side of her mouth lifted. Not much, but enough to send tentative hope soaring through me.

"I believe you, Devora," she finally said. Her voice was soft but firm. "I held on to my bitterness for a long time, thinking it was my *right* to be angry with you." Her brow furrowed as she swallowed.

"But then I realized...I was becoming no better than Lady Reaux. Nox told me you've been invaluable with whatever business you two have gotten up to, and honestly, it didn't surprise me one bit." That infinitesimal smile rose a little bit further. "You've always been capable. You were the girl with a dagger beneath her skirt and liquor down her dress."

I bit my lip as tears sprang to my eyes at her words.

"Everything turned out exactly as it was supposed to be," she said, almost in a whisper. "If I'm being honest with myself, I think I forgave you a long time ago, Devora."

I let out a heavy breath. That simple sentence released *months* of guilt I'd worn on my shoulders like an old cloak. Always there, lingering in the back of my mind. I wasn't perfect, but I knew who I was now. I knew where my loyalties lay and who I wanted to stand beside. But I'd still been holding on to the heartache I'd caused, still dreading that others would always see the worst in me.

You're not the sum of your past.

Maybe Nox was right.

Maybe I could let the self-loathing go.

Maybe I could move forward without the guilt pressing in on my ribs, without the constant struggle to prove myself. Maybe I could stop believing I deserved to be in pain. To be unwanted. To be used.

All I could do was nod, afraid if I opened my mouth, tears would come rushing down my face. Clarissa held out her hand with a small smile, and I crossed to the doors and took it, squeezing tight.

"Congratulations, by the way," I said, then cleared my throat. "I'm so happy for you and Lord Reaux."

Clarissa's nose scrunched. "*Lord Reaux.* That's a title he hasn't heard in a long time. We're just Rissa and Thorne around here." Her eyes sparkled, the same vibrant empress I remembered. I wanted happiness for her now, the same as I had back then.

"You two must be hungry," Rose said from behind us. "We can catch up while you eat. I want to hear all about how living with Nox has been. Has he made you want to rip his head off yet?"

"Daily," I said. The others laughed. I snuck him a look and found him smirking at me, rubbing his thumb slowly along his bottom lip.

"I remember meeting him at the Decemvirate last year and thinking he was absolutely insufferable." Rose gave him a saccharine smile. "But I guess he turned out alright."

"There's the viper I know," he drawled.

Nox and I sat down on the couch in front of a small table with a plate of sandwiches and glasses of water. The others took their seats in various chairs, lounging casually as we talked. Thorne had joined us after putting Marigold to bed, and he rubbed Clarissa's shoulders where she sat by the fire.

When Rose settled in across from me, I asked, "Were you in the Decemvirate, too? With Nox and Arowyn?"

Rose nodded. "I was Feywood's challenger. That's how I met this group of stragglers. Fates, I haven't heard from Arowyn in forever. Is she in Drakorum?"

"Yeah, she's doing great," I said, taking a bite of my sandwich. "Always makes us laugh. And her powers are amazing. She's been a huge help with rescuing Scarven's prisoners, and—"

At my words, Clarissa jerked her head up right as Nox stiffened.

I immediately stopped talking and looked between the two of them. "Did I say something wrong?"

"What's she talking about? What prisoners?" Clarissa's voice was a growl, her dark brown eyes heating to the gold of her fox half.

Nox cleared his throat. "I *may* not have been entirely forthcoming in our chats, Rissa."

"Don't you dare 'Rissa' me. Scarven is taking *prisoners*? What's going on? You told me everything was under control!"

My stomach dropped as I realized my mistake. I turned to Nox and hissed, "She doesn't know?"

He sighed. "Look, Rissa, you were just crowned six weeks ago, and then with the wedding...I didn't know how to put that on you. I've got people helping me. We—"

"Oh, you have *people*. I'm so relieved," she spat. "I'm the Empress of the Veridian Empire, Nox. I could have sent an *army*."

"And that's exactly the kind of catalyst that would start a civil war!" Nox's voice rose. "One I don't think you could win right now. You don't understand what Scarven is doing. How powerful he's grown. If he's provoked, I'm afraid no army would be able to stop him. That's why we're trying to dismantle him from the inside."

"Of course I don't understand what he's doing, because you haven't *told* me anything! Fates, Nox, don't you realize how this looks?" She pointed at her chest. "I've been doing nothing while this man is taking *my* people. For what? What is he doing to them?"

Nox closed his eyes, the column of his throat moving as he swallowed hard. "He's doing experiments. On their magic."

A silence fell over the room. Rose let out a breath and whispered, "Like the ones that were done on you."

He didn't say anything, but his hands curled at his sides. I wondered how much Rose knew about his past. I wondered if any of them knew how his nightmares still tortured him, decades later. If they knew how hard he was working to keep others from the same fate.

"This is *unbelievable*," Clarissa said on an exhale, running shaky hands through her hair. "We have to do something." Her eyes shot back to Nox, desperation evident on her features. "I can't believe you kept this from me. I'm supposed to be the one to *help* these people."

"Rissa, please. I know you're upset. I shouldn't have hidden the truth, and for that, I'm truly sorry. But you know he has my sister." Nox moved forward on the couch, his voice breaking. Clarissa's face softened at the mention of Vera.

"Up until a few days ago, Scarven thought I was on his side," Nox explained. "I was able to get prisoners out from right beneath his nose *and* keep my sister alive. If I had told you, if you had come blazing through Drakorum with the Royal Guard, I would've lost every advantage I had. He would've retaliated five, ten, *fifteen* times stronger. Trust me, I—"

"That's the problem, Nox," Clarissa cut him off. She didn't sound angry, merely resigned. "I don't know how I'm supposed to keep trusting you."

His shoulders fell. The look on his face gutted me—not because he was shocked, but because he *wasn't*. It reminded me of the way I felt when I thought about my "punishment" all those months ago, convincing myself I deserved it.

He didn't deserve any of this.

I gritted my teeth and instinctively moved closer to him. "Look, you have *no idea* what he's gone through." A defensiveness I wasn't used to lined my tone. "You don't know what he's doing to save innocent lives *and* protect his sister *and* still find a way to bring Scarven down. It's an impossible situation. He would sacrifice his life for any single one of you, and you know that."

I looked around the room. "Should he have told you the truth? Probably. But if you've *ever* trusted him, if you've ever put your faith in him because you know how good his heart is, then trust that he had a reason." Turning back to him, my eyes flitted between his as I added, "We have to believe we're more than our mistakes."

Nox's navy gaze shone brighter as he looked at me. His little finger came out to graze the edge of my hand on the couch between us. I thought he would move it away after a second, but to my surprise, he kept it there.

Clarissa closed her eyes and took several deep breaths. The air seemed to waver in her silence, waiting for her response.

"Alright. No fighting. What's done is done, and all we can do is move forward." She opened her eyes and leveled them on Nox. "But you're done hiding things from me. Start at the beginning."

53

NOX

I told them everything. Every moment of trauma I kept buried, every secret, every fear.

Some of it they already knew, or in Rose's case, had guessed. That Scarven had killed my father for his position as governor and taken my mother, sister, and me captive. That we had spent the last nineteen years under his hold. That he still had my sister, and that was the reason I kept doing his bidding and had stayed so quiet about the truth.

When I told them he was my half-brother, Clarissa practically jumped out of her chair. Her fair features blanched, her eyes widening in disbelief.

I pushed through the tension and described the Ashen Order, and how our main purpose was to rescue those innocent lives and give them refuge. Devora stepped in to talk about the Keep and the children who had found a home there. We gave them a shortened version of Devora's role in all of this—the need for her to learn how to use her shadows, her infiltrating Scarven's mansion, how he discovered the truth, and we attacked to get her out.

The longer we spoke, the more my guilt grew at having kept all of this from Clarissa. I *knew* how deeply she cared for her people and that learning how so many of them were suffering would weigh heavily on her heart.

In that moment, I realized how Devora had felt when offered the chance to learn more about her family. Because I would do anything to keep my sister safe—even if it meant potentially losing the trust of those I cared for.

That didn't make it right. Nothing would ever make it *easy*. It just...was. And I would have to live with this decision, good or bad, for the rest of my life.

"We're here now because there was no other way I could think of to finally bring this to an end," I finished.

"And here I was, thinking it was for my wedding," Clarissa said with an exasperated sigh. She looked exhausted. Shame wormed even further into my chest.

"Of course, it's for you too, Rissa," I said gently. "You know I love you both. And Marigold. I didn't want to ruin this time for you. But...I saw my sister." Her lips parted. "Scarven has some sort of compulsion on her. She's completely lost. Things are escalating, and I don't know what he's planning. But we think it could be related to a new herb he's been importing from Mysthelm."

"From *Mysthelm*?" Thorne repeated, brow furrowed at the mention of his home kingdom.

I nodded. "It started a little over a year ago. We saw strange ships arriving in the middle of the night, but were always too late to find out what they were carrying. Until Devora showed up." I shot her a quick look. "She snuck onto one of their ships and discovered it was an herb called fatesprig. She stole some of it, and our Alchemist already went through it all trying to run tests. But there are even more compounds we don't have access to that he's also using. Things Devora found out he's getting from other lands. Rissa, have you had contact with anyone outside the empire and Mysthelm?"

She shook her head. "No. I mean, we monitor the borders, but haven't seen any sign of foreigners trying to make contact. Lark?"

Lark, her best friend and royal advisor, nodded swiftly. "I'll see what I can find out."

"I just wish we knew what he's using to brainwash my sister." I licked my lips and faced Rose. "That's actually why I wanted to talk to *you*, Rose."

Rose let out a long breath. "There's no telling what combinations of charms he's using. The possibilities are endless."

I shifted in my seat. This was the tricky part. "You're right. We don't know what exact ingredients his Alchemist has. But I think it's pretty obvious one thing he *is* doing."

Leo understood first. "Absolutely not, Duma."

I sighed. *Here we go.*

Rose looked between us. "What are you talking about?"

"You're not asking her to practice again," Leo continued. His furry tail came out from behind him and wrapped around the leg of his chair, a habit I'd seen from the half Shifter when he got agitated. Which happened often around me.

Rose's eyes widened. "Oh."

"You know how dangerous *blood magic* is," Leo said to me. "There's always a consequence. Always a price to pay."

"Don't you think those people Scarven has tortured have been paying for long enough?" I snapped.

He gritted his teeth as he stood to face me, a short lock of dark brown hair coming to rest on his forehead at the motion. "There's always another way. You don't know what blood magic can do. It ruins people's lives. My father *died* because of it!"

I jumped to my feet, my dragon half raising its head in irritation. "You don't *know* that, Leo! That's your fear talking. I don't have time for this."

Shadows danced between us, solid enough to hold us back before we pounced on each other. "Settle down, boys," Lark said from the side, shadows billowing from her outstretched hands.

I took a breath and scrubbed a hand down my face, claws pulsing beneath my fingers. This was what I was afraid of. Blood magic was forbidden in the empire because some Alchemists believed it brought dark consequences for taking what was natural and making it *unnatural*.

Leo had used it once when he was young. He cast a spell to try and turn his Alchemist blood into that of a Shifter so he could be like his sister. It worked, to an extent. He gained some Shifter qualities. But the instant the spell was cast, his father dropped dead.

Leo blamed himself ever since. Himself *and* blood magic. He said it was the consequence for upsetting the balance of nature.

"I'm sorry, Leo," I said, lowering my voice. "This was my last resort. I wouldn't be asking if I thought I had other options. And, Rose..." One side of my mouth rose in a sad smile. "Viper, I'd *never* force you to do something you're not comfortable with. You don't even have to technically *use* blood magic. Even just talking us through the basic principles might help spark an idea."

Her emerald gaze fastened onto Leo with that sharp look she always had—the one that earned her the nickname "Viper" in the first place. But it was a tad softer when she looked at him, as if already full of an apology.

"I'll do it," she finally said, facing me again.

Leo reached for her. "Rose—"

"I have to try, Leo," she said, forehead pinched. "If this is something that can help all those people, then what choice do I have?"

From his corner of the drawing room, Chaz let out a grunt. "Well, we're all just a bunch of martyrs, aren't we?"

Leo rubbed the back of his neck, and Rose took his other hand. "I don't like this," he murmured to her.

She smiled softly. "You never do." Standing on her tiptoes, she kissed his cheek, then let her forehead rest against his. "I'll be okay. I know how to control it now. Just trust me."

"Always," Leo whispered. The way he looked at her made it feel like we were intruding on a private moment. I glanced away and caught Devora's eye.

After a pause, Clarissa cleared her throat. "I have one hundred and fifty guests arriving in"—she checked the ornate clock above the fireplace—"sixteen hours. Lark and Chaz, please draft letters and coordinate couriers to initiate contact with the closest king-doms we have record of. If we can get through to the Triad Realm, they may be our best bet. We need to find out more about the substances Scarven may be acquiring."

Turning to her brother, she said, "Rose and Leo, take Nox and Devora to your work room in the basements. Maybe you can get a head start on the Alchemy problem." She stopped doling out instructions to quickly grab Rose's arm, giving it a squeeze. "Please be careful. Don't do anything reckless."

Rose patted her hand. "Leo will make sure I don't put a *toe* out of line."

"And what about me, Empress?" Thorne curved his arms around Clarissa from the back. "What do you need me to do?"

She took a deep breath, then let it out slowly. "You?" Craning her neck, she looked up at him with a soft smile. "I need you to marry me in two days. How does that sound?"

He pressed his lips to her temple. "That, I can do."

Rose clapped her hands. A determined glint shone in her emerald eyes. "Time to out-magic the madman."

54

DEVORA

Rose and Leo led us out of the drawing room and down the lavish corridor until we came upon a set of stairs. Nox and I followed at a distance, and I watched as Leo rested a hand on the small of Rose's back. A furry tail came out and swiped against her calf, almost like a caress.

I leaned closer to Nox and whispered, "Are all of them always so disgustingly sweet?"

He snorted. "You get used to it."

"Did you and Rose ever..." I licked my lips, my stomach suddenly tight.

His eyebrow rose. "Jealous, darling?"

"No, I—just curious, that's all." My cheeks burned when he gave me *that* smirk. The one that sent fire to my core and made my shadows a jumbled mess.

His low chuckle embraced me. "Nothing ever happened between us. We're just friends."

I remembered his words from our sparring match in Tenebra. "Right, I forgot. You don't *fall in love*."

We reached a door at the bottom of the staircase. Rose and Leo walked through it, and as Nox held the door open for me, he murmured, "Things change."

I swallowed hard, but didn't have time to dwell on his words. We entered a huge, dark chamber with stone walls and a wooden floor covered in a myriad of rugs. They were all different patterns of bold, deep jewel tones—amethyst and ruby, emerald and sapphire, with gold accents that matched the standing candelabras around the room.

Ahead of us, Rose whispered a word, and the candles blazed to life.

"Welcome to my lair," she said with a grin. "Leo hates it when I call it that."

"You sound like a villain in a fairy tale," he muttered.

She blew him a kiss. "Rissa let me commandeer this section of the basement to set up a work room. I travel back and forth between here and my own apothecary in Feywood, making healing drafts and anything the hospital wing needs, plus whatever other charms may be useful."

"She likes to come down here and play with her leaves," Leo added. I couldn't help but laugh.

She smacked his arm. "I *like* to experiment." Her eyes widened. "Not like Scarven, of course. But Alchemy is always growing and changing. I like finding new ways to use what we already have, come up with new charms and spells, that sort of thing."

I could see why Nox thought she would be perfect to help. I took in the work room, the tall bookshelves with haphazardly stacked tomes and pieces of parchment, the glass vials of all shapes and sizes, the dried bouquets of herbs and flowers hanging from the ceiling. It smelled like a greenhouse and apothecary all in one.

In the center of the room stood a large desk with a black velvet chair behind it. Three leather-bound books were perched on the edge of the desk, and one was open right next to them with a quill lying on top.

The whole place was teeming with magic. A vibrant energy that spoke of someone who loved what they did and put time into perfecting their craft.

"I love it," I said, drinking in every inch of the space.

Rose blushed. "Thank you." She dropped into the desk chair. "But enough about me. What exactly are we looking for?"

"A way to counteract whatever compulsion Scarven has over Vera," Nox said immediately. "And potentially others."

"Do you think this fatesprig stuff you talked about is connected?" Rose asked.

"I'm not sure. It seems to only affect magic itself. From what we saw of our tests, it didn't have anything to do with controlling people or wiping their minds."

Rose crossed her arms over her chest. "And what type of *tests* did you run?"

"What, you don't trust me?" he asked. Rose continued to stare at him, unamused. Nox sighed. "Fine. I had our Alchemist inject me with it."

I jerked back. "You *what?*" He had said he was considering it in one of our magical message threads, but I never knew he actually went *through* with it. I couldn't stop myself from scanning him, as if there would be some remnant of the test still riddling his body.

Rose threw her hands in the air. "Seriously? The first rule of Alchemy is 'Don't put unknown substances into your body!'"

Nox raised an eyebrow. "I don't know, sounds like a good time to me."

"*Nox,*" she said, a warning in her tone. Nox shifted slightly on his feet—almost imperceptible, if you weren't watching.

But I was always watching. And he was anxious. He often covered his unease with humor—I supposed that was something we had in common.

"It was our last sample, and trying it on a human subject was the only thing we hadn't done yet," Nox finally answered, eyes sliding briefly to me. "It wasn't the wisest decision, but I wasn't in the best headspace at the moment."

I moved closer to him on instinct, reaching out a hand to his elbow before hastily pulling away. Was it because of *me*? Did he take the fatesprig because he was distracted and worried about me?

The thought made my chest both soften and ache at the same time.

"You're an idiot," Rose said. "What did it do?"

He clenched a hand at his side. "It was pain unlike anything I've ever felt. There was this...this *fire* burning every inch of me." A silence fell over the chamber as he paused. "It stripped away my magic for about two days. It was like my dragon half was dead. Mutilated."

I licked my lips. "That's what it felt like for me too. When he— when I was in the cell. The knife he used. And the cuffs. I think it was fatesprig."

Nox's eyes met mine, and the silver slits of his dragon appeared before vanishing just as quickly. My hands twitched with the urge to reach out and touch him. I didn't know when he'd become my anchor, but it was harder and harder to stop myself from needing him.

Rose's voice was quiet as she looked at me and said, "I'm sorry for everything you went through. It sounds horrible."

I adjusted my glasses, trying to brush off the memories. "Yeah, well, I was lucky to get out when I did. Others have gone through much worse." I couldn't help but look at Nox again.

Rose's emerald eyes swept over me. "You care about him. About *all* of them."

It wasn't a question. I simply nodded, more heat rising up my chest. Yes, I *cared* about him. More than I'd let myself admit. I worried when he was gone too long. I felt the emptiness of his absence, sharp and cold, and I craved him when the rest of the world felt too far. I wanted to be *close* to him. To be wrapped forever in his fire and safety and steadfastness. I would rather Scarven string me up in his cells again than betray Nox's trust.

Care was too small a word.

Leo cleared his throat, and the heavy moment passed. "So, he's weaponizing the fatesprig by imbuing objects with it," he said. "If he mass-produces something like this, if he gives his guards or armies—"

"He already is," Nox said grimly. "When we invaded his mansion to get Devora back, his guards had weapons covered in it."

Leo let out a breath. "If he ever decided to go up against the empire, we would be defenseless."

"Which is why we need to find a way to stop him," Nox said. "And anyone under his control. Like Vera. You got anything that can help in that handy Grimoire of yours?"

"If I don't, we'll make one." She grabbed the top leather-bound book off the stack and glanced at me. "This is called a Grimoire. Think of it as an Alchemist's recipe book. This one was my mother's." She placed it on the desk and began flipping through pages.

"Maybe we can make something ingestible," Leo suggested, leaning over her shoulder to read the pages. "Make his sister take it, and it'll fight off his compulsion."

"I love when you talk Alchemy to me." Rose quickly pecked his cheek. "Okay, okay. Compulsion...let me think. I know minor spells that can briefly compel people, but it's not very strong, and they're still cognizant of what's going on. It sounds like what's happening to Vera is in a class of its own." She shut the Grimoire and reached for another one on her desk. These pages were more weathered, the binding fraying at the edges.

"This was my father's," she commented. "He was a little more... *innovative* than my mother."

Leo snorted. "That's one way to put it."

"He did some testing with blood magic," Rose admitted. "Nothing harmful. He was just curious. Tried to see if it could help with problems the empire was facing—diseases, food shortage, that sort of thing."

"What's so bad about blood magic, anyway?" I asked, watching as Rose pored over the old pages, taking in the faintly scribbled words and undecipherable drawings.

"It's unnatural," Leo said. "Alchemy uses what we're *naturally* given—herbs, flowers, stones, the like. While, yes, our bodies are natural, using blood magic requires force. Forcing blood from a victim, taking their bones, cutting their flesh…it's savage. Magic shouldn't be forced or taken. It shouldn't be *harmful*. But people do it because it makes their power stronger by a hundredfold, and they don't care about the consequences."

"Even if it could mean saving lives?" I asked.

Leo sighed. "Once upon a time, I would've said no, that we should never use it under any circumstance. I used to see the world in black and white. Everything was either right or wrong, and there was no in between. I hate it, but I've learned that sometimes there's no other way. You just have to trust the person putting that kind of power in their hands." He laid his hand on Rose's back and softly kissed her temple. "Just be careful, little wolf. You know it will have a price."

I tilted my head in curiosity. "What does that mean?"

"All dark magic has a price. Think of it as a way to balance things out," Rose said, looking up from the Grimoire. "There was this man in my home province who used it to raise his wife from the dead. And it worked, sort of. Her body came back to life, but she was basically a soulless shell. She killed her husband in front of their child, then went on a rampage and killed even more people before she was stopped. There are stories like that up and down our history books, cautionary tales for people trying to conquer forbidden magic."

She looked down at her father's Grimoire, her knuckles white with how tightly she gripped it. "But the thing is, it's unpredictable and not always what you think. It doesn't have to be the person who casts it who pays the price. Like the man who raised his wife. Sure, he died, but none of her other victims had anything to do with it. *They* didn't deserve to die. I can only imagine the suffering Scarven and his Alchemist have caused with how long they've been practicing."

"If it means getting my sister back, I'll pay it," Nox said.

Leo looked at him with a grim expression. "It may not be *you* who pays it, Nox. Are you willing to risk it? Risk *anyone*?"

For the first time, Nox faltered. He looked down at me, and I could see the indecision warring inside him. He was always the first to jump into danger, but the idea of someone *else* being in that danger, something *he* couldn't control, gave him pause.

I swallowed hard and nodded at him, trying to imbue my eyes with encouragement to give him that final push. I knew how desperately he wanted his sister back. "Whatever happens, we'll face it together," I whispered.

His jaw twitched. "Together," he said slowly. When he faced Rose again, his voice was laced with more trepidation than before. "Can you do it, Rose?"

"I don't know. I need some time to study the texts. It's not a *no*, Nox," she said quickly when his face fell. "We have a couple of days. But...there *is* something you could do to help."

"Anything."

Rose reached for a jeweled dagger resting next to the Grimoire, her fingers lingering on the hilt. "I need your blood. It's the closest we have to your sister's, and it might make her antidote stronger."

The air felt heavier, as if the magic wavering in the room knew what Rose was requesting. I swallowed a lump in my throat. A shiver went down my spine, but Nox showed no fear. He strode to the desk and held his arm out.

"Are you sure?" Rose asked, her green eyes cutting to his.

He nodded once, jaw tight. "For Vera."

She took a deep breath, then drew the blade across his palm in a smooth arc. I flinched at the motion, my own hand twitching as if it were my skin being split. Nox's blood welled to the surface immediately, a deep, gleaming crimson. It dripped into a glass vial with soft *plinks*, each one echoing in the lair.

The cut was already healing itself when Rose took the dagger away. She corked the vial and set it on her desk. The tension in the room was still taut when she said, "You two better get some rest. We've got a busy couple of days ahead of us."

Nox nodded. "Thank you. You have no idea what this means to me."

She gave him a tight-lipped smile as the candles around us flickered. "Don't thank me yet, Nox."

55

DEVORA

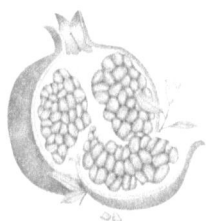

"*Did you think you could hide from me, love?*"

Scarven's words permeated my dream. I could feel him shrouding me, covering me, embedded in the walls of my mind.

"*Did you think you could escape?*" A cold, invisible finger traced down my neck. "*No one ever escapes me. You are mine, Devora.*" He drew out my name, his voice so close now, I could practically feel his breath on me as ghostly fingers clamped over my throat.

The wound on my neck pulsed with white-hot pain. I tried to thrash out of his grip, but the nightmare ensnared me. I was powerless and at his mercy, the way he always wanted.

But then he released me.

The never-ending blackness of my dream gave way to a figure kneeling on the ground. As the shadows pulled it closer, it began to take form. Broad shoulders, thick muscles, unruly dark-blond hair.

Nox.

He was yanked backward by something I couldn't see, forced to face me with a look of silent torment. I reached for him, my heart pumping louder with each passing second. What was he doing here? What did Scarven—

Nox's shirt ripped open, and before I could blink, four claw marks dragged down his bare skin, so deep they cut through muscle until flesh dangled from his open chest.

"No!" I shrieked.

Panting, Nox rolled his head along his neck to stare at me, the light in his eyes dimming. He opened his mouth. "Dev—"

With a jagged slash from an invisible blade, his head was severed from his body.

A scream burst from my throat. Pressure rose inside me, anguish flooding my veins without a way out. My arms vibrated with the force of it, my head pounding and chest crumbling and shadows—

"Devora," a voice whispered, breaking through the storm. "Devora, wake up." It got clearer with every word, and the darkness began to dissipate. I could dimly feel rough hands holding my shoulders.

"It's just a dream. You have to stop," the voice said. I couldn't tell if it was Scarven's or Nox's as my vision bled into reality.

With a whimper, I opened my eyes to find myself sitting upright in a bed, Nox's navy eyes gleaming back at me. His body hovered a foot from mine, his knees pressed into the mattress on either side of me.

And behind him was a wall of shadows.

My eyes widened as I took it in. Surrounding us was a barrier of thick, billowing shadows, so tightly packed, they weren't even able to dance and twist the way they always did. Faint shimmers of red flashed back at me, but they were gone before I could blink.

I looked down and saw wooden shards covering my hands and bed. The headboard had been obliterated. My shadows continued to gather, filling in the gaps between Nox and me, almost as if they were guarding us. They were full of a nervous, violent energy I'd never felt before.

"You have to call them back, Devora," Nox said softly, cupping my cheek. My shadows looped up his arm. "You're going to bring the whole room down."

I squeezed my eyes shut and tried to urge them back to me, but the shock from my dream still lingered fresh in my mind. My shadows responded to my panic. They solidified even more, and the chamber gave a sudden tremble.

"I don't know how," I gasped out. "They—they aren't listening." When I opened my eyes again, Nox inhaled sharply.

"Your eyes." He stroked the top of my cheek. "They're black again, like the night of the Noctus Vigil. Remember what Calyra said? Your shadows are tied to your emotions. Tell me what happened. Tell me what you're feeling."

I let out a small sob and shook my head, wanting to rid myself of the images. Those claw marks, his head rolling in the darkness, his body hitting the floor as blood coated my shadows.

Magic vibrated within me, and I heard something in the room crack.

"Devora," he said firmly. "Look at me." His hand on my neck forced me to meet his gaze.

A tear rolled down my cheek. "It was Scarven," I whispered. "He was there. He said I would never escape him. And then he— you—" My words turned into a shudder, and my shadows lashed out, wrapping around my waist like they could shield me.

"It wasn't real," Nox said. "Whatever you saw, whatever he said, it wasn't real. He can't get to you."

I sniffed and held back another sob. "It wasn't me. It—it was you. He killed *you*."

His throat bobbed as he swallowed, then slowly put his forehead to mine. "He will never take me from you, Devora, darling. I'm not leaving you."

I'm not leaving you.

I knew he couldn't promise it. I knew we had no way of controlling what happened next. But his words still soothed something inside me, still erased the pockets of doubt and fear enough for my shadows to slowly, slowly, slowly make their way back to me.

They swirled through the air as they dispersed, like clouds

moving to reveal the sky. The room came into focus, and I saw the damage I'd caused. Portraits had fallen from the walls, and glass was scattered across the floor. Both bedside tables and the armoire in the far-right corner had been blown to pieces. The wooden mantel above the fireplace was broken on one side and dangling by a few splinters.

Nox started to move away, but I grabbed his arm. I couldn't stand to watch him walk away. Not after that.

Never again.

"Pomegranates," I whispered.

The thread between us tightened. He closed his eyes and furrowed his brow, the look on his face nothing short of pained. His arm shook as I brought his hand back to my cheek, those strong fingers and rough calluses scraping against me.

He still barely touched me. I could feel how much he wanted to, though. I could sense his magic begging to be released, could see how much force it took to control himself. He was *always* controlling himself.

I wondered what it must be like to have all that power beneath his skin. Coiled and eager to strike, but held back by a man who spent his entire life learning to keep it in check.

Scarven had touched me plenty of times. He didn't care about holding back. He didn't care about making others feel safe. Every grasp was a reminder of what he could take.

But Nox?

His touch was one of restraint. Of quiet, unending power. And I ached to be cherished by hands that could bring down mountains.

"Please," I said, voice raspy as I dragged my gaze from his lips to his eyes. "Don't go, Nox."

His gaze flared silver. "After all you've been through, after what he did to you, I just—" He swallowed again, then watched his own thumb graze the top of my cheek. His body leaned closer, heat washing over my neck, even as he said, "You need time, Devora. I should let you heal. You need—"

"Don't tell me what I *need*." The words left me in a rush. The desire to be near him made my chest tighten. "You act like I'm breakable, like one touch is going to shatter me. And maybe it will. Maybe that's what I *want*." I put my palm on his chest, and his heart pounded erratically beneath my fingertips.

His eyes burned into mine, navy and silver and wild and wrecked. A growl crawled up his throat and vibrated through my arm. "You don't know what you're asking for, darling."

He was so close now, his nose grazed mine. When I spoke again, my lips barely brushed his with each word.

"Shatter me, Nox. Break me to pieces. You're the only one who can put me back together again."

With a final breath, his control snapped. His lips crashed into mine like lightning piercing the sky.

Finally.

There was no hesitation. No slowly stepping a toe into the water. This kiss was a storm breaking open. His hand found the nape of my neck, and he threaded his fingers through my hair with a tug. My back hit the broken headboard as his other hand gripped my waist, pulling me toward him. His lips were warm and demanding and fit perfectly to mine.

Fates, he felt like everything we'd been holding back for months. Every angry word, every searing glare, every passing touch. My shadows writhed until they broke free and wound around our bodies, rushing along our skin in waves.

Fingers dug into skin, fabric, hair. Fire and desperation crawled at both of us, the chaos of the last few weeks fleeing our minds and leaving us weightless. My heart raced with a different kind of urgency—not one born of fear or panic, but of *life*.

That was him. *He* made me feel alive. He made me feel reckless and open and free. But mostly, he made me feel *safe*. Even as his power trembled beneath his skin and his grip tightened at the back of my neck, all I could think was that I wanted to be *his*. I wanted to be consumed by him.

When he lowered his lips to the uninjured side of my neck and tenderly kissed every inch of skin, I let the world fall away. Let the ache in my chest from all my pain, my sorrow, my fears, burst into something new.

It didn't feel like breaking. It didn't feel like falling.

It felt like surrender.

And maybe, finally...I was home.

56

NOX

For the second time in as many days, the nightmares didn't find me that night. I did wake up several times, though. Not out of distress or despair. Just because...I wanted to see her.

That red hair like fire spilling across my arm, her curves tucked into my side, the way her nose scrunched in sleep and her toes twitched beneath the covers. I wanted to hear her soft, steady breaths and watch the rise and fall of her chest. To know she was safe and not back in those chains.

I hadn't meant to stay there all night. But I couldn't bring myself to leave.

Until a sharp knock pounded on the door.

"Hey, get up," Rose's muffled voice rang out. "This isn't a vacation. We've got work to do." There was one more knock, and then, "I know Nox is in there. Be downstairs in twenty minutes, or I'm releasing the bride on you."

Devora flipped onto her back with a groan and stretched her arms above her head. I couldn't help but smile when her sleepy eyes met mine. The terrors of her nightmare were still there, but somehow, seeing her like this dimmed their sharp edges. Her bright blue-green eyes were crinkled, an adorable crease appearing at her brow as she fought a yawn.

Her lips slowly pulled into a grin, and it transformed her entire face. "What are you staring at?" she asked, voice still raspy.

"Nothing." I shrugged. "I just never get to see you like this. I like it."

She chuckled. "What, morning breath and tangled hair?"

I propped my elbow on the pillow. I couldn't take my eyes off her. "You're beautiful, Devora. No matter the time of day."

Her smile faltered, a hint of vulnerability sliding into her gaze. She tried to dip her head, but I put a finger under her chin, leaning forward to brush my lips against hers—a promise and a reminder all at once. That our kiss last night had been *real*. That it meant something to me.

When I broke away, she let out a soft breath that sent fire to my core. Her hand came up to the side of my neck to pull me closer.

Another bang sounded on the door. This time, it was a deeper voice that yelled at us. "Rose wasn't kidding. Up. Now."

Devora sighed. Her mouth was still close enough to mine that her breath made goosebumps rise along my neck. "*Leo.* That Shifter hearing is annoying."

I froze with my lips on the edge of her mouth. Heat surged as my dragon half growled, possessiveness boiling to the surface.

I hummed and traced a path down her jaw. "Think very carefully before saying another man's name right now, darling."

She chuckled and pushed my shoulders. "Are all Shifters so territorial?"

"You have no idea," I murmured. That little smirk I loved toyed across her features, and in that moment, I didn't care if Rissa sent her entire Royal Guard to beat down the door. Placing a hand on her hip, I moved back in for another kiss.

My lips met the back of her hand. I narrowed my eyes as she giggled. "We have to go help with wedding stuff, Nox."

"I don't care. It's not like it's my wedding."

She swatted my shoulder. "You're a bad influence." When she

leaned against the headboard, her head hit the back wall. She reached for it with a wince, then snorted as we both remembered her shadows had destroyed the entire bedframe.

"Great, now I have to tell Clarissa about this." She hitched a thumb at the hunk of broken wood. "She's barely forgiven me as it is."

I hauled myself off the bed and lifted my arms high in a stretch. I caught her staring with her teeth dragging at her bottom lip. "You can't keep looking at me like that, darling," I rasped.

She shuffled to the edge of the bed and looped a finger in the waistband of my cotton pants. "Like what?" Her bright eyes flared.

I dragged my nose along her temple, then down to her jaw and below her ear. Her breath hitched when I gently pulled at her earlobe with my teeth. "Like you want me to be a bad influence."

She tugged me closer to her. "I'm probably worse," she whispered. Without warning, she turned her head to capture my lips again, and, Fates, I was helpless. I wrapped her long hair around my fist, then pulled her head back to deepen the kiss.

More pounding at the door. "I swear, if you two don't—"

Devora broke away right as we both shouted, "We're coming!"

She looked back at me, chest heaving, and pointed at the adjoining door between our two chambers. "Go. Now. Before I do something I'll regret."

I chuckled. With one last kiss to the curve of her neck, I pushed away. "Yes, ma'am."

The last thing I saw before I shut the door was her smiling face, and it was the happiest I'd been in decades.

———

WE SPENT the day running around the palace and the central sector of Veridia City, picking up last-minute orders for both the welcome feast and the wedding. Considering this was the first royal wedding since Rissa's own parents were married, the entire capital was buzzing with excitement.

I barely saw Devora all day. She was overseeing floral arrange-ments with Rose, and then delivering gowns and suits to the family. Leo and I were in the kitchen, making sure the food and cakes were on time.

The day passed in a whirlwind of lace, flower petals, and icing, but it was all worth it to see the look on Rissa and Thorne's face when we celebrated them at the welcome feast. I was worried she wouldn't be able to put last night's conversation behind her and simply enjoy herself—Rissa had always viewed taking care of her own needs as selfish—but the smile on her face said it all.

She, Thorne, and Marigold were the perfect family. Happy and adored and loved without condition.

I had a sense of happiness and love with my Order, but this... this kind of love was something I had fought against ever since I learned it could be weaponized. And yet, I felt it trying to slip its way through in a swath of shadows and red waves.

The worst part was that I didn't know how to stop it. I didn't know if I *could* stop it anymore. I knew deep down that I wasn't like my half-brother, however much my own fears tried to twist my thoughts. But part of me wondered if I wasn't my own brand of monster. Knowing the way I felt about someone would only hurt them in the end, and being selfish enough to take what I wanted anyway.

Being with Devora didn't make me forget about the conse-quences—she made me unafraid to face them. She made me feel brave and bold, passionate and slightly irresponsible. She made me feel *free*. Something I hadn't felt since I was taken from my home and forced in a cell.

But in those moments when she was gone, the doubts rose again.

If my happiness was her death sentence, how could I ever let myself keep her?

The welcome feast bled into night, and as the guests made their way back to the guest wing or to their own homes in the capital, our little group found ourselves up in Rissa's personal study with snacks and several plates of cake.

Chaz, the burly guard who was the biggest goof of us all, was laughing with Leo in the corner by Rissa's desk. Rose sat on a nearby settee next to Lark, and every once in a while, Rose would leisurely reach behind and rest a hand on Leo's knee. Thorne was rubbing Rissa's feet in front of the fireplace while she ate small pieces of cake.

The crackling fire sent a pleasant, sleepy haze over the room. When Devora settled next to me on the couch with another plate of sweets, I had to physically restrain myself from pulling her onto my lap. Fates, she looked good. She had on a dark purple pantsuit with sheer sleeves that accentuated her curves, and a cape attached at the waist that gave the illusion of a dress. My eyes kept straying to her, even when others tried to talk to me.

"Who gave these two adjoining rooms, anyway?" Rose said from across the office, tipping her chin toward us. "You know, it would be a shame if someone just so happened to spell your doors shut tonight."

I gave her a lazy grin. "Your little spells can't hold me for long, viper. I'm immune to all your little *tricks*."

Her green eyes sparkled. "That's what they always say."

"What about Grimlock?" Rissa called from her chair, where Thorne still massaged her feet and calves. "Is the mighty dragon Shifter immune to *that*?"

"What's Grimlock?" Devora asked.

"A specialty drink of the capital," Rose said. "I discovered it for the first time last year. It makes you unable to tell lies."

Devora raised an eyebrow. "And people drink this for fun?"

"It's mostly used for interrogations," I said with a shrug.

Lark added, "But *dear* Rissa likes to make it into a game."

"Not this again," Leo grumbled.

"What? It *is* fun," Rissa said innocently when her brother shot her a look. To Devora, she said, "Someone gives you a dare, and you either do it, or take a drink of Grimlock while they ask you whatever they want. I call it Grimlock or Glory. We used to play it at our favorite tavern when we were younger and one of us had snuck in a bottle of it."

I hummed. "Perhaps the night before your wedding isn't the best time to play, Rissa."

She gave me a sweet smile. "I'm the bride." She cocked her head. "*And* the empress, for that matter."

"I mean, I'm down," Chaz boomed from his seat by the desk. He propped his boots on top of Rissa's desk, and when she arched an eyebrow at him, he hastily removed them.

"Fine. Chaz, you go first," Rissa said. "Grimlock or Glory?"

He puffed out his large chest. "Glory. Always."

Rissa held out her empty plate, her lips turning up into a fox-like grin. "Stride to the kitchens and get me more cake." Chaz scoffed and crossed the room to grab her plate, but she snatched it back and added, "*And* bring back the cook's undergarments."

"Done and *done*. I've been trying to get Lyra to go out with me for ages anyway," Chaz said, swiping the plate from her with a salute. "Come on, Rissa. At least give me a challenge." Then he vanished into thin air.

"Alright, Leo, while we're waiting for him, it's your turn," Rissa said in a sing-song voice. "Grimlock or Glory?"

"I've been burned one too many times by you, sister," Leo said. "Grimlock."

Rissa got up and walked to her desk, opened a cabinet, and pulled out a bottle of gray liquid. She poured a small amount into a glass and held it out to Leo. When he drank it, she waited a few seconds before asking, "Who would win in a fight, you or Nox?"

He gave her a bland look. "Seriously? That's not even a good question."

"I don't know, sounds good to me," I interjected.

"You know the rules, Leo," Rissa said.

Leo sighed. "Fine. I guess..." He gave a little growl. "Nox."

Rose snickered, and I barked out a laugh. Leo had slowly warmed up to me over the year I'd known him, but it took a while for the broody half Shifter, half Alchemist to fully trust me. It didn't help that I knew how to push his buttons.

"I'm touched, monkey boy," I crooned, using the nickname Rose affectionately gave him.

"You're a *dragon*," he mumbled under his breath, shifting in his seat as if the words pained him to say. He looked like he was trying to burrow into the ground. "Nobody can beat a dragon. You're too amazing." He clamped his lips shut and glared at me.

My grin broadened. "I *knew* you liked me."

"Fates, as if his ego wasn't already large enough," Devora said with a roll of her eyes, then shot me a wink.

"Your turn then, Devora, darling," I teased. "Grimlock or Glory?"

Devora's smile slowly faded as she looked between Rissa and me, holding our stares for several seconds. Finally, she turned to me. "Grimlock."

The steadfast look in her eyes made all the humor leave me. It felt like a turning point. A full white flag of surrender. If there was any part of me that didn't trust her, this was her way of proving once and for all that she was on our side. The Grimlock would make her spill any secret, any lie.

But I didn't *need* her to prove herself. I trusted her beyond the shadow of a doubt.

The others might have used this opportunity to ask her if she was truly loyal to us. To make sure she regretted her actions with Rissa in Mysthelm, to appease their own worries that she might betray one of us again. That was what Devora *expected*. I could see it in her eyes, like she was preparing for battle.

She was always shielding herself against the words and expectations of others. A quick joke, a sarcastic comment, a defensive stance. Even her shadows liked to guard her, a second layer of skin she subconsciously developed.

I knew I was partially responsible for putting it there, with the way I treated her in the beginning. But I wanted her to know that I didn't need *proof* of the kind of person she was. I knew the truth in my bones.

"Nox?" Rissa held out a glass of Grimlock. I took it, then slowly handed it to Devora. She didn't take her eyes off me as she downed the contents in one go.

"Devora..." I started, lingering on her name. Her heartbeat remained steady, her shoulders straight, her stare unwavering.

My lips tilted into a smirk. "Petunias or tulips?"

Her head reared back. "*What?*"

"Marigold told me I should get you flowers for the wedding. So, which do you prefer, petunias or tulips?"

A soft laugh escaped her, and I could have sworn her eyes misted over before she blinked it back. "Tulips. But only the dark ones."

"Whatever you want, darling." My fingers brushed hers as I took back the glass, then I looked at Thorne. "That little girl of yours is far more perceptive than I gave her credit for."

"And she knows it," Thorne agreed.

Thud. A heavy pair of boots hit the floor as Chaz reappeared. He had a plate piled high with meats, cheese, and all sorts of pastries in one hand, and a pair of black boxers in the other.

When we all glanced between him and the boxers, he grunted. "I thought Lyra would be the cook on duty tonight, but she wasn't. Say hello to Matthias."

He waved the boxers in the air, and we all burst into laughter.

57

NOX

There was a tap at the door separating mine and Devora's rooms as I buttoned the cuff of my sleeve. I crossed the space in three strides and opened the door to find Devora standing in her dress for the wedding, a deep turquoise velvet number.

My mouth fell open as my gaze swept down her form. The long sleeves and bodice clung perfectly to her curves, with gold accents etched into the fabric. The turquoise skirt fell behind her, little gold sequins dotting the length of it and catching the light.

"Tie me up?" she asked.

"I mean—"

She turned so her back faced me. "The *dress*." With a little chuckle, she carefully moved her hair over one shoulder, exposing the criss-crossing pattern of ribbon over smooth skin that ended in two strands down her back.

"You," I stalked toward her and reached for the ribbon, "are trying to kill me." I brought my lips to the curve of her neck and placed a gentle kiss.

"Does it feel wrong?" she asked, her voice a little breathless. "After everything we've been through, after all the people waiting for us...is this wrong? Being happy?"

My brow furrowed. I finished tying the ribbons and snaked my hands around her stomach, pulling her closer. Truth be told, I had the same thoughts. It was difficult not to feel guilty when so many suffered, and here we were, living out some sort of perfect dream in this pocket of the world.

I kissed her temple. "I feel the same way. But that doesn't mean we don't care about the others. It doesn't mean we still won't do everything in our power to help them." I spun her around, and those big, guarded eyes peered up at me. "I don't know what this is between us, but I *do* know it's the happiest I've been in longer than I can remember."

I brushed a strand of hair behind her ear. "I'm selfish when it comes to you, Devora. I've never been able to stay away. I don't know what the future will be, but I want to take any scrap of joy I can from the life that's stolen so much from me."

She nodded. "You deserve that." Her arms wound around my neck, and I closed my eyes when she scratched her nails at the base of my skull. "Happiness."

"I don't know about that, darling." The words slipped out unbidden, my guard coming down with her nails at my neck and her body so close to mine. I didn't talk about these things with anyone besides Tessa and Kieran. I didn't let anyone see the shame and insecurities resting beneath my skin.

"Why would you think that?" She moved a hand to cup my cheek.

I sighed. "You don't know all the things I've done, Devora."

"You mean, all the things *Scarven* has made you do. He may order you to do terrible things to people, but you told me how you get them out." Her voice was so tender, a tone I'd only heard her use with the children at the Keep. "You *save* them, Nox. You take awful situations and make the most of them."

"Not always," I gritted out. Her hands suddenly felt too soft, too pure, too *good* to be touching me. I wrapped my fingers around her wrists and moved them down, then took a step back.

"I've killed people," I said hoarsely, turning away from her. The sounds of their screams still echoed in my head. "I didn't want to, but I've done it. I've tortured them. I may as well have put them in his cells. You were right about me all those weeks ago. I wanted you to think I was better than that, that I was some vigilante or harbinger of justice, but that hasn't always been true." My throat burned with the effort of keeping my emotions from clawing up my throat.

"I once told you *he* was the monster," I said slowly. "But sometimes I think I am too."

There was a moment of silence, and I refused to look at her. Refused to see the disgust on her face—or worse, the realization that she'd been right all along. From the day she spied on me and accused me of hurting our people.

I heard her take a deep breath. And then—

"No."

The word cut through the air like a blade.

My neck jerked toward her. "What?"

"No," she repeated.

"No...what?"

Her arms crossed, chin lifting. "No, you don't get to sabotage this for yourself. Not with me."

The force in her tone rattled me, but then her edges softened. "I'm the last person who would hate you for this. You *know* what I've done. Selfish, cruel things. And I didn't do them for anyone but myself. But *you*?" She stepped closer, eyes flashing. "You did them to protect your sister. To keep your cover so he didn't grow suspicious. That doesn't make you a monster, Nox."

Her voice cracked, wetness glinting on her lashes, but she didn't back down. "Someone who's half the man you are would've given up by now. But you didn't. You endured. You saved who you could. And I *hate* him for making you think you can't have this." She put her hand back on my cheek, and I closed my eyes, trying to take in her words instead of batting them to the side.

"So, no," she whispered. "I won't let you push me away." She ran her thumb along my lips, and they parted on an exhale. "*You* get to be happy. You get to be free. Because if someone like you can't...what hope do the rest of us have?"

I kissed the pad of her thumb, breathing her in. I desperately wanted that to be true.

"Say something," she urged softly.

I slowly opened my eyes. "Okay," I murmured.

She held my gaze. "Okay? Do you believe me?"

I paused. "I believe *in* you." And I believed she meant what she said, which was worth more to me than any touch, any kiss, any stolen moment.

Her mouth tugged up at the corners. "We'll work on that." Lifting up on her toes, she kissed my jaw, then my cheek, then my lips, melting into me as I held her close. I didn't think I would ever see myself the way she did, but she was right about one thing. I had to stop punishing myself. Scarven did that enough for all of us.

"Just one more thing," I said as I stepped through the adjoining door into my room. I grabbed the flower crown Marigold made this morning and brought it back out.

Devora laughed and put a hand on her chest. "For me?"

"The one and only." I carefully set it on her head. The mixture of deep purple tulips and white carnations looked perfect with her vivid hair.

"Beautiful," I murmured. "Are you ready to go watch our disgustingly sweet friends get married?"

She took my hand. "Maybe it's not so disgusting anymore."

THE PALACE HELD nothing back for the wedding. Fresh lilies, roses, marigolds, and irises were placed all down the corridors leading to the grand ballroom. Gold drapes hung from the ceilings, and an Alchemist had spelled them to sparkle like diamonds. The ballroom itself was straight out of a storybook. Rose and Leo enchanted hundreds of candles to hang in mid-air, giving the space a soft, flickering glow. Bouquets overflowing with greenery were balanced on golden pedestals that marked rows and rows of chairs. One of the Lightbender servants had cast beams to refract in the windows, which made the light shimmer like rainbows.

I could see Lark and Rose's hands in all of it. Knowing Rissa, she would've been content to marry Thorne in the back of a carriage. But her best friends wanted to give her the fairy tale she never thought she would have.

Devora and I sat toward the front, watching all the guests from the capital filter in. The buzz and excitement were palpable. People loved celebrating, but more than that, they loved their empress. Clarissa had been such a beacon of light for the empire ever since she took over. It brought a smile to my lips to see how her people fawned over her.

When the magical candles dimmed above us, the crowd hushed. A string quartet in the back played a soft melody that echoed through the chamber. Chaz pushed Lark in her wheelchair down the aisle, the latter looking beautiful in a burgundy gown. Rose followed in matching attire. She sniffed, yanked a handkerchief from inside her flower bouquet, and dabbed her eyes.

Thorne and a priest robed in emerald green stepped onto a raised dais at the front, and my heart swelled when I saw little Marigold holding her father's hand. She wore her own flower crown, the light pinks and whites resting in her bronze hair and framing her face. Their shepherding dog, Mia, sat at her feet, with a flower twisted in her collar. Her tail thumped excitedly against Thorne's leg.

Thorne was barely holding himself together. His features were screwed as if to stop himself from crying, and he kept wiping his cheeks with the back of his hand. I chuckled softly to myself. He wasn't a small man by any means—almost as big as me. His long, thick hair and beard made him appear far more menacing than the hopeless romantic he actually was.

I couldn't stop myself from looking down at Devora. I understood how a great love could bring an unbreakable man to his knees.

The double doors at the entrance opened with a boom, and everyone rose to their feet. Rissa floated down the aisle in a stunning gown of light pink and gold, with a shimmering veil covering her face. On one side of her stood Leo, and on the other was a blonde-and-gray-haired older woman, with the same kind eyes and soft smile of her daughter. Evadine Aris gripped Rissa's arm tighter as she and Leo led her to the dais.

The ceremony was brief but beautiful, and as I watched Rissa and Thorne radiate with that glow of new love, something in my chest ached. I loved my Order, but everything around us was constantly cloaked in darkness and secrets, threats lurking around every corner. They chose to be there because they believed in our cause, but that didn't make it easy.

Devora's hand slid into mine, and I rubbed my thumb along the outside of hers. *This* was easy. She'd come into my life in a blaze of fiery hair and shadows and made things so incredibly complicated...until it wasn't. Until it was just her.

Scarven will come for her.

My muscles tightened, but I pushed that voice away. Let him try. I would *never* let him get near her again.

The ceremony ended in thunderous applause, and a flash of colorful fire shot into the high ceiling as the priest crowned Thorne —now Emperor Consort Thorne Aris. The two strode back down the aisle with Marigold and Mia in tow. Marigold leaped up and down, throwing flower petals that Mia promptly caught and ate.

The next hour was a whirlwind of eating, drinking, and dancing in the adjacent ballroom. I hadn't had this much fun since Everett planned a surprise summer solstice party with the children at the Keep a couple years ago, and we'd spent hours at the beach dancing around campfires and roasting anything we could eat.

I spun Devora in my arms, wishing I could bottle this feeling rising in my heart.

She grinned up at me, cheeks flushed and hair mussed. "I'm going to go get a drink."

I nodded and watched her walk toward the refreshment table, unable to stop the ridiculous smile plastered across my face.

"Nox," someone called. Rose sauntered toward me with a knowing look on her olive features. "Never thought I'd say this, but you two look good together."

"I always look good, darling," I drawled. "And trust me, she looks better."

Rose rolled her eyes. "You know what I mean. You look *happy*. And not that fake-happy, 'oh, I'm so charming' business." She twirled a finger at me.

"I don't know if I should be offended or not."

Patting my shoulder, she said, "Deflect all you want. How did that even happen, anyway? The last thing I saw was you hauling her off to Drakorum, kicking and screaming."

"I don't know." I tracked Devora's red hair as she made her way back to us, my chest warming at the sight. "Some things you just can't explain. I seem to remember you not having the fondest feelings for a certain half Shifter in the beginning," I said with a grin.

"Yeah, well," she shrugged, "the tail does it for me."

"Do I even want to know what you're talking about?" Devora asked as she approached and handed me a drink.

"Oh, nothing important," Rose said, and the three of us clinked our glasses together. "So, I think I figured out something that can help you, Nox."

I instantly jerked to attention. "For Vera?"

Rose nodded. Beckoning us to follow her, she led Devora and me to a small alcove by the exit. She slipped something onto her tongue and muttered a spell. I felt it stretch in the air like a bowstring pulling tight, then it settled into place. The cacophony of the rest of the ballroom faded into a hush.

"Silencing charm," she said. "Anyway, I studied my father's old Grimoire some more and found a weaker form of a compulsion spell. It's for making people compliant in states of distress, not taking away their control completely like what Scarven's doing, but it's close enough to the principles." She brushed a long strand of hair behind her ear as she hurried through her explanation.

"I used a simple breaking spell as a base, then added a couple charms to counteract the ingredients my father listed. Plus your blood. That acted as a binding agent to strengthen it." Rose fished in the pocket of her burgundy dress. After a moment, she pulled out a tiny black pouch.

When she shoved it in my hand, I carefully undid the strings and opened the top. Inside was a small, pearl-shaped red bead, barely the size of my fingertip. It radiated a faint glow, pulsing warmth that reached the tip of my nose.

"What is it?" Devora asked, leaning over to peer inside.

"Get Vera to ingest this, and it should break the compulsion long enough for you to get her away from Scarven," Rose said.

I clutched the black pouch to my chest, gazing at it as hope blossomed inside me. "Thank you, Rose," I murmured. "I don't know how to repay you for this."

She smiled. "Just don't die." The humor faded from her face as she raised an eyebrow. "And stop keeping secrets from us. I could've helped you with this long ago, if you'd only asked."

I rubbed the back of my neck. "I know. You're right, and I'm sorry. I promise to never doubt the all-powerful mind of Rose Wolff again."

"That's more like it." She reached out to pat both Devora and me on the arm. "Please, tell us if—"

She cut herself off and looked behind us to the party still raging silently at my back. I whirled around, muscles tense and waiting.

Devora gasped.

Rose dropped the silencing charm, and sounds came back with a *whoosh*. A couple of surprised screams rang out as a new figure materialized in front of us.

Arowyn.

Panic flared through me when she locked eyes with me and crashed to her knees. Her face was so pale and gaunt, she looked like a ghost.

"Arowyn!" I dashed forward and caught her before she hit her head on the marble. "Did you just stride all the way from Drakorum?"

"Silas—" Her voice was ragged, her breaths labored as she tried to speak. "Silas...is dead."

My heart dropped. My entire body went numb as a ringing formed low in my ears. But in my chest, my dragon half roared—a mournful howl of disbelief.

"He—he broke the wards," Arowyn forced out. Her eyes fluttered shut. "He's there. At the Keep. Scarven is here."

58

DEVORA

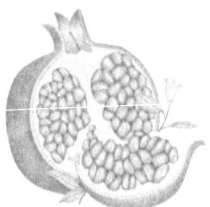

S*ilas is dead.*
He broke the wards.
Scarven is here.

Nox flew south faster than I thought possible. It took everything in me to keep Arowyn and myself atop his back. I called on my shadows to provide a protective barrier, and they slipped around our bodies, weaving us to his scales with an ironclad grip. They pulsed viciously with every breath, desperate to get back. Desperate to act. Desperate to do *something*.

After what felt like an eternity but was probably less than an hour, the eastern coastline of Drakorum came into view. As Nox descended, I saw the familiar outline of my tower, then the top of the mansion, lower and lower until—

My heart stopped.

It was a war zone.

Magic hung in the air, so thick I could taste it, sharp and bitter on my tongue. My own power responded in kind, surging toward the action. Bolts of light and swarms of shadows shot through the clearing in front of the mansion. Figures were illuminated by the bright moonlight and fires burning in the surrounding trees. I could hear shouts and screams, hissing and howling of the various Shifters, steel clashing and reverberating through the air.

Nox landed with a resounding crash. He lifted his head and let out a roar. The nearby trees bowed under the force, flames flickering and branches colliding. Even my shadows cowered at the sight of his fury.

A line of Scarven's men in all black spun to face the new threat, but a stream of dragon fire shot out of Nox's mouth, reducing them to ash.

In front of me, Arowyn stirred. "Wh-what's going—"

"You need to get out of here," I said hastily. "It's a bloodbath, Arowyn."

Her icy blue eyes widened as color rushed back to her cheeks. "I —I can fight. I have to help." She tried to swing her leg over Nox's back and almost fell to the ground. We used his scales as footholds and landed in a crouch on solid earth. When she stood, she gripped my shoulder to keep from keeling over.

"You can't fight," I argued. "You can barely walk!"

More screams made us whip around to face the battle. Scarven's men had grown smarter. Instead of crowding Nox and risking incineration, they plunged into our own people, making it to where one blast would take out as many of our allies as it would our enemies.

Tessa and Kieran fought two attackers each, their weapons a blur as they used their Shifter speed to move as quick as lightning. Behind them were dozens of refugees, some as young as teenagers, all struggling to hold their own against the onslaught.

"Can you stride inside the Keep?" I asked Arowyn. She nodded. "Go make sure the kids are safe."

She turned to face the mansion and disappeared in the blink of an eye.

At my side, Nox shifted back to his human form and grabbed me by the arms.

"You should go. *Run*," he shouted, his eyes blazing silver, wild and frantic. "Get out of here before he finds you."

I shook my head. "I can't run, Nox. This is my family too."

A growl ripped from him as he yanked me closer. His shaking fingers clenched around my arms. "I promised I wouldn't let him hurt you again. I can't—" His breaths were ragged, his chest heaving. "If he takes you, if he—"

I pressed my lips to his to silence him. Magic, shadows, and lightning whipped around us, the wind swirling my hair in the air. My power thrummed to the beat of my heart, aching to join his.

"He won't." I broke away and rested my forehead against his. "I can protect myself. Let me help our family."

He took another deep breath, and I could've sworn smoke came out of his nostrils when he exhaled. "Stay with me. Don't leave my side."

"Always." I kissed him one more time, then we spun and dove into the fray.

As we got deeper, I saw more and more of the battle. A line of our Alchemists—young and old—stood outside the walls of the Keep, with faint, shimmering force fields lifted in front of them. Several bodies in all black—Scarven's men—lay at their feet.

Even though Nox had taken out a group of them with his dragon fire, we were still outnumbered two to one. Refugees from the Keep who weren't holding the shield were fighting their hearts out. Nox had said they were training the older ones in defensive combat, but they were still so inexperienced. Their movements were choppy and delayed, their magic uncontrolled.

One teenage Lightbender and Strider hybrid accidentally shot a beam of light at Nox, who easily dodged it as it sank into the ground, the grass smoldering where it hit. Another one tried to send a shadow whip toward an opponent, only for it to nearly hit me square in the head. A barrier of vines sprang up from the ground just in time to block it.

I whirled to find the source. To the right stood Milo, his hands outstretched and a look of raw, savage grief etched onto his youthful face. His unruly curls were streaked with dirt and whipping around his head from the rush of wind.

After rescuing me, he turned to a new opponent, clasping his hands together and shouting an incantation. Flames ignited on the black leathers of his attacker, and with a jerk of Milo's hand, I heard a loud *crack*.

The man's neck snapped.

He fell like a rock as Milo surged forward to take on two more at once. When he moved, I saw what he'd been standing in front of.

A body.

Linen pants, a tweed jacket over a white button-down now shredded and soaked in blood, a single suspender strap hanging limp on the ground. Cracked glasses. Tawny skin. Brown-and-gray hair covered in dirt.

Silas.

The older Alchemist lay there in a pool of his own blood, with a dagger sticking straight out of his heart. Bile crept up my stomach and stung my tongue.

He was dead. They'd *killed* him. I hadn't believed it until now.

"Devora!" Nox exclaimed sharply. I looked back to find a man in a lion's mask barreling toward me.

I'd never used my magic in combat, besides the training sessions with Thecae. But my shadows were ready. It was like muscle memory, the way my hands rose to form a shield thick enough to absorb the dagger thrown at my chest. I fed my shadows more energy, throwing all my grief and sorrow and anger into it. Several wisps broke away from me to form rows of spikes, solidifying and sharpening with each second.

The man lunged, and I flung the shadow spikes at him. Two flew over his shoulder and dissipated. Two more got caught in the thickness of his leathers, but three of them...

They sank into his neck. He howled and dropped his other weapons as his veins enlarged and blackened. Clutching his face, he clawed his skin, and I watched with wide eyes as my shadows traveled up his head.

I hadn't *tried* to do that. I just wanted to slow him down.

He tried to hurt you, a familiar voice echoed in my mind. It sounded almost like my shadows. *He hurt your people. He deserves this.*

Shadows began to leak from his eyes, his nose, his lips. His eyes bulged out of his head, and his skin stretched, blood pouring out of every orifice as if the darkness was forcing it out.

His screams rattled my brain. I frantically called the shadows back to me, but they kept swirling around him, eager to taste his blood.

Do you really want us to stop? The voice hissed at me again, a chuckle brushing against the back of my mind.

"Devora, look away," Nox said at my side. With a whimper, I spun around, and there was a slice of steel before my victim's cries were abruptly cut off. Only then did my shadows slink back to me, curling around my body like armor. The familiar blackness was tinged with red streaks of blood.

I didn't have time to worry about the way my magic seemed to have a mind of its own—and a vicious one, at that. Several of our fighters were blasted back by a powerful wind spell, allowing Scarven's men to attack with newfound ferocity at our smaller numbers. One of them leaped into the air and shifted into an enormous bear, spit flying from his large teeth as he swiped at us.

Out of nowhere, a black and tan jaguar the size of a lion came soaring toward him. Tessa bared her claws and gripped the bear's head, both of them landing on the ground in a heap. She shredded through his fur with ease, her graceful form able to dart around him while he staggered back to look for her.

"Kieran!" Nox shouted as his second came bounding forward, a sword in each hand. "What happened?"

"They showed up without warning," Kieran said with a grunt, slicing his sword upward to fend off an attack. "A tremor went through the entire Keep when the wards fell from the outside. Silas, he—he ran out to see what the problem was, and—" The stag Shifter swallowed hard, and the image of Silas's body flashed behind my lids.

"We didn't get to him in time. Another man vanished right as we came outside, and then we were ambushed." Kieran and Nox stood back-to-back, each taking on one of Scarven's men. "We held them off for a while"—Kieran grunted and feinted right—"but then we had to either take the fight outside or risk them infiltrating completely."

Nox growled when another man in a lion's mask appeared out of thin air, striding between him and Kieran. The masked man struck Kieran in the side with the hilt of a dagger, then strode to Nox's left, flicking a blade at his neck.

Nox's arm shot out faster than I thought possible. His hand shifted into a claw and caught his opponent around the neck, squeezing until his eyes rolled to the back of his head. Nox flung him to the side.

"Where's Scarven?" Nox asked Kieran, his voice deadly low.

Kieran shook his head. "We haven't seen him. He didn't come with the others."

Confusion swept over me. Scarven wasn't here? He'd caused all of this, and he couldn't be bothered to show himself? To fight back?

One by one, the refugees from the Keep fell, their groans ringing in my ears behind me. I didn't know how many were simply injured or even dead. I couldn't look. I couldn't focus on anything except the bloodshed around me, the magic and teeth and steel that were *this* close to taking away everything I loved.

Someone ran at me with a sword sheathed in lightning, and I used my shadow shield to block. I twisted my arm in the air and commanded them to wrap around the blade. They tugged it out of his hand and I caught the handle midair.

We parried, him with his light magic and me with the sword and my own dagger. Even though I wasn't anywhere *near* proficient with weapons, I was too afraid to use my magic. I'd never been frightened of it before, but the way my shadows hissed with violence scared me. How they'd torn that man apart from the inside out...I didn't even know they were capable of something like that. And they *reveled* in it. I could sense them purring inside me, still tasting his blood, craving more.

Let us out. We can protect you.

My opponent sent a beam of light toward my midsection, and my magic jumped to block it. I feinted left and aimed for his neck, then jabbed at his stomach with the shorter dagger. The blade sank in before he leaped back with a hiss.

A lightning whip flashed from his hand and nicked my shoulder. I yelped as blood loomed to the surface and dripped down my arm. But...it wasn't just blood.

Shadows leaked from the wound, spilling over the sleeves of my turquoise dress and mingling with my blood. I watched with dread as they slowly rose in a cloud of dark gray and red, the scent of copper thick in the air.

Say the word, little one, they crooned. *He will kill your friends if you don't stop him.*

That same sense of bloodthirsty power sang in my veins. They were right. I'd seen what these men did to our refugees—most of them still *children*. And they worked for Scarven. Who knew how many other people they'd harmed?

That's right, my shadows whispered. *He deserves to die. He deserves your vengeance.*

My resolve slipped little by little, the image of Silas's body coming back to me with every breath. My hold on the shadows released ever so slightly.

They instantly solidified into a sharp blade. Before I could blink, it zipped through the air and straight toward my attacker.

It sliced clean through his neck. His head rolled to the ground, and my shadows swirled around the severed skin. I could feel their glee as they lapped up his blood. Could feel their dark satisfaction and hunger for more.

A voice in the back of my mind told me I should be horrified. But this time...I wasn't.

I was curious. Intrigued.

Yes, they chanted. *Give us more.*

A garbled shout reached my ears, and I spun on my heels as a giant hawk Shifter descended from the sky. It stretched out a talon and struck a familiar face, hard and fast.

Everett.

The Illusionist fell to the ground. He pressed both hands to his eye, but it wasn't enough to stem the spurt of blood that spilled over his fingers and onto the grass.

I reacted without thinking. My shadows, now a darker, pulsing red, immediately shot toward the hawk. When they touched his feathers, he let out a shriek and shifted back into his human form. His body convulsed on the ground as his skin turned gray.

I *felt* my shadows consume him. I felt them drain him of his life, leaving him a husk as he went rigid, then limp.

Satisfied with their work, they rushed back to me and twisted up my arms, flitting through my hair as I stalked toward my next target.

Not many of Scarven's men remained standing, but three of them sprinted to the line of our Alchemists holding their magic shields at the walls of the Keep. One of them raised their sword.

"Oh no you don't," I muttered.

I didn't bother holding my shadows back.

I lashed out an arm, and they formed a lasso. It snapped through the air and whipped around the man's neck. When I yanked, he jerked toward me, his back dragging over the grass. A smirk crept up my lips as I squeezed.

The shadows tightened until his face turned red, then purple, his fingers clawing at his neck as he gasped for air. I twisted my wrist, and he fell silent.

Tendrils of my magic branched out from his body to grab the other two men. Shadows wrapped around their bodies and lifted them into the air. I crafted little spikes of darkness that sank into their skin. Their screams filled the night, their blood dripping from hundreds of tiny wounds, and my shadows drank it up before they could fall to the ground.

I thought I heard voices calling my name, but the roaring in my ears drowned them out.

My grin widened as more shadows branched from my feet. They snaked over bodies of the living and the dead, aiming for Scarven's five remaining men. Wind whipped around us like a storm. My shadows tightened around all seven enemies in their grip, the same little needles digging into their skin until they cried out.

"Where is he?" I shouted, a voice I didn't recognize as my own booming around us. "*Where is Kane Scarven?*"

The bodies writhed in the air, struggling to break free from their bonds. None of them responded.

Anger ripped through me, hot and corrosive. He didn't even have the *nerve* to come here. He sent his *lapdogs to* tear down our walls. To break our defenses and our spirits. To *murder* our friend.

Just another message. Another warning.

Maybe it was time I sent one of my own.

My shadows forged their way into my victims' eyes and noses, prying open their lips and burrowing down their throats. Their veins bulged and turned black. Shadows filled their bodies, pushing against their skin until they cracked from the inside.

"Devora!" Nox shouted from behind me. "Devora, stop! Look what it's doing to you."

His words barely managed to break through my anger. I glanced down to find my own veins darkened with black and red, shadows flowing like rivulets down my body.

My breath quickened. Fear returned, only to be slammed back by the force of my magic.

Finish this, it hissed, more powerful than ever before.

Magic rose inside of me, all the way from my feet to my hands. My arms trembled. With a scream that made my throat raw, I slammed my hands into the ground.

All seven bodies crashed with it.

But instead of landing on the grass, they vanished into smoke.

The second my shadows seeped back into my skin, I staggered

backward, the exhilarating surge of power suddenly morphing into terror.

Tessa, Kieran, Everett, and Milo all stared back at me. Their clothes were ripped, their faces bloodied, their weapons limp at their sides. And their eyes...

Scared. Wary. Distrusting.

Nox came into view and kneeled before me, those navy pools full of concern. I realized my entire body was shaking. I could barely draw breath. He slowly reached out and cupped my face in his hands.

"Nox," I whispered hoarsely. "What have I done?"

59

DEVORA

My hands trembled as I washed them in the water basin, watching flecks of dried blood and mud fall away. I scrubbed them until they were raw. Until the pale skin was bright pink and stinging, and even then, I felt the blood from my shadows lurking just beneath the surface.

Why did they do that? Why did I *want* them to? I—I murdered all those men. I *enjoyed* it. I felt powerful. In control. As if it proved I was stronger than the fears I carried with me.

My shadows had never acted like that before. We moved in tandem; they knew what I wanted before I did, and they reacted the way I needed them to. But this time it felt like *they* were controlling *me*. They told me what I wanted. They pushed me to the edge and beyond with their vicious little thoughts.

I gripped the porcelain basin, looking up into the mirror on the wall. My skin was sallow, my hair limp and sagging. The beautiful gown I'd worn to the wedding was torn and covered in blood, and a hint of smoke still hovered around my eyes.

I didn't want to *become* that. I didn't want that sick, twisted part of me that relished in bloodshed to ever consume me like that again.

"Devora, darling?" Nox's hesitant voice came from the door to the bathing chamber. I hastily straightened and wiped my hands as he stepped inside. "Are you—"

"I'm fine," I said, then cleared my throat. "How—how is Milo?"

Nox searched my face for a moment. "Not good. I don't think he's processed what happened. He's taking the lead in the hospital wing, even when we've told him we have plenty of Alchemists who can help."

"How many?" I whispered.

He knew what I meant. "Nine in the hospital wing. Everett took a nasty lash to the eye, but he'll be okay. Two are in critical condition. And three...three didn't make it. Including Silas."

I closed my eyes. *Three dead*. I felt the loss in my core, and I knew the others were taking it even harder.

"How can I help?" I asked, setting the towel down.

"You need to rest, Devora. We don't know what happened to you out there."

I was already shaking my head before he finished. "No, don't do that. You can't keep trying to sit me out while the rest of you face the hardships. I want to help. I *need* to help." My voice rose, becoming more desperate. I looked down at my hands and, for the first time since I'd found them, hoped my shadows stayed hidden.

"I don't know what's happening to me. I need to do something. Something to—to—" I cut myself off and balled my hands, tears springing to my eyes.

Nox rushed forward and took me in his arms. "We'll find a way to stop whatever this is." His lips pressed into the top of my head. "It'll be alright, darling."

I pushed away from him and wiped my eyes with the back of my hand. "How can it be? Silas is *gone*. Our people are in danger, and Scarven can break in at any moment. *Nothing* is alright."

He stared back at me, and I saw him clearly for the first time. He looked so *tired*. So empty. I'd been selfish, so focused on my magic and what I'd done, I missed how difficult this was for him. How his own grief was crushing him.

I cupped his cheek, brushing my thumb beneath his eye as

more tears welled to the surface of mine. "Fates, I'm so, so sorry, Nox," I whispered. "I know what he meant to you. What they *all* mean to you."

He took a shuddering breath, and his shoulders fell as his head dipped. I pulled him against me and wrapped my arms around his neck. His body felt so large next to mine, but his muscles relaxed as he sank further into me. *He* was always the one to comfort *me*. To be my rock when the world became too much to bear. I wanted to be that for him too.

"It's not your fault," I murmured, running my fingers through his hair. After our conversation before the wedding, I knew where his mind would go. He and I were like that, in a way. Always wearing the blame. Always letting the guilt seep in and corrupt us. "There's no way you could have known."

"I should've *stayed*." His voice rumbled through me as his forehead pressed into my neck. "I should've been here. We were off *dancing* while my people were being—"

"You can't think about it like that," I rushed out. "You don't know if us being here would've made a difference. The important part is that we got here when we did."

His hair tickled my cheek when he shook his head. "He must've known I was gone. Why else would he attack now?" He backed away, his features hardening. "This was another game to him. Another move on the chess board. I'm tired of constantly losing pieces while he always has the upper hand."

"I know, Nox. I know. I'm so sorry," I said again, wishing there was something I could do. He'd been through this same cycle over and over again for longer than I could comprehend. Scarven seemed to be multiple steps ahead at every move. I wished there was a way to—

My lips parted as my hand fell away. I let out a curse. I couldn't *believe* I'd forgotten about this.

"What is it?" Nox asked.

Another string of curses left my lips as I darted out of the bathing chamber.

"Devora, what—"

"I know what to do." I fell to my knees before my pile of dirty clothes.

"Would you care to explain?"

I yanked at discarded garments. One by one, I threw them to the side, ignoring his anxious pacing and questions. When I finally found the dirty, ragged pair of black pants, I scrambled through the pockets, barely daring to breathe until my fingers brushed a strip of cloth.

"I got it." My voice was breathless as I rose to my feet. I wasn't sure it would still be there, but the dried blood peeked out on the edge of the cloth. "Scarven's blood."

Nox's forehead scrunched. "How did you get that?"

"It was the night he took me. I told you how I bit his lip and drew blood when he kissed me, remember?"

His eyes glinted with rage as his hand curled into a fist. "I try not to," he said through gritted teeth.

I kept going. "I wiped it on the back of my hand before he healed himself, then transferred it to this cloth when I got back to my room. I thought I could use it to get through the portal to the Hollow, but this is better. Fates, I can't *believe* it was still in my pocket."

"I don't understand how this helps," Nox said.

"You told me Silas cast a spell to see a vision of me, right? That's how you found me in the cell?" I saw the moment realization dawned on him. "You said he needed something of mine to cast it. My sweater. Well, this is a lot better than a sweater."

The corner of his lip tugged upward. "You absolute *genius*," he said on an exhale. He grabbed my waist and lifted me into the air, spinning us in a circle. "You beautiful"—he kissed my neck—"perfect"—I giggled when he kissed my cheek—"nosy little genius."

His lips found mine, hungry and aching and full of both hope and sorrow rolled into one. I gasped against him and wrapped my legs around his middle, letting the world fall away for just one moment. Just a handful of heartbeats in this bubble of solitude.

We broke away panting, and he rested his forehead on my chin. I breathed him in as my fingernails scratched the base of his skull. "This isn't over, Nox," I said quietly. "We can find him. We can strike back."

He slowly lowered me to the ground, his enormous frame towering over me as he tenderly ran a thumb across my cheek. "Thank you," he whispered. "You've given us another chance."

I squeezed his wrist. "Then let's not waste it."

———

WE FOUND Milo in the hospital wing. The scent of healing herbs, disinfectants, and steam from several boiling cauldrons rammed into us as we entered. Some of the older Alchemist refugees were running from bed to bed, wrapping bandages around the injured and murmuring spells at their bedsides. Most of the wounded were sleeping, but a couple were alert and propped up in their beds.

I caught Everett sitting at the edge of one near the entrance. He had a black eyepatch over one eye, with the tip of a bandage peeking out beneath.

"How do you feel?" I asked.

"Like I should be helping, not sitting here," he grumbled. "It's just a cut."

Tessa, who was folding more cloths into bandages at the shelf next to him, scoffed. "You almost had your eye taken out."

Everett pointed to the patch. "She's trying to convince me to leave it."

"It makes you look sexy. In a roughed-up sort of way," Tessa said.

He shot her a scowl. "It makes me look ridiculous."

"At least it's just your eye," a quiet voice said from a bed behind Everett. Milo stood with his back facing us, mixing something in a mortar and pouring it into a glass vial.

Tessa instantly sobered. "Milo, I'm sorry. I—"

"Don't." Milo shook his head. "Sorry. I didn't mean anything. I'm just—" He turned and scrubbed a hand down his tired face. "Let me know if you need a pain spell, Everett."

The young Alchemist ignored Tessa when she tried to reach for him. He headed straight for a bed in the back where Hope, a young Shifter, lay. There was a huge lump on the side of her head oozing black pus, and she winced as Milo gently dabbed oil onto the spot.

"Maybe we should find someone else to do the spell," I said to Nox, turning my back so nobody else could hear me. I didn't want to ask more of Milo. He'd done so much tonight, all while dealing with the loss of his mentor.

Nox gave me a soft, grim smile. "A wise woman once told me I can't keep forcing others to sit out while we face hardships. I'll let him make the choice for himself. He'll never forgive me if we do this without him."

I nodded, and Nox pulled Milo to the side when he was done bandaging his patient. "Milo," he started, his voice tender and careful. "How are you doing?"

The boy rubbed at his eyes, which were bloodshot and weary. Purple circles rested beneath them. His freckles were more pronounced than ever, and a sheen of sweat shone on his forehead.

He didn't look like the same nervous, innocent young man I'd come to know the last few weeks. I watched the nineteen-year-old Alchemist snap a man's neck with a swish of his hand tonight. I wondered if, like me, that was his first time taking someone's life. The first time to feel blood on his hands and know he would be changed forever.

"I think they're all going to make it," he said, wiping his forehead on his sleeve. "It'll be a long night, though."

Nox put a hand on Milo's shoulder. "I asked about *you*."

Milo sighed and closed his eyes. "I don't know, Nox. I can't think about it. He would want me to make sure everyone else is taken care of, so that's what I'm doing. For him."

Nox and I shared a glance. "There's something else we think you might be able to do for him, if you're up for it," Nox finally said.

Milo's eyes shot up. "Anything."

"Hey now, are you three planning something?" Tessa asked. She finished folding the last of the bandages. "I want in."

Everett threw off his blanket. "Me too."

Nox sighed. "Fine. Might as well get Kieran and Arowyn. Where are they?"

"They're burning the bodies out front," Milo said quietly. "Go get them. I'll make sure the healers can take it from here."

Once our entire group was assembled, we rushed to the workshop. Milo faltered when he reached the table in front of the Alchemist's cabinets. Silas's Grimoire was still open to the last page he'd used, his bag of herbs spilling out over the top.

A wave of loss washed over the space. I could still picture his hunched form leaning over those pages, his spectacles fogging with steam from his potions. The way he'd straighten his back and brush his hands on his apron when someone tried to talk to him. How he'd clean his glasses on his sweater in moments of deep thought.

Milo's hand rested on the table. He had *thousands* of those moments with his mentor. I had the sudden urge to wrap this lanky boy in my arms and protect him from the rest of the world. I rubbed a hand up and down his back, wishing I could comfort him, but he flinched away from my touch.

The space was filled with silence when Nox finished explaining our idea, until Arowyn snorted. "Well, Fates. The newbie saves the day again. Where have you been all our lives?"

To my surprise, Milo shot me a glare. I barely had time to register the hurt and anger in his eyes before he looked back at Nox. "If that's the spell I think it is, it's a powerful one. I'm not nearly as strong as him. As—as Silas. Not enough to help you the way he could."

"That isn't true," Kieran said, shaking his head. "Silas believed in you. He *chose* you as his apprentice. I saw you tonight, Milo. You're every bit as strong as any of us."

On my left, Everett stepped closer and put a firm hand on Milo's forearm. "None of us expect you to be Silas. He's taught you well, and you're more than capable of being what this refuge needs."

Tessa gave Milo an encouraging smile and hitched her thumb at Everett, who readjusted his eyepatch. "I'm with Captain Everett on this. You've grown so much, Milo. And Silas was *so* proud of you. More than I think you'll ever know."

Milo raised his eyes to meet Nox's, his lower lids lined with silver. Nox nodded at him. "They're right. And even if you can't do this spell yet, we'll still believe in you."

"Through flame and ash," Kieran added.

"Through flame and ash," Milo murmured, his lips barely moving. With a deep breath, he crossed to Silas's Grimoire, pausing for a split second before turning the pages.

I set the cloth with Scarven's blood on the table as Milo prepared the spell. He gathered ingredients and put them in a mortar, glancing back at the book every once in a while. It felt like we were all holding our breaths. Nox reached over and brushed a single finger down my arm, and I caught it with my hand and squeezed.

Milo took the cloth and smoothed it on the table, then sprinkled crushed herbs on top of it. He muttered a spell, and flames erupted on the surface of the cloth.

"*Vidia*," he breathed.

My heart pounded, my skin tingling with eagerness as we watched the fire dance and flicker. I didn't realize he'd have to *burn* it. This really was our only shot. Once that small bit of blood was gone, we'd have nothing.

I waited, muscles tight and teeth clenched, as the edges of the cloth began to darken and curl in on themselves.

"It's not working," Milo said, his shoulders sagging.

We waited a couple more seconds, and still, nothing happened.

Nox leaned forward and blew out the fire with a blast of hot breath. "Again," he instructed Milo.

The young Alchemist blinked at him. "There's hardly any cloth left. I can't do it, Nox. I'll ruin it."

Nox planted his palms on the table and pierced Milo with his stare. "You *can*, Milo. You can find Scarven. You can find the man who did this to us. To *Silas*."

Milo held Nox's eyes for a heartbeat. Two. Then he reached for his mortar and spread more herbs on top of what was left of the bloody cloth. Nox opened his mouth and let out a small stream of dragon fire, igniting the herbs anew.

One last time, Milo muttered, "*Vidia*."

Nerves churned in my stomach. My pulse raced, beating back the exhaustion that hovered over me like a cloud.

Nothing.

And then—

60

NOX

"Success, all things considered," a middle-aged man with a thick mane of black hair and near-white skin was saying. He stood in a gray room with more bookshelves and cabinets than I could count, and was speaking to someone outside the vision's field of view.

"Yes, it appears so," a second voice said. One that made blinding hatred crash through me. My dragon instantly roared in my chest when Scarven appeared, stepping closer to the other man. "You brought down their wards?"

The man nodded with a sinister smile. "And killed their Alchemist so he can't put them back up."

Beside me, Devora sucked in a breath. "That's Malek Mortep," she whispered. "Scarven's head Alchemist. The one who's helped him create all the experiments. I recognize the room—they're in the Hollow."

Scarven spread his hands wide. "And how is it that *you* alone made it out alive, dear Malek?" His tone was mocking and sharp.

To my surprise, the Alchemist chuckled. The sound made the hair on the back of my neck rise. "You don't keep me around because I fight in losing battles, my lord. You keep me because I *win* them. We both know you didn't want any of those men coming back alive."

Scarven clapped Malek Mortep on the back. "It makes cleaning up far easier, does it not? Tell me, what did you discover?"

"The dragon and the girl showed up in the thick of it, as you anticipated. They do appear to care for one another." At Mortep's words, Scarven snarled, and dread pooled in my stomach. Had this Alchemist been watching the entire fight?

"I must admit, I was skeptical of how all my serums you administered would interact, but it seemed to have a desirable effect," the Alchemist spoke clinically, keeping his voice measured. "The girl's magic was out of her control. Ten times stronger and far more deadly. She killed at least ten of our own without blinking."

Devora shuddered. I looked over to see her grip the edge of the table with a pinched forehead. I instinctively moved to wrap an arm around her waist, but she pulled away.

"And do they suspect anything?" Scarven asked.

"Not that I'm aware of. I expect they'll be tending to their wounded before realizing anything is wrong."

Scarven's dark eyes flashed. "Excellent work. Will our losses cause a delay in the Guardian Forge shipment?"

"No, my lord. Everything is set. We told them to be prepared for arrival in approximately two days."

"Good." Scarven rapped his knuckles on the table. "I need those weap—"

The vision wavered as the last inch of bloodied cloth burned to ash. The fire went out, taking the image of the Hollow with it.

We all stood in silence as smoke curled toward the ceiling.

Milo let out a slow breath. "That man killed Silas."

"That man has done a lot of things," Everett grunted. "I remember him. Scarven's mad Alchemist. We saw *him* more than Scarven himself." The Illusionist's jaw shifted. "He used to come into our cells and torture us with his serums, then collect our blood until there was barely enough to keep us alive."

"What did he inject you with, Devora?" Tessa asked softly,

moving to her other side. She reached for Devora, but she jerked away just as she had with me.

"I don't know." Devora paused and closed her eyes. "There were several serums, but I don't know what they did. I—I passed out a lot." Her voice lowered to a whisper. "I just thought he was taking away my magic. Not—not *changing* it." She looked down at her hands, then wrapped them around her midsection.

What have I done? That was what she'd said to me tonight after killing those men. After her shadows had ravaged both them and her own body, turning her veins and eyes completely black. It was like something had taken over. A cruel, savage version of herself. Had his experiments done this?

What *else* had he done?

"He said there's a shipment. I believe he was going to say 'weapons' before the spell cut off," Kieran said, bringing my focus back. "It's arriving in two days at somewhere called the Guardian Forge. It's important to him; that much is obvious. We need to be there."

I nodded. "This is the first time we have the upper hand. We have to take advantage of it."

Arowyn tilted her head. "But what's the play here? We get there and then...what? We don't know what type of weapons he has or what he's planning on doing with them. We don't even know where it is."

"I do. It's an abandoned weapon's forge built into the Guardian Range," I said. Our previous emperor established stations along each province's border to be used only in cases of emergencies, or when citizens rebelled against his border guards. It was far north, close to the border between Drakorum and Emberfell.

I gave the Order a shortened version of what Devora and I had done in the capital these last couple of days, including my fears about Scarven imbuing fatesprig into weapons and other objects on a mass scale.

"Great." Arowyn crossed her arms. "So we get there before his team, wait for them to bring the weapons, destroy the stash, and kill them all. Easy."

"He's not simply going to allow anyone to walk right into this forge without precautions in place," Kieran countered. "He will have defenses. Magical wards. Guards. Plenty of ways for *us* to get ourselves killed if we are not careful."

"And besides that, how are we supposed to destroy it all?" Tessa asked.

Milo tapped a finger on the table, next to Silas's open Grimoire. "We blow it up."

As one, we all turned to him. Arowyn blinked. "Did *Milo* just say that?"

"Silas and I—we—" Milo cleared his throat. "We've been experimenting with some fire spells. He thought we might need to break into Scarven's mansion one day, and would need something with a bit more...kick."

"Yes, because a fire-breathing dragon wouldn't do the trick," Tessa said, her voice missing its usual sass.

"It's an explosive," Milo continued. "A powerful charm we developed that's dormant in an object until the spell is spoken and it's set on fire. It absorbs the fire, then magnifies it times a thousand." He ducked beneath the table and rummaged for something, then reappeared with a black box. After setting it on the counter, he pulled out a piece of dark red quartz. "We tested a less powerful version down at the shores once. It works."

We all swiftly backed away from the table.

"Whoa, Milo. You can't just whip out your explosives like that," Arowyn said.

Milo gave her a bland look. "It's not activated. I haven't said the spell *or* lit it on fire. This is just a rock right now."

"Is it instantaneous?" I asked, examining the crystal.

"When we tried it, there was about a fifteen second delay as it soaked up the force of the fire and then exploded." Milo shrugged. "It was enough time for us to get to safety, although Silas did land flat on his back," he said with a chuckle, a distant look in his eyes.

It quickly faded as his shoulders slumped. "That was a much smaller scale, though. It covered maybe twenty feet. It could've taken down a small house, but not something like a weapon's forge."

"But it *could*," I pressed.

Milo rubbed the back of his neck. "Yeah, I could get it there. But that kind of power...you'd need much longer than fifteen seconds to get away in time."

"If only you knew a Strider. Oh, wait," Arowyn said, quirking an eyebrow. "Say your spell, give me the stone, and I'll light it on fire and stride out of there. Problem solved. Next?"

"We need to see what kind of defenses he has over the place before barging in," I pointed out. "And before you start volunteering yourself for every task, Arowyn, you literally *just* depleted all your energy to warn us about the attack. I'm not about to let you stride across the province and back without your full strength."

The Strider twisted her lips but didn't argue. For all of her sarcastic jokes, she still looked exhausted. Her skin was paler than usual, and deep circles hung beneath her eyes.

"If we leave first thing tomorrow morning, we can beat the shipment," Everett said. "It only takes a little over a day to get to the Guardian Range. That gives us half a day to scout. I can illusion a couple of us to sneak into the forge and check it out undetected."

"So that's Arowyn and Everett in for Operation Guardian Forge." Tessa looked at everyone expectantly. "Some of us should stay behind. The Keep isn't safe anymore."

Milo swallowed. "I'll stay. Someone needs to try and get Silas's wards back up. Especially if we think they'll keep coming back for *her*." His gaze flickered to Devora, his jaw clenching briefly before looking away.

"Don't you need to activate the explosive charm thing?" Arowyn asked.

"I can do that before you go. Just don't set it on fire until you're ready," he warned.

"I'm going," I said, straightening my spine. "Tessa, Kieran, you stay back with Milo and Devora. Protect the refugees and make a plan for if we need to evacuate. Arowyn and Ev—"

"I'm going with you," Devora interjected, facing me with those fierce, determined eyes.

I sighed. I saw that coming. "No, you're not."

"Yes, I *am*."

Kieran raised an eyebrow. Tessa looked between us and said, "This sounds like something the two of you need to work out."

I kept my gaze trained on Devora, refusing to break her stare. "Go. Get some rest," I said to the others. "Arowyn and Everett, meet me here at sunrise."

One by one, they slipped out of the workshop, leaving the space silent and strained.

"You can't stop me, Nox," Devora finally said.

I let out a low chuckle. "Trust me, darling. I think I can."

She crossed her arms. "I thought we'd moved past this. What was all of that about 'a wise woman once told me I can't keep forcing others to sit out?'"

"Yes, well, that was *before* we found out he experimented on you." I stepped toward her. "He said it made you ten times more powerful. More *deadly*. Whatever he did could *hurt* you, Devora."

"He already did!" she shouted, chest heaving. I stopped in my tracks. "He *already* hurt me, Nox. In more ways than you can understand." Her head shook as she took another ragged breath. "This is *my* choice. I can do things nobody else on the team can. I can *help*. Don't you believe in me?"

I ground my teeth together. Of course I believed in her. She was the most incredible woman I'd ever met. That wasn't the problem.

Now that Scarven and his Alchemist knew of my feelings for Devora, every single step would be a trap. Scarven would stop at nothing to rip her from me, the way he had my father. Vera. My mother. Sage.

I was selfish. I had already signed Devora's fate by falling for her, but I wouldn't be the one to lead her straight to her death. Even if she hated me for it.

I turned away. "It's decided, Devora. You're staying here. I won't risk it. I won't risk *you*."

Her rage washed over me, a metallic and spicy scent mixing with her usual pomegranates. I closed my eyes for a brief moment before crossing to the door, unable to bear seeing the look on her face.

As I reached for the handle, a wall of shadows slammed against it.

I whirled to face her. "What are you doing?"

"You don't get to walk away from me," she said. An angry blush crept up her cheeks. Her shadows slipped from the door and wound around my waist, then fastened in circles around each of my wrists.

I struggled to break free, but she was stronger than I anticipated. "Let me go, Devora."

"No." She flicked her hand, and the shadows tugged my feet closer. Her blue-green eyes flashed in defiance. "You don't get to tell me what I can and can't do, do you understand?"

My heart pounded as her magic called to mine, a furious beat of rebellion and desire and pride all mixed into one. Fates, she was stubborn. Obstinate and hardheaded and absolutely stunning.

I didn't think I'd ever loved her more.

And that was the most frightening thing of all.

A growl worked its way up my throat. "Devora, I—"

"You told me you wouldn't leave me, but that's exactly what you're doing!" she shouted, her magic winding tighter around me.

My dragon thrashed at the challenge as a wave of heat surged through me. "I'm not leaving you, Devora. I'm *protecting* you!"

She threw her hands in the air, and the shadows pulled me forward. "Well, *stop*! Haven't I proven I can take care of myself?" Her voice rose as her magic pushed on the backs of my legs. "I'm tired of this, Nox. Why do you keep trying to cage me?"

"Because *I love you*!" I roared. My arms strained against the shadows, shoving me forward until I had no choice but to fall to my knees before her.

Her mouth fell open. "You—you what?"

My dragon half bashed against my chest, and the workshop faded around us. The only things left were the heightened sounds of our breaths and the echo of her heart thrumming in my ears, as fast and sharp as my own.

I hadn't meant to fall in love. But here I was, on my knees for her over and over.

"I swore I'd never feel this again. I told myself I couldn't." The words were choked, blazing their way up my throat. "But, Fates, Devora, I *love* you. Fiercely. Selfishly. In a way that terrifies me. Loving you makes you a target, but I—I can't do this anymore. I can't pretend I don't want you so desperately, I can barely *breathe*."

Her lips parted, shadows swelling around me as if they were hanging on to my every word.

"I don't care what he tries to take from me this time," I said, voice low and ragged. "I won't let him take *you*."

As if in a daze, she took a single, staggering step to me. Then she fell to her knees and yanked me forward with her shadows, crashing her lips to mine.

I didn't think. I just kissed her.

And, Fates, it undid me.

Her hands fisted in my shirt. I jerked against the restraints with a muffled growl until she finally released me, then gripped her waist and drew her closer. The press of her soft curves against me set me on fire. Shadows coiled around us, licking up my spine with a fervor that made my dragon purr inside my chest. I buried my other hand in her hair, caught between surrender and control.

The world narrowed to just this—her heartbeat, her breath, her everything.

But just as suddenly as it began, she pulled away, lips swollen and eyes blazing. "If you love me, Nox Duma, then you have to understand I won't kneel for you. I'm *not* your prisoner. I refused to be one to your hatred, and I refuse to be one to your heart." Placing a finger under my chin, she tilted my head up. "I'm coming with you. From here on out, I stand beside you."

"But what if I lose you?" I whispered.

Her piercing gaze softened. She swallowed hard, then cupped her hands at my neck. "What if you don't?"

I rested my forehead against hers. "I don't know how to do this, Devora. I don't want to control you, but I don't know how to stop being scared."

Her fingers on my pulse grounded me, like an anchor in a storm. "I'm scared too," she said. "Every time we find out something new, every time we have to face him...I wonder if it's the last time I'll see you. But he doesn't get to control our lives, Nox. *We* do."

I let out a soft exhale. "If anything happens to you—"

She pulled back just enough to look into my eyes. "Then it will happen with me *fighting beside you,* not sitting behind waiting."

I swallowed. I could feel the shift. Could feel my heart warring with my mind, that unbearable tension between protecting her and giving her freedom. I never wanted to cage her. I never wanted her to feel imprisoned again. But now all I was doing was trading one locked tower for another.

She leaned in and pressed her lips to my forehead. "I'm not *her,* Nox," she whispered, and my heart clenched. "I'm not the woman you lost. I know you'll carry that with you for the rest of your life, and I wish more than anything I could take away even a fraction of the pain you've been through. I'm not trying to make this harder for you. But I—I can't live in that shadow."

I moved my thumb to her waist, rubbing back and forth along the sliver of exposed skin beneath her shirt. "You're not her," I said, the words catching in my throat. "But I'm still *him.* The man who couldn't save the people he loved."

Silver lined her eyes. "You're *so* much more than that. You're the man who put aside his own safety, his own *identity,* to protect them. The man who's led countless missions to rescue people who couldn't save themselves. The man who's given *hope* in a world full of darkness." She paused, giving me a gentle smile even as a tear slipped down her cheek. "I want you to see that, Nox. Because you're the most wonderful man I've ever known."

I swallowed hard and slowly nodded, entranced by the tear lingering at the corner of her lips, her warm breath cascading over my nose.

She kissed me again, slow and deep, and I could taste her salty tears. "Oh, and, Nox?" she murmured into the kiss.

"Hmm?"

I felt her mouth curve upward. "I love you too."

The backs of my eyes pricked, warmth spreading through my chest and settling around my heart. I held her close, knowing there was no going back now. Knowing this could be the last time she was in my arms.

Tenderly brushing my thumb along her jaw, I said, "Then go pack, Devora, my darling. We leave at dawn."

PART THREE

THE
SWITCH

61

DEVORA

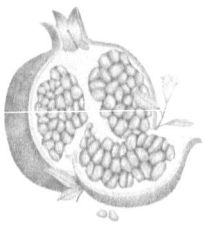

The mountains of the Guardian Range loomed before us, browner and greener than the cold, dark peaks at the south end of the province. This range marked the border between Emberfell, home of the Lightbenders, and Drakorum. On the ride north, the others told me about Emberfell and its jungles, how the coldness of the Shifter province slowly transitioned to lush greenery beyond the mountains.

I could feel the change. It was still cold, but a slight dampness entered the air the further we went, one that reminded me more of the shores back in Mysthelm.

As we climbed higher into the range, the path narrowed into a single, winding trail carved into the mountainside—barely wide enough for a carriage. There was a steep drop on one side and an unforgiving rock face on the other. Moss clung to the stone, slick from the morning frost that was quickly melting in the afternoon sun, and old trees leaned over the path.

Nox came to a halt on his horse in front of me, and that's when I saw it.

Half-swallowed by the cliffside was the entrance to the Guardian Forge. There was still quite a bit of distance between us and it, but I could see the jagged edges of rock, the darkened

414

archway that gaped like a mouth, so flush with the mountainside that it was easy to mistake for a large shadow if you weren't looking. Whoever built this wanted to keep it hidden.

"It looks empty," Arowyn remarked as we all clustered together at a fork in the road. One way led to the forge, and the other to a mountain pass.

I tentatively called on my shadows, sifting and weighing them to see how they responded. I hadn't felt that uncontrollable side of them since the fight, but I was still hesitant to overuse them. When a couple of strands pulled away from my skin and wound peacefully around my fingers, I sent them over the narrow path toward the opening up ahead.

Their movements nudged against my mind, bringing with it sounds of the mountain. Rocks clattering, wind weaving through open spaces, small claws of animals tapping on stone. I felt my shadows crawl through the entrance to the Guardian Forge, then swell and expand in the comfort of the darkness.

I closed my eyes and concentrated. A couple of unfamiliar voices reached me, my shadows whispering their words into my ears.

I faced the others at the same time Nox did and said, "It's just a couple of guards—"

"A few guards on duty. Nothing to—"

We looked at each other, sharing a smirk. "Your shadow whispering is getting good," Nox admitted.

"Yeah, we get it, you're the super cool, super powerful couple of the group." Arowyn waved a hand in the air. "Everett, ready to go?"

The plan was for him to illusion himself and Arowyn to go scout a place to drop the fire quartz, while Nox and I stood on guard duty. Everett nodded, then paused to scratch beneath his temporary eyepatch. The scar had improved, but he still couldn't see very well out of his left eye. It was unfortunate for him, considering Illusionists relied on sight to cast magic. If anything happened to his other eye, he'd be powerless.

"Great." Nox tipped his head at the two of them. "We'll meet back here in an hour and make camp in the mountain pass until the shipment arrives."

Arowyn cracked her neck from side to side. "Sounds good." She put a hand on Everett's shoulders. Giving me a quick wink, she said, "See you on the other side."

They disappeared in a faint shimmer. As planned, Nox and I grabbed the reins of their horses and made our way down the other path until we found a covered area to tie them. I twisted my fingers in the bottom of my fitted leathers, biting my lip as I looked back at the entrance to the Guardian Forge.

"Nervous?" Nox asked behind me.

I let out a hum. "I don't like the *waiting* part."

His hands snaked around my waist. He pressed his lips to my neck, making me tilt my head to the side. "We could do other things to pass the time."

I laughed and tapped his cheek. "We would make *terrible* guards."

"But very productive." He spun me to face him and planted a lingering kiss on my lips. A breeze picked up around us, blowing my hair around our faces. He broke away to lift his nose to the wind, and the movement was so Shifter-like that I couldn't help but smile.

"A storm's coming," he said, sniffing the air. "Hopefully they get done scouting before it breaks."

"Well, aren't you a handy little weather detector?"

He grinned. "My mother was the best at it. She's a raven Shifter, so she has a strong affinity for the sky. She would always pull me aside when she smelled one coming and teach me how to look for the signs." He had a faraway look in his eyes as he gazed up at the darkening clouds.

"I've never heard you talk about her," I said quietly. "Is she..."

"She's alive." A sad smile quirked at his lips. "She's in Tenebra, actually. Scarven banished her five years ago when she tried to help Vera escape. I hadn't seen her since then, until we went several weeks ago."

My eyes widened. "You went to see your mother?"

He nodded. "Before my task for Scarven and going to the capital. It was a quick visit. He has men on her all the time, so I didn't want to be suspicious."

"How was she? What's she like?" I blurted out. I wanted to know everything about this man and his past. I wanted to hear about his childhood. His favorite bedtime stories, all the embarrassing tales of his youth, what life as the governor's son was like. Did he have his mother's eyes? Her smile? Did he get his charm from her, or maybe his compassion?

"She's doing well, I guess. As well as she can be. She made a life for herself in Tenebra, but is still biding her time to be able to come back to Drakorum. To be a *family* again."

The wistfulness in his voice dissipated as he chuckled. "I think you'd like her. And I *know* she'd like you. Even with his men watching her constantly, she still found a way to form her own little rebellion, right under their noses. Father said she was always a troublemaker when they were younger."

I nudged his shoulder. "Now I see where you get it from."

"I could never get away with *anything*. When she was in her raven form, she could hide so easily and catch me in the act. I tried to blame a broken vase on our dog once when I was nine, but she'd seen me sliding down the banister. What she didn't know was that I was trying to fly. I wanted to be a raven, like her."

"Not a lion?" I asked, thinking about his father's form.

Nox shook his head. "I never wanted that kind of strength. A raven is strong in its own right, but it's...it's quiet. Deliberate. A silent force that doesn't demand attention. That was my mother."

The way he talked about his mother and how he yearned for a Shifter form like hers made things that much clearer to me. He was given the power of a *dragon* and all its volatile nature, when that was never what he wanted to begin with.

"I think you still have that," I said. He turned to me with a raised eyebrow. "I know your dragon isn't exactly silent or gentle, but I think, in a way, *you* are. You carry so much power inside you, Nox. You could've easily been like Scarven and abused it."

Something in his eyes flickered, and he turned to stare back at the mountain.

I rubbed a hand on his arm. "But you're *nothing* like him. You're so gentle and compassionate with those kids at the Keep. With *me*, even. You could destroy anything in your path, but you don't. You know how to cherish things. Maybe part of that comes from your mother."

He caught my fingers in his grip and squeezed, then kissed the tips. "Maybe," he murmured. "I wish you could meet her."

"I will, Nox," I said firmly. "I know I will. When this is all over."

He leaned toward me, his gaze latched on my lips, when the air shifted behind us.

"Knock knock," Arowyn said as she and Everett popped back into existence, scaring me so badly, I leaped straight in the air. She chuckled. "Someone's jumpy."

A low rumble of thunder made me glance at the sky. A wave of gray storm clouds inched closer as I said, "Let's just get out of sight before it rains."

———

WE TOOK SHELTER IN A SMALL, hollowed-out portion of the rock face hidden from the main path. Arowyn and Everett quickly explained their plan for placing the explosive, and the four of us sifted through various scenarios to work out backup plans for each. It felt good to be involved in the intricacies of a mission. And this was a fairly straightforward one—stride in, set the charmed fire quartz on fire, stride out. Done. There was always an element of danger, but the more we talked, the more at ease we all grew.

Later, Arowyn and Everett went to check on the horses and relieve themselves. Nox slid out several weapons from his belt to sharpen them against the stone. More thunder boomed through the air, and soon, the soft sound of rain became the backdrop to steel on stone.

I let my shadows rise to the surface, testing them carefully and feeling their normal, playful selves dance around my fingers. As they skated closer to the shadows of the little cave, muffled voices drifted to me on my magic.

"...wonder why Milo didn't want to see his pretty explosives in action," Arowyn was saying.

A beat passed. Then Everett's voice reached me. "He did. He just didn't want to come when she was here."

A weight sank in my stomach. Did they mean *me*?

Arowyn scoffed. "He needs to get over it. She's part of the team."

"Arowyn, Silas *just* died. Have some pity."

"I get that, but it's not like it's Devora's fault."

"He doesn't see it that way," Everett said quietly.

My skin grew cold. I reached up to clasp my throat as I swallowed hard.

"He thinks Scarven sent his men because of his twisted obsession with her. That none of this would've happened if she hadn't been there." Everett's voice was tired and resigned.

Arowyn cursed. "That's ridiculous. Scarven's a ticking time bomb. He would've attacked eventually, no matter what."

"I know. I tried to tell him that, but he's fragile right now. He doesn't—"

Nox's body hovered above me, and their words faded along with my shadows. His jaw flexed as he looked out the cave entrance. "Don't listen to that, Devora," he said.

I blinked rapidly, not even realizing tears had come to the surface until a couple spilled onto my cheek. I swiped them away with the back of my hand. "I'm not."

"You're a terrible liar."

I met his stare, those navy eyes piercing through every lie, every insecurity. I deflated under their weight. My head hit the stone wall behind me as I closed my eyes. "Do you think he's right?" I whispered. "Is it all my fault?"

"Of *course* not. Milo is upset. He's grieving and grappling for anything to make sense of the loss he's feeling."

"But he's not wrong." I played with the edges of my leathers, watching my shadows simmer on my skin. "Scarven had never attacked you before. He still trusted you. He didn't even know about the Keep before *I* blew your cover."

My mind ran through all the ways I'd put them in danger over the past weeks. If I hadn't tried to play the *spy*, if I hadn't rushed into being the hero at the Hollow, if I hadn't given away the fact that I was working with Nox, the Keep would still be safe. Nox's advantageous position at Scarven's side would still be intact.

Silas would still be alive.

Nox dropped to the dirty alcove floor. The sight of his massive frame contorting itself into this small space would've garnered a laugh from me under most circumstances. He wedged his arm behind my head so I could rest it on his shoulder.

"There's only room for one of us with a paranoid guilt complex in this relationship," he said as he twisted a strand of my hair around his finger.

I couldn't help the snort that left me. "Bold of you to assume this is a relationship."

His fingers stopped. They moved to the back of my neck, gripping tight enough to send a shiver down my spine.

"Bold of you to assume I'd ever let you go." Slowly, he angled my head up to look at him, the silver of his dragon shining through his fierce eyes.

"I don't want you to spend another moment thinking *any* of this is your fault." He kissed the top of my cheek, and my eyes fluttered shut. "I want you to think about how powerful you are." His lips moved to my jaw. "How selfless. How beautiful and strong and *brave*." He pressed one last kiss to the side of my throat.

"I want you to think about how much we need you. How much *I* need you."

"You have to say all of that. You *love* me." I drew out the word with a half-hearted smirk, my anxiety from before slowly melting away.

"You aren't those things to me *because* I love you, Devora," he said, carefully moving a strand of hair behind my ear. "I love you because you already *are* all of those things. I wish you could see yourself the way I do, darling. Because you would never blame yourself if you did. You would never question whether you were at fault for *any* of this."

I rested my forehead against his. He leaned forward to skim his lips over mine, as if he felt the same pull I always did. As if he couldn't bear the slightest distance.

"How do you always know what to say? Nobody has the right to be that charming," I said, voice breathless.

He chuckled, but it held no humor. "It's all the things I wished someone would say to me for so long."

My heart twisted. I pulled back so I could see his face. "Would you believe me if I said them now?"

He gave me a sad smile. "I want to."

"Believe that I love you." I swallowed hard. These sorts of epic confessions and moments of raw, open vulnerability weren't my strong suit, but for him...I would do anything.

"Believe that you *are* powerful," I continued, tracing my finger along his jawline, his lips, his eyes. "You have so many people who care about you. You're selfless, and beautiful, and strong, and brave. You're the perfect man to lead us. And I wish *you* could see what *I* see. What I've always seen, even when I didn't want to open my eyes."

I gently kissed him, wishing I could bottle this warmth and fullness in my heart for the days that felt empty. Wishing I could tuck us away into a world without power-hungry governors and half-brothers, without pain and loss and constant guilt.

The sound of footsteps on gravel permeated our little solace, and I broke away from him.

"Can you two save this for later?" Arowyn rapped her knuckles on the stone outside the alcove. Her light hair was drenched and swinging at her waist. "It's time."

62

NOX

Half a dozen black carriages rolled up the steep incline, wheels precariously close to the drop-off as the wind rocked them back and forth. From the thick cover of trees and pouring rain, we watched them make their way over the rocky threshold and out of sight, deep into the forge. The sky darkened rapidly as the sun descended and more storm clouds moved into view.

I homed my Shifter hearing in on the caravan of carriages. We needed to make sure they unloaded the cargo and took it beneath the first level, deep into the underground tunnels where Arowyn found the holding caves. That was where we could set off the explosive charm to do maximum damage to the weapons without killing all the guards on the first level.

Some of Scarven's men chose to follow him, but many were just like his prisoners. Pawns in his games of power. Forced into the role because of what they could do for him. I didn't want to take the chance that we'd hurt a single innocent person, even if it meant sparing some who were loyal to him.

We waited and waited, but there was nothing out of the ordinary that I could hear—instructions doled out by gruff guards, metal scraping against metal, rustling as a handful of guards unpacked the cargo.

Nobody suspected a thing. This was just a regular mission.

Everything was going smoothly. *Too* smoothly. It set my teeth on edge, making my stomach clench with every whisper of movement. I couldn't shake the feeling that there was a bigger play here. Something we weren't seeing. Blowing up this weapon's forge was one thing, but what if Scarven had more? What if this was just a small stepping stone to his end goal?

My burning curiosity and need for control couldn't sit around here and wait while my suspicions were raised. I rocked forward on the balls of my feet. I had to see for myself. Make sure there wasn't something else.

"I'm going to check on things," I said to the other three. Arowyn tried to protest, but I held a hand out. "I'll only be a minute, I promise. Devora, do you have the new piece of enchanted parchment?"

She nodded.

"Good. I'll signal all clear on there, and then, Arowyn, you get in and set the fire quartz. Be careful."

When they all nodded, I slipped on my charmed camouflaging ring, no longer caring about consequences for using Scarven's "gift." I'd already lost that trust.

Rain pelted my camouflaged skin as I left the others and stalked to the entrance. The scent of sweat, metal, and musty stone overwhelmed me, the sharp smell that could only belong to steel filling the air.

There were *hundreds* of boxes disappearing into the forge. Scarven's lackeys worked with precision, forming an assembly line to remove them from the carriages, sort onto wheelbarrows, and roll down the pathways.

I got as close as I dared to one of the boxes whose lid had slipped off. Dozens of daggers glinted back at me, with blades such a dark green, they looked almost black, like oil. I touched one, then immediately recoiled with a hiss as my magic lurched.

Fatesprig.

This confirmed my fear. Scarven had imbued hundreds, if not *thousands* of weapons with the herb. This entire forge was toxic to Veridians, full of objects designed to weaken and detain us before we could blink.

And if he was starting to move them outside his labs...

I gingerly grabbed the hilt of one with the fabric of my shirt, then slipped it into my weapon's belt. It couldn't hurt to have another sample.

A man in a sleek black uniform and daggers strapped to his body marched toward the line of carriages. "Is this the last of it?" he barked at one of the other guards.

The second one nodded. "We're almost done."

"Good," the man in charge said. "Let's pick up the speed. This isn't the only cache we have to move this week." He jerked his head at the carriages. "Make sure they're out soon, or we're leaving you down here when Mortep puts the wards back up."

This isn't the only cache we have to move this week.

The meaning of his words snapped into place, and dread pooled in my stomach. Scarven was putting these weapons into circulation *this week.* He'd hijacked this old forge—who knew how many other hidden locations he'd turned into holding cells? Once he had them in place, he could release magic-dampening weapons over all six provinces with the snap of a finger.

We had even less time than I imagined. Our people wouldn't have time to prepare. To react. Without our magic, we were helpless against someone like him.

Was that what this was all for? So Scarven could make a move on the entire Veridian Empire?

I waited a few minutes for the last of the guards to get back to this top level, then ripped the enchanted parchment and a small piece of charcoal from my pockets, quickly scribbling one word.

Go.

The reply was immediate.

Two minutes, starting now.

Two minutes. That was how long of a headstart we agreed on.

I made my way back to the entrance. Arowyn should have stridden to the caves beneath this very spot, where she'd be counting down the seconds to ignite the fire quartz. As long as everyone was out of the lower levels, we would be—

A scent broke through the haze, drifting to me through the mountain. It was familiar. Like smoke and amber and rose, mixed with something sour.

The world stilled.

Vera.

I turned on instinct, feeling like I was spinning in molasses. My heart beat louder than a drum as ice seeped down my spine.

She was here. My sister was *here*.

And we were about to blow up this cave.

I snapped into motion, weaving around wheelbarrows and darting over boxes, frantically searching for any sign of her. That dirty-blonde hair, those golden eyes, the sharp cheekbones. I tried to follow the scent, frustration mounting as I counted the seconds in my head. How much time was left?

It didn't matter. I had to find her.

Boots hammering on stone, breath burning in my chest, I raced through the dim tunnels, dodging stacks of boxes and flickering torches. The ground declined steeply as it led into an underground system of caves. My pulse ticked faster than the seconds remaining. Every step was heavy, driven by panic and a dread deeper than I'd faced before.

One minute left.

A fork appeared in the jagged path. I barreled down the right side, which opened to a larger cave with shelves built into the walls. Boxes and boxes of weapons were already in place, ready to blow. My eyes swept the shelves, the crates, the shadows between stone pillars. Nothing.

Thirty-five seconds.

Time was running out. This underground level was about to go up in flames. Once I found her, we'd both have to shift to make it out alive, but we could do it. We were powerful enough. I wouldn't leave her again, not after everything.

Then there was movement.

A flicker of color down the tunnel across the cave. Dirty-blonde hair and squared shoulders. I only saw her for a second before she passed, but it was enough.

I ripped the camouflaging ring off my hand. "Vera!" I roared. Sprinting across the cave, my hands shifted into talons, ready to grab her and claw our way out from under the mountain.

Twenty seconds.

I tore through the tunnel opening, breaths ragged. Dragon fire radiated up my chest as smoke filled the air around me. Slowly, so slowly, she stopped walking and turned her head.

But she wasn't looking at me.

I whipped around to peer down the opposite tunnel to find a menacing form staring back at me.

Scarven.

The cave rumbled. Rocks fell from the ceiling and clattered at my feet.

Arowyn had ignited the charm.

"Vera!" I shouted again. I took off down the long path toward her and away from Scarven, but out of nowhere, something yanked my arm. I stumbled backward as Arowyn appeared before my eyes.

"Are you trying to get yourself killed?" she hissed. "We have to go!"

Terror blazed through me, stealing the breath from my lungs. More rocks fell from the ceiling.

I tried to break out of Arowyn's hold. "Arowyn, no!"

Looking back down the opposite side of the tunnel, I saw Scarven's lips curving into a smile.

A thunderous *boom* vibrated in my ears, and the cave disappeared.

We landed in the wet rocks of the mountain pass. I fell to my knees, my claws scraping the ground as I watched smoke envelop the night sky. A frenzy built in my chest.

Distantly, I heard a scream.

I thought it was my sister. An echo of her pain, my own mind crafting her gruesome death under the burning mountain. I bowed my head to the ground and gripped my hair in my talons.

Another shriek pierced the air.

"Nox!" Arowyn grabbed my shoulder. "It's Devora!"

63

DEVORA

I was burning alive.

Flames erupted on the entire left side of my body. My leg, my arm, my neck. I could feel the skin bubbling, nerve endings igniting. My knees buckled as a scream tore from my throat, then choked on my own breath when ash filled my mouth.

This was death. I had to be dying. *Nothing* could ever hurt this bad, like my flesh was peeling from bone, and fire was eating every inch of me. Pieces of my red hair fell in clumps to the ground, burning away until it was nothing but soot and smoke.

And then it stopped.

I was lying flat on my back, panting so hard, I could barely catch my breath. The rain hit my seared skin like acid. I couldn't stop shaking. My teeth chattered, and my vision kept going in and out from the white-hot, blinding pain.

Hands instantly reached for me, but the second they touched my left arm, I let out another scream.

When the ringing in my ears finally dimmed, voices trickled in.

"What just happened?"

"Was she *burned*?"

Then *his* voice, low and pained. "Devora, darling, can you hear me?"

I let out a whimper and pried my eyes open. The world spun around me, the stars twirling above the mountain as rain pounded into the earth. Nox's large body hovered over me and blocked the droplets from hitting my skin.

Without taking his eyes off me, he quickly said, "Everett, get me a pain serum. Now."

A few moments later, another body appeared at my head. Nox took a glass vial from Everett and tore off the stopper, letting a warm yellow liquid ooze onto his hands. When he touched my left arm, I flinched and tried to pull away.

"I know it hurts, but this will help," he pleaded. "Please, Devora. Let me take your pain away."

I swallowed hard, then nodded with another whimper. Nox carefully reached for my left hand and kissed my trembling knuckles. "I'm here, darling. I'm here," he whispered over and over as he began gently rubbing the healing oil on my arm.

I arched my back and let out another cry. It was too much. Every raindrop, every gust of wind, every brush of a cloak felt like daggers driving into my flesh.

"Do we have anything to help her sleep?" Nox urged.

"I—I don't know. Let me look." The image of Everett rifling through our bag of supplies blurred around the edges. Finally, he pulled something out. "This says it's a sleeping draught."

"Give it to me." Nox took the bottle and brought it to my lips. "Here, Devora. Take this."

I let my lips sag open, the taste of raindrops and my own tears seeping onto my tongue. The liquid he poured down my throat was warm. My mind immediately grew dim and foggy, and I was distantly aware that the potion was working, that I was being dragged into a peaceful oblivion.

If this pain was what waited for me, part of me hoped I wouldn't wake up.

———

THE WORLD CAME BACK to me in pieces. First was the feel of my chest rising and falling with steady breaths, each exhale like a quiet burst of wind. Then the sensation of cloth spread over my legs. Fabric rustled against my inner thighs as I shifted, and rocks dug into my shoulder blades. Then warm hands were on my right side, light fingertips resting on my arm.

I slowly opened my eyes to find myself lying in a cave. A fire flickered in a small pit far on the other side, several logs now dwindling nearly to the ground. The sound of flames crackling made my shoulder jerk involuntarily from the memory.

I struggled to sit up, gingerly lifting myself with my right arm as I took in the sight of my left arm and leg encased in bandages. A strong herbal scent filled my nostrils. The burns had dulled to a slight throb instead of the excruciating pain from earlier, and I knew I had our supply of healing serums to thank for that.

Nox stirred at my side when I moved, but didn't wake. He'd fallen asleep leaning against the cave wall with his hand balanced protectively on my uninjured arm. A wave of tenderness poured through me, making my chest ache.

I watched him, my eyes tracing the waves of his unruly hair, the strong jawline, the handsome face that appeared far younger in his sleep. Unburdened and restful. Until his nose twitched and his hand tightened around my arm, a crease appearing in his forehead. With an uneven breath, his eyes fluttered open, instantly finding mine in the dim light of the cave.

"Devora?" he croaked, leaning forward. "Here, let me help."

His hand came to my back, carefully helping me move into a seated position. I grunted at the slight shift of my bandages against raw flesh, but it was tolerable. Nothing compared to before.

"How do you feel?" he asked. "Does it hurt?"

"A little, but it's better. How long has it been?"

His shoulders dropped as he sagged back against the wall, but his hand never left me. "A few hours. We found this cave near the mountain pass and set up for the night to let you heal. It's a network of caves—the other two are down the tunnel." He motioned toward a path beyond the dying fire.

I gazed down at my left arm, still scared of the phantom flames I saw when I closed my eyes.

"Did something happen, Devora?" he asked softly. "Before Arowyn and I appeared?"

"No. Nothing." I shook my head, just as confused as I was hours ago. "Everett and I were waiting for you, that's all. We didn't see anybody, but maybe someone was hiding nearby and—and cast a spell, or something. I thought everything was going well, actually. We felt the mountain shake when the charm was set, but it was like the second I heard the explosion..." I shivered against the memory of the sudden all-consuming blaze. "Everything *burned*."

Nox closed his eyes, and his head dropped against the stone wall. The faint wrinkles around his forehead and mouth were more pronounced than ever, and the puffiness around his eyes...had he been crying?

I furrowed my brow. Something was wrong. Something *besides* my stint as a human torch.

"Nox, what's wrong?"

He slowly opened his eyes, and they took a second to focus on me, as if he were searching for something else. "Scarven was there. Down in the tunnels, when the explosive went off. I saw him just before Arowyn strode us out."

My mouth fell open. "He was *there*? Why? But—wait, that's a good thing, isn't it? Did it kill him?" My mind raced, my injuries forgotten in the light of this victory. We'd never *dreamed* Scarven would actually be here for the shipment. If he'd been down there during the blast, I could only hope that meant he was gone for—

"And so was Vera."

I blinked. "Vera was..." My voice caught. His words slammed into me, my heart sinking at the look on his face.

I brought a shaking hand to my lips. "You saw her? Are you *sure*?"

He nodded stiffly. "It was her. She turned to look at me before —" Cutting himself off, he gripped his head in his hands. His fingers flickered between flesh and talon, and when I saw blood dripping from where he clawed his scalp, I lurched to my knees to stop him.

Pain shot up my left leg, but I ignored it. I grabbed both of his forearms. "Nox, please," I begged. "You're hurting yourself."

"I killed her, Devora," he rasped, eyes glowing silver. "I killed my *sister*."

I shook my head. "No, you didn't. You *didn't*. Nox, look at me. She might've gotten out. Do you really think she and Scarven would've gone down there if he didn't have *multiple* backup plans?" I tightened my grasp on his arms, even when the raw flesh on my left hand screamed at me. "She's *powerful*, Nox. You can't let yourself believe she's gone. You *have* to have faith."

His eyes dimmed, fading back into their normal navy-blue. He took a ragged breath. "What if I can't? What if she didn't get out? How am I supposed to live with myself?"

My heart cracked wide open. I'd never seen him this unsure of himself. I wanted to be there for him. I wanted to be his rock, his support, his anchor when the storms were too fierce for even a dragon Shifter to navigate.

But I didn't know how to make this better.

Wincing, I lowered myself back to his side, placing an arm behind his back. He instantly leaned his head on my good shoulder. I felt a single tear drip onto my arm, and my vision wavered with my own.

"It's going to be okay, Nox. I'm here. I love you. She's going to be okay." I kept repeating the words as I stroked his head, running my fingers through his hair and down his neck.

I didn't know if it was true. I didn't know if Vera had gotten out of those caves. The explosion was fast and powerful, and if she wasn't quick enough...

But I *had* to believe it. I had to have hope, for Nox's sake. Otherwise...this would break him.

His temple rested on my shoulder, and I could tell when sleep finally took him. His breaths evened out as his full weight pressed down on me, soft snores filling the cave. I kept gently kissing the top of his head, my fingers wandering through his hair until I drifted off into my own restless dream.

———

FLAMES BURST FROM THE DARKNESS, dancing and darting around the pitch-black space. I tried to run before they could engulf me, but my feet were rooted to the ground. A scream ripped from me as the fire jumped to my feet.

The pain was numb at first, like my mind was trying to catch up to my body, but then it ruptured. Both searing and cutting at the same time, making my skin bubble as the scent of burning flesh ignited in my nose.

But then, there was a different sort of pain.

A sharp sting broke through the blaze. This was concentrated. Focused. Precise. Not like the chaotic inferno that encompassed every inch of me.

My eyes slammed open as I gasped, nearly choking on my own tongue. My right leg—it felt like someone was cutting me open—

Nox had fallen into my lap in his sleep, but he bolted awake when I jerked my leg. I let out a whimper and pawed at my leathers.

"What are you doing? What's wrong?" He glanced in confusion between my face and my hands clawing at the fabric.

"Get them off, get them *off!*" I cried. There was nothing there, but I could feel the tip of a dagger sinking into me, carving out my flesh.

Without question, he shifted a finger into a talon and used the tip to shred through the leg of my pants.

I slapped a hand over my mouth to muffle my shriek.

On the bare skin of my upper thigh were jagged, bloody letters. It was like an invisible knife was slicing them into me, one by one, and I watched in horror as the last letter dug in deep, sending rivulets of blood down my leg.

A single word shone up at us, red blood glinting in the firelight.

Mine

64

NOX

A roar built up my chest and into my throat, my skin vibrating with my dragon thrashing inside of me.

My rage was consuming. Devouring. Chewing through me like acid, a molten river flowing against my ribs.

Scarven.

I ached with the control it took not to shift then and there. The world blurred in and out of focus—all I could see were the crude, bloody letters cleaved onto her thigh, shredding through her skin.

He was *claiming* her.

My sorrow spilled into this monstrous, red-hot fury until it boiled over, begging to be unleashed. What last night had hollowed out of me now filled with pure, blinding hate.

Tears tracked down Devora's perfect cheeks. Her hand trembled as she pressed on the wound, blood seeping through her fingers. "I'll never get away from him," she whispered, her voice soft and broken. "H-how did he do this?"

Hate wasn't a strong enough word for the way I felt. I didn't know how it was possible, but I *knew* it was Scarven. He'd made her feel unsafe while in his house and locked in his chains, and now he'd taken *this*. Her safety in her own body.

I would kill him for this. I would *burn the world* for what he did to her.

I shifted so I was on my knees in front of her. Her hand still covered the word, and I slowly circled my fingers around her wrist to pull it away. Blood smeared across the jagged edges of the letters and dripped onto the ground.

Mine

Seeing it again lit something feral inside of me.

When I lowered my head to the cut, she gasped. Starting from the edge of the word, I traced my tongue until the coppery tang of her blood burst in my mouth. I wanted it off of her skin. Every drop of blood, every trace of the pain he caused her.

"Nox, what are you—"

"You will *never* be his, Devora," I growled against her. "No word will ever claim you. No mark will ever control you." My tongue dragged across the cut as if I could make the word disappear.

Her breaths stuttered as her tears subsided, and the tremors faded from her body. Her blood was rich and salty on my lips, as powerful and tempting as the woman sitting before me. She deserved to feel that power. She deserved to know that *no one* could put her under their thumb, much less my twisted brother.

I placed one last kiss on the mark, then pushed off from the ground and met her eyes.

"You belong to *no one*, darling. Don't ever let him convince you otherwise."

She closed her eyes, and a soft inhale shuddered through her.

"Do you believe me?" I pushed, remembering the same words she spoke to me when I was at my lowest.

She blinked slowly, eyelashes still wet with tears. "I believe you." There was a pause as she held my stare, then she swallowed. "But that means he's still alive. We have to figure out how he did this."

"I'll talk to Sil—Milo." My fiery anger dimmed as the loss of our head Alchemist swept over me again. Fates, so much had happened in the last two days. My mind was spinning, grappling for purchase as it began sifting through the next course of action.

"Are you healed enough to travel?" I asked.

She flexed her left arm, then peeled back one of the bandages, exposing bright pink, nearly healed skin. "Those tonics worked wonders. I think I can ride."

I nodded. "We need to get back to the Keep as quickly as possible."

Her forehead pinched. "What are we going to do?"

The guard at the forge said they had more caches to deliver *this week*. I knew what came next. What this had all been leading up to. Scarven had his plans, his armies, his tricks up his sleeve. But he wasn't the only one.

We were at a tipping point. The moment before the leap. The weight of everything we'd lost and everything we could *still* lose coiled inside me, tight and electric. There was no turning back. No more hesitation, no more mercy.

"We're going to find out what he did to you." My gaze lingered on the letters on her thigh, and anger crawled back up my throat. "And then we're going to end this once and for all."

65

NOX

Everett and Arowyn were just as horrified by this new revelation as Devora and I had been. They fired off question after question, the same ones I'd been mulling around in my mind.

"I thought you said you saw Scarven in the blast."

"Does this mean he's alive?"

"Are we sure he wasn't in the cave? How else could he do that to her?"

As they spoke, one thought stood out in my mind. A terrible, selfish thought. Part of me was glad Scarven survived the explosion, because there was the tiniest possibility Vera had too. That my sister might not have died down in those caves. And that spark of hope was enough to light a fire under me.

Arowyn and I hastily packed our bags and prepared the horses while Everett applied more healing salve to Devora's burns. "Are we ready?" I called out. I was met with a chorus of confirmation, and I pointed to Everett. "Help Devora onto her horse, and hitch Arowyn's to yours."

Arowyn's pale blonde hair and pink cheeks appeared at the cave's opening. "What am I, chopped liver?"

"You're not coming with us," I said, meeting her at the entrance. "We need to talk. I have a job for you, if you're up for it."

———

By the next morning, Everett, Devora, and I had made it back to the Keep. We immediately found Milo in the workshop and relayed what had happened at the Guardian Forge as quickly as we could while he took a look at what was left of Devora's burns. I could tell she was hesitant around him after the conversation we'd overheard Everett and Arowyn having, but if the young Alchemist was bitter toward her, he didn't show it.

A steady string of spells left his lips, accompanied by more herbs and serums than I could count. The boy looked exhausted.

I put a hand on his shoulder. "You've done wonderfully, Milo. We couldn't have done *any* of this without you."

He gave me a grim smile, then wiped his hands on his pants. The motion reminded me so much of Silas that a pang shot through my heart.

"Look, Nox, about that mark..." He looked down at Devora's thigh, which was covered by a new pair of leggings, then averted his gaze. "I don't know much about dark magic—you know how Silas felt about it. But I—I've read some books." He twisted his lips, as if ashamed of what he was admitting. "I don't know how it's done. But I've been thinking. There are ways to—to *link* people, kind of. Like curses that make what happen to one person happen to another. It's done with blood magic."

"And you think Scarven's Alchemist cursed Devora to link her to Scarven," I said, putting the pieces together.

Milo nodded. "It's the only thing that makes sense. You said he was down in the tunnels right before the explosion? And the second it was set off, Devora caught on fire."

"Almost as if I was there," Devora finished as she stood. She moved her injured arm back and forth, bending it at the elbow without flinching.

Milo continued, "Say Scarven got burned before he could escape. That would explain why it happened to Devora. And then he carved the letters into his own leg, knowing it would appear on hers."

"So anything that happens to him, happens to her," I breathed out.

"How do we break it? This curse or spell or whatever it is?" Devora demanded.

Milo rubbed the back of his neck sheepishly. "You can't. Curses are...complicated. They can only be broken if the person who originally casted it banishes it, or if they die."

"Convenient." Everett's husky voice sounded from across the workshop, where he'd been putting back our weapons. "Because I was going to kill Mortep, anyway."

I raised an eyebrow. "Someone has a vendetta."

Those dual-toned gray-and-green eyes held my stare. "You have no idea what he did in those cells, Nox. He *will* die. And I'll be the one to do it."

A chill settled over the workshop. I'd never seen the Illusionist so ruthless.

It was good. We needed that.

"What if it also works the other way?" Devora suddenly asked. "What if whatever happens to *me* also happens to Scarven?"

"Absolutely not." I shook my head before she could go any further. "Don't you even *think* about hurting yourself."

She held out her hands. "I'm just saying, if we need to weaken him, shouldn't we be using every weapon in our arsenal?"

I growled and stepped closer, my voice low and sharp. "Listen to me carefully. You are not a *weapon*, Devora. You are not *bait*. You are not a *martyr*. We'll find another way."

For once, she didn't argue. She merely shifted on her feet and sighed, those eyes sparking with that defiance I loved so much, even if it was aimed at me.

"Come on," I said. "We need to get the others. We have a new mission to plan."

66

DEVORA

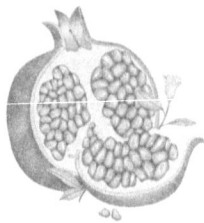

I stood in the workshop, the buzz of magic and purpose thrumming through the room. It was as if lightning had struck the Keep in the last couple of days we were gone—everyone was at high speed, energy flowing, determination and vengeance reignited.

I crossed my arms tight against my chest and dug my fingers into the fabric of my sleeves, as if pressure alone could hold me together.

Every flicker of candlelight, every dark shadow, every twinge on my skin made me flinch. Even with the meetings and preparations to keep me distracted, my thoughts still strayed to the bond, that invisible tether linking me to Scarven.

I knew it wasn't real, but I swore I could *feel* him. He'd done this on purpose. He wanted to mess with me, to mess with *Nox*, and to keep me in constant fear of him. I felt disgusted with my own skin. Each slight motion had me spiraling, wondering if he was doing something to hurt me. Knowing that, at any single moment, he could control me through pain.

I was tired of being afraid.

I was afraid to be alone. I was afraid of fire. I was afraid Scarven could slit his own throat and his Shifter powers would heal him, whereas I'd be left bleeding out on the floor.

The burns had mostly healed now, thanks to Milo. I didn't know if he still blamed me for what had happened, but all that mattered was that we were working together. The last thing we needed right now was for anyone in the Order to be divided.

Because this was our last stand. Our final play. I could tell by the undercurrent of anticipation through the entire Keep that everyone else felt it too. Something big was coming.

Whether it was our salvation or damnation, only the Fates could tell.

"...this cache was destroyed," Nox was saying, his voice steady but tight with exhaustion. "The explosive charm worked like a... well, like a charm. But it's not over. He has more shipments they're planning on disseminating to the other provinces."

He tossed a black dagger at Kieran, who caught it by the handle, then let out a grunt and narrowed his eyes.

Nox pointed at the fatesprig dagger. "I swiped it off the cargo. I hate to say it, but I was right. It has the same magic-dampening effect the fatesprig injection had. There were *thousands* of weapons just like it. Before, it was just us speculating. But now..."

Tessa swore under her breath when she took the blade from Kieran, then dropped it back on the table. Milo, who was scribbling in his Grimoire several feet away, eyed the dagger suspiciously.

Everett leaned against the wall to my left, arms crossed, eye patch gone and revealing a jagged scar across his left eye. "We can't let him distribute this to the entire empire."

"Way to state the obvious," Tessa said, but it didn't hold her usual sarcasm.

Kieran rapped his fingers on the table. He'd forgone his suit jacket this evening, but still wore a dress shirt with the sleeves rolled up his tan forearms. "How much time have we got, Nox?"

"I don't know for sure. They'll be gone by the end of the week."

Kieran's lips thinned into a look of grim determination. "Then we go for the kill. We destroy it all at the source."

A weighted silence fell over the workshop. Outside these doors were dozens of refugees, some still deep in recovery. They represented a fraction of the people Scarven had hurt over the years. A small portion of the ones he still kept locked away in his Hollow. And an entire empire full of innocents who could be harmed by an army of fatesprig.

Nox cleared his throat. "This is the last chance we have to strike. We've been careful up to this point, only making a move when we thought he was looking the other way. But this is different."

"We know the risks, Nox," Tessa said softly, putting a hand on his shoulder. "We always have."

"It's been a long time coming," Kieran agreed. "We're with you to the end."

When the three of them looked at me in expectation, my chest squeezed. I wasn't sure if I'd ever get used to this—people turning to me, *wanting* me, including me.

"I don't even know why you're asking," I said. "I was all in before you even let me leave that tower."

Nox glanced over at Everett, still leaning against the wall. Everett lifted his chin. "You know I've made promises. I'm not giving up on the ones I care about who are still in there. As long as we get them out, I'm in."

Nox nodded. "Of course. We'll make sure we get every single prisoner out, as well as anyone who's been working for him against their will. And then—"

"Then we blow it sky-high," Tessa said, rubbing her hands together.

"It sounds like you don't even need me to make a plan this time," Kieran remarked.

Nox gave him a lazy smile. "I'll always need you, Kieran."

"What say you, oh mighty Alchemist?" Tessa asked Milo, propping her elbows on the table to face him.

"Someone's got to stay behind," Milo said. "I'll keep a team of Alchemists here to ward the Keep. We can't leave it unprotected."

"Are you sure?" Nox asked.

"You know I don't like fighting." Milo smiled pensively, hints of the grief he still bore shining through. "Silas wasn't a warrior either. He taught me protection is just as powerful as destruction. I'm where I'm meant to be."

Tessa reached for his hand across the table. "He would be so, *so* proud of you."

"We'll need more people," Kieran said. "If this it to be where we make our stand, we cannot do it alone."

Nox nodded. "Already three steps ahead of you. Everett, evaluate who among the refugees is fit to fight, and we'll give them the choice. Tessa, get everyone outfitted with weapons and protection charms. Milo, we'll need at least one strong fire quartz and an Alchemist who can activate it when we're ready."

I shifted on my feet, my eyes glued to him taking charge and doling out instructions. I knew this was serious. I knew *everything* was at stake, and we were walking straight into the arms of the enemy.

But, Fates, if watching Nox in his element wasn't the hottest thing I'd ever seen.

The faint shimmer in the air was the only warning before Arowyn popped into existence in the space next to me. I let out a yelp and jumped to the side.

"Well, it's good to see you too," she quipped, but I didn't miss the way she reached for the table, her legs unsteady as she tried to get her balance.

When Nox looked at her with a raised eyebrow, she nodded. "It's done."

I barely had time to wonder what that little interaction was about before Nox squared his shoulders and said, "Good. Everyone knows their assignments. We leave in twenty-four hours."

The room sobered even more at his words, if that was possible. Eyes wandered, exchanging glances mixed with trepidation and resolve. We were all in this together, and that bond we'd formed snapped stronger into place at the thought of what lay ahead of us.

Nox cleared his throat. "This is what we've worked for. This is what we've *survived* for. Each and every one of us, in our own ways. Scarven thinks he's built a world he can rule through fear, and has tried to break us down bit by bit." His navy eyes met each of ours, and I felt my shadows stir in response. "Maybe parts of us *have* broken. But we used every loss, every wound, every scar to forge something new. Something *unbreakable*. And you—"

He cut himself off. He swallowed hard, the emotion in his voice making my own throat clog. After taking a breath, he continued, "Before the Order, I was heartbroken and lost, driven by ego and vengeance. But each of you came into my life and made me a far better man. When I need to be put in my place—" He motioned to Arowyn, who let out a soft laugh, and then he cast a look at Milo. "Or when I need a reminder that goodness and innocence still exist in the world."

Nox's gaze settled on Everett. "As much as I wish you had never been through what I went through, you give me strength because of it. You give me joy," he added, reaching out to squeeze Tessa's arm. She hastily wiped her cheeks with the back of her hand. "And loyalty—" He clapped a hand on Kieran's shoulder.

Then he turned to me, eyes burning through to my soul. "And you give me peace."

Taking in the room, he said, "Whatever happens tomorrow, I want you all to know that fighting with you has been the greatest honor of my life. And that's something he can't take from us."

My heart swelled. I had to swallow the lump in my throat as I watched everyone's spines straighten, their eyes brighten, their faces settle into steadfast resolution.

"Practice that speech in the mirror, did you, Nox?" Arowyn's words broke the weighted tension, and a chorus of chuckles rang through the workshop.

"Through flame and ash," Kieran said, nodding firmly at Nox.

"Preferably *our* flame and *Scarven's* ashes," Tessa added.

Everett snorted. "I could drink to that."

———

I TRACED a circle on the mug of hot tea in my grip, staring at the sunrise out the window of Nox's chambers. His windowsill was large enough for me to curl up on with a warm blanket and a pillow propped at my back. There was frost on the glass, and when I exhaled, puffs of hot air clouded the inside of the window.

For just this moment, I didn't want to think about Scarven. I didn't want to think about the bond, or the scar still marking my thigh, or my uncontrollable, violent shadows, or the fact that tonight...everything could change.

We might not come back from this.

Stop thinking about it, I chided myself. I focused on the faint pink-and-orange hue settling over the rocky shore, the blue-and-gray waves crashing onto the sand, the solitude of the morning before the storm hit.

Nox silently slipped up to the window. He squeezed my ankle, and I moved to give him space to sit. The golden sunrays highlighted the dark blond of his hair, making his tan skin glow as he fixed his gaze on the horizon.

I loved seeing him like this. Soft and muted, without all the hard, anxious lines and tense muscles. I didn't think many saw this side of him—they either got the ferocious dragon and rebel leader or the cocky, silver-tongued charmer. And I loved all of it. All of *him*. But this version of him...this was mine.

I nudged his leg with my toe. "What's on your mind?"

He hummed. "Just thinking about how it'll feel to watch that mansion burn."

"How romantic," I said with a chuckle.

"What can I say?" He looked at me. "Listen, Devora, tonight will be dangerous, and—"

"If the rest of that sentence involves you asking me not to go, you can stop right there," I said, quirking an eyebrow.

It was his turn to smile, but it didn't reach his eyes. "I learned my lesson the last time. But I'm still allowed to be worried about

447

you." He repositioned his legs and patted the spot in front of him. I set my mug down and grabbed my blanket, crossing to sit between his legs. My back was flush to his chest, and his chin rested on top of my head, his arms wrapping around me.

"How has your magic been?" he asked.

I shrugged. "It's been fine. Normal. Nothing like the night of the fight. Maybe it was temporary."

"We'll just have to be careful tonight." He pressed a kiss to my temple. "Hopefully, it won't come down to fighting at all."

I craned my neck to look at him. "You don't believe that, or you wouldn't be prepping over a dozen refugees for battle."

He sighed. "We have to be ready for the worst."

"Trust me, I get it." I nestled back into his chest. "But have you thought about what happens if we win?" I asked, more quietly this time.

"Darling, I've dreamed about that every day for the last nineteen years."

I turned so I could face him. I ran my fingers through his hair, marveling at its softness as his eyes fluttered closed.

"And what does the famous dragon Shifter dream of doing with his freedom?" I whispered.

"Seeing my mother and sister. Being a family again." His shoulders relaxed slightly as he spoke. "Not having to look over our shoulders at every turn. Traveling the world because I want to, not because I'm forced to." He let out a breath, slowly opening his eyes to meet my gaze. "Waking up next to the woman I love without wondering if today is the day I lose her."

I brushed my thumb across his cheek. "You will never lose me, Nox."

He caught my thumb with his lips and kissed the pad. "Never is a long time, darling."

"It's not long enough," I murmured. "Not with you. I want forever."

The idea should've scared me. Being this vulnerable, placing my heart in someone else's hands, trusting him so implicitly when I'd only ever been used and cast aside in the past.

But I wasn't scared. I couldn't imagine anyone I felt safer with.

He smiled, slow and aching, and he reached up to grasp my hands. "If we make it through this, then I promise you, Devora, darling..." He kissed the tips of my fingers. "Our forever will start tomorrow."

I took a deep breath and nodded. Closing the gap between us, I rested my forehead against his.

Tomorrow.

67

DEVORA

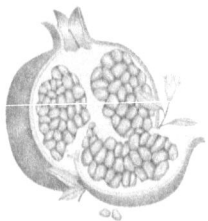

Scarven's manor loomed ahead. It was all black spires and sharp edges, with darkened, empty windows that looked like unblinking eyes. Watching. Waiting. It made the cut on my thigh prickle with awareness.

We moved like shadows across the bridge leading to the property, the crushed gravel crunching beneath our boots. Mist curled low around our feet. Creatures scurried by in the distant trees surrounding us, and thick wind whistled through their branches.

Milo stayed behind, as he said he would, but the rest of the Ashen Order was armored up and ready to go, along with more than a dozen older refugees who had volunteered to help.

Everett and two other Illusionists were a few steps ahead of the rest of us, using their magic to conceal the entire group as we neared the mansion. To anyone looking, they would see straight through us and to the forest beyond.

We all wanted to believe it would be simple. Get to the Hollow to find where the weapons were being hidden, rescue the remaining prisoners, set the explosive charm, get out.

But we were dressed for battle, and I feared that was the only way this would end.

Nox glanced at me, his eyes holding a question. When I

nodded, he looked over at Tessa and Kieran, then the others, meeting each of their stares with a quick nod of confirmation. Then he pointed two fingers at Everett.

According to plan, our ranks began to spread. Kieran led a small group west toward the stables that hid one entrance to the Hollow, while Tessa and her group went south. The rest of us kept straight toward the front of the mansion, prepared to fend off any defenses that may be in place.

Everett, Nox, and I stepped forward. The second my boot landed in the hard grass, I felt it.

A spell. It skittered across my skin, tightening in my chest and making the hair on the back of my neck rise. I jerked toward Nox, whose jaw was clenched.

"My illusion," Everett said beside me. "It's down."

"Well, I guess he knew we were coming," I muttered.

We all tensed, the air suddenly shifting around us. My breath quickened as the shadows cast by the towering mansion became more sinister. They crawled across the ground like spindly fingers reaching for us. Wind rustled my hair, howling in the distant trees.

"Nox, what should we—" I cut myself off with a sharp gasp.

Something struck.

But it wasn't someone attacking. It was from *inside* my leathers. Like something invisible was clawing at my skin beneath my shirt.

I quickly ripped the sleeve up my right arm, my stomach crashing to my feet when I realized what it was.

"It's him," I breathed out, watching in horror as, once again, words were carved into the sensitive skin of my inner arm. Nox yanked me toward him. Fury radiated from him in waves, and my shadows sprang to my fingertips in response.

Blood beaded and pooled around two crimson words.

Look up

My head snapped up. It wasn't *shadows* from the mansion that were inching closer.

There was a flash of glowing eyes, claws of steel catching moonlight, and then three of them dropped from the rooftop.

Shifters.

Before I could blink, they attacked.

68

DEVORA

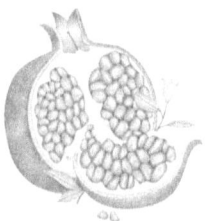

Clawed feet hit the courtyard with a *boom*, and the entire world trembled. I sucked in a breath when they came into view—black-and-red veined and inhuman, like someone had warped them.

The first had the head of a wolf while his massive upper body was still in his human form, with clumps of fur scattered across his bare chest. His pants were torn at the legs where his feet had shifted into enormous paws. When he opened his mouth, his jaw came unhinged, opening wider than possible and exposing lines of serrated teeth. Thick black veins pulsed around his black eyes.

These weren't like any Shifters I'd seen before.

The second one made me stumble backward. She was a serpent Shifter, with slick green scales covering her entire body and whip-like coils in the place of arms. Even her long hair took the form of snakes, each strand ending in a head with a forked tongue and sharp fangs. Her waist morphed into the body of a tiger. Muscled legs crouched before flying into the air, straight at Everett.

She sent him crashing through a stone statue in the courtyard with a sickening *crack*. The wolf Shifter blurred, moving faster than my eyes could track, and struck Nox to my right. The third...

A thick wing barreled into me, knocking me off my feet. Three reptilian tails lashed out and wrapped around my wrists and ankles. I struggled to catch my breath, my temples pounding as a welt formed on the back of my head. But even my shadows stilled when I saw what stood before me.

This Shifter was easily eight feet tall, with a face that shifted with every blink. Feline, avian, reptilian. Its glowing black eyes transformed from thin slits to wide, round orbs, with scales turning to fur then to feathers.

My magic pulsed in my bones, erratic and scared. It whispered a warning: *Wrong, wrong, wrong.* There was something wrong with these Shifters. Unnatural.

It bared its teeth and stretched its bat-like wings, pointing a sharp wingtip straight at me. My shadows reacted instantly. They shot around me like a solid barrier, thick enough to block any weapon.

But the Shifter didn't slow. It punched through my wall of shadows like it was mere smoke. I quickly rolled onto my side. Dirt sprayed my face when the wingtip pierced the ground.

While it was distracted, I summoned my shadows and formed them into spikes, hurling several at its body. They hit their marks across its abdomen and wings. Black, viscous blood poured from the open wounds. Victory shot through me as its hold on my wrists loosened.

But within seconds, the skin stitched itself together, barely leaving a mark.

The tails bit into my skin, and I gasped against the pain. The voices in my head grew louder and louder with each passing moment.

Let us out, little one.

You know we can protect you.

My shadows taunted me, begging for release. Panic swept over me. I couldn't do that again—not like last time. I didn't have to fight that way. I didn't have to—

The Shifter lifted me into the air by its tails, my body stretched so taut, I thought it was going to tear me in half.

Let us help you, my shadows hissed.

No! I shrieked back at them. The fabric of my leathers snapped as the Shifter's tails kept pulling at either ends of my body, stretching me. The strain on my limbs was almost too much to handle—

A dagger soared through the air and sliced all three tails clean off. I crashed to the ground as the Shifter screeched at its new opponent.

Nox's eyes were silver and molten, with navy scales shimmering in the starlight as his wings unfolded in a flash of fury. He tackled the Shifter and dug his talons into its flesh, flaying its chest open and ripping out its heart.

Its twisted, blackened heart.

Bile crept up my throat. What had Scarven *done* to these creatures?

All around us, the battle spiraled out of control. There were only two of his mutant Shifters left, but their power was undeniable. At least three of the refugees who had come with us were lying on the ground, and an Alchemist was kneeling over one of them, trying to revive him.

Everett took on the serpent Shifter alone. His dual-toned eyes were locked in fierce concentration as he sent illusions the rest of us couldn't see, making the serpent rear back with an ear-splitting cry.

The handful of refugees who hadn't gone with Tessa or Kieran's groups were battling the wolf hybrid, but their combined magic was barely putting a dent in the Shifter's massive form.

Arowyn strode between the two fights, her movements as quick as lightning. In one breath, her sword glinted off the serpent's scales as she struck, and in the next, she was plunging it into the wolf's side. Even though she was getting good shots in, each wound healed faster than the last.

My chest burned as I watched. Shadows pommeled inside me, the pressure rising like boiling water.

I couldn't lose control. I couldn't become *that* again. One wrong move, and someone I cared about could die.

A shout rang out ahead, and time stilled as Everett stumbled away from the serpent Shifter. In his momentary distraction, she lunged, sharp fangs glinting and slicing through the air.

I jumped forward, but Nox got there first.

He shoved one of his wings between the Shifter and Everett, catching a fang in the translucent underside. Clutching at his back, his wings instantly shifted out of view. He dropped to his knees as a trail of dark green veins crawled up his neck.

The serpent smiled, then attacked.

A scream tore from my lips. "*No!*"

Her hair of writhing, coiling snakes dove for his head, hundreds of tiny teeth bared and sharp enough to break skin. They latched onto his head. He let out a terrible roar of pain that shook the ground at my feet.

I snapped.

An ocean of darkness exploded from my skin. I thrust out my hands, and a solid wall slammed into the serpent. It wrapped itself around her body, cutting off the snake's heads in her hair and flinging them to the ground. Her body was swathed in shadows, completely swallowed by the darkness until—

Blood sprayed, coating Nox in black-and-red ink. The Shifter's scream ended in a wet gurgle. When my shadows unraveled and rushed back to me, her body dropped in a dozen pieces to the ground, hunks of scaled flesh now ripped to shreds.

I dragged in a breath. As before, my shadows were now tinged in red and humming with dark satisfaction. They twisted around my limbs and filled me with an overwhelming sense of power. It flooded my veins, trickling through my blood and steeling my spine.

It felt *good*.

A whisper, cold and low, brushed my ear. But it wasn't the familiar whisper of my bloodthirsty shadows.

"*Exquisite,*" the voice said.

My euphoria halted. I knew that voice.

"Scarven," I breathed out. Whirling around, my shadows scattered into the night, seeking out the source of the voice. But he wasn't there. The battle raged on around me as if no one else had heard him.

Laughter echoed next to me. I swung out a hand, but again, nothing was there.

"You grow more beautiful every day, love," his voice murmured. "I almost forgot how stunning you are when you *break*."

"Where are you?" I shouted, shadows circling in anticipation. "Show yourself!"

"You can't see me, Devora. But I see you. I always have." Magic pulsed around me, and on the outskirts of the surrounding forest, more shadows emerged.

"You were the first," Scarven whispered. "We thought fatesprig was meant to *take* power. But I changed that. I *gave* you power. I made your magic bloom into something I could only dream of. And look how glorious you became when you stopped fighting it. When you *submitted* to it."

My knees threatened to buckle. I pressed my fingers to my temples to try and block him out. "You turned me into a monster," I spat.

"I turned you into a masterpiece," he hissed back. "And I've done the same thing with the rest of them. There is no limit to what I can do." A sharp pain dug into the cut at my thigh. "You are *mine*. By the end of the night, the rest of you will be too."

The sensation in my leg dimmed, and his presence disappeared. The shadows that lurked on the edges of the tree line elongated and widened as several more creatures came into view.

"Nox!" I shouted. I ran forward into the thick of the fight between him, Everett, and the wolf Shifter. Nox spun at my call, and I was relieved to see he'd already healed from the serpent's wound.

He grabbed my forearm. "What happened? Was it your shadows?"

I glanced down at my hand to see black veins, identical to the ones on these mutant Shifters.

"It's Scarven. He was here. He—he talked to me." I shuddered. "Whatever he did to make my magic so uncontrollable is the same thing he did to all of them," I explained, brandishing an arm to the battlefield. "They're stronger than us, Nox. And there's more coming."

His eyes followed my hand when I pointed toward the oncoming opponents.

There was no fear in his gaze, like the kind I felt in my own bones. Only resolve. His features hardened as he said, "The prisoners. You and Arowyn have to go—*now*."

"But there's too many—"

"We'll hold the line. We *have* to get the prisoners out, Devora. Stick to the plan. Finish what we came here for."

I met his stare and swallowed hard, willing my shadows to calm. My eyes took in the courtyard, the broken Shifter corpses, the fallen refugees. I nodded slowly. He was right. We had to try.

Arowyn appeared beside me with her blood-smeared sword and dirt speckling her pale hair. "You ready for this?" she asked.

I clenched my hands into fists and spun to face Nox again. "You promised me tomorrow." Grabbing the back of his neck, I forced him to meet my eyes. "So you will *not* die today."

His answering smirk shot straight to my heart. "As you wish, darling."

He claimed my lips with his, a heady flood of desire, fear, and unspoken promises lingering between the blood and sweat. When he broke away from me, it took all my strength to let him go.

I straightened my shoulders and shook off the rising dread. He would be fine. He *had* to be. I couldn't let myself think otherwise.

"Alright, Arowyn." I gripped her arm. "Take us to the Hollow."

With a faint shimmer, the battlefield disappeared.

69

DEVORA

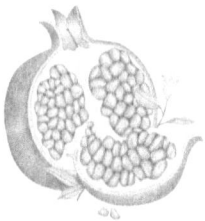

Arowyn strode us straight to the stables on the west side of the property. The first thing I noticed was the destruction. Clawmarks were scratched into the floor of the stables, wooden doors were ripped from their hinges, and the earth surrounding the area was torn up, as if something had trampled through. I crept to the hidden trap door leading down into the Hollow, expecting there to be wards blocking us out, but the door was already blown open.

"I guess the question is whether someone was trying to get *in*," Arowyn mused, "or *out*."

I wasn't sure which was worse.

We hurried down the steps, the lack of any wards or defenses particularly unsettling. Rattling chains reached our ears when we made it to the first tunnel. I bit back panic as memories from similar cells crept in.

Arowyn and I snuck silently down the path, taking in the wooden doors lining the hall, with tiny windows allowing a view inside the cells. Each one had a steel bed with leather cuffs and tables with trays full of sharp weapons and empty syringes. Several of the doors were already cracked open, and when we peered inside, the cells were empty.

We exchanged a glance. A shiver went down my spine. I had a feeling that wasn't a good thing.

We came across the first locked door, and I pressed my face to the window. Another empty room. Where were—

A hand slammed against the glass.

I jumped back with a yelp. Fingers slowly slid down the window and were replaced by a gaunt, sallow face, with dark brown hair hanging limply down a thin neck. The girl stared at me with her head low, dull eyes boring into mine.

"Well, *she* looks friendly," Arowyn said before disappearing in a faint shimmer. She popped into view on the other side of the door, took the girl's arm, and strode back to me.

The girl—barely a teenager, if I had to guess—staggered backward in alarm. Sparks flew from her hands as she caught her balance. She wore a raggedy piece of cloth that hung to her knees, with straps so worn, they hardly held it up on her shoulders. Wide eyes glanced between the two of us, changing color from gray to orange and back again.

"It's okay, don't be frightened." I held out my arms in a gesture of peace. "We're here to help get you out."

"O—out?" she rasped, blinking rapidly. I wondered how long she'd been down here. What torture and experiments she'd been exposed to. Whether she still had *family* waiting for her.

I nodded and made my tone as gentle as possible. "We're getting all of you out. Every single one. What's your name?"

Sparks flew erratically from her hands. "I—I don't remember."

My heart clenched uncomfortably. "That's okay. My name is Devora, and this is Arowyn." I pointed to Arowyn, and the girl's eyes followed.

"We're going to take you far away from this place," Arowyn said. "You just have to trust us and stay beside me. Do you think you can do that?"

The girl looked at us, then back at her cell, and a shiver racked her body. "Yes," she finally said. "Yes. Please...please help me."

"We will, sweet girl. I promise. Come here." I held out a hand.

She took a deep breath, and her sparks slowly subsided. When she placed her hand in mine, her bones were so brittle, I thought I would crush them if I squeezed too tight.

This close, I could see her skin was riddled with scars and puncture wounds. Some looked like little crescent moons. I glanced at her fingernails and saw blood caked beneath them, and sorrow surged through me.

"We're going to get the others now, okay?" I said. When she nodded, the three of us tiptoed down the tunnel to the next cell.

"Mmm," the girl suddenly hummed, brow pinching. "Mmm. I think my name starts with an M."

I rubbed my thumb reassuringly on the back of her hand. "Okay, how about I call you Mae until you remember?"

"Mae," she said, drawing out the name. She tightened her grip and nodded shyly, dark hair draping over her shoulder.

Arowyn got three more prisoners out of their cells in the span of the next few minutes. One was a Strider and hawk Shifter hybrid named Theo, who was in his thirties and seemed to have a better understanding of what was happening. Another was Elynor, a twenty-year-old female Illusionist with a black cloth draped over her eyes and tied behind her head. She explained that Malek Mortep had blinded her and studied how to get her illusions to work without the power of sight. Her story made my blood boil and my stomach twist into knots at the same time.

The last one was the youngest yet—an eleven-year-old boy with fox ears and a reptilian-like tail who kept asking us for crackers.

I put my hands on his upper arms, rubbing them up and down. They all looked so cold. Their skin was paper-thin and pebbled with goosebumps, and the rags they wore did little to protect against the winter chill. "We'll get you some crackers and anything else you want as soon as we get the others, okay?"

His little fox ears wiggled when he nodded, and my heart cracked further.

Now that we had another Strider, we were able to move a little quicker. Theo and Arowyn worked together to whisk others out of their cells and into the hallway, and soon, we'd covered three tunnels and had about a dozen scared but hopeful prisoners trailing behind us.

"How much bigger is this place?" Arowyn hissed at me.

Before I could respond, Elynor appeared at my side. "There's another tunnel this way"—she pointed to the right, where the path veered up ahead—"and one more beyond that, but it doesn't have any cells. It just leads to the main laboratory."

When I glanced at her in surprise, she smirked. "You're wondering how I know that, aren't you?" She gently touched the cloth covering her eyes. "Mortep did a lot of tests on me. I never let him figure out they actually *worked*. I can't see with my *own* eyes, but I can see through *others*. When he would take me out of my cell and to his lab, I could see everything he saw. I have these tunnels memorized."

Arowyn crossed her arms. "Why in the world have you been letting *me* lead, then?"

Elynor chuckled and motioned the rest of us forward. The stone walls looked darker the farther we went. It was mustier and colder, with the soft *drip drip drip* of water echoing down the path. We collected a couple more prisoners and were about to turn back when Theo threw out a hand to stop us.

"Do you hear that?" he whispered.

Our eyes swept the darkness, and we all held our breaths. I pulled Mae and the youngest boy close, holding them to my side as my shadows trickled protectively along my arms.

I felt a quick, sharp stab of pain on my forearm. When I hissed and looked down, there was a small cut with blood blooming to the surface.

I didn't have time to dwell on it long before I heard a sound.

Footsteps, distant at first, then loud and thunderous as they pounded against the stone. A low snarl tore down the path. More heavy steps rumbled, menacing growls following in their wake.

Arowyn and I forced the younger children behind us. I stared into the shadowed tunnel, barely able to see a few feet ahead. My shadows swirled around my arms when I held out my hands. They, like me, were waiting. Breathing. Watching.

The footsteps slowed, and the first pair of glowing yellow eyes pierced the darkness.

"Stay back!" I shouted at the kids, molding my shadows into two blades in my hands. I put my right foot forward and braced myself as Thecae had taught me.

Two enormous, fully shifted beasts stepped into the firelight. My eyes landed on the nearest one, and I had to hold back a gasp. It was some sort of canine with *two* heads, each baring rows of razor-sharp teeth.

It locked eyes with me and let out a growl that sent waves of musty heat rolling over me. Heart hammering, I held my shadow blades up to my face.

The first creature charged.

It flew through the air and collided into my chest. Its hot saliva slid down my neck. I barely managed to erect a shield before its teeth sank into my shadows. The weight of its giant body crushed me, making it hard to breathe.

I tried to strengthen my shadows to force it off me, but it was too strong. When I blocked one head, the other lunged, snapping at my neck. I jerked to the side and felt it grab a mouthful of my hair.

Its jagged tail whipped around and lassoed my wrists together. I stared into its maw of sharp teeth, its black eyes, its flared nostrils. My heart battered against my ribs. I had to get out of this. I couldn't let it get the children—

Without warning, my body fell.

It felt like I was freefalling as I sank straight into the darkness beneath me, then popped back out from the shadows behind the beast.

"Whoa," I muttered, steadying myself from a spell of dizziness.

"Whoa," Arowyn echoed in agreement.

Shadow melting. I grinned. "Oh, I'm *so* doing that again."

The creature whirled on me, but this time, I was ready. I formed a sword from my shadows, my smile widening as it hesitated. With a snarl, it swiped a paw at me, and I swung my sword through the air.

It leaped back, its tail so long, it nearly hit Arowyn and the group of prisoners. I taunted it, trying to lure it toward me and away from them.

"Come and get me." I brandished my shadow sword and stepped backward.

A low growl behind me made me stop in my tracks.

I forgot there were *two* of them.

"Okay. This is not good," I muttered as both beasts converged on me from either side.

Out of nowhere, a streak of darkness sailed through the air and landed on the one behind me.

I gasped as the black-and-tan jaguar the size of a horse tore into the two-headed dog's throat, teeth digging in and ripping.

The beast went still.

The other creature hesitated. The jaguar faced it with blood spraying from her mouth, letting out an earth-shattering roar.

Claws skittered on stone as it tucked its tails and ran the opposite direction.

In the blink of an eye, the jaguar leaned onto its hind legs as its body shortened and limbs withdrew into the familiar form of Tessa.

"I had them right where I wanted them, you know," I said through gasping breaths.

"Sure you did." She picked at her tooth with a fingernail and shot me a wink. "Just thought you could use some help."

70

DEVORA

"I've never been happier to see you," Arowyn said.

"I get that a lot. Is this all of them?" Tessa took in the dozen people behind us.

Elynor stepped forward. "Should be. The only hallway left leads to Mortep's laboratory."

Mae and the boy ran back up to me and clutched my waist. I patted their backs as I said, "Tessa, can you get them to safety? Arowyn and I should check out the main lab."

Mae clung to me, looking up with wide, scared eyes. "It's okay, sweet girl," I said, smoothing her hair. "Tessa will take care of you, and I'll see you soon. I promise."

Her gray eyes shifted to orange again, and her body heated with her lightbending powers before she blinked it away and extricated herself from me. I hated leaving them when they were still so traumatized, but the important thing was getting them out of the Hollow.

Tessa, Theo, and Elynor took the lead and helped the younger ones back down the way we came. I watched until their footsteps receded and Arowyn and I were left alone.

"This way," I said, following the directions Elynor gave us to the final tunnel with Mortep's lab. It was eerily silent without the heavy breaths and footsteps of the others. I could hear every tiny creature scurrying along the tunnels, every echo of dripping water, every distant rumble.

We turned down the last hallway. Torches lit the path, showing a few empty cells along the walls. All the way down the long, narrow tunnel, I could see the faint pinprick of light coming from Mortep's laboratory.

As we walked, there was a slight shift in the air. My breath caught, awareness prickling at my skin. Everything felt...heavier. Darker. Thicker. My shadows responded, but they were slower than usual. It was like they were trying to wade through molasses. They moved in lazy circles inside my chest and around my hands, instead of their usual lively dance.

"Do you feel that?" I whispered.

Arowyn nodded solemnly. We kept walking, my shadows resting across the tips of my fingers.

But as we got closer to the door, they flickered. Gone one moment and back the next.

I could feel my magic straining, pushing against some invisible force attempting to snuff it out. Alarm flooded me. I tried to send my shadows ahead of us, but they barely moved. Only a faint wisp stretched its little fingers into the darkness beyond.

We were almost at the door. I shuddered as the *wrongness* of the air got even heavier. Dark energy rolled over us, and no matter how hard I tried to summon my shadows, they were a fraction of their normal strength. I met resistance with every step forward, as if the tunnel itself was exhaling and pushing us back.

The torch at the end of the hall hissed and sputtered low, casting strange, flickering shadows over the floor. I grabbed the handle to the lab's door and twisted.

It flew open with a bang.

At the table in the center stood Malek Mortep, with his mane of dark hair and those pure white eyes staring back at us with sadistic glee.

But he wasn't what made my heart leap in fear.

In front of his outstretched hands, amid the shattered glass vials and pools of blood, was a huge sphere of black and red shadows.

Shadows wasn't the right word—it was more like energy, a tight ball of flickering magic, lightning, and darkness. The air crackled with power as black and red tendrils twisted over each other like a den of snakes. Dark magic permeated the room. The sensation of my magic being sucked out of me was overwhelming, an infectious curse spreading through the lab and into my veins.

"Welcome back to the Hollow, *Miss Nyte*," Mortep jeered. "You were a bit earlier than we expected."

"What are you doing?" I shouted at the mad Alchemist, watching his lips move soundlessly as he held the sphere between his gnarled fingers.

"Me? Oh, I'm simply the decoy." His white eyes met mine, and he cocked his head with a sinister grin. "It's too bad you'll miss the show."

With a powerful thrust of his arms, he threw the ball of magic at Arowyn and me.

It collided with us, instantly obliterating our magic and sending us flying backward out of the lab. I crashed into the stone wall and slumped to the ground. Everything went gray as a throbbing pain exploded in my head.

When the spots in my vision cleared, I saw the swirling ball of dark magic hurtle past us and down the hall, leaving shadowy wisps of black-and-red energy in its wake. A dark fog descended over the entire corridor, pulsing and suctioning all magic from the air.

"Arowyn?" I called.

"Right here," she answered with a groan to my right. "Where'd he go?"

I scrambled to my feet as quickly as my head would allow and staggered toward the lab, only to find it empty. The opposite door was swung ajar.

"Gone," I said, rubbing the back of my head. "What just happened?"

Arowyn limped to me and dusted off her leathers. Several scrapes marked up her cheeks and neck, but other than that, she appeared unharmed. "I don't know, but I draw the line at some freaky ball of death."

"Can you stride at all?"

She shook her head. "No. I can't do anything. My magic is gone."

"Mine too." I slowly swept my eyes over the lab, taking in the cloud still billowing around us, with its flickering red and black shadows. Broken glass vials were strewn all over the floor. Tufts of shredded green leaves littered the space. When I opened one of the enormous cabinet doors, I found box after box overflowing with fatesprig leaves.

"This is where they keep the fatesprig," I said. "I wonder if the rest of the weapons are down in these tunnels too—"

Before I could finish my thought, a resounding *boom* echoed from somewhere above, shaking the ceiling and sending rocks flying to the ground. Arowyn and I both looked up.

"Well, that doesn't sound good," she said.

"Mortep *did* say this was just the decoy." I tried to summon my shadows again, but that well inside me where my magic rested was still empty.

Something inside the cabinet caught my attention before I turned away. One of the only syringes left unshattered in the mess of the laboratory, filled with a dark green serum.

It looked...familiar.

I quickly swiped the syringe and shoved it in my pocket as more high-pitched, animalistic screeches drifted down the hall.

"Come on," I said with a shiver. "Let's get out of here."

71
NOX

W e hadn't been ready for this. There were *dozens* of them, these red-and-black-veined, unnatural creatures with dark magic flowing from them in droves. As several more refugees fell to the onslaught, the weight in my chest sank lower and lower.

This was my fault. *I* brought them into this. I led my people straight to their demise.

We had to hold on. Just a *little* longer.

More shouting and clanging steel rang through the air, and I saw our two other groups that had split off at the beginning now being pushed back to us by Scarven's mutant creations.

"Nox!" Tessa shouted, wielding two shortswords against a Shadow Wielder covered in dark veins. "What are these things?"

"Mutants," I growled over the noise. "Stronger than normal Veridians. Looks like he has an army of them."

"You can say that again." She grunted, lunging forward to pierce the Shadow Wielder's wall of magic.

There was a tremble at my feet right as a brilliant white stag burst through the clearing, impaling someone in a lion's mask with his antlers. Kieran flung the body to the side and charged again. Several of Scarven's men backed away in a group to avoid the sharp antler tips.

"It's like they're lining up for me," I said to Tessa, watching them gather together.

"How nice of them."

"Kieran, *move!*" I bellowed, and he darted out of the way. I unleashed a stream of dragon fire on them. The air heated, the red and orange flames illuminating the fight around us. I closed my mouth and watched their ashes fly away in a gust of wind, then turned back to the others.

More mutants had arrived, along with some of Scarven's men in their lion masks. I lost track of how much time had passed as I barreled through mutated shifters and hybrids of all kinds while still keeping an eye out for Devora and Arowyn to return.

"Tessa!" I called to my third as she took out another opponent. "Go check on Arowyn and Devora. Make sure these things don't get to them."

With a nod, she hurried through the fray, disappearing in the wave of fights.

Someone shouted my name, and I spun around to see the same half man, half wolf Shifter from before launch himself at me. Claws swiped at my face, but I grabbed his wrist and snapped it in half. He didn't even howl as the bones popped themselves back into place. He was so close now that I could see the black-and-redness of his veins swirling like liquid, the same darkness reflecting in his pure black eyes.

Spit clung to the wolf Shifter's teeth as he unhinged his jaw and bit at me, narrowly avoiding my neck.

"A little help over here!" I heard Everett yell from somewhere. I rolled my neck along my shoulder, relishing the crack and pop of joints, then shifted my hand into talons.

The wolf threw himself at me again, and I shoved my talons through his chest and out his back, severing his spine. For good measure, I pulled my arm back and yanked his heart along with it.

Black blood and red entrails covered my talons. I threw the organ on the ground and pivoted to find Everett.

What I saw stopped my heart.

Was that—was that my *mother?* How could she possibly have gotten here?

She ran through the flailing limbs and weapons, clutching something to her chest. Her gray-and-blonde hair whipped behind her as she sprinted. She kept glancing over her shoulder with a look of absolute terror on her features.

"Mama!" I shouted. I pushed forward, finally getting a glimpse of what she held in her arms.

A baby.

Confusion blurred my senses, taking me back twenty years ago, when I watched my mother twirl that same baby in the living room of our house. That was *Vera.* But that wasn't possible. Vera wasn't a baby anymore.

I reached for her, so close I could almost grab the ruffled sleeve of her dress, when she let out a scream.

A sword rammed through her chest.

I opened my mouth, but there was no breath left to scream. It felt like someone had ripped the air from my lungs. Her body slumped to the ground, revealing a man with a curved sword in his grip.

I blinked away my shock and staggered backward. Something was wrong. It couldn't be—

"Father?" I whispered, taking in his short dark brown hair, the gray streak on the side, the sharp chin and jaw. A face I hadn't seen in nineteen years.

"So sentimental, brother," my father said with a sneer. Slowly, his face morphed into Scarven.

Illusions. It had to be. All of it.

Wrath replaced my shock, and a snarl worked up my throat. I gripped the dagger at my waist and took a few steps toward Scarven. "You *bast*—"

He disappeared. I stopped short, spinning in a circle to find him. His chuckle burned my ears. I whirled again, but he was gone.

I could still hear the fight raging around me, could still see my comrades locked in battle, but all I could focus on was *him*. This was my chance. I was so close, I could taste it.

There was a flash of his dark hair, and I lunged.

My dagger fell through thin air. I let out a growl of frustration.

"Looking for me?" Scarven asked, reappearing several feet away. He cocked his head and stared at me as I pounced. I wrapped my hands around his throat, but all he did was smirk.

"I thought you were the mighty dragon Shifter, slayer of enemies and lord of the skies," he taunted. "Where's that *fire*?"

I squeezed his neck harder, feeling his muscles work to draw breath and watching his veins bulge from the pressure. With a roar, my dragon fire climbed up my throat in an intense wave.

This was it. *Finally.*

But someone was shouting. With a gasp, a familiar voice spluttered from Scarven's mouth.

"Nox, it's me!" the voice said. "What are you—Nox—"

Scarven's face flickered, and suddenly, I was staring into Kieran's eyes. His face turned purple beneath my hold, his fingers clawing at my arm as I crushed the life out of him.

I instantly dropped him.

Disgust poured into me. I almost *killed* him. My best friend.

He fell to his knees, and I caught his back, my hands shaking. "Kieran, I—I'm so sorry. I thought you were Scarven. He's here. He's—"

"Are you sure, brother?" Scarven whispered behind me. I set Kieran down as he recovered his breath, hunting for the disembodied voice. "Are you sure I'm truly there? I could be anywhere. Any*one*."

There was a mass of dark curls and full red lips, and suddenly, Sage was standing before me. She swished the skirt of her dress and flashed me a smile. "Did you miss me, love?" she crooned. "Or have I been replaced so easily?"

The image wavered and shifted to Devora, red hair tangled down her back. She was bound and gagged, that horrid fatesprig collar back around her throat. Tears streaked down her dirty cheeks as she stumbled to her knees. I *knew* it wasn't real, and yet I couldn't stop myself from reaching for her, the fear so visceral, I thought it would eat me alive.

Her body vanished. In its place was a single, rolling head. It came to a stop, the gaping mouth and vacant eyes of my father staring back at me.

"Get out of my *head!*" I roared, gripping my hair.

"What does it feel like to have everyone you have ever loved leave you?" Scarven's voice echoed across the space. The vision of my father's head was quickly replaced by a younger version of my sister and me holding hands. My breath faltered.

"Even your own *sister* doesn't know who you are." In the span of several seconds, the younger Vera changed, aging by a decade as her features hardened. She glared back at me with those bright golden eyes full of venom.

"She's dead," I choked out. "Vera's dead. I saw her at—at the forge. I couldn't save her."

Scarven's deep hum rumbled the earth. "Did you, now? Did it look like this?"

The world tilted. I was back in the tunnels of the Guardian Forge, staring at my sister down the hall. She looked back at me for a split second before the caves erupted.

Was all of it an illusion? Had she truly not been in those caves, or was *this* the lie?

My head spun. My dragon half ached inside my chest, begging to be free and carry me away from this. I didn't know what to believe. I couldn't trust my own sight, my own mind. The pressure built in my chest as my stomach tightened.

More and more visions slipped by, each of them more gruesome than the last. Memories of the past mingled with my present —Kieran, Tessa, Devora, the Order, all of them ripped from me in a haze.

He was trying to make me crazy. He was trying to make me *snap*. My people needed me, and here I was, captive to my own mind. Useless. Helpless.

In the blink of an eye, the visions stopped. I gasped at the abrupt change.

In their place stood Everett, black fighting leathers coated in blood and dirt. I wasn't sure if this was real until I saw what he was holding.

With one hand, he gripped none other than Malek Mortep by the throat.

"He's an Alchemist," Everett said, slowly turning to me. "*And* an Illusionist."

Clarity struck me. The answer was so simple.

Mortep had *two* magic types. *He* created the illusion of Vera in the forge. Scarven was using him to mess with us tonight.

"You know the key to stopping an Illusionist?" Everett said, glaring back at Mortep. The scar across Everett's gray eye stood out brighter in his fury. "You go for the eyes."

With two strikes from his dagger, he tore out Mortep's eyes.

72

NOX

ortep's wail ripped through the night. I froze as Everett dropped him, then threw his own eyes back at him. Mortep shielded his face with his hands, blood seeping through the cracks of his fingers.

A dagger appeared in Everett's hand. "This is for me," he seethed, "*and* for her." He raised the blade to Mortep's chest.

A mass of fur, hard muscles, and sharp claws burst from the side. A great lion rammed into Everett, and he sailed through the air. The lion roared and shook his wild mane, spit flying from his maw.

He was *enormous*. Easily twice the size of any normal lion, with bronze fur that rippled in the wind and dark eyes that burned with both cunning and rage. Muscles coiled beneath its hide with every step as it stalked toward me.

Scarven.

At the sound of Mortep's loud groan, I took my eyes off Scarven to catch the half Alchemist, half Illusionist groping aimlessly at his chest until he pulled out a small silver box.

I realized too late what he was doing.

With trembling fingers, Mortep placed something on his tongue and muttered a string of words. There was a flash of smoke, a tightening sensation stretching in the air, and then—he was gone.

"No!" Everett shouted, struggling to rise as he stared at the spot Mortep had disappeared from.

I didn't care about the Alchemist. When the lion lunged for me, there was only one thing going through my head.

Devora.

I couldn't hurt him. Anything that happened to him, happened to her.

Once again, my hands were tied behind my back. He was untouchable.

He soared through the air and slammed his paws into my chest, and we went crashing to the ground, a tangle of claws and fur. I shifted my wings and slammed the wingtips into the ground to stop our momentum, spraying dirt around our bodies as I caged him beneath me.

He struck first. He swung his paw at my face, but I blocked with my shifted hand, careful not to strike him. Sparks flew when his claw hit my steel talons.

Scarven snarled. Rearing his hind legs up, he shoved at my chest and threw me off him. The force made me yank my wings from the ground to steady myself.

Back on all fours, Scarven shook his mane again. This time when he charged me, his body shifted midair, bronze fur morphing into a trim black suit, dark hair with that streak of gray, and gleaming eyes that held my gaze.

"Something wrong, brother?" He sauntered forward, casually buttoning the cuff of his sleeve as if there wasn't a battle raging around us.

"You're a coward," I spat. He was powerful, sure, but he'd never been a match for me. He *knew* it. It was why he hid behind others. First me, then Vera, now Devora.

He shrugged. "You call it cowardice; I call it practical. I haven't made it this far by picking fights I couldn't win."

"Break the bond," I demanded. "Whatever you did to Devora, break it and face me like a man."

"Ah, you see, there's just one slight problem." He brandished a hand. "It looks as if the only Alchemist who *could* break the curse is nowhere to be found. How unfortunate."

I closed my eyes. Milo told us only the original caster could undo a curse, unless they died. If only Everett had finished the job.

I quickly switched tactics. "You're out of plays, Scarven. You've lost your Alchemist, and I'm done being your pet. There's only one way this ends."

He raised an eyebrow and looked around him. My attention strayed to the weapons and magic flying, watching as Kieran battled a mutant levitating on a cloud of shadows, to Everett fending off both a Lightbender and a Shifter, to a group of our refugees slowly being surrounded by half a dozen mutants with dark, swollen veins.

All their faces bore the same expressions: exhaustion. Fear. Grim resignation. Even as they fought for their lives, for *our* cause, they were being overcome.

My heart sank. *Just hold on a little longer*, I wanted to plead. *I have a plan.*

"It doesn't look like I'm the one who needs to worry, does it?" Scarven said. "I am not too proud to admit your little rendezvous at the Guardian Range set things back a bit, but it's no matter. Tell me," he took a step forward, a smirk lighting his features, "how is my dear Devora?"

My lips peeled back from my teeth as I let out a snarl. "Stay *away* from her."

He moved closer, and my arms shook from the effort it took not to unleash my dragon on him. He lowered his voice. "And what are you going to do about it?" Pushing up the sleeve of his shirt, he shifted the tip of his finger into a claw and pressed it to his arm. "I can do anything I want to her, and there isn't a single thing you can do to stop me."

His skin dented from the pressure until a bead of blood

bloomed to the surface. My hand whipped out to grip his wrist, wrenching it away without breaking bone.

He smiled in triumph.

I released him. Hopelessness surged through me, cold and numb. It always ended up in the same place—with me back beneath his feet.

"You truly care for her, don't you?" Scarven asked, that inquisitive, cunning gleam back in his eyes. Slipping a dagger from his pocket, he twirled it between his fingers. He tauntingly slid the edge along his own throat, down his chest and back up again. My muscles clenched with every motion.

"How far would you be willing to go for her?" he asked.

A million thoughts penetrated my mind. He and I have had this conversation before. *How far would you be willing to go to save your sister?*

Flashes of the people I'd hurt, the blood I'd shed, the lives I'd ruined came back to me in a rush. The myriad of things he would ask me to do. The paths he'd force me down to keep Devora unharmed.

Everyone was always in awe of the all-powerful dragon Shifter. The first in two centuries, the impossible miracle. But what they didn't know was how utterly powerless I was. I never had a choice—not with my sister, and not with Devora. I loved her with my entire being.

And love made me a monster. It made me a *weapon.*

I hated myself before the words even left my mouth. "What do you want?"

"From you?" He hummed and leaned away. "Nothing, brother. You've outlived your usefulness. In fact, you've been nothing but a thorn in my flesh these last few months. I simply wanted to remind you of your place."

I went on instant alert. What was he planning? Why go through all of this just to let me go?

"Here's what's going to happen." He put the knife back and

steepled his hands in front of his face. "I'm going to kill every single one of your friends. I'm going to make your *precious* empress watch as I drain her people of magic one by one until they have no choice but to bow at my feet." Every word was enunciated, each one lighting his eyes with glee. "Magic is not a *birthright*, brother. It's a *privilege*, and only those loyal to me will be able to wield it. But do you want to know the best part of it all?"

His smile widened as a wave of heat rushed over the space. The sound of powerful wings flapping behind me made my heart turn to stone.

"You won't be alive to see any of it."

I slowly turned to find bright orange, yellow, and red wings burning through the tree line and heading straight toward me.

My sister landed in a crouch among the dirt and leaves, fire licking from her sharp, brilliant wings and into the sky. She clutched a sword of lightning in one hand and shadows in the other. Her golden eyes blazed with power as she faced me.

She was alive.

And she was aiming straight for me.

"Vera, listen to me. I know you're in there," I said, raising both my hands in a sign of peace. I was acutely aware of the small bulge in my pocket where the blood bead Rose made rested, the one that could break Scarven's compulsion on her. I just had to get close enough.

Vera tilted her head and swirled the lightning sword in one hand. "I don't know you." Her voice was hard, but it was still *her*. My sister. She was in there somewhere.

To my surprise, a figure stepped out of the battle beside me. Everett's eyes were wide as he stretched out a hand, reaching for Vera.

"Songbird?" he whispered, his words choked. "Is—is that *you*?"

I blinked. "How do you know my sister?"

He looked as if he'd seen a ghost. "*She's* your sister?" When I nodded, he dropped his arm.

"That's my girl. My songbird." His eyes were glued to Vera. "She's the one I left behind."

Without warning, my sister launched at us.

73

DEVORA

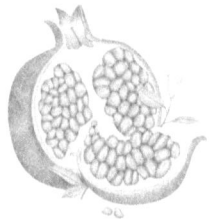

Everywhere we looked was chaos. Blazing, burning, deadly chaos. Arowyn and I had outrun the web of dark magic and gotten our powers back, but the Hollow was slowly turning into a vacuum, a pit of darkness that consumed magic with hunger.

I wondered if it would keep spreading. If it would soon overtake the entire battlefield. The entire *province*.

I shoved the thought out of my mind and focused on what lay before us. In our absence, *hordes* of Scarven's mutant creations had joined the fray. Not just Veridians, but also the creatures he'd created in his labs. Our side was fighting valiantly, yet for every one of the mutants they took down, three more took their place.

My eyes darted from fight to fight. Kieran battled a two-headed dog with one sword while evading an attack from a Shadow Wielder with another. Next to them, two Illusionists on our side stood back-to-back, blades in their hands as their opponents dodged illusions only visible to them. Another refugee was kneeling on the ground beside a crumpled body, tears streaming down their face.

A hawk Shifter with the legs of a deer charged the grieving refugee. I shouted in warning, but before I could reach them, the refugee looked up. She shielded her face with her arm, then grabbed the dead body and strode out of sight.

But not before the hawk Shifter sliced his sword through the air and cut her hand clean off.

The severed hand fell to the ground as she disappeared, leaving trails of flowing blood and the echo of a scream in her wake.

I gasped and halted in my tracks. The Shifter turned to me and let out an ear-splitting squawk. I clapped my hands together and pulled them apart to form a wall of shadows right as he jabbed his sword at my chest. The blade ricocheted off my shield. In turn, my shadows surged, wrapping around his body.

I felt that same rush of violence that was always creeping at the surface of my magic, but I shoved it down hard. I knew now I was the first of this particular brand of Scarven's experiments, and I didn't want to become like his others. I *couldn't*.

I wouldn't let it consume me this time.

So, while my shadows shrieked inside of me, showing me visions of all sorts of torturous ways they could end this Shifter, I ignored them. I yanked them away from him and brought them back to me. He lost his balance and swayed on his four legs, and when he opened his eyes, I was struck by how *human* they still were.

I furrowed my brow. All of them were just...humans. Veridians, like the rest of us.

I could've easily been in his place. One of Scarven's vicious puppets. These mutants were once innocent people with lives, families, and homes to go back to.

I dropped my dagger even as the hawk Shifter's gaze latched on to me. He barreled through the short space between us.

I quickly threw up another shadow shield and found Arowyn, still nearby but locked in battle with a spider. "Arowyn!" I called. "Arowyn, come here!"

"Little busy at the moment!" she shouted as she blew a strand of hair out of her face.

With one hand holding my shield steady, I thrust my other

toward her and sent a wave of shadows over the spider. They muffled its high-pitched shrieks, and when I flicked my wrist, they sent it flying across the property.

"Well, that was easy." Arowyn brushed her hands off.

"Can you stride me and this guy to the Hollow?" I asked, straining against the force of the hawk Shifter trying to break through my shadows.

She raised an eyebrow. "Any particular reason why?"

"He's not the enemy," I grunted. "Scarven made him this way. He made *all* of them. It's not their fault, and we can't keep killing innocent people. But that magical suction charm thing down there—"

"You think it can suck the dark magic out of him," she finished for me, realization dawning on her features.

"It's worth a shot."

"Say it doesn't work, and he turns around and kills us?"

I huffed and pushed more magic into my shield. "At least we go down together."

"That's not comforting." She looked me up and down. "Fine. You better be right." Without another word, she stood directly between the hawk Shifter and me, placed a hand on each of us, and we all disappeared.

When we rematerialized in front of the familiar trap door in the stables, Arowyn gave a mighty grunt and shoved the Shifter into the dark hole.

I waited with baited breath as he landed on the ground. Dark wisps of that same cursed energy flitted near him, summoned by the presence of more magic.

The second they touched his skin, he froze.

And then he screamed. A harsh squawk that made me clap my hands over my ears as he thrashed in the dirt. Those black veins got even *bigger*, pushing against his skin so hard, I thought he was going to split open.

This was a mistake, I thought to myself. We weren't curing him. We were *killing* him.

But his veins didn't burst. As the dark magic swarmed around him, it literally *pulled* the poison from inside of him. Arowyn and I watched, unblinking, as little by little, the blackness was purged, sliding from him like a noxious gas.

His screams slowly subsided as his four legs shifted back into two human ones, his top half shrinking and shedding its feathers. What was left was a young man huddled on the ground, shaking in his torn clothing.

"It worked," I breathed out. "He's—he's cured."

Arowyn exhaled loudly. "You were right, Devora. These people have absolutely no idea what they're doing."

A small seed of conviction took root inside my chest. "Find the other Striders and get as many of the mutants down here as you can." I turned to face her. "We can save them. *All* of them."

She nodded tightly, and I took off.

The sight that greeted me back at the courtyard sent my hopes crashing to my feet. Somewhere on the other side of the property, a violent flash of lightning illuminated the sky. Shouts rang out as more mutated Veridians crawled from the shadows of the surrounding forest.

Where were they *coming* from? It was like every time I looked, there were more. Stronger, faster, fresher. While we, on the other hand, were losing steam.

The faces of my allies were haggard, and their magic was slowing. What were once fast reflexes a couple of hours ago were now drained and sluggish, barely able to stop blow after blow that kept coming from the enemy.

I darted between fighters as quickly as I could, focusing on defense. I raised shadow shields in front of the refugees and pushed back against their attackers. But still, it wasn't enough.

Where was Nox?

A roar burst from somewhere close by, rattling the ground. A couple of mutated Shifters descended from the roof of the mansion.

My mouth dropped. They were easily four times my size, each

with the body of a snake, feet of a lion, and strange, mismatching reptilian wings. Almost like Scarven had pieced them together to fashion a crude version of a dragon.

Two of them crashed to the ground, expanding their enormous, bat-like wings. At the same time, they opened their mouths to reveal rows of jagged teeth and long, forked tongues. Plumes of smoke issued from them and cast the grounds in darkness. It smelled musty and foul, stinging like ashes as it coated my lungs.

The first set of screams rang out. I couldn't see a single thing. The coppery tang of blood filled the air, and fear coiled inside me, so thick I could barely breathe past it.

Shadows flickered in all directions. The occasional outline of a blade slashing through the air was silhouetted against the darkness. Another scream shattered the night. My lungs burned, my shadows hissing against this foreign smoke.

Something furry brushed my arm, and my heart jumped up my throat as I yelped.

"Hush, Devora. It's me. On your left."

I blinked twice. I recognized that voice. There was *no way*—

A small flame burst to life in front of me. My jaw fell open.

Before me stood two figures. One was shrouded beneath a dark hood, with glowing rings on his fingers and a furry brown tail coming beneath the cloak to brush my arm. Beside him was a raven-haired beauty with magical flames resting in one palm and crushed leaves in the other.

"Easy there," Rose said with a wink. "We brought backup."

74

NOX

Vera descended on Everett and me in a cyclone of fire, her phoenix wings ablaze and her eyes as molten as the sun. When her feet hit the ground, it sent up a shockwave of light. I quickly shifted my wings and spun to cover Everett right as she struck.

I braced against the impact, the force of her light sword scorching the outside of my scales.

"What happened to her?" Everett asked, eyes still fixed on her over the tip of my wing.

"I have a few questions of my own," I grunted. "Namely, what do you mean, *that's your girl?*"

His neck jerked up. "Watch out!"

A shower of shadow blades fell from above, and we barely leaped apart before they embedded themselves into the ground, one after another with quick *thwacks*.

I whirled to face my sister. She blinked out of existence, then reappeared mere inches from my face. Her expression was blank. Unknowing. Unseeing. Just another one of Scarven's puppets. She wrenched out a hand and wrapped her long fingers around my throat.

Searing pain surged through me as she pushed her light magic into my skin.

"Come on, Vera. We've done this before," I hissed as I gripped her wrist and yanked it back, shoving her chest with all my might.

She went flying backwards. Her blades of shadow and lightning soared from her reach as she hit a tree all the way across the property.

"Nox!" Everett snarled. "Don't hurt her!"

I cracked my neck back and forth. "Trust me, I didn't hurt her. I just pissed her off."

A bolt of lightning flashed across the sky. Flames erupted along my sister's entire body as she stalked toward us, fury in her gaze.

"That doesn't seem any better," Everett mumbled.

"If you have any ideas, I'm all ears," I snapped back as I grabbed my blade from its sheath. My hand brushed over the blood bead in my pocket.

Vera threw out an arm, and her discarded light sword flew into her grasp. She raised it to the sky as another bolt of lightning crashed around us, illuminating the entire battlefield.

I growled and broke into a run, unfurling my scales across my skin—not a full shift, but enough to give me protection. My talons and fangs shifted to partial length as I lunged for her.

We clashed in midair. Fire with fire, lightning against steel. She brought her sword down, and it sang through the air as it bounced off the hardened scales on my upper arm.

She summoned a small shadow dagger and tore after me. Her blows were deadly and precise. She aimed to do whatever her master commanded. She aimed to *kill*.

I never struck back. I countered with my own blade and talons, redirecting blow after blow, waiting for an opening. Our motions were a blur in the night, with her fire shimmering around us.

"Come *on*," I gritted out. She spun in place and delivered a strike to my stomach with the hilt of one sword, then swung high to reach my throat. I instantly shifted the scales on my neck to block the blade and seized her outstretched wrist. "Come on, Vera. This isn't you!"

Her eyes flickered. Just for a moment, barely a breath, but something changed.

Then she vanished.

I stumbled forward and let out a roar.

I felt the heat from her flames behind me. I spun to catch her, only to find a bloody finger raised to her lips, a spell on the tip of her tongue.

"Wait—Vera, wait." I dove at her, and she turned both hands toward me in defense. Shadows and light coiled around her fingers, the opposite magics forming beautiful, glowing threads. She weaved a net of light and darkness between her palms and shot it at me.

I unfurled my left wing and rammed the edge of it into her.

She dropped with a gasp, skidding across the ground. I threw myself on top of her. Locking her wrists in my grip, I covered our bodies with my wings to block out the noise of the battle.

For a heartbeat, our eyes met. Her lips parted in a snarl as phoenix fire built in the enclosed space between us.

"Vera, *please*."

A blast of her fire hurled me backwards. I slammed into the side wall of the mansion. Stone and bone both cracked, the sound reverberating in my ears as my shoulder screamed in pain.

She was stronger. Faster. Deadlier. Scarven had turned her into his unbreakable weapon.

But she was *my* sister.

Scarven took her from me once before. And I left her there. I claimed that everything I did was for her, and that was true. But I hadn't done *enough*. I hadn't fought for her the way I should. I followed his orders and kept my distance, lying to myself that it was the best thing for her, when I should've rescued her long ago.

I was done making excuses for myself. This ended now—either with her sword in my chest, or with her shackles off for good.

I dragged myself upright, feeling my Shifter healing kick in and mend the broken bones in my shoulder. I fingered the blood bead in my pocket and tucked it in my palm.

One chance.

I took a deep breath and folded my talons away. I let my scales of armor fade, felt my fangs and wings receding back into my skin.

Fire danced in my vision as Vera appeared before me again, golden wings spread out wide, her body a living, breathing flame. She brandished her lightning sword and drew her arm back, aiming for the killing blow.

I knelt to the ground.

"I won't fight you," I whispered. "Not because I can't, but because I *won't*. You may not remember me, Vera, but I remember you." Snippets of our brief time together as a family flooded me. "You—you loved the water. Even as a baby, your favorite place was the ocean. We'd go down to the cliffs to watch the waves roll in, and you were mesmerized."

Her features were full of wrath as she stared down at me, but she stilled with her sword pointed at my chest.

I kept going. "When Scarven took us away from the sea and into his home, the first thing you found was the fountain outside. You took your first steps there." I licked my lips, my voice growing hoarse. "And—and you loved stories. Mama would bring us to the fountain when we were allowed to be together, and you begged for story after story. I always pretended they were too childish for me, but truthfully, I loved them as much as you did."

Memories and emotions I hadn't known I buried suddenly burst to life inside me, making the backs of my eyes burn.

A small smile tugged at my lips. "And when you got older, you used to sneak down to—"

Without warning, Vera struck.

Light emitted from her fist as she slammed it across my cheek. I grunted and fell to all fours, coughing blood onto the ground. Her sword fell from her grip, and I looked up to see her body trembling.

She lifted her fist again—and hesitated. The flames in her eyes shuddered.

"Vera—"

Her fist swung, landing another punch and flinging my head to the side. This time, however, the force brought her to her knees.

She was close. *So close.*

When her eyes met mine again, they were full of so much pain, it made my heart twist and shatter.

I surged forward and wrapped an arm around her, pulling her close. She thrashed in my grip, fire blazing back to life in her palms, but I brought my lips to her ear.

"*I'm sorry.*"

In one swift motion, I shoved the blood bead into her mouth and clamped her lips shut.

75

NOX

Vera froze. She blinked up at me once, twice...and then her entire body convulsed. Magic pulsed through the air, violent and bitter on my tongue. My brow pinched in horror as her *skin* shook—not her muscles, but the actual skin.

Her veins grew darker with the same blackness that bulged out of Scarven's mutant experiments, but this time mixed with gold instead of red. I watched, refusing to let go of her, as the black and gold pushed beneath her skin until it *erupted*.

Magic oozed from her like oil, black shadows leaking from her flesh and pouring into the ground. I kept holding on to her as she trembled with wave after wave of dark magic exiting her body. She let out a shriek that turned into a mournful bird's song, and the sound splintered my heart.

Then she went slack in my arms.

Fear shot through me. I strained to hear the sound of her heartbeat, weak but steady in her chest.

"Vera?" I whispered frantically, placing her on the ground. "Vera, can you hear me?"

Another figure rushed over. Everett's hand shook as he reached for her. "What happened to her?" His voice cracked, full of raw emotion.

"What happened to her?" His voice was raw, cracked, full of more emotion than I'd ever heard from the Illusionist.

I didn't say anything. I simply waited, my hope draining out like the sludge of magic that drained from her body.

Something grazed my knee, and I looked down.

Her finger flinched. The tip of it brushed my knee again, and then she gave a shuddering gasp.

Her eyes flew open to reveal that bright, beautiful, golden light, void of the emptiness that had taken her captive.

"N—Nox?" she murmured.

My heart soared. I gripped her shoulders as a tear slipped down my nose. "It's me, Vera. It's me. You're safe now." I pulled her into my chest and repeated the words over and over until they became unintelligible.

"Nox, I—I'm so sorry," she said with another gasp. "I almost killed you. I ki—killed so many people—" She cut herself off and clutched her dirty-blonde hair in her hands.

"No, you didn't," I pressed. "None of that was you. It was all him. It's *always* been him. But you're free now, and he can't get to you ever again."

Her eyes were still frantic, golden tears lining the lids. "But I—I remember it all. It was *me*, Nox. I still—I still did those terrible things—" She looked down at her shaking hands, and I wondered if she was picturing them covered in blood.

I went to reach for her again, but before I could, different hands replaced mine.

Everett sucked in a breath as his fingers traced a path along her jaw. Slowly, so slowly, she followed his guide and turned her head to face him.

I had no clue what was happening. My mind still refused to wrap around the fact that Everett knew my little sister—that he was *in love* with her. But I watched, transfixed, as Vera's eyes searched his, that crease at her forehead deepening even further.

Her lips parted on a ragged exhale. "Swift?"

It was like the clouds had parted to reveal the sun on Everett's face. "It's me, Songbird," he whispered. He cupped her face in his hands. "I'm so sorry. I wanted to come back for you. I tried for so long, but you—"

"He moved me," she croaked out. "Right after you—after you left. I thought he..." Tears spilled from her as she gripped Everett's wrist. "I thought you were dead. Mortep told me you were *dead*."

"No, no, sweetheart. Please don't cry." Everett's husky voice broke as he collected her in his arms, and she buried her head in his shoulder. "I'm right here, Songbird. I'm not going anywhere."

A beat passed before I said, "You two"—I pointed between them—"have a lot of explaining to do."

Vera twisted away from Everett and threw herself at me, embracing me in a hug so tight, I thought she was going to pop my head off.

"I missed you, big brother," she breathed into my neck.

"I missed you so much, Vera." I couldn't believe she was here. For the first time in nineteen years, we were both free.

Almost.

She broke away, determination ringing those golden eyes. But the fire didn't wipe away the pain, the gaunt cheeks, the hollowness from an entire life of torment and captivity.

"Where is he?" she asked, her voice low and scratchy. "Where's Scarven?"

"He's here. Somewhere. I don't—"

"He's *mine*, Nox." The very air around us seemed to crackle with her newfound vengeance. "Scarven is *mine*."

I swallowed hard. "You can't kill him, Vera. Not yet."

"Watch me."

"No, I mean—he did something. He has someone else. Someone I—someone I love." I imagined my sister burning him alive with her phoenix fire, and watching Devora burn with him.

"What are you talking about?" she growled.

"He cursed her. Everything you do to him will happen to her too," I said, and she blinked as understanding dawned on her

493

features. "I'll explain everything later, but *promise me* you won't hurt him," I pleaded. "Not until I can get her safe."

I could've sworn my sister's fingers sparked. There was such endless hatred in her eyes as she held my stare. For a brief moment, darkness flickered there. I wondered if she wouldn't care. If her years under his hold had dimmed some of the humanity that once shone so bright.

I didn't think I could blame her if it had.

"I wouldn't be asking if it weren't important to me, Vera." I gripped her shoulders. "Please. Wait just a *little* bit longer."

That thin, sharp jaw clenched. Her nostrils flared as she glanced behind me, then back again. "Fine," she gritted out. "But when it's time, *I'll* be the one to do it."

76

DEVORA

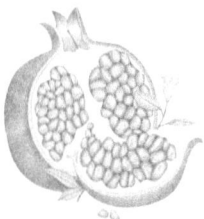

Words caught in my throat at the sight of Rose and Leo. "What—*how*—"

"Nox," Rose said simply.

Her eyes scanned the darkness behind me, and she raised a chunk of herbs to her lips, whispering a string of spells. A fierce wind tore through the field. The toxic smoke around us rippled then blew back, spiraling upward like a cyclone as Rose held her arms out wide. With a thunderous *boom*, a second magical blast of wind cleared the smoke completely.

Gasps rang out among our numbers as we could finally see again. Motion flickered in the corner of my eye, and I whipped around to see one of the mutated snake Shifters grip Tessa by the throat. It reared back, ready to sink its elongated fangs into her neck.

With a faint shimmer of light, none other than *Chaz* appeared next to her. He drove his long sword into the Shifter, shoved the body aside, then whirled toward us with a quick wink.

"What's even *happening* right now?" I mumbled in awe. "How did you know to come?"

"Nox sent Arowyn to us a couple days ago," Rose explained. "Told us he was preparing for something big and to be ready."

"It nearly took her out to stride that far again, but it gave us time to get things in order," Leo added. "And not a moment too soon, it looks like."

"Finally!" a tired voice said behind us. Arowyn threw her hands in the air. "Fates, it took you long enough. Hey, you. Strider." She jerked her head toward Chaz. "I need your help."

"Hello, there," he said, a smirk stretching across his dark features. "I'm all yours."

The two of them blinked out of existence. Around us, at least ten more creatures appeared with gnashing teeth. They snarled, their muscles grotesquely stretched and veins glowing.

"What *are* these things?" Rose asked, her face screwed in disgust.

"Scarven's experiments. It was worse than we thought." I quickly explained the fatesprig mutations, and how it made them all stronger and more bloodthirsty, completely beholden to Scarven.

As I spoke, the remaining snake Shifter with wings landed at Rose's feet. Leo jumped into action. His tail flicked out to wrap around its front leg, yanking it forward. Leo gripped the hilt of his sword and swung it in an arc at the Shifter's neck.

"Wait! Don't kill it!" I rushed out. Leo faltered, his sword hanging in the air as the beast's serpentine head reared back to strike. With fast reflexes, Rose put something to her lips and muttered a spell, and the snake froze in place.

"Don't *kill* it?" Leo repeated, pointing at the poison dripping from the frozen snake's fangs. "Seriously?"

"They're still *human*. They didn't choose this," I insisted. "We've found a way to cure them—that's what Arowyn's working on. So, for now, just...just incapacitate them. But don't kill, if you can help it."

Leo let out a sigh. "This is the most high-maintenance rescue operation I've ever seen."

"Devora, watch out!" Rose yelled.

I whipped around to see a ball of crackling light aimed straight at me. I didn't even have time to raise my shadow shield.

But I didn't have to.

A wall of shadows formed within inches of my face, so strong it knocked me to the ground. It swallowed the lightning sphere whole, then molded to the shape of the ball, growing and shifting with power. A second later, it reversed direction and sped back through the open air. With a powerful clap of thunder, it collided with the mutant Lightbender across the field, sending him and two others flying back into the forest.

Thecae emerged from the pool of shadows at my feet.

My mouth fell open. He wore deep red fighting leathers and a belt full of weapons, his hands outstretched with shadows dancing between them.

Shock overwhelmed me. I couldn't believe what I was seeing right now. Even *Thecae* had come?

He quirked an eyebrow. "What've you gotten yourself into, girl?" he asked in that hard, gruff voice. I hadn't realized how much I missed my shadow trainer until now.

I jumped and threw my arms around his waist. His muscles tensed at first, then he awkwardly patted me on the back. "Think we can save this for later?"

I cursed and gathered my bearings. "Right. Fates, okay." I looked out at the horde of glowing eyes, the dark magic hanging thickly in the air, and the menacing growls from the dozens of mutants still left standing in the field.

I gestured at them. "So basically, we just need to—"

"I think we got it," Rose said with a smirk.

Tessa and Kieran leaped toward us in their animal forms, shifting midair and landing at my side in a crouch. Tessa rolled her neck along her shoulders as she pulled a shortsword from its sheath. With a nod at the others, Kieran fell in line and brandished his weapon.

My heart kicked as I took in the sight of them. *All* of them.

"Through flame and ash," Kieran said, raising his sword. "Form ranks!"

And they attacked.

The battlefield exploded into motion. Thecae shadow melted straight into the ground, appearing behind enemy lines with blades of shadows in his hands. He carved a path through the chaos faster than I could keep up. He aimed for nonlethal points—the legs, the arms, the occasional swipe at their sides.

All around him, creatures fell, and Thecae erected barriers of shadow to keep them firmly stowed behind until Arowyn or Chaz could get to them.

Rose and Leo each took on two Shifter mutants, wielding both daggers and spells in tandem. Rose cast a rapid-fire string of spells, and vines ripped from the ground to wrap around her opponents. She blew a powder in their faces that made them yowl in pain. Thin pricks of blood trickled down their skin from thorns embedded in the vines.

I had to admit, the Alchemist was a little vicious. I liked it.

Kieran, fully shifted once more, lowered his antlers and plowed through a trio of creatures. Tessa's snarls accented the night as she launched herself into the air to take on a wolf Shifter.

In between the fighting, Arowyn and Chaz were striding every couple of minutes to pull the incapacitated Veridians to the Hollow.

I summoned my shadows, and they swelled around me with new strength. The battle was no longer collapsing around us. It was *turning*. Shifting. Changing in our favor.

We could *do* this. Together.

But a small flicker of panic crossed my mind as I took in the field. Where was Nox?

A roar echoed over the grounds, followed by a flash of brilliant light to my right. Sounds of another battle rang out, taking place around the side of the mansion. My breath quickened. What if he was—

"Go," Rose said at my back. "We'll be fine. Get your boy."

I nodded and took off as another roar sounded. When I could see around the edge of the property, I stopped short. A figure, both human and bird-like, shot into the air, feathers igniting as flames encompassed her body.

Vera blazed a trail across the sky, letting out a low, beautiful song as she dove back down.

Nox and Everett stood beneath her, weapons raised high. At first, I thought Vera was targeting them. I put on a burst of speed, ready to throw out a shadow shield.

But when she landed, she spread her glorious, golden-fire wings wide, blocking Nox and Everett behind her as a raging lion burst through the air.

She pulled her two long swords free, one encased in lightning and one in shadows. She was *protecting* Nox.

Did that mean he'd saved her? That the blood bead from Rose worked?

Scarven, in his lion form, swiped a paw at Vera's face. She dodged, and they began to weave around each other, him with his claws and her with her swords. While he aimed to kill, I could tell she was merely defending herself, never taking an opening to do damage even though I knew how talented of a fighter she was.

Nox must have told her. Guilt swam to the surface. She was holding back for *my* sake. Because they didn't want me to get hurt.

How were we ever supposed to stop him if we had to walk on eggshells for *me*? They couldn't even get a hit in. Scarven had gotten exactly what he wanted, *again*. To be untouchable. Invincible.

We were never going to win with both hands tied behind our backs.

Scarven's snarl of frustration brought me back to the moment. His anger made him sloppy, and when he swung his paw at Vera's stomach, she lifted her light sword to block it.

A sting shot through my right hand. I looked down to see the singed edge of my thumb, with a thin trail of smoke rising from the wound.

We knew this bond, this *curse*, worked one way. If he was hurt, I was hurt. But what we *didn't* know for sure was if...

I clamped my lips together and dug my other thumb into the burn, grunting against the stab of pain.

Several yards up ahead, the lion stumbled backward, holding his right paw to his chest—the exact same spot as my wound.

It worked.

My thoughts raced. Whatever happened to me *also* happened to him. My pain could be a weapon. A way to gain the advantage.

But before I could dwell any more on that, the lion shook out his mane with a growl, and then he began to change.

It was slow at first, and I thought my eyes were playing tricks on me. But he was *definitely* getting bigger. In the same way Tessa could alter her size in her jaguar form, Scarven was making himself larger.

Within seconds, he towered over Vera. A single leg was twice the length of her entire body. His shadow engulfed Nox, Everett, and Vera, dimming the light of her wings as his tail brushed the branches of the nearby tree line. Fates, his paw *alone* could flatten a wagon, with claws as long and gleaming as a blade.

To her credit, Vera was unfazed. With a powerful flap of her wings, she rose in the air to meet him at eye level, swords crossing defensively in front of her face. He caught the side of her leg with a paw, making her cry out and fly backward a few feet. Rearing up on his hind legs, he batted at her with both paws, one after another in quick succession.

I jumped forward to try and send a shadow shield up right as four claws embedded themselves in her phoenix wing, shredding it to ribbons.

Her piercing wail was the most mournful song I'd ever heard.

The other wing flapped furiously, trying to compensate for its sagging counterpart. Vera barely kept control as she shot to the ground and rolled, then banished her wings. Everett sprinted to her and fell to his knees at her side.

Everything after that seemed to happen in slow motion.

Scarven raised his monstrous paw above Vera and Everett, its shadow swallowing their still forms. Right as he brought it down to crush them, Nox appeared in its path.

"Nox!" I cried, thrusting a solid wall of shadows at them.

Out of nowhere, a large jaguar leaped into action and planted its front paws on Nox's chest, shoving him out of the way. Tessa and Nox rolled on the ground as my shadows slammed into Scarven's paw, shifting it just enough to crash into the ground right above Vera's head. Rocks went flying, the forest floor trembling with the force.

Tessa shifted into her largest jaguar form, which still barely reached Scarven's chest. But she was faster than him. She reared up and swatted at his neck, drawing his attention away from the others. When he lunged for her, her claws caught him in the upper chest, and he let out another roar.

I gasped and staggered back at the sting.

Blood seeped from beneath my leathers. The fabric clung to my chest, digging into the claw marks that now marred my skin.

Nox finally saw me. His head snapped at the sound of my cry, and his eyes widened. "Don't hurt him, Tessa!" he called out.

Tessa's feline eyes found mine, and that was all it took.

Scarven pounced. His blade-like teeth wrapped around Tessa's outstretched limb...

And ripped it clean off.

Devastation tore through my body, punching the breath right out of me.

I would never forget the sound that came from Tessa's mouth. It wasn't a roar, but not quite a scream—it was a ragged, guttural bellow, the kind only spawned by gut-wrenching, unexpected pain. Tessa's jaguar form buckled and crashed to the ground, her wail morphing into a human's cry as she was forced to shift back.

Blood flowed from the gaping hole in her arm, the wound too deep for even her Shifter abilities to heal her. She hunched over her knees in a ball as she trembled on the ground.

I had to get to her. *Someone* had to help her.

I raced across the grounds separating us, dodging Scarven's larger-than-life paws and keeping my sights set on Tessa's face, which was becoming scarily ashen from blood loss.

I was almost to her when the massive, bronze legs surrounding us disappeared.

Scarven landed at my feet in his human form. Before I could blink, his hand whipped out and closed around my throat.

He cocked his head with a smirk. "Hello, love."

His voice sent a chill through me, echoes of moments at his side whipping through my mind. I swallowed them down and met his gaze.

"We both know you won't hurt me," I said, feigning bravado. "Anything that happens to me, happens to you."

"That's true. But I'm no stranger to pain." He squeezed harder, enough to make the muscles in my neck clench under the pressure. I watched the column of his throat as he swallowed hard, his nostrils flaring with the same sensation.

"Why are you—doing this?" I gasped, struggling to breathe.

He loosened his hold and leaned in closer, that stench of sweet, slightly soured wine bringing back all the horrible memories I tried to bury. My arms trembled, and my lungs constricted. I *hated* the way even the sound of his voice invoked such panic.

"Because I tire of this *insolence*," he rumbled. He swiped his nose along my jawline and into my hair, inhaling deeply. A familiar low snarl reached my ears from somewhere behind him.

"And because I know how to make it end." His words were rushed now, heating my skin as his rough lips scraped me. "He's always been so predictable, your *dragon*. You just have to know what nerves to strike. Three, two, one..."

Before I could register his words, Nox appeared directly behind Scarven, his eyes wild with possessive rage.

It happened faster than I could draw breath.

Scarven yanked my dagger from my thigh sheath, whirled in place, and plunged it into Nox's stomach.

77

DEVORA

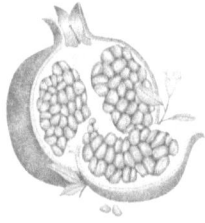

The world tilted as I crashed to my knees.

He will heal. He will heal. He will heal.

The blade sank into his side. His lips parted in stunned silence, his eyes scrambling to find mine as two dark blooms soaked the front of his shirt.

His mouth formed a single word.

"Tomorrow."

Our forever will start tomorrow.

My stomach turned inside out, the air torn from my lungs like I'd been gutted. When Scarven pulled the blade out again and rammed it into Nox's chest, all sound vanished.

I forgot how to breathe. I forgot how to do anything except scream. The world dimmed around me, and I barely saw the cloaked figures emerge from the shadows behind Vera and Everett, stopping them from racing forward.

My body wouldn't move, wouldn't run, wouldn't do anything but shriek uselessly at the sky. My magic, however...

Shadows flailed inside me, a tidal wave of despair unlike anything I'd ever felt. They swelled and collided against my ribs, and I no longer cared about holding them back.

Magic *exploded* from me in a blast of energy, so strong my hair whipped around my face, and my chest caved in from exertion. A ripple of shadows coursed over the ground. It trembled beneath the dark wave, kicking up dirt and sending weapons flying through the air.

But the power was short-lived.

Something cold and hard bolted around my wrist, and as quickly as it hurtled from me, my magic died. The shock of its loss sent me reeling backward into a cloaked figure.

My head snapped to the black cuffs on my arm. *Fatesprig.*

Not again.

I can't lose him. I can't lose him. I can't—

My stifled magic made my chaotic, raging emotions claw up my throat, trying to get out. They were going to flood me. Drown me.

When Scarven heaved the dagger from Nox's chest, the blood glinting off the steel practically blinded me, making my vision go gray at the edges. I felt myself struggling against the cloaked man holding me, but it was as if I was watching it from afar as a soundless scream escaped me.

Scarven moved the dagger to Nox's throat, and I lunged forward with all my strength.

When my assailant grabbed my waist to yank me back, something in my pocket shifted. I blinked, thoughts racing as quickly as my pulse.

The fatesprig serum.

I dug in my pockets for the cool metal cylinder and hauled it out, needle tip glistening in the moonlight.

Nox's gaze met mine as he stumbled to his knees. Even in his pain, even facing his own death, he didn't attack. He didn't defend himself.

He was protecting me, as he always did.

My fault.

Nox's eyes widened. His lips curved around my name, his blood-stained hand reaching for me.

I didn't think. As I watched Scarven put the blade to his throat, I plunged the needle into my heart.

The last thing I heard was the deafening, soul-wrenching roar of a dragon.

78

NOX

I could taste my own blood, a sharp, metallic tang coating the inside of my mouth. The blade had partially slid across my neck when Scarven froze, eyes wide.

He looked down in shock. He gritted his teeth and dropped the dagger as the veins in his neck and temple bulged, then slowly darkened to a thick, green sludge. The toxin Devora had injected herself with was also working its way through *his* system.

But I couldn't care less about him.

Behind him, Devora crashed to the ground. Her body spasmed as she cried out my name.

All thoughts splintered. There was only the pounding in my ears and my heart ramming into my ribs. Even the immense pain from my wounds dimmed as I watched the agony of the fatesprig injection consume her.

I let out a roar as my dragon took over. My back arched at an unnatural angle, blood spurting from my neck and rolling to the ground before the wound could fully heal. Scales burst from my skin, and my wings ripped out of my back, lifting me into the sky.

The shift was slower, sluggish, battling through waves of anguish as my body attempted to heal itself from so many fatal wounds. My limbs elongated, my claws sharpened, and my horns emerged, all while the battlefield and Scarven's mansion shrank beneath me.

And then there was her.

Two of Scarven's men were holding Devora's limp body down, those black cuffs wrapped tight around her wrists and dark green veins running over creamy skin. She writhed on the ground, her hair billowing around her like a cloud of blood as she screamed.

I *felt* her pain. Fates, I remembered that night I'd injected myself with fatesprig, how every single cell in my body burned and wished for death. My dragon flinched away from the memory. When she shrieked again, it cut a gaping wound down my chest, worse than any dagger Scarven could stab me with.

I'd promised to protect her, and I failed. She had done this for *me*.

I was tired of people I loved paying the price for my life.

When the cloaked figures behind her reached for her again, I dove without thinking. My wings flapped at my side, sending a powerful gust of wind over the field, and I snatched both men in my teeth in one fell swoop.

I clamped my jaws over them, severing their bodies in half, then jerked my head to the side to send the pieces flying into the forest. The bitter taste of their blood made my bloodlust hum with pleasure.

A muffled shout rang out from my feet. I craned my long, snake-like neck back to find two more of Scarven's lackeys detaining Vera and Everett with the same black cuffs. Another knelt to the ground next to Tessa, whose blood stained the earth red. Her features were ashen, and her head sagged to one side as she clutched her shoulder.

I hadn't seen many injuries that severe on a Shifter before. I knew we weren't invincible—there were some wounds that even powerful Shifter blood couldn't heal.

But she would be fine. She *had* to be fine. I refused to lose anyone else.

A growl rumbled from deep in my throat as I opened my

maw, inches from their assailants' faces. The scent of piss filled the air as the one reaching for Tessa went slack-jawed in horror, while another thrust Everett at me and raced off in the other direction.

I let him get several yards away. Let him think he had *hope*.

Then I lifted one of my legs and brought it on top of his head, crushing him straight into the ground.

I took the one hovering over Tessa and launched him deep into the forest, then ripped the other from my sister. I raised him high to meet my eye level, his small body wrapped inside my talons. He shook with terror, lips moving in a silent plea as if any of his prayers to the Fates or his *master* could save him now.

I tore his head off with my teeth and dropped his decapitated body to the ground in front of Scarven's feet. My half-brother was clawing at the dirt, his teeth gritted as the fatesprig grew darker in his veins.

I shifted into my human form and quickly looked at Everett. "Help Tessa!" I jerked my head to my third. "Get her to an Alchemist. *Now*."

He nodded and helped her to her feet while I turned my attention back to Devora, hurrying toward her in panicked strides.

Her eyes rolled into the back of her head with every spasm, her head jerking and body curving inward. I gathered her in my arms and pressed my face into her hair. "Devora, darling," I murmured. "What am I going to do with you?"

I held her tight and rocked her through the waves of pain, some of my tension releasing when I saw the dark green veins begin to lighten.

"That was the most thoughtless, irresponsible, impulsive thing you have *ever* done," I whispered.

Her hands curled around my arm. "I'll take that as a 'thank you,'" she said with a groan. "Are you okay?"

"I'll be fine. I've almost healed, thanks to you." I pulled her further into my lap, wishing I could burrow her into my very skin. "But never, *ever* do something like that again."

"You can't tell me what to do," she mumbled into me. "You promised me tomorrow. I was holding you to your word."

My heart squeezed. I leaned back slightly to take her chin in my fingers. "*You* are my tomorrow, Devora. And every day after. I couldn't live with myself if something happened to you."

"He was going to kill you," she said, forehead creasing. "Just like in my dream. I did what I had to do."

I sighed. "This is what I get for falling in love with the most stubborn woman in the world."

She winced as she disentangled herself from me, and I helped her slowly rise to her feet. I glanced back to find Scarven on his knees with my sister looming over him, a fiery, winged angel of vengeance holding both of her swords at her sides.

Apprehension coursed through me. She promised not to hurt him, not while he was still bound to Devora. But the look on her face…

"Vera!" I shouted in warning, my voice carrying above the mayhem around us.

Her eyes met mine over Scarven's head, then shifted to Devora and narrowed.

A shiver crept down my spine. She was still my little sister, but those years in captivity had changed her. And that furious look in her eyes, the one that said she would scorch everyone who stood in her way…part of me wondered how much of the girl I'd once known was left.

And if she would take Devora down to get her revenge.

Scarven chuckled and shook his head. "What's the problem, phoenix? Have I finally burned that fire out?"

Vera shoved her shadow blade forward, holding the tip to his throat. I sucked in a breath.

"You have *nothing*, Scarven," my sister snarled in a voice I didn't recognize. "No magic, no power. No hold over me. Mortep is gone. Your men are being slaughtered." She brandished her lightning sword to the battlefield at the front of the manor. "You're *finished*."

"Then why am I still alive?" A slow grin unfurled across his features, smooth and oily. "Ah, yes. Because your brother couldn't *dream* of losing his precious pet. Just another thing he gets to have while you get nothing. Isn't that right, my phoenix? All those years he lived in freedom, traveling the empire, sleeping in his own bed. He left you behind faster than you can say 'family.'"

The words were a blow to my chest. I locked eyes with Vera. Was that what she thought of me? Was that the lie he'd been feeding her all these years?

It's the truth, a dark voice in the back of my mind leered. *You did leave her.*

I left to ensure her safety. I left to obey his every command, with the threat of her death hanging over my head to keep me in line. I would have taken her place a *million* times over if it meant she could be the one to get away.

"You know that's not true." I stepped forward. "Everything I did was to prot—"

"To protect her, yes, yes, we've all heard that before." Scarven scoffed. "But who are you protecting *now,* brother? It certainly isn't your sister."

Fear and anger poured over me. He was trying to pit us against each other. Trying to claim one final pound of flesh before losing it all.

"It's not going to work, Scarven," I snapped. "It's *over.* Whatever future you think you've created for yourself, whatever life you imagined, it's not going to happen." I shook my head as I thought back to the lives he'd ruined in the last two decades, then to the brave souls who risked it all just to bring justice to a dark land. "You've taken everything from our people to grow your own power, but you will *never* be stronger than all of us united."

"How beautiful," Scarven mocked. "Such a noble start to your quest of redemption, truly. I hope all those who have died because of you would feel the same."

I flinched as if I'd been struck. A smile shadowed Scarven's sweat-slicked features. His expression grew hungrier, like a lion readying to pounce on its prey.

"That's always been your problem, Nox. So worried about how others perceive you, holding on to the hope that they'll see a *shred* of something good to salvage in you, all while battling for everyone's loyalty. I have always known exactly *who* and *what* I was loyal to." He leaned in closer, dark eyes glinting. "*Myself.* Perhaps that's something we both inherited, as you seem rather intent on your own self-interest over your sister."

I turned to Vera. "Don't listen to him. You know this is what he does. He—"

"Yes, she *does* know, doesn't she?" Scarven hummed. "Because *she* was the one by my side all these years. Oh, how I made her sing. My sweet phoenix." He was practically crooning at her, a wild look in his eyes that was more frightening than any of his cold, calculated ones.

He *wanted* her to kill him. He knew this was over, and he wanted this one last victory. To take *one* more thing from me.

Lose my sister's trust, or lose the woman I loved.

A ripple of fury crossed over my sister's face. The wind picked up, stirring the ends of her hair.

"Did you enjoy being the little bird in my gilded cage?" Scarven looked up at her from his knees, the harsh wrinkles around his eyes more pronounced. "I almost forget that we share the same wretched father too. You looked so pretty on my mantel. So pretty in my—"

"Enough!" Vera bellowed, heat rising from her in waves as she lashed out and punched him across the cheek.

At my side, Devora gasped and fell to the ground. A bruise quickly formed on her pale face.

I reached for her. "Vera, please—"

Scarven's low laughter cut me off. "You see where his loyalty lies? Where his heart belongs?" His cheek turned bright red as a trickle of blood oozed from between his lips. He spat it at Vera's feet.

"Do you even know who you are, phoenix?" he taunted. "You've been denied your freedom, your *identity*, for your entire life. And now he's denying you *this*. The one thing you dreamed of every night you spent in that cold, dark cell."

"I told you his life was yours, Vera," I rushed out. "I just need to make sure Devora's safe, and then I *promise*—"

"He *promises*," Scarven mocked. "Just as he *promised* to rescue you. You don't need his promises, sweet phoenix. I didn't raise you to need anything from *anyone*."

Vera visibly flinched at those words, and my heart jumped into my throat.

"But maybe you're just as weak as the rest of them," he growled. Tension and heat rose in tandem. The sound of Vera's pulse thumped loudly in my ears.

"All that power, all that potential, and look at you." Scarven finally staggered to his feet so he was face-to-face with her. "You can't even get this right. No wonder your mother and brother *left* you."

Vera raised her lightning sword, flames crackling along her skin.

I lurched forward to yank Scarven a few inches back. "Vera, wait—"

"Just *stop!*" she cried out, closing her eyes as her arm trembled above her head. Wind and magic surged around us in answer to her distress.

Scarven wrenched himself from my grip. He snarled in her face, spit flying from his lips. "*Do it!*" he roared. "Kill me!"

I threw myself to her side and wrapped a hand around her elbow. "Please, don't—"

She let out an ear-piercing shriek as she swung her sword at his neck.

In that split second of frozen time, the air shimmered between us. Pale hands reached out to clutch both Scarven and Vera.

Before I could blink, the three of them disappeared, taking me with them.

79

NOX

My feet hit hard ground. It was as if no time had passed, yet we were suddenly in a different place, the chaos and heat from before now replaced with cold, dank darkness.

My mind didn't have time to catch up with the change before I saw Vera and Scarven standing across from me in the same position they were just in—him baring his teeth in her face, her with her sword stretched to his neck.

Vera's battle cry still rang in my ears as her sword sliced through the air.

And cut Scarven's head clean off.

"No!" I roared, eyes bulging.

Devora.

My knees slammed to the floor.

She's dead.

The world went gray, my vision going in and out as I saw her lifeless blue-green eyes staring up at me from Scarven's severed head. I saw his blood as the rushing red waves of her hair, saw her body crumple in the reflection of Vera's sword.

My entire heart was torn from my chest, the pain so visceral I couldn't draw breath.

"What"— I gasped out, hands digging into the stone—"have you *done?*"

My sister dropped her sword. She stared down at her hands, eyes wide and full of horror. "Nox, I—I'm so sorry—"

"I have to get to her." My voice was distant, echoing around my head. "I have to find her."

I summoned my dragon, only to be met with a wall of silence. Then I realized my magic had been completely snuffed out, leaving a hollow pit deep in my chest. Confusion swarmed me. Why was my magic not working? Where was I?

Where is she?

More footsteps clattered around me, and I whirled to find Arowyn standing several feet above. I slowly began to recognize our surroundings—the trapdoor in the ground, the stone steps leading to the surface, the hay bunched at her feet.

We were at the entrance to the Hollow. The stables where Devora and I had rescued those prisoners almost three weeks ago.

Devora. My misery pooled and formed itself into resolve, like liquid silver solidified in fire.

Arowyn stared down the steps. "This was the only thing I could do, Nox."

"Where did you take us?" I growled.

"You're in the Hollow. There's this spell Mortep cast," she said. "Magic can't exist down there. It's siphoned out the second you cross the boundary."

I flexed my hands at my sides, wishing I could feel the imprint of my claws. "I don't care, Arowyn," I gritted out as I stepped onto the stones leading aboveground. "*I need to find her.*"

The instant my feet reached the surface, magic flooded back into me like a dam had broken. I looked down in shock. My dragon was back, as if it had never left.

Arowyn stopped me with a hand to my chest. "Magic can't exist down there," she repeated. "The *bond* can't exist."

I blinked again. My lips formed her words, saying them back to her slowly. "The bond can't..."

"She's alive, Nox. Devora is alive."

A buzzing sounded low in my ears. "I—I don't understand."

"It's some sort of siphoning spell. Mortep casted it when we scouted out where to set the explosive charm," Arowyn explained, the words tumbling out of her faster than my muddled mind could keep up. "It takes away our magic. I've been bringing the mutants down here, and it cures them of his magic. I thought it might work on the bond too. It was a crazy hunch, but—"

"Take me to her," I demanded, barely registering her story. All I could hear was "*she's alive.*"

I had to see for myself. I had to get the image of her head cleaved from her body *out of my mind.* My control was hanging by a thread.

Arowyn abruptly shut her mouth and nodded. When she grabbed my arm, the ground disappeared for a heartbeat before we landed back in the field.

At first, there was nothing. My dragon thrashed with hopelessness beneath my skin. But then—

A body slammed into me, the scent of pomegranates and sunshine enveloping us. My hand immediately gripped the nape of Devora's neck and slid into her hair. Was she really here? Was this *real*?

"Nox," she murmured, and the sound broke me.

My other hand crushed into her back, pulling her as tightly into me as possible. I closed my eyes and breathed her in. I didn't realize how badly I was shaking until her small hands on my back steadied me.

She was alive. She was *here*, whole and soft and safe.

And mine.

"What happened?" she asked, her voice still weak. "Where did you go? Where's Scarven?"

"Arowyn." That was the only word I could get through the tightness of my throat, my relief so all-consuming, it clogged every cell.

Devora pulled back, studying me with that little crease in her forehead, and I couldn't resist the urge to lean forward and kiss it.

Swallowing hard, I finally said, "Arowyn strode us to—to the Hollow. Something about a spell, and our magic..." I shook my head, thoughts still fuzzy.

But comprehension lit Devora's face. "Is Scarven...is he—"

Next to us, Arowyn made a squelching noise and slid her thumb across her throat.

Devora reached for her own neck with a look of alarm. Her normally bright skin was ghostly pale with a hint of green still lingering in her veins. "The spell took the bond away?"

"And not a second too soon." Arowyn whistled. "You better be glad I'm quick on my feet. I just saved your life, Shadow Wielder."

"Arowyn, I—" My voice cracked with gratitude, and I cleared it. "I don't know how to—"

"Don't mention it, Boss," she said, offering me a small smile.

The air wavered again, and a moment later, my sister strode into view, clutching Scarven's severed head the same way I clung to Devora. Her eyes darted frantically until she found me.

She dropped his head and staggered forward. "She's okay?"

My Vera was back, the voice of the sister I remembered from so long ago. Regret flitted across her face, erasing the coldness of the phoenix who hungered for Scarven's death.

I didn't blame her. How could I? Everything Scarven said was the truth. She was the one to suffer at his hands for her entire life, never getting an ounce of freedom, never finding herself or truly *living*. He knew all the ways to goad her, all the right nerves to press. He'd always been a master manipulator.

But...she had almost killed Devora.

Both things could be true. Both things were solidly ingrained in my mind, as firm as any foundation. And as I stared at Vera inching toward us, I couldn't help but turn protectively in front of Devora.

I nodded. "She's okay. There was a way around the bond Scarven had with her. It's over, Vera."

Those three words made tears swim to the surface of her

golden eyes. Her shoulders slumped as her chin fell to her chest, and I could practically feel the weight of her twenty-one years of life settling over her.

When she looked back up, I held my arms out on instinct. There was a brief moment of hesitation before she barreled into me and clung to my sweaty, blood-soaked leathers, whispering apology after apology.

Something snapped into place in my chest. I clutched her tighter, hardly remembering what it was like to hold her. *My family.* My little sister, finally—*finally*—free from her cage. How could I fault her for what she'd been through? For the decisions she made? Fates knew I had done worse.

"I don't blame you, Vera. It's okay," I said. "I love you. He's gone for good."

No matter what future obstacles we'd have to overcome, what nightmares would linger in the backs of our minds...*that* would never change.

It was over.

Arowyn cleared her throat behind me. "There's another problem with your plan, Nox."

80

NOX

"That magic-siphoning spell we told you about?" Arowyn said. "It started way down in the Hollow and has already reached the surface. Unless someone knows where that creepy Alchemist went, we don't know how to stop it."

I released my sister. "What are you saying?"

"It's *spreading*," Arowyn explained exasperatedly. "Quickly. Like, *too* quickly. It was slow enough for Devora and me to outrace it at first, but now..." She bit her lip and glanced off toward the west, where the stables lay. "Can't you feel it?"

It was difficult to feel anything after the events of the last few minutes, but as I looked beyond her to the battlefield, something in my magic stirred. There was a shift in the air, a different type of urgency unrelated to the mutants and the smell of bloodshed.

Something darker. Thick and pungent, hanging heavy in the night and slowly coiling around the property.

Dark magic.

"It's bad, Nox," Devora whispered at my side. My eyes hovered over her downturned lips and scared eyes. "It's like the fatesprig, except *everywhere*. The second we came into contact with it, our magic was gone."

"We have to get the others," I said, gaze snapping to my Ashen

Order still fighting in the courtyard, unaware of Scarven's death and the new threat lurking around the corner.

"Wait, Nox, I've been thinking about it, and—"

Arowyn tried to get my attention, but I was already halfway to the battlefield. My people had certainly held their own against the swarm of mutants and Scarven's men. But as we got closer, I no longer saw clashing swords and whirling magic.

The remaining mutated Veridians stood in the aftermath, smoke and the occasional crackle of flames wavering in the air. Weapons hung at their side as they glanced at one another in confusion. One half tiger, half antelope had its horns locked with the unmistakable form of Kieran's white stag. It dropped its head and stumbled backward, shifting into a frightened teenage boy.

A boy. Barely older than I'd been when Scarven captured me.

That was who he had fighting for him. Innocent victims who were forced into a battle they wanted no part in. Pawns in his schemes, disposable property he experimented on and sent out to do his dirty work.

Just like me.

All around us, swords dropped to the ground, a slow wave of surrender rolling over the courtyard. It seemed whatever hold Scarven had over them had faded with his death.

Rose stepped out of the fray. "Nice of you to join us," she called out to me in her sarcastic tone.

Behind her, Leo knelt over Tessa, hands hovering above her arm and lips moving with wordless spells. To the right stood Thecae, with his thick, menacing shadows binding several of Scarven's men. Dark wisps of rope were wrapped around their arms and stuffed in their mouths to gag them.

An overwhelming sense of gratitude flooded me. *They made it.* Arowyn's messages worked. I wasn't sure when I sent her to deliver warnings to both the capital city and to Tenebra if they would have enough time to get here, but they had come through for us.

Kieran bounded forward in his stag form and shifted mid-stride. "What happened?" he asked sharply.

"Scarven is dead," I said, barely believing my own words. His eyes widened. "But we're not done yet. The original plan is still in place. We need to destroy the Hollow."

That was the only way I could think of to get rid of the fate-sprig supply before Malek Mortep came back to finish his master's job, *and* to end this siphoning spell he cast over the place.

I gazed out onto the courtyard at the dozen or so mutated Veridians, then to our own wounded, and to the hordes of ragged prisoners clustered at the edge of the forest behind them all.

"Your master is dead," I called out, my voice carrying over the distance.

At my side, Vera raised Scarven's head, and the entire courtyard sucked in a breath.

I met each of their stares, both ally and foe, as I said, "We know what he did to you. We know how you've suffered, and that many of you are just as much a victim as we are. There doesn't need to be any more bloodshed tonight. We want to help you, but we have to work together for what comes next.

"There's a powerful spell that Scarven's Alchemist cast before he fled. One that can take away our magic." My words were met with quickening heartbeats and uncomfortable shifting. "We need to get everyone as far away from the property as possible."

"About that—" Arowyn started, but I turned to my Order to dole out instructions, my mind racing through the plan.

"Chaz, Rose, and Leo—get the wounded to the nearest village. Thecae, are those the only ones left who are loyal to Scarven?" I pointed to the men still bound in his shadows with lion's masks over their faces. Thecae nodded. "Good. Keep an eye on them and get them past the property line. We'll deal with them later."

Arowyn cleared her throat. "Nox, you need to know—"

"Kieran, you and Everett get the innocent ones out to the village," I said, my attention snagging on the figures lingering at the tree line. "We can regroup and take them to the Keep once this is over."

I turned on my heel and pointed to Arowyn. "Arowyn, stay with me. Once everyone is clear, we'll set the explosive and—"

"Would you shut up for one second?" the Strider rushed out, swiping her blonde hair away from her face. "That's what I've been trying to tell you. The plan won't work. Magic can't exist down in the Hollow, *remember?*"

"Yes, I know, that's why we have to break the—" I cut myself off.

My back slowly straightened, thoughts blurring as I worked out what she was saying, piece by piece.

The spell siphoned all magic. Magic wouldn't work in the tunnels.

We needed the explosive to break the spell and destroy the fatesprig and weapons.

A Strider had to be the one to set it, so they could get out quick enough to avoid the blast. And—

My stomach crashed to my feet.

A Strider had to have *magic*. If their powers didn't work in the Hollow, they wouldn't be able to escape in time.

Arowyn's lips formed a grim line. "If we want this plan to work, someone won't make it out."

81

NOX

Silence filled the air, heavy and churning with both oncoming dark magic and the magnitude of Arowyn's statement. The others exchanged uneasy looks as they shifted back and forth on their feet.

But I wasn't scared. In fact, I was calm. Resolute. Because I knew not a single one of the people I loved would be harmed today.

I realized with glaring clarity that this was my purpose all along. How many years had I spent talking about a better future? About ending the injustice and violence caused by my brother? How many times had I claimed everything I did was for those I loved?

I wouldn't accept a future in which I lived while someone else sacrificed their life for me.

I pointed to the Alchemist Milo had trained on activating the charm in the fire quartz. "You still have the quartz?" The young man nodded. "Good. Do the spell and give it to me. Everyone else, your roles are the same—get to safety and stay as far from the property as possible."

Rose blinked, then narrowed her eyes. "Why does it sound like you're about to play the hero, Nox?"

"I'm not *playing* anything." I took the fire quartz and a piece of flint, rubbing the rough, warm stone with my thumb. "I'm protecting my own."

An uproar broke out. So many voices blended together that I couldn't pick them apart.

"You can't be serious."

"Nox, you're *not* going down there."

"Wait just a moment and let us figure out a different plan—"

"You're *such* an idiot. Do you really think we'd be okay with this?"

I shook my head and took a few steps back, needing to clear my mind. "This isn't a *debate*." I forced an air of cold finality into my voice. "I vowed to lead you through this, and that's what I'm doing. The longer we stay here, the longer this curse has time to spread. You need to go."

Kieran stepped forward. "You expect us to stand by and act like we don't care? You are not simply our *leader*, Nox. You're our friend. Our brother."

I balled my hands into fists at my sides. "And would you not do the same for me?"

"In a heartbeat!" he exclaimed, glaring back at me.

"Then what's the difference? Why is it so wrong for me to do this, if any of the rest of you would take my place? Why should I let one of *you* go instead?"

Kieran swallowed hard, nostrils flaring as his jaw clenched. But he remained silent.

"Nox, please," my sister said, and heat flared at my back. When I turned to meet her gaze, her eyes sparked with flames. "Let *me* go. I'm strong. If you tell me what to do, maybe I have a better chance of—"

"Absolutely not." I was shaking my head before she even finished her sentence. "You're finally free, Vera. *You* of all people deserve to start over. To live the life you never got to have." I gripped her hands, so small in my own. Just like when she was younger. "What kind of brother would I be if I sent you off to die?"

She squeezed my fingers. "I just got you back," she whispered. "Please don't go."

My lips tilted up into a sad smile. "If not me, then who?"

Her eyes flitted behind me to the people she'd never met, but who had risked everything to come save her and countless others. Then her gaze strayed to Everett at her side, who had been silently attached to her hip since the moment she came back to herself.

I knew what she was thinking. There was no right way to condemn someone to their death. No way to offer someone else in my place.

Vera threw her arms around my neck and pulled me close, infusing me with her warmth. I closed my eyes and rested my chin on her shoulder. Her freedom was the most important thing. She would get to *live*. She would get to dream and wish and love whoever she wanted. That was the only ending I could've asked for.

At least I'd done one thing right.

"Go get Mama," I whispered. "She's waiting for you in Tenebra. Everett knows the way." I kissed her cheek before backing away and taking a deep breath.

My dragon half recoiled in disgust when something dark flooded my nostrils. My magic was slow and tired, no longer a vibrant pulse. All around us, dark wisps of black and red filtered through the air in a fog, licking at our skin like it wanted to taste us.

"It's coming from the west," Arowyn said, squinting toward the end of the property where the entrance to the Hollow lay. "The spell is spreading faster."

It was a gradual suffocation. An infection working its way through our systems, pushing and pulling at our powers.

"We're out of time," I said curtly. "You know your orders."

Leo took Rose by the arm, but she paused and reached out to me. "There has to be another way," she murmured, her green eyes holding so much sadness. "If there's one thing I've learned with Alchemy, there's *always* another way."

"Maybe so. But we don't have time to sit around and find it." I took both of her hands in mine. "Be good to each other, viper."

Rose nodded once, a little furrow appearing in her brow as she took her hand away and wiped her nose.

Urgency was beginning to pick up in the courtyard, with the threat of the dark magic closing in. Rose, Leo, and Chaz gathered the wounded as Thecae made his shadow cages float toward the edge of the property. Every few seconds, his shadows would flicker out and then come back, as if growing weaker and weaker.

I could barely feel my dragon anymore. I couldn't put off the inevitable any longer.

But as I turned toward the Hollow, another hand fell to the small of my back. It was a touch I'd know anywhere, and the only one I couldn't bear to face.

"You said you wouldn't leave me."

Devora's voice was quiet, but hard as stone. I slowly turned, keeping my gaze at her shoulder, unable to meet her eyes. To see the betrayal I was sure marred her beautiful features.

"Devora, darling, I—"

"Don't you 'darling' me," she snapped. "You weren't even going to say goodbye."

I licked my lips. "You know I don't have another choice."

She scoffed. "Well, I'm selfish, Nox. You may be willing to sacrifice yourself, but *I'm* not."

"This is the only way, Devora."

"Then *think of something else*." She stepped closer, forcing her face into my line of sight. I closed my eyes and turned my neck. "You vowed to lead everyone through this, but what about the promises you made to *me*? What about *us*? What about our tomorrow?"

Each word was a blow to the chest, but I stayed silent, unmoving. There was nothing I could say. She was right. I should've never made promises to her I wasn't sure I could keep.

I could smell her anger, but more than that, I could smell her desperation, even as my Shifter magic struggled to maintain itself.

Her voice cracked as she said, "Do I mean so little to you that you won't even *look* at me?"

My eyes snapped to hers, to those blue-green pools that shattered my resolve, begging me to kneel and plea for her forgiveness. The pull between us tugged me closer until my fingers found the nape of her neck. I closed my eyes and pressed my forehead to hers, breaths ragged and racing.

"I *can't* look at you, Devora. If I do, I'll choose you. Every time. Even if it means the rest of the world turns to ash."

"Then choose me," she whispered, voice hitching. She bunched the top of my leathers in her fist. "Choose *yourself*. You don't have to go."

I gently kissed her forehead. "I love you so much, Devora. You brought sun and light and *hope* into my cold world, and that's all I could've ever asked for." A tear tracked down her cheek. The backs of my eyes burned when she trembled in my arms. "And I'm so sorry, my darling."

I looked over her shoulder and met Kieran's hardened stare, giving him a single nod. As I let Devora go and backed away, she tried to snag my arm, but Kieran stepped forward and held her back.

She screamed my name. The sound was so gutting, I had to turn away to force myself not to run into her arms.

Each step was like swimming against the tide. The dark magic was pungent and biting, strong enough now that I knew it wouldn't be long before my powers stopped working completely.

My feet and my heart begged me to turn around. The sound of Devora fighting against Kieran squeezed the breath from my lungs.

This is for her. This is for all of them.

I could see the stables, where the black magic vibrated and twisted more fiercely than ever. The prisoners had been evacuated from the tree line, as well as all the wounded and the remaining mutated Veridians. I would give them a couple more minutes to get clear of the blast.

Maybe I could survive, a hopeful part of me thought. There was a fifteen-second delay on the explosion. If I set the fire quartz close enough to the edge, there was a small chance I could beat the blast.

Without your magic? another voice asked. *Without your speed?*

It didn't matter. I would try. For Devora and for myself.

When a couple minutes passed and I could no longer see or hear our group beyond the property line, I took the flint and fire quartz from my pocket. Almost as if it could sense I was about to cross the border into the dark magic's hold, my dragon gave one final twitch inside my chest, urging me to stop.

I ignored it and took a step.

There was a small rush of wind at my back, and suddenly, a hand was on my arm.

I spun to find Kieran and Arowyn. "What are you—"

Kieran grabbed the flint and fire quartz from me. "You have fulfilled your duty a thousand times over. Let someone else take care of things this time, brother."

Alarm blared through me. I realized too late what was happening.

"Kieran, don't you *dare*—"

"Through flame and ash." He tipped his head at Arowyn and sprinted off toward the Hollow.

I was still yelling his name when Arowyn squeezed my arm and the world vanished.

82

DEVORA

My whole body was numb. Numb, yet still in pain. I pressed the heel of my palm into my chest where I'd shoved the needle, slowly massaging it to try and take the ache away. Every injury Scarven sustained in the fight lingered over me—the burn on my thumb, the claw marks on my chest, the bruise on my cheek.

The aftermath of the fatesprig made my entire body weak. That pain had eaten me alive, burned me from the inside out as it ripped away my shadows. I hadn't felt them since. Everett promised me my magic would come back, but right now, it all seemed hopeless. Like there wasn't a point to drawing breath.

Everything *hurt*. Everything was *wrong*.

But nothing was more painful than watching him walk away.

Rose, Leo, Chaz, and Thecae had gone ahead into the village with the prisoners and those who had surrendered. They took Tessa with them, who was still passed out. The gradual draining of our magic had made her healing process slow even more.

The rest of the Ashen Order and I stayed as close to the property as we could risk to avoid the blast. They tried to convince me to go with the others since I was defenseless without my shadows, but they would've had to pry my dead body away.

A part of me still believed I'd see Nox appear from the rubble. That he'd come back to me. That he'd keep his promise.

"You must be the one he loves so much," a voice said from behind me. I turned to see Vera twisting her fingers together, little sparks of lightning flying from them.

I thought I was, I wanted to say, but I didn't have the heart or energy to respond.

"He was willing to die for you, you know," Vera continued in her soft, sad voice. "To protect you against Scarven. It takes a lot to earn that kind of loyalty from my brother."

I thought I nodded, but I wasn't really sure if my head moved. I kept my eyes on the dirt at her feet as I croaked, "Doesn't really matter now, does it?"

She paused for a moment. "I think it's the *only* thing that matters. In the end."

The end. Because that was what this was. An ending.

It was supposed to have been our beginning.

There was a rustle ahead, then Kieran and Arowyn's aggravated voices caught my attention.

"—to do it. Before it's too late," Kieran was saying.

"Are you sure about this?"

Kieran grabbed Arowyn by the shoulders. For the first time since I met the man, his clothes were ruffled and dirty, his dark brown hair messy and tousled. "You know it's the right thing."

Before I could muster the strength to ask what was going on, they both vanished into thin air.

Vera and I shared a look, and she braced a hand on Everett's arm. I eyed the two of them. Past me would've already asked a million questions about *what* in the world that was about. But right now—

The air shimmered, and Kieran and Arowyn came hurtling back through space.

Except...it wasn't Kieran.

It was Nox.

All of us jumped in surprise, and my mouth dropped so hard, I thought it would hit the ground.

"Take me back there *right now*," Nox snarled at Arowyn, his navy eyes turning to silver slits.

"What's going on?" Everett asked.

The pieces clicked together, and I raised a shaking hand to my lips. Kieran had—he was—

"I'm going to wait for him," Arowyn rushed out, backing away before Nox could grab her. "There's still a chance, Nox. I'll stay as long as I can."

He lunged for her, but she was quicker. His arms wrapped around thin air. He let out a roar and swiped his fingers through his hair, then staggered toward the manor.

Fear lurched up my throat. I thought he was going to make a run for it. "Nox, don't—"

But he didn't run. He merely crashed to his knees with his hands splayed across his thighs. His neck dropped to his chest.

"He took my place," Nox said, so quiet it was hard to hear. His sorrowful gaze met mine. "Kieran took my place."

Tears pricked the backs of my eyes. Fates, I was *so mad* at him, I wanted to strangle him with or without my shadows. But I also loved him so much, I could hardly think straight. And he was about to watch his best friend die.

I lowered myself in front of him, and he instantly crushed me against him. His silent tears dripped down my neck as his fingers tangled in my hair. I melted into him, letting my own tears overwhelm me. Tears of relief, of disbelief, of love, of mourning.

"I'm so sorry, Devora," he whispered into my hair, his voice choked. "I'm sorry I left you."

I swallowed hard and clung to him tighter. "Shh, it doesn't matter right now. I've got you. I'm here."

When the first resounding *boom* shattered the quiet night, his body recoiled. I pulled back to grip his face and forced him to meet my eyes. "Just look at me. Right here. I'm with you, Nox."

I could see the flames out of the corner of my eye as another explosion rocked the air. Smoke rose in a mushroom cloud, hanging over the surrounding forest. Tears tracked down Nox's dirt-stained cheeks, but he kept his sights set on me, his shoulders shaking and hands curling into fists where they held me.

I counted the seconds in my head. Each tick took me further and further from hope.

The blast was so strong, we could feel the heat even from this distance. Cracks echoed around us as the house succumbed to the fire and began breaking down on itself. The sky was blanketed in a smoky haze, blocking the stars and coating us in darkness.

A few more seconds passed. Nox closed his eyes, and the weight in my heart sank.

Until—

"*Nox*," Vera said with a gasp. We both jerked toward her, then followed her finger pointing a little ways out.

Arowyn appeared on the ground, her hands blackened with ash as she crawled across the grass. Parts of her long hair were singed and smoking, soot covering her from head to toe. Fire had eaten through the sleeve of her right arm and burned the skin beneath.

Nox and I hurried to help her to her feet. When she doubled over with a cough, tufts of smoke spewed from her lips.

"I—I waited," she said in between more coughing fits. "I waited as long as I could. I'm sorry, Nox."

A lump formed in my throat. There was nothing more we could do.

Kieran was gone.

Nox threw his head back and roared into the sky, a deep, unending sound full of grief and heartache that made my own heart break even further.

I clutched a hand to my chest and looked out onto the collapsing mansion. The wind whipped my hair across my face and scattered the flames further into the forest. The snapping of limbs was a backdrop to Nox's cry, and my own tears slipped freely down my face.

But then I saw something.

It was so brief, I thought I'd imagined it. I blinked and rubbed my eyes, then squinted.

My heart stopped.

"Nox," I breathed out.

In the distance, rising through flame and ash, was a pair of white, glinting antlers.

83

DEVORA

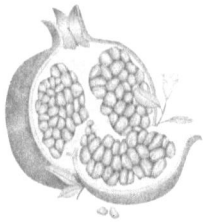

The theme of the next few weeks was obvious.

Regroup. Rebuild. Restore.

That looked different for everyone. For the prisoners who escaped from the Hollow, it was healing. It was discovering what trust and safety felt like after years of being denied their most basic rights. It was visits to the healing wing and having food coaxed down their throats because they were nothing more than skin and bones.

For the mutated Veridians who had been released from Scarven's ironclad grip, it was solitude. It was figuring out how to live in the quietness of their own mind after hearing *his* voice in their heads. It was coming to grips with the fact that their magic was forever changed, and learning how to control it instead of being filled with self-loathing and shame.

For the Ashen Order, it was moving on. It was mourning our losses and memorializing the sacrifices made by so many. It was late-night meetings in the workshop where our gazes lingered on Silas's missing space, where the circles under our eyes grew darker, but the purpose in our hearts grew stronger.

For me, it was...finding myself.

I was no longer Devora the orphan, the lady's maid, the spy, the prisoner, the bait, the bonded. For the first time, I had the choice of the name I wanted to make for myself.

Who did *I* want to be, when nothing was pulling my strings?

"Rora!" a high-pitched, irritated little voice called behind me. "Tilly stole my bear!"

I balanced atop the rolling ladder in the library and, without turning around, flicked my shadows through the air. They found the offender—a sweet six-year-old Strider named Tilly—and plucked the stuffed bear from her arms.

I glanced down the rows of bookshelves at the pouting girl. "Did you ask if Eliza would share her bear, Tilly?"

Tilly's lower lip puckered out. "No."

"Next time, ask first, okay?" My shadows carried the bear back to Eliza, then swiped away the tears under her eyes. I carefully descended the ladder to kneel before Tilly. "There are plenty of other toys by the window. Let's find something you like."

That first week after we destroyed Scarven's property, I spent most of my time with the little children. Once a couple of them latched on, it was like I couldn't get rid of the rest. I actually kind of enjoyed it. They all thought I was hilarious, and the little girls liked to play with my hair. Who could say no to that?

Those initial days were *hard* for them. I put out fire after fire (metaphorically and literally—those Lightbender kids were menaces) and settled more fights and tantrums than I could count.

I wondered if they felt a kinship to me. I knew what it was like to seek attention in whatever way you could because you'd never been shown that you were special. I knew what it was like to test boundaries—not out of disobedience, but to see if you could still be wanted afterward. If you could still be loved.

So that's what I did. I loved the *Fates* out of them.

"Devora, I could use some help," Tessa called from the other side of the library. I made my way over to help her with a stack of books. After the battle, her shoulder did eventually heal itself, although she lost her arm for good.

She was still our *Tessa*. Still cracking jokes at every opportunity.

But I saw it hit her sometimes. When she thought no one was looking, she would let her bubbly mask fall into something else. The loss, the suffering, the mourning. A different kind than what we felt for Silas, but grief all the same.

"Thanks." She tossed her long braids over her shoulder. "We've had so many book donations lately, we're going to have to build another library."

"Hey, no complaints here," I said as I scoured through the new titles.

Tessa and Kieran were focusing their efforts on expanding the Keep now that we no longer had to lay low. They rallied the nearby villages and set up several refugee camps to house the homeless, wounded, and those who just wanted to get their lives back. People had been *flooding* us with donations of all kinds—food, books, clothes, furniture. It certainly kept the two of them busy divvying it all up between the new camps.

We *all* stayed busy, both out of necessity and because sometimes...if the world stilled, even just for a moment, the reminder of what we'd been through crept in.

I still had visions of that night. I would watch Scarven stab Nox with my dagger, then the moments right before he almost slit his throat. I would see Nox running toward his death as Kieran held me back. I could feel the scratchiness of my throat as I screamed, like claws scraping down the inside.

I looked around the library, my gaze snagging on familiar navy blue at the entrance. Nox leaned against the doorframe with a smile as he watched me. My chest always eased when I saw him. He grounded me in those moments when the memories took over, reminding me that this was real. *He* was real.

We had survived. And we could finally let ourselves be *happy*. We could let ourselves dream of a future not cloaked by fear or consequences.

But with the light came brief spots of shadows. Not everyone was healing in the same way we were.

"Ready for dinner?" he asked.

I nodded and gathered the children into single-file lines so we could make our way to the dining hall. Tessa led the group while Nox and I took up the rear. "Is Vera coming?" I asked quietly.

He shook his head, and his jaw twitched.

I sighed. We'd tried to get her to eat meals with us, but she preferred to be alone most of the time. Nox was concerned about her. *None* of us knew what Vera was going through. None of the others had been as close to Scarven, had been under his mind control for as long, nor had taken as many lives at his command.

A vast majority of the refugees bonded over their trauma and found ways to help each other through it all. But Vera kept distancing herself. Nox was the only person she felt even remotely comfortable with. I thought something was going on between her and Everett, but he quickly disappeared to complete a task for Nox a couple days after the battle, so I didn't get the chance to snoop my way to the bottom of things.

I rubbed a hand along Nox's arm. "Maybe next time," I said reassuringly. "It only takes one time."

He gave me a soft smile, but it didn't reach his eyes.

Every day, we felt her drifting further and further away. And every day, I saw it weighing on Nox like an anchor. He was a *fixer*. He liked to take what was broken and make it whole again. It was why I thought he loved carving his wooden figurines so much. It was why he offered to take responsibility for me all those months ago instead of letting Clarissa do it, and why he formed an entire *rebellion* to save the weak and lost.

But he couldn't *fix* his sister, and that was killing him.

Little did I know, my dragon had a plan.

Ten days after we destroyed Scarven's mansion, Everett returned to the Keep. And he wasn't alone.

84

NOX

Most of us were leaving the dining hall and making our way to the workshop, like we often did in the evenings. I had *finally* convinced Vera to join us for a nightcap. The doors to the entrance hall burst open as we passed, letting in a blast of icy air and flutters of snowflakes onto the rug.

Everett was back.

Laughter echoed down the hall from some ridiculous joke Tessa had just told. Devora leaned further into my side to escape the chill, and I wrapped my arms around her, waiting. Holding her tight enough to hold myself together for what came next.

"Where you been, Ev?" Arowyn called out when his familiar form came into view, silhouetted against the night sky.

Tessa turned around in surprise. "Oh, would you look at that? I didn't even know he was gone."

"*Tessa,*" Kieran sighed, shaking his head.

But when another woman hesitantly stepped out from behind Everett's broad form, cloaked and travel-worn, everyone came to a halt.

Her blonde-and-gray hair was flecked with snow, her frame even leaner than the last time I'd seen her. And yet her eyes were as sharp and steady as ever.

Vera gasped at my side, and I looked down at her. The air warmed as her gaze burned gold. For the first time since Scarven's death, I felt that restless energy in her still.

I took a staggering step forward, my chest squeezing. Our mother didn't speak. She simply crossed the floor with surprising speed and pulled me into her arms. My body shook against her, my head bowed to her shoulder like I was a boy again, not a man who had carried a rebellion on my back.

She pulled away and patted my cheek, tears glistening in her eyes. "Hello again, my son."

"Welcome home, Mama," I choked out.

Her gaze trailed over my shoulder, and I turned to see Vera still standing there, arms crossed tight and flames flickering in her eyes. She looked ready to bolt, to vanish into the shadows the way she did when the world pressed too close.

I shifted to the side to let our mother move past.

Vera's lip trembled. For a long, painful moment, she was frozen. And then, slowly, haltingly, she stepped forward. Mother held out a hand, and when Vera finally took it, the sound that broke from her chest was raw and keening, like a bird lifting up its song.

Mother pulled her close. Both of their shoulders shook as they held each other.

My throat strained with the effort of holding back my own tears. I didn't think this day would ever come—the moment I'd dreamed of, had worked toward ever since we were ripped from each other's lives.

I threw my arms around both of them. Meeting Everett's eyes over their heads, I gave him a quick nod. *"Thank you."*

He bowed his head low, and the first tear leaked free from my eye.

"My beautiful children," Mother said, her voice cracking. "No more running. No more fighting."

I kissed the top of each of their heads. "Never again," I promised.

At last, after all the years and battles, all the suffering and isolation, all the blood spilled and tears shed...we were home.

———

OUR MOTHER'S reappearance evidently wasn't the only visit that would shift our world over the next few weeks.

We had all finally settled into a rhythm here at the Keep—Devora and Everett with the children, Tessa and Kieran and I handling community outreach, Milo with his new apprentice, and Arowyn doing...whatever Arowyn did in her free time.

Vera, Mother, Devora, and I spent most of the evenings together over the last two weeks, eating dinner around a fire and taking walks along the rocky shoreline when it wasn't snowing too hard.

I was hanging my cloak in the workshop one night after our walk when a pounding came from the front door. A minute later, one of the servants popped his head into the room.

"There's a guest at the door, sir. She said she needs to speak with you immediately."

Devora turned to me with a devilish smirk. "A late-night *lady* caller? Should I be worried?"

I leaned forward and nipped her earlobe playfully. "As if I could handle another woman." Looking back up, I asked, "Who is it?"

The servant scratched the back of his neck. "It—it's Her Majesty. The empress."

85

NOX

"Well, well, well. To what do I owe this pleasure?" I drawled, bracing my arm against the doorway as I stared across the threshold at Rissa and Thorne.

Her burgundy cloak was wrapped tight around her shoulders. Delicate snowflakes fell from the sky, landing in their hair. The heavy chill in the air promised another storm.

"Cut the chitchat; this place is *freezing*." Rissa patted my arm as she strode past me and into the Keep. "It's good to see you, Nox."

Thorne chuckled and followed after her. I shut the door, the hinges creaking. "How's married life treating you?" I asked.

"Why, are you interested?" There was a twinkle in Rissa's dark eyes. Her gaze strayed to the other side of the entryway, where Devora stood bundled in a blanket. The empress's lips turned into a feline grin. "Oh, *hello,* Devora. I didn't see you there."

Against my wishes, a blush crept up my cheeks. "Have you been traveling all day? I can make you something to eat."

Rissa raised an eyebrow. "Nox in the *kitchen*? Now this I have to see."

"I think she means 'thank you,'" Thorne interjected with a laugh.

Rissa nodded. "Sure, that too."

"I'll have you know that I make a mean bean soup." I shot Devora a wink, who stifled a laugh with her hand.

I led them down the winding corridors and to the kitchen, where the scent of baked bread and roasted meat from dinner still lingered. A fire dwindled in the massive fireplace. Several iron kettles hung above it, casting shadows on the floor. Tables were spread across the large space, with spots of flour dotting the wood.

Devora poured four cups of hot water from one of the kettles, then dropped tea bags into each of them while I found an extra loaf of bread.

"So," I started, grabbing a knife and slicing through the center, "I assume you two didn't come all this way because you missed my beautiful face?"

"Not exactly." Rissa shifted on her stool. I figured their visit had something to do with the battle over three weeks ago. Rose, Leo, and Chaz had gone back to the capital a couple of days later, and Rissa and I had exchanged some letters since then, but we hadn't had a chance to talk in person about what transpired.

"You know we destroyed all the fatesprig and the weapons," I assured her as I walked to the pantry and took a wedge of boar's cheese. "I sent a team to put out the fires and check all the underground areas. Everything is gone. You don't have anything to worry about."

"I believe you. But what about that Alchemist?" Rissa asked.

"Mortep?" I scowled. I cut a slice of cheese a little too hard, and the tip of the blade got stuck in the table beneath. "No sign of him. But we're looking."

When he wasn't with the children, Everett had made it his life's mission to track down the mad Alchemist. It was also one of the only topics of conversation that made Vera come out of her shell. Their vendetta against the man who had created such twisted experiments lit the bloodlust in her, and while it was understandable, I was worried for my sister. For the rage and vengeance I saw consuming her.

"Good. That's good." Rissa twisted her fingers together. "Well, it's not good that you haven't found him. But it's good someone is looking. I have a sect of my guard searching too. We've put out a warning to all the governors to be on the lookout in their provinces."

I laid slices of cheese on the open-faced bread and sprinkled it with the rosemary that hung by the window. As I set it on the hearthstone over one of the fireplaces, the scent of Rissa's nerves mixed with something *else* reached my senses.

Hmm. That was new.

She cleared her throat. "Speaking of governors…"

I blinked, slowly turning to stare at her as all other thoughts left me. I should've seen this coming. I should've *known* she'd come here for this.

Her shoulders slumped as she sighed. "Listen, Nox. I know this isn't your favorite subject, but Drakorum needs—"

"I never asked to be its governor," I interrupted. "It doesn't matter if it's my birthright. That may have worked well for you, but not all of us were meant to follow in our father's footsteps."

"I couldn't care less about your birthright." She was using her no-nonsense empress voice now, the one that could convince a fish to walk on land. "You're the kind of man this province needs, *not* because of who your father was, but because of who *you* are. No— don't scoff at me. Name one person who cares about these people more than you. Name one person who would sacrifice more than you to make sure they're safe, provided for, and *heard*."

Devora slipped up behind me to rub a steadying hand along my back. "She has a point, Nox," she said. "You're an incredible leader. We would follow you anywhere, you know that. But only if it's what *you* want."

I licked my lips, a myriad of emotions brewing inside of me. Denial, resistance, doubt. There was a sudden drop in the pit of my stomach, bringing with it the urge to step back.

Who was I to lead these people? Rissa and Devora looked at me with admiration, but they didn't see all the things I'd done. The ways I'd hurt people at Scarven's command.

But with that fear came another thought. *If I walk away, who takes my place? Who keeps them safe?*

I had already felt the weight of this province's fate on my shoulders for years. It had never been a burden, but a responsibility. One I thought would end when I got rid of Scarven.

Perhaps that kind of duty never truly ended. These people would always be sewn into the fabric of my heart, the foundation that kept me strong.

My eyes fell to the table. "I never wanted power."

Rissa's words made me look up. "I know, Nox. I think that's what makes you perfect for it."

I would be lying if I said I'd never imagined myself taking up my father's legacy. I just never felt worthy of it. Of walking in the great Caius Duma's footsteps. But even he made mistakes. *Huge* ones. I always wondered if Scarven would have turned out differently if my father had taken responsibility for his actions all those years ago.

"You're not the sum of your past," Devora said quietly, standing on her tiptoes to brush her lips against my jaw. They were the same words I said to her once upon a time. I turned to catch her forehead, planting a kiss there before tucking a strand of hair behind her ear.

The way she looked at me made me believe it. Even after how I treated her in the beginning, after all she'd learned about me, after seeing my good and bad and everything in between...she looked at me like she saw through it all.

I stayed quiet as I took the tray of bread from the hearthstone, breathing in the melted cheese and fresh herbs. I set it on the table and eyed the empress.

"There are going to be some changes around here," I warned.

Rissa's lips curved into a grin. "Does that mean you'll do it?"

"On one condition." I took the cutting knife and held it blade-up between us. She reached for it, but I kept it in my grip as I stared her down. "You name your baby after me."

Thorne cursed beside her, and Devora gasped so hard, she choked on her tea.

Rissa merely chuckled. "I *knew* you'd figure it out."

"Shifter senses never lie." I tapped my nose with a grin.

"We *just* found out," Thorne grumbled. "I thought we could keep it a secret for at least a little while."

"There are no secrets among friends, lover boy." I set the knife down and rounded the table to envelop Rissa in a hug. "I'm so happy for you, Rissa."

"Thank you." She squeezed hard, then pulled back. "And now that you're governor, we'll get to see a lot more of each other. I'll need regular updates on the state of the province, and I'm convening a quarterly meeting with all the governors at the capital."

"Yes, yes, I get it." I waved her off. "Business talk later. Now, we celebrate." I raised my mug of steaming tea, and the others joined it. "To baby Nox Aris and the health of your beautiful family."

Thorne snorted into his tea. "We are *not* naming it Nox."

I took a sip. "You're right. What if it's a girl?"

"To baby Aris," Rissa repeated, eyes twinkling at me. "*And* to you. The new Governor Duma."

The title made the smile fade from my face. Governor Duma. *My father's title.*

But a small bloom of pride rose from the weeds, filling my chest with warmth.

Devora wrapped her free arm around my back with a wicked little grin. "Hmm," she hummed lazily. "I've never been with a *governor* before."

I kissed the tip of her nose. "Get used to it, darling. You're stuck with me."

She rested her head on my chest, a smile in her voice as she said, "I think I can live with that."

86

DEVORA
FIVE WEEKS LATER

"Close your eyes."

"I'm not sticking my finger in it again, Nox."

His chuckle wafted over me, warming me to my toes. "It's not that. Just trust me, darling."

I shot him an unimpressed look, then sighed and closed my eyes. "Okay, done. Now what?"

I felt his presence shuffle across the floor of his chambers, then I heard something scrape against the wood. With a smirk, I sent my shadows drifting toward the sound, trying to scope out what he was doing.

"Stop that," he grunted.

My shadows whisked back to me as I laughed.

Finally, his footsteps drew nearer. The bed dipped beneath me, and his thigh brushed mine. "Open them."

I blinked my eyes open to see his lips tilted into a shy grin. When I looked down to his lap, there were two planks of wood, each with the bust of a silhouette carved in its center.

My brow furrowed. I recognized those silhouettes. I remembered seeing them in the shadows the night of the Noctus Vigil back in Tenebra. There was a man with short hair and broad shoulders, and a woman with a quill raised in the air and a long braid running down her back.

My mouth went dry. "Is that..."

"Happy birthday, Devora," Nox murmured.

I blinked. "*What?*"

I'd never known exactly when I was born. When they found me on the shores of Mysthelm, the healers and midwives estimated my age, but they could only guess around what season: spring.

"I may have talked to Thecae and his mother." Nox rubbed the back of his neck sheepishly. "They remembered when you were born. The spring equinox. Your parents always told everyone you were their new beginning, the warmth after the winter's cold."

My gaze dropped back to the silhouettes. I reached forward and traced the outline of my mother's hair, feeling every smooth dip in the wood.

"And Thecae also gave me the wooden plank," he said, even softer this time. "It's a remnant from the shipwreck. The only thing that survived, besides you."

I steepled my hands, pressing my fingers into my lips as I exhaled. A tremor shuddered through me.

For so long, my past had been a shadow. Faceless, unreachable, slipping through my fingers. I'd uncovered more of myself all those weeks ago in Tenebra, but even then, we had a mission. We had to keep moving, and I couldn't let myself get caught up in ancient history.

But they were *always* here. My mother and father, carved from the wreckage that stole them from me and shaped by the hands of the man I loved. A man who *saw* me, who knew what I'd lost and had wanted to start something new.

Our new beginning.

Tears slipped free before I could stop them. They traced the curve of my cheek and fell onto the wood, staining the corner of my father's silhouette. My fingers hovered just above the plank, not quite touching it this time.

"I don't..." My voice cracked. "I don't know what to say."

"You don't have to say anything." Nox leaned forward to kiss my forehead. "I just wanted you to have a piece of them. They would be so proud of you. *I'm* so proud of you."

"You have to say that," I commented with a choked laugh, wiping a finger under my eye. "It's my birthday."

Something occurred to me, and my back snapped straighter. "You didn't throw a surprise party for me, did you? Nobody's going to jump out from under the bed?"

He chuckled. "I certainly hope not. If so, they've been there for a while. Do you *want* a party?"

"I don't know." I shrugged, then carefully moved the planks of wood out of the way so I could settle in his lap. "Maybe a dinner. But I want *lots* of gifts."

He snorted at that.

"Or just you," I murmured as I tucked my head under his chin. "We could sit like this all day. No meetings, no couriers delivering messages to the *illustrious* Governor Duma."

He leaned us back onto the pillows propped against the head-board. "I think I can arrange that. They can all wait until tomorrow."

I craned my neck to meet his gaze, taking in the little flecks of silver glinting in the navy pools. His lips found mine, warm and soft and unhurried. Like the hint of springtime spreading across the cold, cracked winter.

Tomorrow, I thought to myself.

Our tomorrow had finally come.

EPILOGUE
VERA

I rubbed the two letters in my grip, the smoothness of the parchment at odds with the roughness of the contents. It was fitting, I supposed. Pretty things often hid the harsh reality beneath.

As if I hadn't already read them a thousand times, I flicked the first one open, my eyes scanning my own handwriting in the low torchlight of the docks.

> *To Mother and Nox,*
>
> *Thank you both for everything you've done to get my life back to some semblance of normal. Being with you again has reminded me what it's like to have a family, and I love you more than you could possibly know.*
>
> *But nothing about my life has ever been normal. And for so long, I've been forced to do what others wanted me to. I need to figure out where I go from here, and I don't think I can do that in Drakorum. There's too much pain there. Too many memories.*
>
> *I'll come back when I'm ready. Don't try to search for me. All I want is for you to live your lives—you deserve that as much as I do.*
>
> *I love you,*

Vera

Would my big brother listen to my request? I didn't know. But I doubted he'd be able to find me anyway. Not where I was going.

A rustle of wind shook my hair free from my cloak's hood, blonde waves streaked with red dye blowing in front of my face. I gazed out at the moon hovering above the waters of the Sea of Scarab. The gangplank shifted beneath my feet, urging me to make a decision.

Backward or forward. Past or future.

I glanced down at the second letter, caressing its edges with a gentleness I rarely felt these days. This one was shorter. Barely worth opening.

Swift,
Please forgive me.
Your songbird

Taking several herbs from the pouch inside my cloak, I placed them on my lips and murmured a spell. Instantly, both letters erupted into flames and vanished from my grasp.

My boots creaked on the wood as I crossed onto the looming ship. A sort of dark, expectant eagerness shifted in the air, making my stomach tighten in anticipation.

"Where ya headed, miss?" the captain called to me.

I swallowed and put my hand to my hip, feeling the outline of the map and a bag of gold through my cloak. "North," I replied, voice raspy.

"To Emberfell?"

My lip twitched, a string pulling the corner into a ghostly smile. "Not quite." His features screwed in confusion until I threw a money purse on the deck in front of him. "How far north out of the empire will this get me?"

A low whistle left his lips. "For that, I'll take ya to the skies itself."

"Perfect."

I finally had a mission. A purpose.

And I wouldn't stop until I burned him to the ground.

Also by V.B. Lacey

The Elementals of Iona:

Long Live

Forever Reign

Wildfire: A Prequel Novella

The Veridian Empire

In the Wake of the Wicked

Of the Curse or the Crown

From the Silence of the Shadows

By the Flames of Her Fury

ACKNOWLEDGMENTS

All glory and thanks be to my God for His blessings in this life and for the opportunity I have to share my words and live out this epic dream of mine.

I want to first and foremost thank my husband, Taylor, for continuing to support my publishing career. You've always believed in me (more than I did in myself) and pushed me to go after what I wanted. I love you 3000.

To my family and friends, who are just as excited for me today as they were on day 1. I don't take for granted how fortunate I am to have you in my corner.

Thank you to the amazing editors and artists who contributed to making this book shine - Krista with Mountains Wanted Publishing, beautiful covers by Fay Lane and Charlie Arpie, and the stunning maps and interior art by Andrés Aguirre and Ana Maria Sandru.

This series wouldn't be what it is today without my wonderful street team! Thank you for your messages, posts, encouragement, and excitement throughout the last year and a half. Your love for the Veridian Empire and these characters keeps me going. You truly don't know the impact you have on authors like me, and I'm so lucky to have you.

This specific story is close to my heart for a number of reasons. I'm sure I'm not alone when I say I've struggled with dark thoughts of loneliness, insecurity, and even self-loathing. Nox and Devora both travel down difficult paths that lead them to embrace their emotions, the good *and* the bad, and learn to love themselves.

This is still something I work on (and often fail at) every day. If you're like me, I hope their words and love for each other strike a chord with you and reassure you that you're not alone.

Thank you, dear reader, for coming along with me on yet another journey (and I finally got to write a DRAGON). What epic winged creature might I tackle next?

Stick around...

About the Author

V.B. Lacey is an office manager by day and an avid reader-turned-writer by night. She grew up on stories of Jesus, magic, love, and sarcasm, and has always dreamed of being an author. She lives in Texas with her supportive husband and two rambunctious dogs. When she's not writing about morally grey characters and far-off kingdoms, you can find her reading (mostly fantasy and contemporary romance), playing board games, or spending time with friends.

Visit her online at www.vblaceybooks.com, or follow her on Instagram and TikTok: @vblacey.books.